CHARLES EGAN was born in Nottingham, England of Irish parents.

When he was five, the family returned to Ireland, as his father had been appointed Resident Medical Superintendent of St. Luke's, a psychiatric hospital in Clonmel, in County Tipperary.

Every summer they visited his father's family's farm, outside Kiltimagh in County Mayo for a month, where his grandmother and uncles spent many evenings, talking about family and local history.

The family subsequently moved to County Wicklow, where he initially attended the De La Salle Brothers School in Wicklow town. He then went to the Jesuits' Clongowes Wood College (James Joyce's alma mater), and subsequently studied Commerce in University College Dublin, graduating in 1973.

After an initial career in the private sector, including Marubeni Dublin, (where he met his future wife, Carmel), he joined the Industrial Development Authority (IDA) in Dublin. After a few years, the desire to be his own boss, led him to resign and set up his own business, which ran for 30 years.

His main interests are history, film, and worldwide travel.

Also by the author

The Killing Snows
Cold is the Dawn

THE EXILE BREED

CHARLES EGAN

SilverWood

Published in 2015 by SilverWood Books

SilverWood Books Ltd
14 Small Street, Bristol, BS1 1DE, United Kingdom
www.silverwoodbooks.co.uk

ISBN 978-1-78132-452-3 (paperback)
ISBN 978-1-78132-453-0 (ebook)

British Library Cataloguing in Publication Data
A CIP catalogue record for this book is available from
the British Library

Set in Sabon by SilverWood Books
Printed on responsibly sourced paper

'Lord John Russell, have you no better occupation for Her Majesty's troops than employing them in a useless war against the dying people of Mayo?'

The Telegraph & Connaught Ranger
County Mayo, March 1848

For Carmel

Preface

The Irish had been emigrating for centuries. Before The Great Famine though, the majority of emigrants were Scotch Irish. These were settlers from Scotland who had settled the northern Irish counties, and then emigrated again, using their own means, because they saw opportunity in North America.

The Great Famine migration was of a totally different order. The starvation of 1845 and 1846 and the devastating epidemics of early 1847, induced a sense of panic in Ireland.

Many other factors encouraged this movement out of Ireland. One was chain migration, where family members already settled abroad, sent home money, or the 'American Ticket' to encourage their family members to join them. A second factor was that the Workhouses, desperate to clear their colossal over-crowding, chartered ships to clear out the people. These ships were a very low quality and there was nothing awaiting the people in either cash or work when they reached their destination. The landlords too, cleared out their surplus population in this way, though the numbers here were very much less.

For most of the rural underclass though, none of these options were available. These were the families of men who had no land at all, either freehold or by tenancy. They lived in mud cabins, and they and their families represented a population of well over a million. By the end of the Famine, most had been wiped out. The landless labourers hardly exist as a class today.

For those who left, the story of the Atlantic journey was a horrific one, though not all ships were as bad as the appalling coffin ships travelling from Liverpool or Cork, especially those going to Quebec. Many migrants lost their lives on the ocean. Soon after they arrived, a disastrous financial crash hit both sides of the Atlantic. Few could gain employment, and many of those who had, were soon thrown out of work. Even worse, the famine fevers followed them, and thousands died in the Irish ghettoes of Liverpool, Manchester and London; in the Emigrant Hospitals of Quebec and Montreal; on the back-roads of Canada and the United States; and in the tenements of Boston, New York, Philadelphia, St. Louis, New Orleans and many other American cities.

Years later, some of the Irish in America had become farmers, whether in Canada or the United States. In both England and North America, many of the women had become domestic servants, derisively known as biddies or bridgets.

For most of the men, those who gained work were to be found in backbreaking labour, whether as dockers, miners, lumbermen, or railway navvies, still living in the city slums, the mining camps, the forest shanties, and the hovels and shacks along the railways.

The experience of the Irish Famine migrants was a hard one. This is their story.

Charles Egan

Luke's Family

Luke Ryan
Winnie, his wife
Michael, his father
Eleanor, his mother
Pat, his younger brother

Murty Ryan, Luke's uncle
Aileen, Murty's wife
Danny, their eldest son
Nessa, their daughter
Murtybeg, their youngest son
Brigid, Nessa's daughter

Sabina McKinnon, Luke's aunt

In County Mayo the county towns of Castlebar, Claremorris Westport and Ballina are real, but the East Mayo towns of Kilduff, Knockanure and Brockagh are fictitious, as are the settlements and mountains around them. In Pennsylvania the mining town of Lackan is also fictitious.

A note about italic use in this book. Where the dialogue is in italics, the character is understood to be speaking in Irish.

Prologue

The sea was still running wild, but the wind had dropped. More sails were going up as the ship sailed past the ice. Close enough, a hundred yards perhaps, but the danger was over.

The iceberg's stillness seemed unreal in the early dawn. All around it, waves crashed into its white cliffs, gnawing in under it. Rivulets flowed down its flanks, running off the skirts of ice at its base, sheets of white water pouring into the ocean. Spume flew high into the sky, caught in the early sunlight and blown on the wind like smoke.

Like white smoke over a white mountain.

He leaned against the rail, watching. His heart had ceased its pounding, but still he felt a fear he could no longer explain.

Remember Mayo?

Two thousand miles behind? Could be more. They were nearer to America now. He was losing track of time too. Hundreds of people crammed into the cargo hold, sickening, praying and dying. More deaths every day. He wondered how many would survive the voyage of the Centaurus.

Would he?

What a fool he had been, travelling on a lumber ship. Another few pounds, and he could have been on a real passenger ship. But he had thought the money would be better feeding his own family in Mayo. Was it? They were depending on him to reach America, and send his money back. Money for food, and money to bring Winnie and the baby out to join him. How many more weeks of fever 'till there would be no one left on board? Then there would be no money from America.

Remember Mayo.

Croghancoe. The snow covered mountain, still and silent. Mud cabins strung across it, white smoke rising. Unseen people, dying and dead from famine, fever and cold.

The endless drifts. The frozen lakes. The killing snows.

The power and the terror.

County Mayo.

Chapter 1

Tyrawly Herald, Ireland, July 1847:
From the promise of an early, and, where the seed was sown, of a plentiful harvest, it was seen as if the Almighty was mercifully to shorten the days of our calamity. But in the sanguine anticipations, which are but natural, wherever the land is cropped, we are debarred from sharing to the same extent on witnessing entire tracts have been left unseeded and desolate in Galway and Mayo, and no doubt in other places.

It was dark as he left Carrigard for Liverpool and Quebec.

Luke knew he had left most of his family forever. His father, his mother, his brother and his little sister, these he would never see again. But Winnie would follow on. Their baby too. But the question was when?

It was not as if there was anything unusual about this. Many Mayo families had suffered the same, and now in the midst of famine and fever, many, many more were suffering. America was different to England. Men and women worked the summer season in England. Some returned after a few months, but many stayed for years, working as navvies on English railways. But post to England was rapid. You could expect a reply to a letter within eight or ten days.

America or the Canadian provinces – they were different. Five or six weeks sailing each way – it took three months to even get a reply to a letter, and no one ever returned.

But Winnie would follow him to America. That much was certain. So many men, at least in normal times, travelled to America to settle. They brought out their wives and families when they had the money and a fixed address. The address was crucial. He knew many stories of men who had crossed the Atlantic, and were never heard of again. Men who never made money, who never settled long enough in one place. Men who could not even write. It was a hard thing for any family to be waiting for the American letter for news, or for money to stop the hunger, or to bring wives and families across to America. Often, the letter never came.

*

When he reached Knockanure, the sun had risen. The first houses were only mud cabins with straw roofs. These were the sure signs of the desperate poverty of the West. He stopped in shock as he saw a dead body on the road, rats already sniffing at it. He was well used to such sights. He pulled it into the side of the road and walked on.

In the town, the Workhouse had the usual crowds outside, clamouring for entry. It was only a few days since he had last seen his brother, but even so, this was his last chance to see him or Sarah. Inside the high gate of the Workhouse, two inmates with sticks ensured that no one climbed the gate. Luke pushed through the crowd to one of the inmates and explained he was Pat Ryan's brother. The man only nodded, and Luke clambered over the gate, dropping down the other side. He was directed to the back of the Workhouse, and went around, passing the fever sheds towards the mass grave. He saw Pat there, directing the inmates, back-filling soil into the grave. As he watched, two more inmates carried a body past him and threw it in. He shouted at his brother without going closer. Pat waved and came across.

'I don't want to go any nearer,' Luke said, 'but I couldn't pass by without seeing you and Sarah.'

Pat nodded. 'I can understand you not wanting to go closer. It's awful, but you get used to it.'

'How are you getting on here?'

'Well enough, but little else has changed. The Workhouse is in a dreadful way, though better than it was some months back.'

'How's that?'

'The fever is less. They cleared out hundreds on the boats to British America, and hundreds more died, but they didn't let so many back in. They knew the crowding only killed more from fever. So the Workhouse isn't as packed, and the fever isn't killing as many as it used to. They're still dying, but nothing like it was. I'll tell you this though, Luke, 1847 will never be forgotten in County Mayo. Black '47, that's what they're calling it.'

They walked over towards the Administration block. Luke was thankful. He had no desire to see the death pit again, nor the inside of the Workhouse either.

Sarah was working, adding long columns.

'Look who's here,' Pat said. Sarah glanced up.

'Luke!' She ran and embraced him. 'How's Winnie? How's the baby?'

'Both are well, though the baby is far enough away. Sometime early next year. March, they're reckoning.'

'She'll join you in the summer, will she?

'That's what we're hoping anyway, if they're both well enough before the shipping season is ended, and if I'm well settled, she'll join me. But for all we know, the American ports might still be closed to the ships from Ireland or Liverpool, and I sure as hell wouldn't want her and the baby to come in by Quebec, and have them travelling down to New York or Pennsylvania by land. And I'd have to be settled enough wherever I'm going so as to make sure I'd still be there whenever she arrives. We'll see.'

'But if she doesn't make next year...'

'Yes,' said Luke, 'it would have to be the year after. God only knows.'

'1849,' Pat exclaimed. 'But you'd be two years apart then.'

'Don't I know it, but...?'

'Why don't you just go over to Stockport?' Sarah asked. 'Work with Danny?'

'Danny, is it? Our dear cousin, the roughest labour contractor in England. Helping drive Mayo men into the ground with starvation wages? No, I'd never do that. And anyhow, from all we hear, Mikey and the boys are earning good wages out in America.'

'But Danny would have you as a ganger, surely?'

'He might, Sarah. Still I reckon I could earn more in America as a labourer than I would with Danny as a ganger. And anyhow, I don't want it. No, the only future for me – for any of us – is America. Why don't you come too?'

'To America? I couldn't leave mother. And with Pat working here as a clerk, sure, we're not starving.'

Luke nodded.

'Fair enough, so. There's only one thing I'd ask of the two of you. Keep an eye on Winnie and the baby too, when it arrives. And let's all pray the famine and fever has run its course.'

Soon, he was on the road again, heading east out of Knockanure. He saw gangs of men, women and children in the uniform of the Workhouse, repairing roads. There were few of them, and nothing like the many thousands who worked on road building and repair before the Relief Works were stopped. And the weather was warm, with none of the freezing cold of the winter that had killed so many thousands of starving people. The potato crop looked good, but he could see that very little had been planted. He knew starving people had eaten their own seed potatoes. The hunger would go on.

Many times he passed impoverished groups of men, women and children walking towards Dublin. Some talked of the Dublin Workhouses, but most were travelling to Liverpool, and then on to America. Luke wondered how many would get to Dublin, let alone Liverpool or America.

He was walking the same road on which he had returned from England, just over a year ago. Seven years working on the English railways, but then he had to come back to farm his father's farm. Even before he left England,

Mayo had frightened him. When he arrived, he could see why. Even then, he could see the early signs of hunger following the lesser potato failure in 1845. But no-one had expected the terrible starvation and cold of the bitter winter of 1846, nor the savage fever epidemics of 1847. Connaught had been devastated.

Oh God, Winnie, when will I see you again?

Knockanure to Ballaghaderreen to Frenchpark. Everywhere, the abandoned mud cabins, their people dead or gone. Sodden thatch collapsing on sodden walls, returning to the earth. He remembered how many of those he had seen around Brockagh, Ardnagrena, Knocklenagh and, worst of all, the mud villages strung out across Croghancroe. The dying and the dead.

Belllinagare and Tulsk. Strokestown. He walked down the wide main street, the Big House at the end of it. There was a strange silence in the town. He stopped at a bar outside the town, and it was here he heard stories of a mass eviction. Fifteen hundred people sent to Dublin and Liverpool, and on to Quebec, only two months before. Nothing had been heard from them since, though, as Luke reflected, it would have been too early to cross the Atlantic and expect letters back in that time. There were also rumours of more evictions to come. He thought of the Lucan evictions at *Gort-na-Móna*, just above Kilduff. How many of those might have been sent to Quebec out of those who were admitted into Knockanure Workhouse, or any of the other Workhouses. They might have been lucky to be sent to Quebec instead of the mass fever graves in the Workhouses.

He reached Termonbarry and crossed the Shannon, leaving Connaught behind. There was less devastation in the Leinster counties, fewer mud cabins to abandon, but there were still crowds outside the Midlands Workhouses, and more crowds of people walking towards Dublin. Luke noted from their accents that most were from Connaught. County Mayo and County Roscommon sending their people to England and America.

Longford, Edgeworthstown and Mullingar.

Kinnegad, Enfield and Kilcock.

After five days of hard walking, he reached the edge of Dublin, herds of cattle streaming toward the Cattle Market at Smithfield. On the other side of the Liffey was the huge Guinness brewery with its greedy appetite for thousands of tonnes of barley to brew the black beer. How many thousands upon thousands of families could be fed from that barley?

He walked along the quays, all wet and stinking from the cattle manure. At the North Wall Docks, three cattle boats were tied up at the pier. He watched the flow of cattle into the boats, hundreds of ragged people squeezing in with them. At first he considered taking one of the cattle boats – thruppence only to Liverpool. He saw a passenger ship though and considered the matter. He knew he had to save as much cash as possible for when he arrived in Quebec, but even so, he did not want to arrive in Liverpool streaked with cattle manure. He went to the passenger ship.

A man with a table was collecting fares.

'Six shillings.'

'Six shillings,' Luke exclaimed. 'It was only...'

'Forget what it was. It's six shillings now.'

Luke hesitated, and the next man pushed him out of the way. It had only been a shilling and sixpence when he had crossed from Liverpool last year. A quarter the price. Reluctantly, he walked towards the cattle boat.

'A shilling!' The price here had quadrupled too, but there was little he could do. He paid.

As he joined the long line of families waiting to board, he took off his shoes and rolled his trousers up. He knew well the conditions he would find inside a cattle boat.

The crossing was pathetic and disgusting. Walking barefoot through manure was bad enough, but even so, he could not protect his clothes from the filth. The low keening of the women, mixed with the bellowing of the cattle, left him no opportunity to sleep, even if he could have found somewhere to do so. It was the keening that upset him more than the cattle. He had heard it many times before, as the women scrabbled through the potato fields, though they already knew from the colour of the leaves what they would find.

The crossing was calm enough, so he was not seasick, though many around him were.

It was strange, he reflected, that he had never travelled on the cattle ship before. Even when he first crossed to England in 1840, it had been on a passenger ship. When he had been working on the railways, nothing less was acceptable. But this Famine was even worse than 1840. The shipping companies were taking advantage of the enormous demand from the Famine refugees by packing them in and multiplying the prices four times over.

Three days later, they arrived in the Clarence Dock in Liverpool. The gangplank dropped. The police were waiting at the end. Beyond them, more police surrounded a crowd of hundreds of tattered people.

As the people disembarked from the ship, two men in civilian clothes stood forward and started watching the crowd. From time to time they pointed passengers out, and these were dragged away by the police, their families following. Whenever anyone protested, they were clubbed.

Neither of the selectors glanced at Luke, and he walked past the crowds.

Across the road from the dock he spotted a bar and was surprised to see a statue of Saint Patrick outside. Curious, he crossed the road and saw the bar was crowded. Two men were standing outside, drinking ale. Luke recognised the Irish accents.

'Do ye know what's going on over there?' he asked.

'They're the fellows going back to Ireland.'

'Not of their own free will, by the looks of it.'

'Damned right. There's no question of free will about it. It's the Workhouses, terrified of fever they are. The powers-that-be reckon the fever is coming from Ireland, so they're sending the Irish back out of the Workhouses. Now they reckon the best thing is not to allow them in either, so they're watching the ships, and any they think might have fever, or are too weak to live, them they're sending back too.'

'God,' Luke said, 'Liverpool has changed this past year.'

'That it has.'

He left and found his way down some steps beside the Mersey. He went down, washed his feet and rubbed down his trousers. Then he took off his shirt and greatcoat, and washed them in the river too. He knew his shirt would dry on him fast enough in the summer heat, and the greatcoat could wait 'till later.

When he had his shirt back on, he climbed back to the dock and went across Vauxhall Road up to Scotland Road. He saw white crosses on many doors. Everywhere, there were crowds of dirty, ragged people, some standing, many just sitting or lying beside the road. On Scotland Road he found Buckleys', where the Mayo men had always stayed, coming and going from England. Three policemen were outside, turning people away. Luke noted too that some houses had white crosses on the doors. Fever?

He turned back. What now?

A cart rattled ahead of him, two corpses in the back. It stopped. The driver jumped off and knocked at one of the doors with white crosses. A woman looked out in fright. Her face was gaunt, her clothes thin and ragged. She nodded. A minute later, she and the driver carried out a naked corpse and threw it into the cart. Then the woman brought out the body of a baby, and carefully placed it by the other corpses. Luke could see inside the room. There was no furniture except a wooden chest. The beds consisted of straw thrown on the floor. There were half a dozen more children, and one man raving.

He returned to the Clarence Dock and made his way through the crowds, asking for the Centaurus, the ship that he had booked for Quebec. But no-one knew of the Centaurus here. Luke had been through Liverpool before, and knew the vast extent of the port. He started walking south along the

Docks, questioning people about the Centaurus. The Canning Dock and the Liverpool Dock. No one had heard of the Centaurus. At the Albert Dock, he asked some sailors, but they did not speak English.

The Dukes Dock, the Kings, the Queens. No luck.

He found a bar by the Coburg Dock. It was crowded, but he sat at a small table in a corner and ordered a pint of ale and a pork pie. Two seamen on the next table were eyeing him. He could see by the insignia on their cuffs that they were officers.

'Hey Paddy,' one shouted. 'What are you doing in this country?'

Luke did not answer.

'Paddy, I'm talking to you. You're Irish...'

'What of it?' Luke asked.

'You shouldn't be here. All you're doing is costing the fair city of Liverpool to send you back home again. You don't believe that, do you? Three hundred of them they've shipped back in the past days. Why should our Workhouses be paying for the likes of you?'

'They only come to work.'

'Yeah. The ones who get away, that is. If they don't bring us fever, they're off working as navvies on the railways. Lowering wages for everyone, all of God's honest Englishmen. That's what they do. Damned bastards.'

Luke's ale had arrived. He sipped it, saying nothing. The barman had stopped and was listening.

'Now lads, no need for this.'

'And there's another damned Paddy,' the officer said, recognising the barman's accent. 'You're all damned bastards, the whole lot of you.'

Luke stood up. 'Outside.'

'What...?'

'You heard me.' He strode to the open door and stood outside, fists raised. The bar was silent. The seaman stood.

His comrade put his hand on his arm. 'No, John. Not that one.'

The other glared at Luke, then sat down abruptly, muttering 'Irish bastard.'

Luke came in again and sat at a small table beside the door. The barman brought out his pint of ale.

'Good move, that, asking him outside.'

'No point in staying and wrecking your bar, was there?'

The bar was loud again. Soon, the two seamen left.

His pie arrived. He paid for it, thinking of starving Irishmen being brought in to work for starvation wages on the railways, pushing English wages down. He knew it was true. Danny did that and lived off starving Irishmen.

'I'm looking for a ship,' he said to the barman. 'The Centaurus. Bound for Quebec.'

'It's those two fellows you should have asked,' the barman replied. 'They'd have known.'

'I don't think they'd have answered me.'

'No, but they're on the Centaurus.'

'But where…?'

'She'll be sailing out of Brunswick Dock, next one down. She's a lumber trader.'

'Lumber?'

'Carries lumber out of Quebec, she does. They change them into passenger ships for the homeward run. They're not designed for passengers, but they pack them in anyhow. Most of them Irish too, just like yourself, though you look better than most of the poor devils we see coming through for the lumber ships. Half starved, the most of them.'

Luke thought of what he had been told. A lumber ship! He should have known it. He had heard stories of these, and the many who died of fever on them. Yes, he had booked 'below decks' for his crossing, but he had thought that would have been on a passenger ship. He swore softly, thinking of the agent in Kilduff who had sold him the ticket, knowing full well the conditions on the lumber ships.

He walked to the Brunswick Dock, noting the huge timber yards landward of the ships. There were no passenger boats there, only two enormous cargo vessels unloading heavy lumber. He watched in wonder as bundles and bales of planks, boards and railway sleepers were discharged. Further down, massive squared logs of incredible length and weight were being hauled onto a sloping quay, which led to more timber yards behind.

He went up to the first ship. He saw the name on the prow. The Mary Emma. The next was the Centaurus. He could see the age of the ship by the appearance of it. It was patched in places, planks replaced in parts of the hull.

When he reached the ship there was no one there. Unsure what to do, he looked around and spotted the dockmaster's office. He knocked on the door but there was no response. He knocked again. The door opened. 'What in hell do you want?'

'The Centaurus…'

'Won't be leaving for a few days yet.'

'But…why?'

'It'll take days to rebuild the inside of it, and they haven't even started.'

Luke shook his head, still puzzled. Hoisting his pack over his shoulder, he walked back towards the city. He had two immediate purposes. One was to find lodgings, the other was to buy food for the voyage.

On the docks, he spotted the Mersey Ferry to the Wirral Peninsula. If, at least, he could get away from the city, he might find better places to stay. He paid his farthing to Birkenhead.

He leaned on the rail as the ferry began to move. Then he noticed the two men beside him were speaking in Irish. He listened closely. County Mayo. He was sure of it.

'*Well, where are ye lads going?*' he asked, speaking in Irish.

The two men looked around in surprise.

'Birkenhead.'

'*Are you working out that way?*'

'*We are. On the* Birkenhead & Chester Railway. *You know it?*'

'*I do,*' Luke replied. '*They're still building it, are they? I'd heard it was finished.*'

'*So it was, but now they're adding a second track, all the way from* Birkenhead *to Wallasey. Is it work you're looking for?*'

'*No. It's America I am headed to. I'm only going to* Birkenhead *to see if I can find a bed for the night.*'

'*You're Mayo, aren't you?*' the second man asked.

'*Indeed,*' Luke said. '*The best county. I've worked the railways too in my time.*'

'*Well, if you're a railway man from Mayo, you may come and stay with us, if you wish.*'

When they arrived in Birkenhead, they walked along the tracks snaking towards Wallasey. Birkenhead was crowded, but closer to Wallasey, it became less so. They passed potato fields, and Luke noted that there was no blight on the leaves.

They came to a shack. Inside, there were two other men, a woman and a baby.

Poitín was passed around. Luke sipped at it.

'*Why don't you stay working on the rails yourself?*' one of the men asked.

'*I've been thinking of it,*' Luke answered. '*My cousin works the rails too. I don't think I'd be too welcome.*'

'*Your cousin?*'

'Daniel Ryan.'

There was a silence. 'Daniel Ryan *is your cousin?*'

'*He is, and I don't want to meet him again. He's destroyed the name of Ryan on the railways.*'

'*He has too,*' the woman commented. '*A savage man.*'

'*Perhaps I shouldn't have told you so, but I can't help being his cousin, we were born as cousins. My own family are decent enough. Danny's family too. But Danny's a tough man, and I know if I stayed in this country, I'd end up working for him, and I don't want that.'*

'*None of the fellows around here want that,*' the woman replied. '*The men who work for him are fast enough getting away.*'

Luke groaned. '*They are. And now you understand why I can't work the rails here. They say there's better chances on the rails in America though.*'

'*So we've heard,*' one of the men said. '*And sure, if you're not having anything to do with* Daniel Ryan, *you're welcome to stay here.*' He raised a glass. '*Your health.*'

That night, Luke tried to sleep, listening to the low snoring of the men. The baby started to cry, but the woman fed him, and he quietened.

Watching her in the light from the embers of the fire, Luke felt intensely lonely. Winnie, his family and friends were behind him. The business with the seaman had sickened him. It had come very close. He knew he had no friends in Liverpool and none on the crossing, nor in Quebec. Again he thought of travelling to Danny in Stockport and working with him. Yes, and make good money too. Danny would have him as a ganger, not as a low-paid navvy. It could be a better choice, in that he could send money back to Mayo sooner and leave travelling the Atlantic until it was easier to do so. But Danny was no longer the young man he had known when they first worked on the railways together. His savage reputation had shocked Luke, and the fact that even a woman in the Wirral despised Danny so much was no longer a surprise. America was his only choice.

Next morning, he joined his hosts for a breakfast of porridge and tea. He felt relaxed with these people. This was County Mayo as he knew it. Even the men were gentle in their ways, though Luke knew just how tough and strong they had to be to work on the railways.

They spoke of railways they had worked on up and down Britain, and sometimes they spoke of County Mayo. No one mentioned famine or fever. As Luke left, he paid them tuppence for his lodgings. At first, they refused, but in the end the woman took it.

'*You must understand one thing,*' she told him as he left. '*You should be careful of mentioning the name of* Daniel Ryan. *There is great bitterness against him on the railways. You cannot help being born as his cousin. We understand that, but others might not.*'

'*You're right,*' he said. '*I'll not mention his name again. For me, he is dead.*'

He walked to Birkenhead and took the ferry back to Liverpool. He wanted to check the ship again, but first he had to write home. He found a post office, bought paper, an envelope and a penny stamp. He paid an extra farthing for the use of the pen and ink on the counter, and began to write.

Dear Winnie, Dear Father and Mother,

I am now in Liverpool and thought to drop ye a note before leaving for America. I visited our ship yesterday, and it is indeed a well-built one and will make Quebec without difficulty, but it may be five or six weeks before it arrives. I will, of course, write to you at once, but you may not hear from me for three months. But please not to worry.

I must also tell you that the potato fields in this country look most healthy. I hope they will continue so, both here and with ye.

I remain your loving husband and son,

Luke Ryan

A well-built ship? Who knows? No point in mentioning it was a battered old lumber ship. Why worry them? He bought his food for the voyage – a stone of porridge oats, flour, butter, salted beef and a small pot, and returned to the Brunswick Dock.

The Mary Emma was loading, long lines of people waiting to board. More people were walking from the direction of the city to join them. He could see by their filthy clothes that they had come from the Dublin cattle ships, others coming direct from Westport, Ballina, Sligo and the other ports of the West of Ireland, the real centre of the famine and fever that killed, and went on killing.

He made his way to the Centaurus. No-one was boarding. He showed his ticket to a ganger.

'Sailing in three days,' the man told him.

'This is for Quebec, isn't it?'

'It is.'

'But it isn't a passenger ship.'

'Not now, it isn't,' the man replied. 'It will be, you just see. Lumber from the Canadas, passengers back. How do you think they make money? Ship them out by the ton, that's how.'

'That's what I thought,' Luke said. 'See you Wednesday so.'

'Where are you going?'

'Birkenhead. I've some friends there on the railway.'

'You've worked the railways, have you?'

'Six years…'

'Six years? You'll be well used to heavy labour so. We might have some use for you. Two shillings a day if you're interested.'

Luke hid his surprise.

'Of course I'm interested.'

'Go on up so, and ask for John Starkey. Tell him I sent you.'

Luke climbed the gangplank. He saw that carpenters and seamen were working inside the hold, where a second floor was being built. All around the sides, bunks were being built, three high. Down the centre of the ship were two double rows of bunks.

He spotted an officer.

'I'm looking for John Starkey,' he said. The man swung around.

'Who asked for me?'

'The officer below told me to...'

Their glances met.

'By God, if it isn't our fighting Irishman.'

'I was told you were looking for workers.'

Starkey laughed. Then he shouted to another officer.

'Louis, look who's arrived.'

He turned back to Luke. 'Well, you may work on this ship, but by God, I'll break you. You don't talk to me like you did in the bar. Not here. Not now. Do you understand?'

'Yes, Mr. Starkey.'

'Mr. Starkey, Sir. And don't you forget it.'

'No, Mr. Starkey, Sir.'

Starkey turned to the other officer. 'Remember this fellow?'

'Yes, Sir.'

'Let's see now just how tough he is. No need to waste him hammering nails. Get him over there, and start him carrying the timber.'

'Yes, Sir.'

'And make sure you work him hard.'

'Yes, Sir.'

Luke followed the officer to a high stack of timber.

'Don't worry about Starkey,' he told Luke, when they were out of hearing. 'More bark than bite, though don't say I said that. Still, he'll work you hard so long as you're in his clutches. Just stay with me and you should be fine.'

'He was all game to fight me there, yesterday.'

'I know, but he had drink taken. That's why I stopped him. I reckoned you had the build of a man who might flatten him. And whatever you do, don't try that here. You'd be flogged. He's the First Mate. Sailed the seven seas he has, and sure as hell doesn't like being on this boat. He's a Liverpool man. Speaks naught but the Queen's English. No French, nor would he want to, even if he got it for nothing. He hates French speakers, hates all the Irish.'

'They all do.'

'I know, I know. But what about you. Who are you? Where are you from?'

'Luke Ryan, I'm called. From County Mayo, if you've heard of it.'

'Heard of it? Haven't we all heard of it? Seems half our passengers are from County Mayo. See that lot behind the stacks.'

Luke saw another group of workers. Men, women and children, gaunt and dirty, the men all bearded.

'They're from Mayo?'

'They are. They're working their passage, unpaid. Not enough strength for real work. Unlike you. Now, Starkey is watching. Let's get you working too.'

Luke followed him again. Child workers! No different to Famine Relief Roadworks. And not even paid here, not even tuppence a day. How many would survive the passage? How many already had fever?

They crossed the hold to where a bundle of sawn timber had been un-roped. Two men loaded a beam on to his shoulders, and watched as he carried it across to the carpenters. He spent hours carrying timber, as instructed. He did not take off his pack, fearful it would be stolen.

A break was called. Luke sat down, sweating heavily. Starkey saw him.

'I was thinking how long it would take to break you.'

'I'm not broken,' Luke said. 'Mr. Starkey. Sir.'

'Not broken? We'll see about that. Fine, rest a few minutes, then back to it. What's your name?'

'Luke, Sir. Luke Ryan, Sir.'

'Luke Ryan, aye. Well I'll tell you this Luke Ryan. I'll have uses for you. And, by God, I'll make a sailor out of you, long before we get to Quebec.'

They worked on. As of habit, Luke counted the number of beds down the side and multiplied it across. Three hundred on this floor alone! Six hundred people on two floors, where there had only been lumber before.

When the final whistle was blown, Luke sat on a bundle of planks. The other officer sat beside him.

'You've been counting have you?'

Luke looked up in surprise. 'How did you know?'

'The look in your eyes and the way you were pointing, when you thought there was no one was looking. So what's the number?'

'Of bunks?'

'What else.'

'Near to six hundred, I'm reckoning.'

'And you could do all that in your head? You're good. I'd been thinking you were just a simple fellow from Mayo and you reckon like that. Have you schooling?'

'My uncle used to teach us. Not a Government kind of school, you understand, but good enough to reckon numbers.'

'It's more schooling than I ever had, I can tell you that. Still, I had to learn to get my Mates Ticket. Hard enough it was, and it makes a man know the value of learning.'

'I know what you mean,' Luke said.

The officer took out a pipe, tamped the tobacco in, and slowly lit it.

'We educated men must stick together, even if neither of us have been to proper schools. But one thing I must tell you, Luke. I'm the Second Mate, name of Tyler, and as long as you're on board the ship, you have to call me 'Mr. Tyler'. Or 'Sir' if you prefer. Otherwise call me nothing. It's not that I want it, but that's the way that it is. So don't ever think of calling me 'Louis'.'

'I understand,' Luke replied.

'An odd mixture, you might say. 'Louis' because my mother was Quebec. French speaking. The Tyler bit is from my father.'

'English, I'd guess.'

'An English-born sailor from one of the Medway towns. Chatham, right beside the docks. He was a tough fellow by all accounts. Ended up in the Workhouse, and so to the Merchant Marine and Quebec. When I was still only nine, he vanished on a voyage. Whether he was drowned or just ran off from my mother, I really don't know. One way or the other, it finished my schooling.'

'So what did you do then?'

'By the time I was eight, I was working the winter in the forests, and spending the summer on odd jobs. After my mother died, I ended up on the street. That's where half the Quebec sailors come from, those that don't come out of the jails.'

'You've worked in the forest, Mr. Tyler?'

'I have, though at the age of eight I wasn't earning much. They wouldn't let me out cutting the timber in the bush, they just kept me in the caboose shanty, peeling potatoes and the like. So with damned little earnings, when the spring came and the logging was over, I'd make my way back with the other fellows to Quebec. Then one day, I decided to try my hand as a sailor. There's no future in that though, so I decided to go on for my Mate's Ticket. Took me long enough too, but I got there in the end.'

'You've had a hard life, Mr. Tyler.'

'Not as bad as some, Luke. The poor devils we take to Quebec, they're the ones that have it worst. They're the reason that you're working as you are. It's almost impossible to get sailors for a wreck like this.'

'A wreck?'

'A wreck is all it is, and none of the sailors in Liverpool, nor Quebec neither, have any wish to be working on her. They're terrified of fever, and I can't say I blame them. So, since Press Gangs are out of fashion now, that's why we're desperate for men like you. Sharkey would never have taken you, except he knows he has to.'

'It makes sense,' Luke said. 'Still, we're being paid.'

'Aye, ye are. What are they giving you?'

'Two shillings a day.'

'Not so bad, you might think. They didn't tell you they were Canadian shillings, did they?'

'No...'

'Not quite the same as shillings sterling. Your two shillings are more like a shilling and eightpence when you work out the difference.'

'Not that I've much choice, do I, Mr. Tyler? It's still far better than any wage in Mayo.'

'None of us had much choice, Luke. I'll tell you one choice we have though, and that's not to ship out on this wreck again. The moment we hit Quebec, I'm off.'

After the carpenters had left, and the sailors had gone to their quarters, Luke was alone in the hold except for the huddled group of men, women and children in one corner. He already knew that he would not be allowed to sleep in the sailors' quarters due to the terror they had of fever being carried by the Irish. He went to the other end of the hold from the Mayo families. There he wrapped himself in his greatcoat, lay down in a soft heap of sawdust, and slept.

Next day, he worked on, helping the carpenters to swing the heavy beams and floorboards into position to finish building the second floor. Then more carrying timber, upstairs and across to where the bunks were being made. On the third day it was finished. He went to the second floor and found himself a bunk alongside the ladder leading up to the hatch onto the outer deck. Arms aching, he climbed up to the top bunk and lay on it. He knew these were safer, since the mess from men or women in fever could drop down on those below. Using a piece of spare rope he had found, he tied his pack onto his bunk and knotted it well.

At daybreak loading began. Luke leaned on the rails, watching the crowd of humanity entering the dock and flowing up the gangway into the hold. Tyler came alongside.

'Self-loading cargo,' he said. 'Costs a lot more to load the ship at the Quebec end, I can tell you.'

'Sometimes I think you're a little mocking, Mr. Tyler.'

'Maybe I am, Luke. It's just the way it is though, isn't it?'

Luke went down into the hold. Already fighting had erupted as people fought for the best bunks. Alarmed, he went to his own bunk. His pack was still there. He climbed up, and lay down, his head on his pack.

There was a tap on his shoulder.

'Luke. For God's sake, get up.'

'I didn't know you needed me, Mr. Tyler.'

'Need you! You're working now, and don't forget it. Come on.'

Luke was assigned to one of the bars on the anchor capstan, and heaved hard with the other sailors as the anchor rose.

The captain had come to supervise the weighing of the anchor. It was the first time Luke had seen him. He saw Luke, and came over to him. 'New, aren't you?'

'Yes sir.'

He muttered a few words which Luke could not hear. Then he prodded a finger into Luke's chest.

'And this is my ship, and don't you forget it.'

'No sir,' said Luke. He could smell the rum on the man's breath.

After the anchor was secured, Luke was assigned to coiling the ropes on deck. He watched as the docks of Liverpool slipped by on the right, the Wirral peninsula on the left. As soon as they left the Brunswick dock, their place was being taken by another ship. He recognised it at once as another lumber trader. As they passed long lines of other ships, he picked out another seven lumber ships at anchor.

Most of the passengers stayed below, but there were a few dozen on top. Again, there was the eerie keening from the women. One of the sailors swore in French. The other sailors glared at the women. They too were unnerved by the keening.

Chapter 2

Cork Examiner, August 1847:
Surely the Government will not allow the feeling from the disasters attending the poor Irish in a foreign land to pass away with the miserable deaths of the victims. Will there be no enquiry into the causes, immediate or remote, which produced all this loss of life? Into the modes of transport, the state of emigrant vessels, the abominations of emigrant agents, and all the etceteras which have become and are accessory to the deaths of the Irish poor. Out of the 2235 who embarked for Canada in those wretched hulks, called emigrant vessels, not more than 500 will live to settle in America.

The voyage of the Centaurus started well enough, with quiet seas, though it was very slow. As Liverpool disappeared astern, they sailed into the Irish Sea, they passed the Fylde Coast on the starboard side. Over the next few days, Luke saw the mountains of Westmoreland. The Isle of Man visible to the west, outlined against the setting sun.

Past the Kintyre Peninsula to starboard, the Glens of Antrim and Rathlin Island to port, the last they were to see of Ireland.

The long procession of mountainous Scottish islands to starboard. Islay and Jura. Mull, with tiny Iona at its tip. Tiree and Coll.

Then the open Atlantic.

Luke soon discovered what his duties were, and just as important, what they were not. He had been taken on as a swabbie, not as a sailor. The sailors were all Quebecers, and only knew French, which they spoke in their own argot. Luke was glad he was not expected to climb the rigging and furl or unfurl the sails. That was strictly reserved for sailors, and in any case, it would be dangerous for him because he did not understand their speech.

One of his jobs was cleaning the outside deck timbers with the rough limestone bars of holystone. This meant long hours on his knees scrubbing. He spent time too stuffing oakum between the timbers to keep them watertight, often under the sharp eye of Mr. Starkey.

His main duty though was manning the bilge pumps, often working two separate stretches of four hours each in a day, between his other duties. He suspected strongly that this was the reason he had been taken on, and it was the hardest. Pumping meant long hours in semi-darkness, pushing and pulling the handles of the pump up and down until his back ached with the effort. The stink was appalling. There was always a sailor on the other handle, but it was a duty that the sailors despised, and the more that Mr. Starkey could keep Luke on the pump, the more gratified the sailors seemed to be.

Many of the planks in the hull were rotten, and the gaps between them had not been caulked before they left port, nor could they have been unless the ship had been hauled on its sides to expose the bottom of the hull. Always, the water was seeping into the bilge hold to mix with other foul fluids and slops from the ship, though most of the filth from the shit buckets went overboard before it hit the bilge hold. At times, Luke feared that he would contract fever from the bilge, though, as he reflected, the passenger decks were probably more dangerous.

Working the pump went on all day. During squalls and storms, the pump was manned all night as well. Often, Luke worked at the pump right through the night as the ship pitched and rolled.

His bunk was a good one, well above the bilge hold. He could never get away from the stink of the hold though, nor the sounds of the people relieving themselves into the buckets, night and day. Every morning they slopped out, and this was a job for the passengers who were working their passage. 'Sloshers', the people called then. Every morning they carried the buckets outside and threw the shit and piss overboard. When the sea was rough, they also had to scrub down the passenger decks and scoop the shit into the buckets, before carrying them up. During storms, when the hatches were down, none of this was done and the stench got worse.

The bunk beneath was occupied by a young man, who never spoke. Instead he turned his head to the hull, and seemed to sleep for most of the day. Luke had seen this kind of misery before, the misery of a man who had already been broken.

Luke himself spoke to no one, except when necessary, and he told no one of where he was from and where he was going, nor did he ask. There was no point either in talking of conditions on the ship. That would only depress him. In any case, he had little time. Most people were asleep when he left the passenger decks to start work in the mornings, and asleep again when he returned.

The women's keening had stopped when Ireland had dropped below the horizon. The only disturbance now was the wailing of babies, and the crazed whine of an old man, all through the night. That apart, the ship was quiet, and he slept well enough.

Cooking was not easy. At first, he had enough to eat from what he had bought in Liverpool, and he added to it by buying cabbage from the ship's stores. But the vegetables on board ran out very early, and after that, he never ate anything green.

The kitchen had a long narrow bin, filled with sand, with a log fire built on top. Often the smoke of the fires forced them out of the kitchen. Luke had been frustrated by this, and also by the time he spent standing in line for the kitchen, especially since he never had enough free time.

His rations were simple now – porridge with water in the morning, flat bread with butter and smoked meat at mid-day, and sometimes porridge in the evening. Then he began to buy ship biscuits, picking out the weevils, though in the end he ate them too. As time passed, he rationed himself to save money and food.

He never ate with the sailors, who kept well to themselves.

There was little enough water for cooking and drinking, but none for washing or shaving. At first, the prickling of his beard irritated him, but as it grew, he became used to it. When it grew too long, he borrowed a Sheffield scissors to cut it back.

He had one change of clothes, and this helped, but he quickly became rather repulsed with himself. He got used to it though, and slept in his clothes every night, his single blanket wrapped around him, inside his greatcoat so it could not be stolen.

He watched anxiously for any signs of disease. There was enough sea sickness in the early days, that was for sure, but no obvious evidence of fever then. But that was to change.

As he made his way to the pump one day, he passed a screaming woman. He saw her head was swollen, and her face was hideously deformed. Her cheeks were red, but the rest of her face had turned white. Her feet were swollen too, and covered with putrid, black spots. He could smell the reek of decaying flesh. Now he knew for the first time that there was fever aboard ship.

He thought back on the desperate winter days in the mountains, watching people slowly dying from fever. The screaming. The unmistakable stink of gangrene.

And Alicia's death too, years before the hunger came.

A few days later, he saw the ill woman's corpse being man-handled up onto the outer deck. A priest accompanied it, and it was laid on the deck. He made the form of a cross on the woman's forehead.

'Per istam sanctam Unctionem...'

Through this Holy Unction, May the Lord free you from sin, and raise you up on the Last Day.

Luke went down on one knee. The corpse was wrapped in a shroud, and weights attached. Then it was passed over the side of the ship.

When all was finished, Luke walked over to the priest.

'It's started."

'It has,' the priest replied. 'And more to come before we make land. Her husband has it.'

Yes, Luke thought. How much further would it spread? How many would survive the voyage?

Would he?

There had been many days and nights of wind and rain, but then the first storm came.

It began with a rising wind, and the sails were lowered. The sailors worked fast as the masts swung from side to side. The passengers were sent below, and the hatches were battened down.

The wind was still rising, and the rain became torrential. The outer deck flooded, and the rolling of the ship flushed it through the gaps between the hatches and the deck. Seawater poured down into the two passenger decks. Soon the water was ankle deep in the lowest deck, and it sloshed from side to side as the ship bucked and rolled. There was more sea sickness and the screaming of frightened children.

Luke spent much of that desperate night at the bilge pump. Now there were two men on each handle, working the pump far faster than before, as the water from the decks cascaded into the bilge hold. For some time, it seemed that the water kept rising as the ships timbers flexed before the waves, and water came in through the splits in the ship's timbers.

After two desperate hours, Luke was relieved, and staggered back to his bunk. He nibbled on his smoked beef, but it was not enough, and for the first time since the winter in the mountains, he felt the bite of hunger.

He was only able to count the days by the chinks of light coming through a little crack between the cover and the hatch at the back of the ship, where the water sloshed in as the waves hit.

For four days they ran before it, the sails wrapped tight on the masts, the decks stripped bare, the hatches battened tight. Four days in the darkness, women and children screaming as the ship lurched up and down. Four days living with the foul smell of vomit and shit in the passenger decks, and even worse at the bilge pump.

Then it was over, and they were in the gentle swell of the North Atlantic. Starkey allowed them outside for the first time. As Luke made his way towards the ladder, he passed another woman screaming on her bunk. He noticed again the reek of decaying flesh. Now he knew for certain that fever was spreading through the ship.

Within a few days there were other cases, and the woman was showing clear signs of gangrene, and her face and legs were bloated. A week later, she and two more were dead, including the husband of the woman who had died before the storm.

Now Luke had a new duty. Starkey ordered him to supervise the disposal of the corpses. The sailors had refused to undertake this duty, and even the threat of a flogging had not moved them. They knew full well the dangers of contagion. So did Luke.

The irony of this struck him. He was now a ganger again, even if it took little of his time. He thought back to the building of famine roads across Croghancoe, supervising people who were desperate for money, but hardly able to work.

Every morning now, he walked between the bunks. Any corpse found had to be manhandled up the ladders to the outer deck. At first, Luke tried to have this done by the family, knowing that they had been closest to the infection, and not wishing to infect other passengers. This proved to be impossible though.

The bodies were wrapped in shrouds, and weights attached, before they were thrown into the devouring sea. As the fever killed more, the corpses were thrown into the ocean unweighted.

Again and again the priest repeated the blessing, as Luke and the families dropped to their knees.

'*Per istam sanctam Unctionem...*'

'*How many dead now?*' the priest asked him.

'*Seven.*'

Next day.

'*How many?*'

'*Ten.*'

Day after day.

'*How many?*'

'*Fourteen.*'

'*How many?*'

'*Twenty two.*'

Then there were no more shrouds. For some days, he was able to use old sails, which he had cut up to use as shrouds, but these too, ran out. Bodies were stripped of clothes by the families, or those nearby, and the victims were dispatched to the sea stark-naked.

The clothes were sold by auction. Clothes were valuable. Sometimes fights broke out at these 'auctions', and then it fell to Luke to supervise them, sometimes taking the bidding himself. He had no interest in buying clothes himself, knowing well the risk of fever.

And still the fever spread. He spent hours picking the lice out of his clothes and blanket, fearful that they were carrying fever. He knew the only way to kill them properly was to boil the clothes, but there was little chance of that. Sometimes, he wondered whether the lice were the real cause of the fever, or just a superstition he had picked up in the mountains in County Mayo. But who else would understand the reason for boiling clothes, far less dispose of them without selling them?

They hit a second storm, but after two days, it too had calmed.

Then the third storm came. This one lasted longer and was far more violent. For some time, Luke stood at the stern, watching the lightning flashing from horizon to horizon. It became continuous and the thunder roll went on without a break. Then the rain came, pouring down in a torrent of water. The wind rose and the waves became mountainous. Still Luke stayed above, drenched to the skin, but almost exultant. It brought to mind the Big Wind of 1839. He knew he was in danger, but the sheer power of the storm overawed him.

'Luke, in the name of God what are you doing?' Tyler grasped him by the shoulder and pulled him back sharply.

'Go down to the hold, now. That's an order. We've got to get the bilge pump working.'

'It's not working?'

'The sailors have refused. They won't go downside – they know there's fever. They say the passengers should be doing it. Damned bastards, but I just can't shift them. Get the passengers working. Do it now.'

Luke went to do as he was ordered, but when they came to the hatch he had to help Tyler to open it. He scrambled in as Tyler shut the hatch after him with a crash.

The women and children were screaming, convinced they were to die. Quickly, Luke selected some of the healthier men and ordered them down the ladder to the pump.

'*But we're paying passengers,*' one man protested.

'*Aye, and you'll be dying passengers if the ship sinks.*'

They were not strong, but they set to, two to a handle, working until they were exhausted. Then Luke had them replaced, sometimes after only half an hour, and sent them back to the decks to find more men. When he was convinced the pump was working well, he climbed back up. For fear of fever, some of the sick had been deserted by their families. Abandoned or not, there was no way of cleaning them in the darkness, and the water between the bunks swilled their filth throughout the deck,

The air was already fetid, and became worse. The stench was unbearable, but it had to be endured. By the third day, Luke was finding it difficult to breath, gasping and inhaling deeply to gain sufficient air for his lungs. Now he had four men working each handle on the pump. He wondered how much longer he could keep the pump going.

The fever patients, already weakened, no longer had the strength to breath. More died during those days, but the hatches remained locked, and the stinking bodies lay where they were, putrid with gangrene.

On the fourth day the hatches were opened, and they were let out – men, women and children clambering onto the open deck, staggering and falling as the ship pitched violently. Some made their way to the rail, holding tightly as others grasped them from behind. Many lay where they were on deck, breathing the fresh sea air,

The storm died down, and as the waves died away, the ship steadied.

More funerals.

'*How many dead now, Luke?*'

'*Thirty one.*'

Next day.

'*Forty.*'

Next day.

'*Forty six.*'

One morning, as he was stuffing oakum into cracks, Tyler called him to the rail.

'Still alive, I see.'

'Just about, Mr. Tyler.'

'I'm sorry I can't see you as often as I would like. I have to oversee all these fellows, you know. Takes all my time when they're up the rigging. Mr. Starkey won't do it. He reckons it's not his business, that's for the Second Mate. But the real reason is a different one. I'm the only one of the officers that speaks French. All the sailors are out of Quebec, and he can't speak a word to them. They're devils, they are. They pretend not to understand English, even when they do. Not that they need much overseeing when they're on the bilge pump, and they know their lives depend on it.'

'No,' said Luke. 'But now they know they can get the passengers on the pump. Isn't that it?'

'Yes, and we may have to keep it that way. The sailors are terrified of fever if they go down. One of them has fever already. And whether you like it or not, we're short of sailors to work this damned ship, and we can't afford to lose any. We've lost enough passengers already.'

'I know. Fifty eight by my count.'

'Counting again?'

'Yes, Mr. Tyler.'

Tyler shook his head. 'You're some fellow.'

'I don't know about that. But there wouldn't be so many dead, nor much call for a pump if the ship weren't leaky, would there?'

'There'd still be need for one, but only an hour or two a day on the better vessels, very little on a passenger ship. But this is a lumber ship, and no one gives a damn if it sinks. It would be easier for the bastards if it did. The ship's worth damned little, the passengers even less, and all they cause is trouble when they land at Quebec, carrying fever and whinging about the way they were treated and all that have died. I'll tell you this Luke, it wouldn't be like this going to an American port, that's for sure and certain.'

'Why not, Mr. Tyler?'

'Because the Americans inspect them all the time, that's why. The ship-owners, they know damned well they won't let them in with fever, so they make bloody sure that there isn't any. Even the Mayo ships carry fever, but there's nothing like the numbers. Do you know, just before we left Quebec the last time, we saw the Dew Drop coming in – a Westport ship. And do you know how many had died on the crossing there? None. None at all. And she didn't even have to stay over for quarantine at Grosse Île. But you see, she wasn't a lumber carrier. The Dew Drop was built to take passengers. That's not to say all passenger ships are fine, some can be just as bad as this wreck. But the ones going to Boston and New York, they have to be a better class of ship altogether.'

'But how?' Luke asked. 'How in God's name…?'

'They don't cram them in, that's how. But Quebec will let them in, all packed like sheep for the slaughter, just waiting to die in the quarantine sheds. I'll tell you this, they wouldn't dare to treat men like that unless they were going to Quebec. Like I say, the shippers don't give a damn. All they're doing is taking you as ballast – lumber out, passengers back. Human cargo – and no-one cares. Nothing matters to them now. Big ships they are, they have to be for the tonnage they carry. And for that reason they go into the big ports – Cork, Dublin, but most of all, Liverpool. And when they get there, when they've got rid of their cargo, what do they have to carry back? Quebec doesn't need that tonnage of cargo. So you crush hundreds of them in the cargo hold, doesn't matter how they fit them in. There's hardly any English among them either. All Irish, that's what they are, taking the cheapest passage to Quebec. Through Liverpool. The Liverpool ships, they're filthy. And they're murderous. They all are, not just this wreck. Listen, I saw it myself in Quebec. The end of May it was. The John Bolton, sailing out of Liverpool. I saw what she was like when she came into Grosse Île. Damned near the half of them died at sea, and I reckon half of the ones who survived the sea, died at Grosse Île, either on the ship, or in the fever sheds. That ship was a disgrace to humanity. And even last year, there was nothing like this in the Quebec ships.'

'So you're saying it's only Quebec,' Luke said. 'And worst this year.'

'Dead right, it is. God knows I've crossed the Atlantic many times, and I've never seen it like this. Back in the spring, it began. This is my third time in the Centaurus, and I wouldn't be here if I could have gotten off it sooner. I'll not sign with this one again, and that's an end to it.'

'Where will you go?'

'Damned if I know. New York, if I can. Boston maybe. But it's not easy. Who knows, I might have to go to New Bedford, and go on a whaler. It's a damned rough life that though.'

'I'd heard that. You've been whaling, have you?'

'Indeed. I've whaled all over. The southern oceans, that's where I spent my years on the whalers. Chasing the southern right whale along the Roaring Forties. All round Antarctica, and back through Cape Horn. Doubled the Horn three times, I did, Valparaiso to Rio. But it's a young man's game, so I shipped home to Quebec, trying to find easier work. The lumber ships, they were good work then. But then I ended up on this wreck, and it's worse than any whaler I can tell you. Same with all the Quebec fleet. So it's back to whaling for me, I'm thinking.'

He nudged Luke.

'So what about you? What are you planning?'

'I'm trying to get out to some lads I know working the rails out in Pennsylvania. I worked with them on a gang back in England. Six years building railways in every part of the country. From what we've heard back in Mayo, there's good money on the American railways, and that's where I'm aiming to get. It was one of my friends – Martin Farrelly – that advised me to come this way. Wrote a letter from Pennsylvania saying it was impossible to get into the American ports, and advised Quebec. Some of the Irish fellows I knew on the railways have worked the forests, just like you told me. Then they crossed the border into America to work the rails with Martin. I might try the same. First the forests. Then the railways.'

Just before dawn the following day, two corpses had been dragged up by Luke and the other men, and lay on the deck awaiting the priest. It was only when he saw the panic among the sailors, he realised they were in danger.

The ship was running at high speed in the early dawn, driven by a strong wind behind, when out of the sea ahead of them loomed a huge mountain of ice. An iceberg – and they were heading directly for it. There was chaos as sailors ran up the rigging. More tumbled out of the boat, half dressing themselves as they did so. But they were very slow. Luke knew more of the sailors were down with fever, and wondered how strong the others were. He felt a moment of pure panic. To come all this way and die in the freezing Atlantic! He watched the sailors in the rigging, awed at the complexity of what they were doing. Tyler was hanging on one of the spars, screaming directions to the sailors as Starkey screamed directions to him from the deck. The captain was nowhere to be seen.

Gradually, the ship reduced speed, and slowly – ever so slowly – began to change direction. Luke was sure now they would hit it broadside on, but as it grew in size he realised that the iceberg was further away than he had thought. For endless minutes he watched it approach.

Abruptly, the danger was over, and he saw they would miss the iceberg. As they passed it, he stared at it, half bewitched by it. The size of it, the sheer overwhelming power of it.

It was only then that he realised how he was shivering, whether from cold or fear, he could not tell. He wrapped his coat tighter around himself, thinking back on County Mayo. They were depending on his letter and the money it would bring, both to feed them through the rest of the famine and to bring Winnie to America.

There would be no letter to Mayo if the ship had sunk.

Chapter 3

Mayo Constitution, July 1847:
On the 7th instant, the Emily Marie of Skerries, a smack laden with Indian corn, was attacked near Inniskea, but the captain having applied to the commander of the Emerald Cutter, now stationed in Broadhaven, for the marines which were on board, the people made so desperate an attack that the marines resolutely defended the property under their care, and shot four of the plunderers dead, and wounded several others. It is to be hoped that this melancholy occurrence will put a stop to plunder on the Erris coast.

Ireland. Luke had left Mayo because he had to leave. A vicious famine two years long – that was reason enough for hundreds of thousands to leave. But for Luke there were other reasons.

Winnie knew that. And Eleanor was finding out.

Eleanor had been surprised by Winnie. Luke had chosen his wife well, there was no doubt about that. She had perhaps been a little quieter before, though forceful enough when alone with Eleanor and the other women. She had taken intensely to Brigid, Eleanor's grand-niece. That was no surprise. All the women were close to Brigid, projecting their hopes and aspirations on an orphaned child, not two years old.

Through the growing horror of fever and famine, Winnie's character seemed to only grow stronger. She was determined that the Ryans at least would survive. She had been devastated by Luke's emigration, but she, like Eleanor, knew that there was no other way. Winnie was determined not to show how distressed she was, though there were times she could not hide it.

She had become protective of her mother-in-law. Whenever corn had to be bought, Winnie would take it upon herself to go up to Kilduff and join the scramble outside Dillon's shop. Eleanor knew that this carried a risk from fever, but Winnie would not allow Eleanor to leave the farm unless it was necessary. For fear of fever, they no longer even went to Mass.

Not that that was necessary to understand what was happening. Eleanor always insisted on Winnie telling her what she had seen and heard. Rat-eaten bodies in the streets, people lying in the open with horrific signs of fever, the people outside the shop showing the late signs of starvation. Mud cabins beside the road pulled down over dead families with no burial at all. There were stories of bodies buried in turf banks, rumours of new evictions to come, and much more. Always, Winnie would talk of these things in a flat voice. Trying to hide her own sense of shock, perhaps? Eleanor did not know. But still, behind it all, there was the brutal resolve that the Ryan family would not suffer such horror. But could they avoid it?

Always, Eleanor felt a dull, grey fear.

Yes, the potato crop was looking good, but it had been the same last year. Then the blight had struck again, and destroyed most of the crop – even those that had already been dug. Now desperate people were convincing themselves that the blight was gone, but Eleanor was not so sure. The next weeks would tell much. What if the blight returned a third time? What would that mean? That the potato was finished forever as food? What then?

Yes, they had survived the past two years. During the worst of it, Michael had been working the quarry, but more important their two sons were working, Luke as a ganger on the Famine Relief Works in the mountains, and Pat as a clerk at Knockanure Workhouse. So they had had enough cash for corn, right through the devastating potato failure. Now they would have no money from Luke until he reached America. But Pat had been kept on as a clerk in the Workhouse, and he had become the family's sole source of money. They could still pay the rent and buy corn.

At times, Eleanor felt guilty about this, and she suspected Winnie did too. Many families had no income at all, and very few could pay the rent and have enough left for food. It was not that the Ryans were well-off. They had never been that, and over the past two years, Eleanor had slowly been cutting back on what the family was eating. Michael had become thin, Eleanor even thinner. Still, they were not suffering the vicious agony of outright starvation. Michael had come close to dying of fever, but after weeks of cruel pain and wild nightmares, he had survived, and she was not a widow.

The two women started to prepare the dinner. It was mostly cabbage with very little turnip, only one old potato each, and no meat. When had they last tasted meat, even chicken?

'*You're looking worried,*' Eleanor said. '*What's on your mind?*'

'*A letter.*'

'*It'll be a long time before we see that.*'

'*Ach, I know, I know, but still.*'

'*Still what?*'

'*Three months married and he went…*'

'*I know it's hard on you. But…*'

'But yes, I couldn't have asked for better. You treat me as your own daughter, you do, yourself and Michael.'

'That's easy enough. You're great company for an old woman. We'll miss you when you go.'

'No more than I'll miss you. And you're not old, so don't be saying it.'

'Oh, I don't know about that. And stop your fretting – you'll have Luke waiting for you in America. You know that.'

Winnie put down the turnip she had been peeling.

'If he gets there.'

'Don't be silly. He'll be there.'

'But what if gets fever?'

'He won't. He's been close to fever enough many times in the mountains. If he was going to get it, he'd have had it by now. But it's your baby we'll have to worry about. If your baby catches the fever, it will surely die.'

Winnie sat, patting her stomach.

'Well, that's far enough away yet.'

Eleanor sat at the table across from her. She reached across, placing her hand on Winnie's arm.

'Now you're to stop worrying about it all, child. Luke will write again soon enough. You've got the baby to think about, and sure we've both got Brigid to look after too. Time will pass quick enough. Come this time next year, Luke and yourself and the new baby will be together in America.'

Winnie quivered.

'Oh look mother, I'm sorry, but I still can't help thinking. There's terrible stories about the ships to Quebec. There are some that say half the people on them died.'

'And you believe stories like that, do you? Isn't it the right amadán you are?'

Or is she? Eleanor thought. Who knows? Do I?

One morning, Michael was out digging potatoes for the first time. Winnie was inside with Eleanor, clearing up scraps after breakfast and mashing them for the hens.

Everyone is saying it's a great crop,' Winnie said.

'It is,' said Eleanor. 'Would you ever have thought it after the past year?'

'I'm still not sure though. I'd thought the potato was finished forever?'

'It's easy worried you are, child.'

'Oh, I don't know – we might see the rot yet. There were many last year looked well enough when they were dug.'

'Will you stop that now? If they were going to rot, they'd have begun by now. Don't you know that?'

41

Why did I say that? she thought. *Do I really believe it? They've still not rotted these past weeks, but are we really clear of it now? Is it really too late for the blight to return? Should I believe it now?*

Winnie had said nothing. Could she believe? Why worry her now?

'The blight is gone, Winnie.' Eleanor said. 'We'll have enough potatoes now. Michael always kept his faith, never let us eat the seed potatoes, always made sure there were enough planted.'

'Yes, yes,' Winnie replied. 'I'm sure you've the right of it. But what of everyone else? Sure there's hardly any potatoes planted at all. The people, they're dying all around us and they'll stay dying. The Food Kitchens are closed, the Relief Works are closed. Sure enough, the price of corn is dropping at last, but it won't drop far, and there's not much of that they'll get if they have no money. And the poor creatures are getting desperate. Roaming the country at night, digging at potatoes wherever they can find them.'

'I know, I know,' Eleanor said. 'Ours would all be gone by now, but for Michael sleeping out among the potatoes to guard them, though I doubt he gets much sleep out there. Thank God the nights are warm, God only knows what kind of shelter he'd get in that little hut if the rain comes.'

Winnie picked up the bucket of mashed scraps and went out to feed the hens. She returned with an empty bucket.

'They keep pecking at me.'

'Maybe they want to eat you!'

'I wouldn't blame them for that. God knows, they're scrawny enough. Still, if we have enough potatoes being dug, they won't be hungry much longer.'

She had started to make a brown bread loaf, putting the flour into a bowl and adding the baking soda. She poured in the buttermilk and mixed it all together, then turned it out onto the table to form into a cake.

Leave that a minute and sit down there,' Eleanor said. *'I want to talk to you.'*

'What's that?'

'Tell me about Luke. What really happened the months he was in the mountains with ye?'

Winnie shook her head. 'It's hard enough to tell you. Working as a ganger was hard on him.'

'But how?'

'Well, the first thing – the pain and suffering he saw. We think we've seen it with starving people passing the road and working the Relief Works and queuing at the Kitchens.'

'Indeed' said Eleanor, 'but that was before they closed them all. It's worse since.'

'It is, but you must understand, Luke was seeing that every day – hunger, fever and cold. Starving people being forced to work in the snow, dying every day. It's hard for any man to watch that, far worse to have to do the forcing. And they hated him on the Works. He was their ganger, and they hated him.'

'Yes, I can understand that,' Eleanor said. 'They were cruel, the roadworks were. But the Government wouldn't let them earn money any other way, and the Workhouses were full. And coming into the time of the snows – that was desperate...'

'It was. But worse than that, there was the going to the houses. When the people didn't come back, he'd go around the houses to pay them, or whoever was left after them. Him and the priest, God only knows how they did it. I think that was the worst of all. It's bad enough watching people dying of hunger, what it does to their bodies, to the children's faces. But worse again was the fever. It's a terrible way to die. Their faces and legs swell up, the fever eats at them, and they die screaming. And the stink of it.'

'I know,' Eleanor said. 'Didn't my own daughter die of it?'

'I'm sorry. I didn't mean...'

'Of course you didn't, alanna. But what of Luke?'

Winnie gulped.

'It was everything all coming together. The suffering, the cold, and the hatred they had for him. He thought he was going mad, and I don't know, maybe he was. There was something strange in the mountains, something that terrified him. You know Croghancoe, the mountain?'

'I've heard of it,' Eleanor said,' but I've never been over that way.'

'He kept on telling me he saw something behind it, but there was nothing there. Something so powerful, it frightened the hell out of him.'

'Something that wasn't there?'

'Well, that's what he said. Like some class of a vision.'

Eleanor thought of that.

'It wasn't any kind of a vision' she said, 'more some kind of madness. Something that only lasts a minute or so, isn't that it?'

'I don't know. But one way or another, whatever it was about Croghancoe, there was something that scared him witless. Who knows what it was?'

Michael came back, carrying a sack load of potatoes. Excited, Winnie took one out. She sliced it straight through. Good white flesh, and still no blight.

That evening, they ate a good dinner for the first time in a very long time. Eleanor almost felt bloated. Long months without potatoes had accustomed her to being satisfied with very little.

Next day, Luke's letter arrived from Liverpool.

'*He's saying the ship is a good one,*' Winnie said.

'*Well, that's something to be thankful for,*' Eleanor said.

'*And he says there's no blight on the English potatoes either. We're going to be lucky this year.*'

'*We are,*' Eleanor said.

'*And isn't it the right pity, Luke couldn't have stayed in England. I'd be there with him.*'

'*And work with Danny, is it? No way would he do that. God knows, Danny would take Luke quick enough, and pay him well too, but he's a rough man, and I reckon his ways of working men are rough too. Pays his gangers well, but the men are on starvation wages.*'

As Winnie returned to Carrigard one day, she spotted Kitty Brennan ahead of her. She ran to catch up.

'*God with you, Kitty.*'

Kitty turned around, startled. '*You shouldn't be sneaking up on me like that.*'

'*I'm sorry.*'

Winnie was startled by Kitty's appearance. Thin, yes, but the bruising on her face had returned, and her shift was far more ragged than before.

'*Going to see Brigid, are you?*' Winnie asked.

'*Aye, and the rest of ye. And sure, why wouldn't I?*'

When they arrived at Carrigard, Eleanor was in the kitchen.

'*Kitty, child.*'

Brigid ran across the room screaming '*Kitty, Kitty...*'

Kitty drew the child up, and hugged her. Suddenly the baby drew back, fingering the bruises and cuts on Kitty's face, and began to cry.

'*There, there,*' Kitty said, '*stop crying, alanna.*' She handed the child over to Winnie who glanced across at Eleanor. Both women knew what had caused the bruising.

Kitty sat at the table, trying hard to laugh. '*I hope ye like my new dress.*'

'*What happened?*' Eleanor asked.

'*Fergus reckoned my last dress was too good for me, so he sold it. He said we needed the money for food, but the half of it he spent on poitín. He told me too he needed the money for his father's funeral expenses. Not that much went on that – he was buried under the turf, poor man.*'

Winnie went into her bedroom. She came out with a dress. '*Here, take this.*'

'*Indeed, I will not. It'll only go on whiskey and poitín, don't you know that?*'

Eleanor placed a cup of buttermilk in front of her. She buttered a slice of brown bread, and put it alongside. '*Here, you might as well eat while you're here. At least he can't sell that.*'

Kitty ate and drank. Then she took Brigid from Winnie and put her on her knee, gently rocking her up and down. Brigid started as if to cry again, but did not. Within a few minutes she was asleep.

'*Are things so bad on the Mountain?*' Eleanor asked. '*What are you hearing?*'

'*Worse than here, that's for certain. The people from the Gort-na-Móna evictions, the half of them are dead. The rest of them, they're sleeping in bog holes with branches and sods of turf over them. They've no chance, and wherever they go, they bring the fever with them. The people from Currach-an-Dúin tried to run them away, fighting them off with sticks and stones, but where else could they go, poor devils. And there's no food for them, none at all. When they came off the Mountain, we had to stand guard over our corn and what was left of the potatoes. Every night. Fergus or me, depending. At least it meant I had a bed to myself some of the time. In the end, we had to dig the potatoes and bring them inside, the donkey too. There's not many donkeys left now. They were all killed and eaten, raw the half of them, every bit they could, fresh or rotten. That's killed a lot of people now, vomiting up all they ate. If they had horses, they'd be gone too, but they've no horses on the Mountain.*'

'*We'd best watch over our own so,*' Eleanor said.

'*You'd better,*' Kitty said. '*There's scarce half a dozen sheep left on the Mountain, I hear.*'

'*You don't surprise me,*' Winnie said. '*Even down here I've seen and heard all those kind of things, but we're hoping it will get better. The potatoes at least are looking good.*'

'*Indeed,*' Kitty replied, '*for those who had potatoes to plant.*'

She hugged the baby, still breathing gently on her breast.

'*And at least there's one little angel isn't too worried. Look at the smile on her face, and she not even awake.*'

'*Long may she smile, so,*' Winnie said. '*And we're the ones who are going to keep her smiling. We'll school her, she'll be a teacher. We will do it, even if they all think we're mad. If we can't have hope in Brigid, Mayo is finished.*'

'*True for you,*' Kitty said, '*but she's not our only hope. There's your baby coming – there's other chances too.*'

'*Yes,*' said Eleanor, '*but not in Ireland.*'

'*What does it matter if it's Ireland or not,*' Kitty said. '*It's a future for Irish people, isn't it? And anyway, there's good money there, and whatever ye have left to send back will help everyone here.*'

When Michael came in the meal was ready. He sat at the table, glancing at Kitty. 'I'd heard Fergus' father was dead.'

'That's right,' Kitty replied, speaking in English now. 'We buried him three days ago.'

'I'm sorry we couldn't make it.'

'Sure if you tried to make every funeral, you'd never get any work done,' Eleanor said. 'There aren't enough hours in the day for all the funerals. If they even get funerals.'

Brigid had woken. Eleanor took her from Kitty, and started to feed her buttermilk. At first Brigid refused the spoon, but then she swallowed it down.

'Well Michael, do you still think we're mad?' Eleanor asked.

'I don't know,' Michael answered. 'Having a teacher in the family, sure it's pure mad. But for God's sake, don't tell anyone else, they'll all be laughing.'

'Let them laugh so. They'll be laughing the other side of their faces when she comes back here, and she a teacher. Isn't that so?'

'Damn it to hell,' Michael replied, 'you're infecting me with your madness now. I still don't know how we'll do it, I don't know where the money is to come from. I don't even know how long we'll feed ourselves. And none of us knows if the baby has the brains for it.'

'...brains...' Brigid repeated.

'And there's your answer,' Winnie said. 'Trying to talk already. There's brains there right enough.'

Eleanor passed a plate to Kitty. 'Here, if your husband's not feeding you, we'll have to get something inside you.'

Kitty took the plate, as Michael passed her over a potato.

'Tell us this,' she asked, 'what are ye hearing about Pat? Has he been over lately?'

'Not for two weeks now,' Michael replied, 'but we're reckoning he'll be back tomorrow night.'

'And thank God for that' Eleanor said. 'You're going to need help with the potatoes with such a great crop.'

'*Arra,* hell,' Michael said.

'No, *a ghrá.* You take help where you get it. I'm sure Pat'll stay out with the potatoes for a night or two, keep an eye on them, and let you sleep. Isn't that what sons are for?'

Eleanor had been amazed at how accepting Michael was of Kitty. He certainly had not accepted her at first, when he had learned of the affair between her and Luke. But that had been over a year ago, and in that year Michael had come to despise Kitty's husband, and had come to respect Kitty in a way that Eleanor had never expected. Now he would defend her against

46

anyone who made sly comments about the past liaison between Luke and Kitty. Not that many made such comments anymore. Famine and fever gave them other things to think about.

Eleanor had been even more surprised at Winnie's relationship with Kitty. Winnie knew Kitty had been Luke's lover, she knew too of the scandal it had caused, and yet she accepted her. At first this had been because of their shared ambition for Nessa's orphaned daughter, but now Eleanor knew that it was deeper than that. Much deeper.

Chapter 4

Mayo Constitution, September 1847:
The Unions throughout our county being in debt, and without a vestige of credit, what is to become of the people? Are they to starve by the wayside? Are they to be left to plunder and rob, and turn our prisons into poor house Bastilles? Are the Government determined to try one or other experiment in the shortest period of getting rid of the surplus population? Are they determined to admire once more how 'nobly these Irish die?'

Pat's position in Knockanure Workhouse was a good one, and he knew it. A clerical position at thirty five pounds a year was one of the most sought after positions in the county, and even more so given the fever and starvation around. Looking at the hundreds of inmates in the Workhouse, and the dozens who died every month, he knew he was lucky indeed. Yes, he had to work hard, but that was only to be expected at a time like this. Still, his position was a secure one, or so he hoped. It was permanent, unless he did something terrible, and he certainly did not intend that, especially given his growing rapport with Sarah.

One morning, he sat in the office with her.

'You're nervous, Pat,' she said.

'Maybe I am. Not so much nervous though, just concerned that I get everything right. Mr. Voisey needs these figures to persuade the Guardians to keep the place going. And the Workhouse is going through money at an awful rate, given the times that are in it.'

'I know.'

'Yes, and Clanowen was never a man to let anything by, or have anything put over on him. And this Trinder fellow, what do we know about him since he's taken over as Master? No, it's going to be a difficult meeting and Voisey's depending on me.'

'And hundreds of others depend on you too.'

'Oh God, don't remind me.'

Twenty minutes later, one of the inmates called for him. Pat gathered up all his papers, and went to the Boardroom for the Guardians Meeting.

At the head of the table sat Lord Clanowen, by far the largest land owner in the area, whose estate covered much of the land from Knockanure up to the lower slopes of the Ox Mountains. Pat had once considered him as a fair man, but his opinion had changed after the Clanowen evictions. For Clanowen, as for the Workhouse, money was the key issue.

Pat knew that many landlords in Mayo were being bankrupted by the Famine. Many of the smaller landlords could not afford to pay the Rates, no matter how hard they squeezed the small tenant farmers under them. It was the tenants who paid the rents, and the landlords who paid the rates that paid for the Workhouses. And even if Clanowen himself could pay, the Guardians included a number of other smaller landlords and magistrates, and Pat had no idea who among them could pay, or who could not.

Cecil Trinder, the new Master of Knockanure Workhouse, was an unknown factor too. Sarah's own father had been Master, until he had died of fever, like so many hundreds of the inmates. Since then, the Workhouse had been running without any Master, until Trinder was promoted from an assistant position in the South Dublin Workhouse. But Dublin was not Mayo, and Pat wondered how long it would take Trinder to appreciate the difference between common Dublin poverty and the outright starvation and brutal fever that was crushing Mayo and the rest of the West.

Voisey had been the Poor Law Inspector for Knockanure Union since the beginning of the Famine in 1845. Pat always thought of him as a deeply religious man, more concerned for the welfare of the inmates than the landlords were. Still, it was a delicate balancing act, maintaining the stinginess of the Guardians against the voracious demands of the Workhouses for cash.

'Do you have the sums there, Pat?' Voisey asked.

Pat handed out ten copies of a single page, which he and Sarah had only just finished transcribing. It contained the key figures for the Workhouse's accounts, with total spending for the month at the bottom.

When Clanowen received his copy, he glanced down and shuddered.

'I thought our rate of spending was supposed to be dropping.'

'Damned right, it should,' said one of the other men. 'What's the explanation for this?'

Everyone looked at Pat.

'There are a number of reasons,' said Pat, 'but the main one, as you will see, is that the number of inmates is going up again.'

'Why is that?' Clanowen asked.

Pat was about to respond, but Voisey put his hand on his elbow.

'I don't have to tell you about the closing of the Soup Kitchens.' Voisey answered. 'That's forced a lot of families back to the Workhouse. Also, there's been a number of evictions locally.'

Including Clanowen's, Pat thought. How many families did his agents throw on the road?

'So what have we now?' Clanowen asked, sharply. 'How many?'

'Over nine hundred,' Voisey answered, 'which, with respect, is an improvement on April when we had well over twelve hundred. Some weeks ago, it had dropped to eight hundred, as I told you. But since then, the death rate has been dropping, and more of the inmates are living, and increasing the numbers.'

'A pity, that,' another man interjected. 'Fever helps keep the numbers down.'

'Though not in a Christian way,' Voisey said.

'It's true, nonetheless.'

'Enough of this,' Clanowen said, abruptly. 'Pray continue, Mr. Voisey.'

'Yes, well. As you know, we sent two hundred inmates to Quebec back in May, mostly from Lord Clanowen's estates...'

'Surely we can do that again?' the other man asked.

'Yes,' Clanowen said. 'We chartered the ship, we...'

Pat was about to speak, but Voisey silenced him again.

'In all Christian conscience, I don't think we should do that again.'

'But why not?' the other man asked. 'Didn't we send them out through Westport? And not that many died on the passage. Nothing like the deaths on the Liverpool ships.'

'That's as may be,' Voisey replied, 'but it's the Canadian side, that's where the problem is now. The fever we suffered here has followed our brethren to Canada. They've some dreadful quarantine station in Quebec which is killing thousands. It's just as bad, if not worse, in Montreal, Bytown and Toronto. Tens of thousands are dying of fever in British Canada, and the people are blaming the Irish migrants.'

'But how do you know all this?' Clanowen asked.

'Mr. Edmundson, who went to direct the journey. He has sent me a page from one of the Quebec papers. It's true, right enough. Like I said, the fever is killing tens of thousands. The doctors, the nurses, the nuns, are all working hard to stem the tide of death in the fever sheds, but they too are dying. In their hundreds.'

There was a silence around the room. Then Trinder spoke.

'At least if they died in Canada it wouldn't be at our cost. Nor on our conscience either.'

'I don't think we can see it that way any longer,' Voisey said. 'We've got to do our best with them here, not send them three thousand miles away for burial in Canada. This is a Christian country.'

Silence again. Clanowen was thrumming his fingers on the table. Pat knew it was not his place to speak. He was thinking about Luke. Tens of thousands dead in Canada. And on the Liverpool ships too. Would Luke get through?

The silence dragged.

Voisey whispered to Pat. 'That's fine, we're finished with you now.'

He turned back to Clanowen, as Pat left the room.

'Well, how did it go?' Sarah asked.

'Damned if I know,' said Pat. 'I hardly said a word.'

For an hour, he and Sarah worked on long columns of figures. Pat was relieved that his attendance at the meeting was over, but it had been replaced by other concerns.

An hour later, Voisey came into the room.

'You did well there, Pat.'

'I barely said anything.'

'No, but your report gave them the facts pretty straight, and I think the Workhouse might survive for a month or two longer. '

'That's great,' Pat said. 'But tell me just one thing. What's this you were saying about Canada?'

'Canada? Frightful entirely. The quarantine stations are overflowing. The Mayo ships aren't so bad though. The lumber ships out of Liverpool, they're the ones. They're in a terrible way when they reach Canada. The reports from St. Johns and Quebec are of ships arriving with a quarter or half their passengers dead, and spreading fever everywhere.'

Through August, everyone watched in fear as the potato was harvested, but there was no blight.

Then some of the inmates trickled away from the Workhouse. Some made their way home to fathers or sons who had kept their holdings, and many, who had no such choices, made for Dublin and Liverpool. Some begged as they went, or worked their way digging the harvest for the bigger farmers in the east of the country.

Even as people left the Workhouse, there were more waiting for admission. Many families had eaten all their seed potatoes as a result of the blight of 1846. They had planted no crop for 1847. Many no longer believed in the potato after two years of blight. But the Workhouse admitted very few.

So the hunger went on.

Every second weekend, Pat went back to Carrigard, walking through the dark on Friday nights, no matter what the weather. Some nights he arrived drenched to his skin.

One Friday evening, he finished his work and left his desk in the Workhouse to walk to Carrigard. As he walked across from the Administration block towards the Workhouse gate, he could see the death pit, still edging closer to the front wall, day by day. Even so, it was slowing from what it had been. The fever was killing fewer people in the Workhouse than it had been in March and April.

He nodded at the three inmates guarding the gate from the inside, quickly pulled himself up the bars to the top, balanced over the spikes, and jumped. There was still a crowd of gaunt men, women and children outside the gate, but less than it had been even a few weeks before.

He walked fast out the Kilduff road. It was raining already, and got heavier. It was two hours before he reached Carrigard, and well dark. He pushed the door open.

'God with you, mother.'

Eleanor spun around.

'Pat! I wasn't sure you were going to come. It's late enough.'

'I know. I'd far too much to do, and perhaps I shouldn't be here at all.'

'You're drenched. You should take better care of yourself.'

'Arra, what. Sure it has to be done.'

'Not at the cost of your health.'

He took off his coat, and Eleanor draped it over the back of a chair by the fire.

'Where's father?'

'Up guarding the potatoes.'

He poked at the fire, and the flames soared.

'And Luke? No word from Luke?'

Eleanor reached over to the dresser and picked up Luke's letter.

'Here, read this.'

Pat read through it quickly.

'He seems to be doing well enough so far. But you've nothing back from Quebec?'

'Sure how could we have heard from Quebec in this time? God, you're as bad as Winnie.'

'As bad as who?' a voice said from the hall. Pat turned around.

'By God, Winnie, is it? Hiding out in the back room were you?'

'Just making sure Brigid was asleep.'

She sat at the table.

'Have you eaten,' Eleanor asked.

'I have, and well,' Pat said. 'Don't be worrying about me.' He reached into his pack. 'And I brought you a sackeen of corn. It's not much, but it might help.'

'It surely will,' Eleanor said. 'But tell us this, how's the Workhouse?'

'*Oh, I'll tell you about it some other time,*' Pat replied.

He went to the door. The rain was lessening.

'*I'll go and see father first. See how the potato patch is getting on.*'

'*You're still wet.*'

'*I can't get any wetter so.*'

He took his coat again and left.'

'*He didn't seem too happy about the* Workhouse,' Winnie said.

'No, *he didn't*' Eleanor replied. '*I reckon we'll hear all about it soon enough though.*'

Both women knew the desperate stories of Knockanure Workhouse. Pat had told them enough about it, and Winnie herself had witnessed it, even if only briefly. They too knew that the real killer in the Workhouse was fever rather than direct starvation or cold. Black Fever. It brought back to Eleanor all the horror of the death of her daughter Alicia at the time of the Big Wind of 1839.

Fever was part of Mayo life. Most women had watched their babies die. It was something that they just accepted, even in normal times. Still, as Eleanor had explained to Winnie, if her daughter, Alicia, had not died of fever, and her niece, Nessa, had not died in childbirth seven years later, she herself would never have fostered Brigid and raised her as her own daughter.

For Eleanor, Knockanure Workhouse had come to symbolise the horror of Black Fever, right across the county. If Pat was to be believed, the epidemic had been killing hundreds of the Workhouse inmates during its horrific climax in March and April of 1847. And the epidemic had spread far beyond the Workhouses, killing thousands of people in all the villages of Mayo. Eleanor had heard enough of that from Michael's brother-in-law who had travelled around the county working as a surveyor for the many Famine Relief Roads. In the end, the fever had killed him too. Both women knew well that fever spread fast anywhere that people gathered. Workhouses, churches, bars – they avoided them all. But Pat still worked in Knockanure Workhouse as a clerk, and this terrified Eleanor.

Pat walked across to the potato patch. It was still raining.

'Father,' he shouted.

'Over here' Michael called from the darkness. Pat went across, and down between ridges. He found the hut. He could just see his father's figure. He sat alongside. Rain dribbled through the heather scraws and down the back of his coat.

'Any more stolen?'

'Not since a few weeks. And that wasn't much anyhow. I wouldn't worry about it.'

'Maybe ye should dig them all and take them into the house.'

'We'll do that soon enough,' Michael replied. 'There's still growth left in them, I don't want to lose that. Might give us another few hundredweight yet.'

'The crop's well enough, from what I can see here in the dark.'

'It is. One of the best ever. For those who have planted it.'

'Yes, I know. A good crop, but the hunger is going to get worse.'

'It is,' Michael said. 'And what happens then, I just don't know.'

He stood.

'Come on, let's go back to the house a while. The potatoes can look after themselves. There'll be less fellows out in this rain.'

Eleanor poured out four cups of *poitín*.

'I'm delighted you brought him back in so fast,' she said to Michael. 'I hadn't even the chance of talking to him, and he was away out the door.'

'Talk away,' Pat said, as he sipped the harsh spirit. 'There's not much I can tell you that would cheer you up.'

'How's the county? What are you hearing?'

'Well, the Poor Law is in a terrible way. We're still seeing it in the Workhouse. They're not dying as fast as they were, but the fever's still there, and the Workhouse doesn't even have the money to feed them all.'

'Not as overcrowded though?' Michael asked.

'Not as bad as it was. It was in a terrible way after Clanowen's evictions on the Mountain, and the evictions he ordered over by Killala made it even worse. But the crowding is less now. They just don't let them in, so the crowds outside aren't like they were. They know they can't get in, so they don't come rattling the gates like they used to.'

'So what's happening?' Winnie asked suddenly. 'What about Brockagh…?'

'Brockagh's not as bad as you might expect. Sure, there's fever and hunger, but it's not as bad as everywhere else. So I'd reckon your people are fine.'

'And the area around?'

Pat sighed.

'Oh God, I don't know. Knocklenagh, Lisnadee, all that area, all the way up to Croghancoe, it's in a terrible way. They were depending on the Soup Kitchens for feeding them, but now they're gone. They know the Workhouse is full, so they don't bother coming. I heard a crowd of them went walking to Sligo a while back. Some talked of ships going to Quebec after some clearances up that way. Some government minister in London, Palmerston or something, he was chartering ships, clearing his own land…'

'A damned absentee?' Michael said. 'They leave it to the agent, that's the way, isn't it?'

'So I'd guess,' Pat replied. 'But anyhow – the story got around that there was room on the ship, and because it was a chartered ship no-one would have to pay. How many others got on, or even if any others got on apart from the Palmerston lot, I just don't know. There were stories of bodies along the road from Knocklenagh all across the gap by Croghancoe, and down to Sligo itself.'

'That's enough now,' Eleanor said. 'Just drink your drink. And would you be leaving him alone, Michael, he's enough to be thinking about.'

Pat sipped the *poitín*, saying nothing. The silence dragged.

Michael poked at the fire. 'Surely they could have gone over by Westport?'

'Westport's too far,' Pat said.

'So's Sligo. There isn't much difference in the distance between the two from Knocklenagh.'

'More than you might think.'

'Killala then. Killala is surely closer.'

'Yes, but they charge for the crossing from Killala. The people high up the Ox, they've no money at all.'

Pat put his cup to his mouth. He had noticed that no one else was drinking.

'What's wrong with ye all? Are ye not thirsty?'

Michael shook his head.

'And what about the west and all over that way? What have you been hearing?'

'Desperate stories. Whenever the fellows from Castlebar come over, we hear all about it. Partry, Achill, Erris, they're all in a terrible way. Worse than the mountains, if you could believe them all. And the landlords, they're all near bankrupt out that way. There's talk of evictions coming.'

'And Knockanure?' Winnie asked. 'What about...'

'Near bankrupt.'

There was a shocked silence. Eleanor was the first to speak. 'But...if the Workhouse goes bankrupt, where does that leave you?'

'God only knows, mother,' Pat replied. 'For the moment, no one is saying anything, and they're still paying me. But as to how long it will last, who knows. So ye'll understand why I can't get back late to Knockanure, or leave early.'

'I understand it well,' Eleanor said. 'It's hard on you though, and we all depending on you. It's not fair, is it?'

'*Arra,* he's well able for it,' Michael said.

'It's not a matter of fair or not fair,' Pat said. 'It just has to be done. For as long as it lasts. Isn't that it?'

All through the evening, Pat was thinking of Canada and fever, but said nothing. Perhaps he lacked courage. On the other hand, there was nothing any of them could do, and if Luke survived, and a letter arrived from Canada, he would only have upset the family for no reason.

As everyone went to bed, Michael made for the door.

'Someone has to guard the potatoes.'

'I'll go,' Pat said.

'No, you've had enough of a drenching already.'

Pat spent the next two days helping his father around the farm, and guarding the potato patch. He insisted on doing so on the Saturday night, and thought he saw some figures moving through the bushes. He stood and shouted, and then there was silence.

On the Sunday night, Michael insisted on guarding the potatoes himself, while Pat slept in the outshot, beside the kitchen fire.

He was up early the following morning, but Eleanor was already in the kitchen, preparing breakfast.

'What you said about the Workhouse, it worries me,' she said.

'Me too,' Pat replied.

'And what about Sarah? How's Sarah taking it?'

'Much as you might expect. She's helping me all the time with the figures, but she's terrified of her mother working in the fever sheds. God knows, we've heard enough of them dying in the sheds – matrons, doctors, what have you, the fever gets them all in the end.'

'And you?'

'Oh, I don't go near the fever sheds, Sarah neither. Nor the death pit. So you needn't worry about either of us, we'll live.'

'You'll have to bring her over again someday. She's a nice girl.'

'She is, mother, she is.'

Pat finished the porridge that Eleanor had prepared for him. Then he embraced her and walked back to the potato fields. After a quick farewell to his father, he walked out the Knockanure road, and back to the Workhouse.

The relationship between Pat and Sarah Cronin intrigued Eleanor. Pat had brought her to Carrigard before. Sarah was in a different class to the Ryans. Her father had been Master of the Workhouse before he died, and her mother was Matron. Pat would hardly be seen as the best chance for Sarah, but the fact that he was working in the administration of the Poor Law Union, and in a clerical position too, meant he could, in time, do better than being a tenant farmer. What was odd, in Eleanor's eyes, was the easy relationship between Pat and Sarah, together with the way they pretended there was nothing between them. But why else should Pat bring Sarah to meet his family. Time would tell. But was it wrong to be thinking of such things as the hunger deepened around them?

She thought of Luke and Winnie. They had married at the height of the fever epidemic in the spring. At first, Eleanor had been shocked at this, but slowly she had begun to see it differently. Through the horror of the Famine and fever in the mountains, neither Luke nor Winnie had ever given up. Nor would she.

One night she woke from a nightmare of being buried alive. She lay awake, listening to Michael's gentle breathing. It was the first time that he had been in the bed for two weeks.

But it was Luke Eleanor was thinking most about. What Winnie had told her was disturbing, though she knew some of it already, and suspected much of the rest. She had not been able to forget it, every day it came back to her. The horror, the hatred, she could understand that. But Luke, tough and all as he was in so many ways, had been living on the edge. Or beyond it? What Winnie had told her about Luke's experience on Croghancoe did not surprise her either. She knew it was no vision though. So what now?

Now Luke was out on the broad Atlantic, with no one for company but desperate people fleeing a cursed land. How many had fever? Could he survive it? Even if he did, what would be the state of his mind? Winnie was right to worry, much as Eleanor herself had comforted her. Yes, it was hard to wait, another seven or ten weeks at least until the first letter came. If it came.

Other matters gnawed at her. Michael was getting old, and she knew he would not be able to work two farms for much longer. Perhaps not even now. And two quarries too, patching up roads for the County and the Barony. Almost impossible.

But this put more pressure on Pat. Five days working for the Union at the Workhouse, and then two brutally tough days on the weekend helping his father to catch up. She wondered if he could last the pace. More important, when Michael finally could not work the farm, would Pat become the farmer? Not as long as he had a paid position at the Union. But if he did not work the farm, who would?

She thought of the stories of the death pit at Knockanure Workhouse. And the Union – what if Pat lost his position? If it was bankrupt, how long could they keep him? What if the price of corn went up?

What if the potato failed again?

Chapter 5

London Daily News, August 1847:
The Railway Mania, and railways were in the field long before short food crops were heard of, or suspected; and in fact, but for the enormous disbursements occasioned by the imports of food for a starving population amounting probably to some thirty millions in all, freights included, during the last year and the present, the capital required for the railways might all have been supplied with little comparative inconvenience.

England. Danny put down his pen, and looked out at the driving rain. In the distance he could see the high red arches of Edgeley Viaduct leading from Manchester into Stockport Station. He felt uneasy.

An envelope lay on his desk. It had been hand delivered, addressed simply to Daniel Ryan, and marked 'Most urgent. Attention addressee only'.

At length, he opened it, not knowing what to expect. He read it with stunned amazement.

Brassey was asking Edwardes & Ryan to enter a contract.

And what a contract!

The envelope contained a detailed map, which illustrated plans for a cutting on the North Staffordshire Railway, together with a series of calculations.

Attached was a brief letter.

'For the attention of Daniel Ryan.

We have determined that Edwardes & Ryan might be an appropriate labour contractor to undertake the attached contract. A price of £22,000 has been determined.

Please confirm that you are willing to undertake this work, and address your response to Mr. Simon Johnson, senior clerk, acting on behalf of Thomas Brassey & Co. at Birkenhead.'

Danny had known about Thomas Brassey for many years. He knew that Brassey was the biggest railway contractor in the world, said to be employing fifty or a hundred thousand men, mainly in Britain, but also across Europe and further afield.

Long before that, Danny had been working for Brassey, though in a different way.

Since he was twelve, Danny had been one of Martin Farrelly's gang of ten or fifteen men from the Kilduff area, who worked up and down England for various different railway and labour contractors. But the contractors varied, and often the gang had found themselves working with men they truly despised. But whenever they worked with Brassey's managers, they knew they were working with honest men.

The only difference was that he had been a navvy then. Now he was a labour contractor himself, and Brassey wanted to work with him.

He knew that if he signed this contract, it would be the greatest break he would ever get. But it would also be the greatest risk he would ever take.

How long was it since he had come to England? 1838. So long? He had not been back to Mayo in that time. He thought of all the years working as a navvy with Farrelly and the others. Great years, but he was the only one with the ambition to break away to form his own business.

England was where the future lay. It gave a man chances – the chances to fight all the way to the top as a contractor. Not even two years in business, and he, Daniel Ryan, was employing four hundred men.

Anderson & Sons had been his first customer. Andersons were railway contractors, handling local contracts in the Stockport and Manchester area. The firm was owned by Roy Anderson, who had become a friend.

Anderson was building a number of stretches of railway in the Manchester and Stockport area. This was where Danny's main sites were. Up to now, Anderson was his only customer. Danny had just finished a contract near Gatley two weeks ahead of time, and precisely at the price agreed. He was now working on three more contracts for Anderson, one on the Lancashire & Yorkshire Railway, another on the Liverpool & Bury Railway and a third on the Leeds, Dewsbury & Manchester Railway.

Danny intended to finish these contracts ahead of schedule, and preferably at an even lower cost and higher profit.

These three were straightforward. More contentious though, were the Works Danny was carrying out at Oxford Road, in Ancoats, which was almost in the centre of Manchester City. This again was a contract from Roy Anderson, though Anderson did not wish anyone to know of his own involvement. He was perfectly happy therefore to let Danny front the operation for him.

Oxford Road was part of the Manchester South Junction Railway. It was to be driven straight through 'Little Ireland', which was known as the worst ghetto in Manchester, and perhaps in all of England. It had developed a reputation in countries far beyond England too, and had become a major embarrassment for Manchester. The city fathers were delighted at the prospect of demolishing it, and the Manchester South Junction Railway gave them a perfect excuse.

Whatever of Ancoats, it was through the other Anderson sites that Danny was developing his reputation. Word had begun to spread among the larger contractors too. Brassey, Peto, Mackenzie and the rest of them, were forced to deal with Irish labour contractors, but most of those were semi-literate, if that. At a time like this, Edwardes & Ryan could be invaluable to any main contractor who had little desire to deal with Irish navvies directly. Danny was literate, highly numerate too, as were his most senior gangers. They would know well how to deal with the agents working for the big contractors. He had always intended to approach Brassey directly, but he had never dreamt that Brassey might approach him first.

The Railway Mania from 1844 to 1847 had created a bewildering profusion of railway construction, as new railway companies built lines in a frenzy of competition all over England. Many said there would be no end to it until England was crossed and criss-crossed by railways, connecting every city, town and village.

It was surprising to Danny that such a boom should continue in England while Ireland was starving. The two countries were detached to a massive degree – a roaring boom contrasting with a murderous famine. A voracious demand for labour against an endless supply of men willing to work for starvation wages. And this gave Danny his greatest opportunities.

The question was – how long would it all last? Could the boom collapse?

Up to now, he always had sufficient workers, which meant he could always bring contracts in on time. If they were running late, he could just hire more workers, and pay them as little as he liked. He did not supply shacks on the Works, and most of the navvies built their own mud cabins alongside, much as they did in County Mayo.

Edwardes & Ryan could undercut any bid from the other labour contractors, and guarantee time of completion. So long as he had a supply of cheap labour.

Unlike the other Irish contractors and gang-masters, Danny read the newspapers obsessively.

Until he met Irene, he had little concern for the outside world beyond the railways and railway contractors.

But that had all changed when he started living with her. For a woman, she was highly educated.

Also, she came from Manchester, and now every day the Manchester Times arrived in the house. Then Danny ordered the main Liverpool and London papers too. He had never read newspapers before. On the gangs, no one else cared, and back in Carrigard, no one could afford to buy papers. Sixpence was too high a price.

Danny took it as a great opportunity to broaden his horizons. News of parliament in Westminster absorbed him, and the wider reports on political developments in Europe and America fascinated him. The Kaffir Wars intrigued him too. He wondered how much rail building there might be in southern Africa.

The Manchester and Liverpool papers covered mainly the North West of England. The London papers covered the world. He had started reading the financial pages through his interest in the railway companies, the banks that supported them, and the trading companies that supplied them. There were many words he did not understand at first, but he had learnt a lot. Literacy was a major advantage, and Danny's quick mind grasped the key concepts rapidly.

But railways were his key concern, which all the newspapers covered in depth.

Railways, railways, railways.

Some papers claimed Railway Mania was over, but Danny was not convinced either way. If it continued he did not want to miss out. But if the market crashed, he could be highly vulnerable.

The problem was, how to finance it all. From the start, he had the backing of the Manchester & Salford Bank. He had the strong support of Anderson & Sons in all his dealings with the Bank, and Roy Anderson had accompanied him to the early meetings with the Bank. Now he would have to deal with the Bank on his own. If he was to run gangs with other contractors, Danny's dealings had to be confidential to each contractor and the Bank. He would have been stretched financially if he won any new contracts. Now this massive opportunity with Brassey would stretch him even further. It was essential to talk to the Manchester & Salford before he accepted the Brassey contract.

Best talk to Irene first.

He observed her sharp profile. A beautiful woman, no doubting that, but a tough one too. Wasn't that what had first attracted him to her? The toughness showed in the way she dealt with everyone.

As English as they came – he admired her for that too. His lover, soon to be his wife.

She had come to Edwardes & Ryan as his secretary, but now she was far more than that. Everyone had at first thought of her as some kind of clerk, or perhaps an assistant to Danny, but they soon discovered otherwise. She was a hard woman, working now in a men's world.

All dealings with the main contractors and with the Manchester & Salford Bank, she left strictly to Danny. But dealings with timber merchants, builder's providers, horse breeders, wagon makers and quarrymen were increasingly Irene's own responsibility, as they soon found out. Edwardes & Ryan had a ravenous appetite for shovels and picks for the navvies' horses and wagons for the cartmen and graded stone to prepare the permanent way for the main contractors. Irene knew well that the smaller local suppliers were more dependent on Edwardes & Ryan, and she was well able to push prices down, particularly with the quarrymen.

Her ability with accounts also amazed him. She could glance through accounts – payrolls, trial balances, profit & loss statements, balance sheets – and pick the key figures out at once. And her speed of reckoning, that surprised him too. He had thought he was able to reckon numbers, and he knew his gangers could, but Irene could out-reckon them all.

'You know,' Danny said to her, 'there are a lot more contracts coming. Which could well be a problem.'

'I thought you said to be careful.' she replied. 'You said railway construction was dropping.'

'That was back in April, but it's back up now. Parliament has been pushing railways hard. The past few months alone, there's been eighty Royal Assents for new railway lines. Eighty! Can you believe it?'

'Looks like Railway Mania again to me,' she said, sharply.

'Might well be.'

'We have plenty or orders though?' she asked.

'We have.'

'So what's the problem?'

'Hard to know. There's a lot of contradictions in what they all say. Sure, there's lots of new lines to be built. But can they afford it? The government has spent a fortune on the Irish Famine. So now there's a money shortage. Railways fighting everyone else for cash. The ironworks have to pay cash on the nail. No cash, no iron ore, no rail. Worse than that, the saw-mills are really in trouble, especially the fellows importing lumber. If they can't get bills of exchange from the Liverpool banks, the Quebec banks won't pay out in Canada. No cash, no lumber, no sleepers. No railways to be built.'

'I think you read the papers too much,' she said. 'They're always in a panic.'

'Maybe. Or maybe not.'

'So what can we do? What of Andersons? That's where our money comes from.'

'Indeed, and I'd like to finish off our contracts there as quickly as possible. Two reasons. First to get the money.'

'Naturally.'

'But there's a second reason,' Danny said. 'There's some question of some of some of the Liverpool & Bury Works being suspended.'

'Suspended!'

'Nothing certain, only a rumour, and even if it happens, they're saying it'll only be for the rest of the year. But I'm not sure that I believe that. If it's suspended, it could be for years.'

'So what then?'

'Finish our contract on the Liverpool & Bury as soon as possible. At least we'll have cash in the bank.'

'Does Roy know about this? Will he have any of his contracts suspended?'

'I don't know. He should know though. Roy's smart enough.'

'So what now?' she asked.

'Brassey. We'll work for Brassey.'

'Brassey!' she exclaimed. 'Stop dreaming. We've a business to run.'

'Take a look at this.' He placed the letter on her desk. Quickly, she read it, eyes opening.

'Twenty two thousand!' she gasped. 'Are they serious?'

'Deadly serious. This is the biggest chance we've ever had. We've just got to get it.'

'But...how do we bid?'

'We don't. Brassey has approached us to act as a labour contractor. And you don't bid with Brassey on this level. He decides what the contract is worth, and it's our decision to accept or not.'

Irene shook her head.

'I don't understand all this,' she said.

'It's up to us to check his figures, and see the site. Decide if we can make money on it. If so, we accept.'

'But...will we have the money?'

'We'll have to ask the Manchester & Salford.'

'Where Roy will support us.'

'I'm not so sure of that. Up to now, we've either been working for Roy, or other small contracts around which were of no interest to him. If we work as a direct contractor for Brassey, we're becoming a competitor. I'm not sure Roy will like that.'

'He won't.'

'So I've got to meet the Bank myself. On my own. Prove to them we're worth lending to.'

'How will you prove that?'

'Two ways. One is the very fact that Brassey has approached us on a contract of this size. That speaks volumes. The second point is to convince them that our ways of doing business are superior to anyone else. In our normal business, we can undercut most of the other fellows. On a contract like this, I think it might be even better. I think we might be able to make an enormous profit. And that would certainly interest the Manchester & Salford Bank.'

'It would,' Irene said.

'But there's another thing that worries me. Getting the workers. We're already running short with the work we have. We'll need more, and with a Brassey contract, we'll need them damned fast.'

'But Liverpool…? Isn't the Workhouse supplying us with enough?'

'They are. Or they were. The problem is to get Mayo fellows. But the Workhouse see no reason to sort them out. Murtybeg says it's nearly impossible to get that type of gang now. They're insisting we take all kinds of fellows – Kerry, Donegal and the rest of it.'

'And what's wrong with that?' she asked.

'First, we're trying to keep them together as gangs, and if they're all mixed up, there's no loyalty to each other, and they'll drift off in ones and twos. Second, they can't understand one another. Donegal and West Cork Irish are different enough. It's hard to give orders, the gangers are complaining of it. And third, they're insisting we take English speakers, and by God, we won't have that.'

Irene shook her head.

'No,' she said slowly, 'you're right. We can't have English speakers, can we?'

'Under no circumstances.'

'So what then?' she asked.

'Damned if I know.'

'You know, Danny, the real problem we're going to have here is one of time.'

'I know. We've got to deal with Brassey, deal with the bank. Find more workers too, and that's getting tough. We've all our existing sites to run. And in the middle of it all, we're to be wed? How'll we have time to organise a wedding? We haven't even booked a hotel yet.'

'I know. And it'll have to be a top one too. The Midland Hotel at the very least.'

'I agree, and there's no way on earth we're going to be able to do all that over the next few weeks.'

'Are we committed though?' she asked. 'Have we booked the Registry Office?'

'Not yet.'

'Sent out invitations?'

'No, though there's a few that know. Murtybeg, and he'll have told mother and father by now. The gangers know too. But what of that? Roy

Anderson is the only other one who knows.'

'We've no choice then. We'll have to push it back. A few months at least.'

'I agree.'

Danny felt relieved.

Even before the arrival of the Brassey letter, he knew that labour was becoming tighter as the demand for navvies soared around the country.

Every week he sent his brother to Liverpool to recruit. Murtybeg did this directly off the cattle boats coming in from Dublin or the West of Ireland, with hundreds of starving Irish mingling among the cattle. Sometimes, if they wanted stronger men, Murtybeg would go direct to Liverpool Workhouse, which was desperate to get the flood of Irish paupers out of the Workhouse, and preferably sent home to Ireland. Murtybeg gave them another welcome option. He packed all his recruits into railway wagons, and brought them back to Danny's Works on the railways around Manchester or Stockport.

Here, Danny paid them marginally more than they had been earning on the Famine Relief Works back in County Mayo, slowly paying them more as they became stronger. Still it was less, far less, than English or Welsh navvies were being paid.

Often, the stronger Irish navvies drifted away to better paid work, but up to now, that had been of no great concern to Danny. There were, after all, hundreds of likely recruits coming into Liverpool every day. But Danny's need for labour was increasing faster than before.

The real key to his business was Mayo. The county had been badly hit by the Famine, far worse than any other Irish county. It had been bad in the east of the county, especially in the Ox Mountains, bordering County Sligo. But Mayo suffered most from the Irish Famine, and west Mayo worst of all. Men from these districts were the men Murtybeg was searching for when he visited Liverpool. He knew the accents, he could distinguish the accents of East and West Mayo. This was vital to Murtybeg and Danny.

Danny knew that he already had a savage reputation on the west coast of Mayo. This did not concern him. As long as he was not recruiting underpaid men from east Mayo, especially Kilduff, Carrigard and the area around, his family and friends had no reason to complain.

The savage conditions at Little Ireland might be of more concern to him, since many of the inhabitants were from County Mayo. They were not the kind of people to write home though, and Danny doubted that many would hear of his involvement, particularly since his ganger on the site was not from Mayo. In any case, fever would kill most of them.

Little Ireland had been settled by dirt poor Irish emigrants from the mid-1820s, and by 1847 conditions were appalling, with hundreds of people crammed in tiny rooms and cellars, which, combined with the filth of the surroundings, gave it one of the highest death rates in England. Now it was to be flattened for the railway. Where the inhabitants would go, was a question that occurred to few.

The work here consisted of more than railway cuttings. First, the houses had to be demolished. To do that, the occupants had to be evicted. Danny's half-starved navvies were incapable of this, and he was content with this. Evictions he left to the police, but after the evictions, the demolitions were carried out by his own gang. It was dangerous work. On occasions, the buildings collapsed without warning. There had been many injuries on site, but, as yet, no deaths.

A second problem Danny had was that he had to find a special ganger. Finding Steele had been the key to working the site at Oxford Road.

He could not use any of the men he knew from Mayo. Many of the people being evicted came from Mayo themselves, often victims of previous evictions in Ireland. Through contacts, and contacts of contacts, he finally located Samuel Steele, a hard-bitten ganger from Dublin. Where he was originally from, Danny had no idea, but he spoke in a guttural northern Irish dialect when necessary. He had never visited County Mayo in his life, and never wished to. Nor did he involve himself with any other activities of Danny's business beyond Oxford Road. He was the only ganger who never attended the meetings in Stockport, and Danny had no wish that he should.

Danny suspected that Steele was a Freemason, and if he was, this was an advantage. Edwardes & Ryan had to have a close relationship with the police, and many of these were rumoured to be Freemasons too. They had no qualms about carrying out evictions, nor even guarding Danny's gang from the wrath of the evictees.

One irony of the Oxford Road site was that in the worst area for joblessness in Manchester, Danny could use none of the locals. They would not assist in evicting them themselves. Even here, he was still left with the problem of finding enough labour.

There was a knock on his office door.

'Come in.'

Three men entered and sat the table.

Most of Danny's gangers were from Kilduff and Carrigard. These were the men that Danny knew from his own time working as a navvy on the English railways in the early 1840s. They were men he respected, and it was from here he recruited his gangers to supervise the West Mayo navvies working on his contracts. Roughneen, Lavan and McManus were among the best in England, each supervising a single stretch of railway, mostly running gangs of a hundred men or more.

'Your reports, gentlemen,' Irene said. McManus looked at her in surprise. He glanced at Danny, who nodded. McManus handed his report to Irene. She skimmed through it.

'I don't like the look of this report, Mr. McManus' she said, abruptly. 'We're behind time on this contract.'

'There are reasons for that,' McManus said.

'Picks? Shovels? Wagons? You're not undersupplied, are you?'

McManus glared at her.

'It's not that,' he said. 'It's a shortage of workers, that's our problem. The stronger fellows, they're drifting off to the other contractors. They're paying up to three shillings a day now.'

'Three shillings!' Danny exclaimed.

'They're desperate for workers.'

'They won't last long, paying three shillings,' Irene commented. 'Not if we're paying a shilling and thruppence at the top end. We are, aren't we?'

'We are,' McManus answered.

Danny had been flicking through the reports.

'So what do you fellows suggest?'

'We need more cheap workers and a hell of a lot of them,' McManus said. 'That was never a problem before, was it?'

'It wasn't,' said Danny, 'but it seems it is now. And it'll be a hell of a lot more of a problem if we get more contracts.'

'You're bidding for more?' Roughneen exclaimed.

'One or two,' Danny said, not wishing to mention the Brassey contract yet. 'I don't want too many contracts until I know we have the cash and the workers. If the other fellows are paying three shillings a day, they won't last long, and we might be taking over bankrupt contracts too.'

He handed the report sheets back to each of the gangers.

Lavan glanced through his sheet. 'What about your brother?' he asked. 'I haven't seen him lately.'

'No,' Danny replied, 'Murtybeg has been over in Mayo. I'm expecting him back soon though. We'll send him back to Liverpool as soon as we see him. Scour the Docks and the Workhouse and make sure all of you have cheap labour. We must complete these contracts on time. Our good name depends on it.'

'What's he in Mayo for?' Roughneen asked.

'He's bringing my mother and father over here.'

'The Master!' Lavan exclaimed. 'But...'

'The school has closed.'

'Closed!'

'They're building new schools in Ireland now,' Irene said. 'They're using trained teachers.'

Roughneen, Lavan and McManus looked at each other. Their own knowledge of reading, writing, calculating, and even the English language, had come from hard years of study under Danny's father in Carrigard. That was one of the key reasons they were gangers, paid six shillings a day. That – and the fact they had been known and trusted by Danny for all their lives.

'But what will the Master do?' Roughneen asked.

'Work here, I'm hoping. Accounts and the like. He's an able man. As well you know.'

'So it'll be a while before we see Murtybeg again,' Lavan said. 'What will we do for workers in the meantime?'

'Just wait,' Danny replied. 'Murtybeg should be here in a few days, a week at the most. We'll send him to Liverpool straight away.'

The men rose to go.

'Oh, one other thing,' Danny said, as they made their way to the door. 'I think some of ye knew that Irene and I were to be wed.'

Roughneen smiled. 'So we had. We're still waiting for the date.'

'I'm sorry to tell you, it'll be a while yet. With all our labour problems, and the new contracts we're bidding on, we just don't have time to arrange it.'

When the others had left, Danny spent some time going through accounts with Irene, bringing the figures for each of the Works up to date. She carried them out to the clerk in the next room, instructing him to make two 'fair copies'.

Then they checked the figures on the Brassey contract.

'This could be very profitable,' Irene exclaimed.

'It could,' Danny said.

'I wonder what they're paying the rest of their workers.'

'Twice what we are,' Danny replied. 'More.'

'So it'll still be profitable, even after allowing for contingencies.'

'What?'

'Contingencies. Extra costs we don't expect.'

'Oh, I see,' Danny asked, still unsure. 'Like what?

'Over-runs. Anything that takes longer than usual, or uses more carts than you might expect. Also back-handers.'

'Back-handers?' Danny exclaimed, astonished again. 'What the devil...?'

'Kickbacks. Special payments.'

'We'd hardly have that with Brassey,' Danny said.

'I don't think so. It's the other ones though, Peto and the like. They might accept back-handers. Though it could be more useful to know what our competitors are bidding. Then we just undercut.'

'And how would you find that out?' he asked.

'Never mind. Just tell me what other contracts we're bidding, apart from Brassey.'

'A cutting at Ormskirk, on the East Lancashire Line. The invitation to tender just came in this morning.'

'That's Mackenzie, isn't it? He's the main contractor on the East Lancashire.'

'He is,' Danny said. 'Another top contractor.'

'Not in Brassey's league yet.'

'Not quite, but even so...'

'Baxendales are bidding Mackenzie for the labour on the Ormskirk Cutting. They're the competition on this one.'

Danny knew well who Baxendales were. An English labour contractor, far bigger than Edwardes & Ryan. They had a worksite alongside McManus' site.

'I don't know if they are or not,' he said.

'I'm not asking you, Danny,' Irene said. 'I'm telling you.'

'But...what...Baxendales! How in hell do you know that?'

She ignored the question.

'They've come in at just over seven thousand pounds, and I understand that's the lowest. So if we bid, say, six thousand, seven hundred, we'll get the contract. And at our wage rates, there'll be a good profit on that, even allowing for contingencies.'

'Irene, how in the name of God, do you know all this?'

She met his eyes, challenging him.

'Not for you to know, Danny. The less you know, the better. Then if anyone asks you, you'll be able to deny all knowledge, and you won't be lying.'

Danny shook his head in total bewilderment.

'You seem to know a lot about Baxendales.'

'I do.'

'But how?'

'Just trust me,' she replied.

They worked well into the night. When the calculations were finished, they made two copies of every document.

It was only when Danny was totally convinced of his facts and figures that he decided to talk to the Manchester & Salford Bank. He wrote, requesting a meeting. A response came two days later, suggesting a meeting the following day.

He went to Stockport station and took the train to Manchester Piccadilly. He walked through the rain, sheltering his satchel of documents under his greatcoat, to the Head Office of the Manchester & Salford in Mosley Street.

'Mr. Ryan. How good to meet you. James Winrow.'

Danny slipped off his greatcoat.

'We haven't met.'

'Not yet. The directors have appointed me to your account.'

They commenced work at once.

'Looking for further loans, Mr. Ryan?'

'Yes, but not today. We're considering a few new contracts, and I'll need to know I'll have your backing for whatever we get.'

Winrow leant back in his chair.

'I see. And how is the business going to date?'

Danny slipped the original of the accounts across the desk.

'These are the accounts for the year so far,' he explained. 'Six months only, but as you can see, we're making good money.'

Winrow checked the figures.

'The bottom line seems quite satisfactory.'

'To be honest, it should be better,' Danny said. 'We've been slipping behind on one of our contracts. Nothing dangerous, we will finish on time. We've a good name for delivering on time, and we must keep that.'

'Any reason for being behind?'

'We've been low on workers. My brother is in charge of finding workers. He's been in Ireland for a few weeks. As soon as he arrives, he'll be going back to Liverpool to find more workers. We'll need at least a hundred for the present contracts, probably another four hundred to start for the new contracts.'

'New contracts?'

Danny hesitated. Best to start with the less important contract perhaps, and see how Winrow reacted.

'Peto's agents have been in touch with us. Mackenzie's too. And others. They're all anxious for us to bid on new contracts, but I don't want to give them hard figures yet.'

'Where might the contracts be?'

'There's this cutting at Ormskirk, on the East Lancashire line. Just north of Liverpool. Mackenzie is the main contractor. That's where I'd have the best chance of having my bid accepted. At a good profit of course.'

Danny laid another sheet in front of Winrow.

'These are very rough figures on some of what we're bidding.'

Winrow looked down the sheet.

'This is a big one? Think you can handle it?'

'I can,' Danny replied. 'But only if we have the backing of the Manchester & Salford Bank.'

'I don't know,' Winrow said, without commitment. 'Let's see what else you're bidding.'

'This one here, this is the most interesting. The one we have to get. The one we will get.'

He handed the Brassey contract documents to Winrow, who scanned the first page.

'The North Staffordshire. Yes, I know...What! Twenty two thousand pounds. Who...?'

'Brassey.'

Winrow glanced up at Danny.

'Brassey wants you to act as a labour contractor?'

'I won't say we're certain, Mr. Winrow. He may have approached other fellows too. But I doubt it. And this is the biggest chance Edwardes & Ryan have ever had.'

Winrow shook his head, still astonished. 'And your own costings?'

'I scribbled a few figures down for you.'

He slipped the calculations across the desk.

'This will be most profitable,' Winrow said.

'It will, won't it?'

'What will you bid?'

'No need to bid,' Danny said. 'Brassey doesn't work that way. Twenty two thousand pounds is his figure. All we have to do is accept.'

'So what loans do you need?'

'Three thousand pounds should cover the Ormskirk Cutting for Mackenzie. The Brassey contract could be as much as five thousand.'

'A lot for one single contract.'

'It is. Brassey takes time to pay. But we know he will pay.'

'Indeed, Mr. Ryan. So you are looking for eight thousand in all?'

'Exactly. So the question now is – will we have the approval of the Manchester & Salford?'

'I can't say as yet, Mr. Ryan. I will discuss these projections with the board. You are well regarded within the bank. The one problem I foresee though, is that this Mackenzie contract, together with the Brassey one, would represent far too big a risk for the bank, especially with a new business such as yours. It may be necessary to drop one.'

'In that case, I would have to say the Brassey contract is by far the most important,' Danny said.

'Yes, I can understand that. Let's work on that one, shall we, and see if we can convince the board? It is definitely the contract that would be of most interest to them.'

When Danny returned to Stockport that evening, he spent an hour with Irene, telling her of Winrow's responses.

'The good news is regarding the Brassey contract. Winrow seems sure the bank will support it. I think in fact, he was surprised when I mentioned it to him.'

'He doesn't know much about Brassey so,' Irene said. 'From what I hear, Brassey's are using many Irish labour contractors. Maybe he reckons we're the best.'

'Maybe he does. One way or the other, it impressed him.'

'So what now?'

'We have to wait 'till we get confirmation from the bank.'

'So while we're waiting, what of the Ormskirk?'

'I don't think they'll lend on it.'

'What!'

'They just won't do it.'

'Did he tell you why not?'

'It's just to do with the bank. Winrow reckons one contract of this kind of size would be enough for us. They won't lend on both. So when pushed to it, I said the Brassey contract was by far the most important, and I'm sure you'd agree with that. The Ormskirk is not as vital to us as the Brassey contract, even with Mackenzie as contractor. The bank have great confidence in us, but they think we're still new to contracting. They want us to take it slowly. They still see us as unproven.'

'Unproven?'

'For now, my love. But let's not worry what might have been. The Brassey contract, that's all that matters, and I reckon if we play our cards right, we could become Brassey's preferred Irish labour contractor. And you know what that could mean? More contracts, Irene. A hell of a lot more.'

She shook her head. 'That might be so. Still – there's this business of the Ormskirk Cutting with Mackenzie. Then we'd be working with two of England's top contractors.'

'I know. But...'

'You know that Baxendales bank with the Manchester & Salford.'

'They do?'

'Yes, and I reckon Winrow would never have told you that.'

Danny was astonished again.

'But, Irene, how do you know...?'

'Never mind how I know. But I can understand it. That's the reason they won't lend to us. Baxendales are far larger than us, and an important bank customer. The bank won't support us against Baxendales. What worries me is this. Are we always going to lose out to bigger contractors?'

'We've still got Brassey, Irene. Mackenzie can come later.'

*

The Facility Letter from the Manchester & Salford Bank arrived, but only for the Brassey contract.

'So now we've got to get Brassey's to approve,' Irene said.

'Yes,' Danny replied, 'and damned fast.'

The next few weeks were busy ones for Danny.

He wrote to Brassey's, confirming his acceptance of the contract.

Two days later, he received a letter, requesting his presence. He went into Manchester, and took the train to Chester, travelling first class. He changed onto the Birkenhead & Chester, where he noticed that it was being expanded to take a second line.

When he arrived at Birkenhead, he went directly to the Brassey & Co., head office, where he was received by one of the clerks. They spent the next hour going through the figures in detail, to ensure that both sides were satisfied. At no time did Danny mention the low wages he was paying.

As he was leaving, he saw a man alighting from a carriage.

'That's Mr. Brassey,' the clerk told him.

Danny looked back after him. The biggest contractor in England.

If Brassey could do it, he could do it.

He spent that night at home in Stockport, explaining the details to Irene. The following morning, the Brassey contract arrived, together with a request to visit the site.

'And who should handle this contract for us,' Irene asked.

'Roughneen. Best by far.'

Next day, he visited Roughneen's site. There were long lines of men with picks, hacking the side of the cutting. Alongside, there were more, shovelling soil and shale onto a line of horse-drawn carts. Every so often, one came out of the line, and drew the cart down to a ramp alongside the rail, where they were off-loaded into wagons. It brought to mind all the long years he had spent working as a navvy himself. Hard work. These navvies were not working as fast, but he was well aware of that, and they were working for very low wages. But he was feeding them well, far better than what they would have in Mayo. Slowly, they would toughen up.

Roughneen came over to him.

'Everything going well?' Danny asked.

'No problems yet, Danny. We're well on time and should be fine as long as we get new workers over the next week or two.'

Danny changed the subject.

'I'm going down to Staffordshire tomorrow,' he said. 'I'd like you to join me.'

'Another contract?'

'Yes, and it'll be our biggest. I'll want you to take it over.'

'Our biggest!' Roughneen exclaimed.

'By far. Are you interested?'

'Of course. But…where is this contract.'

'It's a new cutting on the North Staffordshire. We're working for Brassey.'

'Brassey!'

'Yes, Johnny. No agents neither. Direct. This contract will be as big as all the rest put together. That's why I want you to handle it.'

'Of course, Danny, I'd be delighted.' He stepped aside as a horse drawn wagon passed. 'But if it's as big as you say, it must be quite something.'

'It is,' Danny said. 'That's why I reckon you're the man to run it, and I'll be putting you up to eight shillings a day.'

'Eight!' Roughneen exclaimed.

'Eight, I said.'

They walked towards the completed end of the cutting, where the horses were dragging the wagons for tipping onto the rising embankment.

'The second question is this, If you take it over down there, who is there right here who'd run this site?'

'Not a sinner,' Roughneen replied. 'There's not one of them would be up for it. There's only a few have the slightest smattering of English, and none of those have any arithmetic, nor any other book learning. How on earth could they run a site like this on their own?'

'I see,' said Danny. 'We'll have to think of something. Let's leave it 'till tomorrow, and you just sleep on it. I'll see you at Stockport station, say seven o'clock.'

'See you then,' Roughneen said.

Next morning, they boarded the Birmingham train, second class.

'I've been thinking of that business of getting a new ganger,' Roughneen said. 'I think there's only one answer. Go back to our old gang around Leeds. Farrelly's fellows.'

'Yes,' said Danny, 'I was thinking the same myself. It's a long time since I was on the gang though. I'm sure many of them will have left since then.'

'Including Farrelly himself. Gone to America.'

'Not the only one, neither. Though that's a different matter. So who would you think might be best?'

'There's a few fellows could take it over. But of them all, I think Tim Kearney would be the best. Joe Gilligan would be good too, if we can't get Tim.'

'Yes,' Danny said, 'I think you're right. And we might have call for more of them in time.'

They got off before Birmingham and found where the North Staffordshire railway was being built. Using the Brassey map, they located where the cutting would be. They walked the length and breadth where it had already been marked out. Danny measured distance, as he had trained himself to do for so long, by the simple method of counting his own steps. Roughneen did the same, and they compared their estimates. They estimated the depth of the cutting at different parts, confirming the estimates by talking to navvies and gangers further down the line. It was essential to understand, not only the number of cubic yards involved, but also the type of material to be removed – soft soil, clay or rock.

'This'll be one hell of a contract,' Roughneen commented.

'It will.'

'How many navvies will we need?'

'Three or four hundred, I'm guessing.'

Roughneen nodded. 'Yes, I think that'd be about right. And already we're short of men.'

'I know,' Danny said. 'I know.'

It was the following night before Danny arrived back in Stockport.

'Well?' Irene asked.

'I'll tell you this,' Danny said. 'There's money in that cutting. A lot of it. Contingencies or not.'

Again, they worked through the accounts.

'I think you're right,' Irene said. 'We'll make a lot of money on this one. And do you know something, Danny? By the middle of next year, we're going to be rich. Really rich.'

'Far beyond anything I ever dreamed of,' Danny said. 'We make a strong combination, you and me.'

Over the ensuing days, Danny visited his worksites for further discussions with his gangers, McManus in particular. His site was falling further behind, and Danny was concerned.

'It's the lack of workers, Danny,' McManus told him. 'The less workers we have, the slower we are.'

'We'll sort out something,' Danny said.

His last visit was to Newton, where he finalised negotiations for the purchase of the site for his new house. Here they would, at last, live as man and wife, away from Manchester, but close enough by train. It was beside Earleswood Junction, where the Grand Trunk Railway from Birmingham joined with the Liverpool & Manchester Railway.

'Fifty pounds!' Irene exclaimed that evening. 'For three acres. Pricy.'

Danny laughed. 'Maybe I should send you to do the talking next time.'

'Maybe you should,' she said, derisively.

'But don't forget, it's close to Earleswood Junction. Links us into the whole rail network.'

'But when do we start building?'

Danny hesitated.

'I'd like to say at once, and it's not as if we don't have the money, but we'd have to hire an architect, and for the kind of house we want to build, he'd have to understand what we have in mind. It'll all take time. I think it might be best to leave it 'till after the wedding. Where we're living isn't so bad. What do you think?'

'I'd agree with you,' she said. 'Not that I want to put it off much longer, but it would be mad to start it while we've so little time.'

'I know. And it's not just for one house. It's for the cottage too.'

'Yes, the cottage. I wanted to talk to you about that too. We're building a cottage for your parents.'

'So? They have to live somewhere.'

'Why not leave them in Mayo? This idea of bringing them over here. It's mad.'

'It's not mad. They're my parents. I have to support them. They'd only starve in Ireland.'

'Couldn't you just send them over the money, they'd have been happy enough.'

'And get no return on our money? Is that what you want? No, don't forget what I told you. My father ran his own school. He has a brain in his head and we're going to use it.'

'The Board of Education didn't think much of your father's school. They're opening proper schools right across Ireland. English speaking schools. That's what you told me. That tells you what your Education Board thinks of the Irish language and Irish schools.'

'Maybe you're right. But my father can still have a role to play in this business. A very important one. He can read, write and reckon, far faster than most. Dealing with the gangers too – he's taught them all. No, he'll have his work cut out for him here. Don't you worry about that?'

'And Aileen? Your mother, what about her? Can she read or write? Add or subtract?'

Danny thought about that. Aileen had been brought up on the Mountain. No one there had ever gone to school, and he had never seen his mother with a pen.

'I don't know that she can,' Danny answered. 'They had no teaching where she came from.'

'And your father? All those years married, couldn't he have taught her.

She was married to a schoolmaster. What a chance they had.'

'I know,' Danny said, 'and I agree with you. At that time, it wasn't seen as a woman's place to have book learning. Her duty was to take care of her family.'

'And what will her work be here?'

'To look after father.'

'And not earn any money?'

'Earn? Where could she earn?'

'There's a mill just across the way.'

'Weir Mill! Are you serious?'

'Why not?'

Danny shook his head.

'You're a hard woman, Irene.'

Chapter 6

London Standard, August 1847:
This scarcity of labour is easily accounted for. First from the deaths which occurred during the past winter among the migratory hordes that previously poured in at harvest from the counties of Mayo, Galway, Sligo and Roscommon; secondly the vast emigration to America and England of the same and rather higher classes of labourers; and thirdly the vast increase of tillage in their own localities which offers employment at home.

Danny's parents were already on the road to England with Murtybeg. Danny had spared no expense. And, unlike Luke, they had travelled across Ireland in some comfort. Murtybeg had rented a private coach to take them from Carrigard through Castlebar and Ballaghaderreen to Castlerea, where they met the Bianconi coach service and travelled through Roscommon to Athlone. Aileen being tired, Murtybeg had booked two rooms in the Prince of Wales Hotel, the best in the town. The following day, they travelled by Bianconi coach as far as Enfield, where they stayed in the Royal Oak Inn. It was not the quality of hotel that Murtybeg might have liked, but it was certainly adequate, and the following morning they left for Dublin. This time they travelled by rail. As Murtybeg explained, the rail service had only just reached Enfield. His father was intrigued by the train, since he had never travelled on one before. Murtybeg explained how the railway itself was constructed, and Danny's part in it as a railway contractor.

When they arrived at Kingsbridge Station in Dublin, Murtybeg called a cab and asked for the Gresham Hotel.

'Best again, I presume?' Murty commented.

'Of course.'

'And this is what Danny insists on.'

'It's what he's used to himself.'

Murtybeg left his parents in the hotel, took a cab down to the docks and bought tickets for first class on the City of Dublin Steam Packet to Liverpool. That night, he slept soundly in the Gresham.

*

The crossing was a calm one. Aileen stayed in her cabin, while Murty and Murtybeg stood at the stern, watching Dublin receding. As with the railway, Murty was fascinated by being on a ship.

'I was expecting sails,' he said to Murtybeg.

'This is a steam ship, father. Times are moving.'

'They are indeed.'

They arrived at the Clarence Dock in Liverpool and stayed that night at the Adelphi, the best hotel in the largest port on earth, as Murtybeg explained it. That evening, he and his father ate alone.

'Where's Ma?' Murtybeg asked.

'Up in the room. She says she isn't hungry.'

'She's always that way. And she hardly ever talks.'

Murty put a hand on Murtybeg's wrist.

'Don't be worrying about it. All the business about the school closing. That worried her. And she's fearful of all this travelling. The big hotels like this, they're far better than she's used to. They frighten her too.'

Murtybeg sipped his wine.

'Yes, I can understand that. It takes a little bit of getting used to, doesn't it?'

'It does,' Murty said. 'Even for me.'

'But there's more than that, isn't there?'

'Maybe there is, but whatever it is, it's in her own head, and there's no way any of us will ever understand that.'

Murtybeg decided not to pursue the matter. He said nothing, as his father cut into a steak.

'Damned good,' Murty said. 'I wonder where they get their meat.'

'On the hoof from Ireland, I'd say. They bring them over on the cattle boats. And you can just thank God you weren't on one of them.'

'Yes,' Murty said, 'I'd heard about them. There's a lot of cattle coming into Liverpool then?'

'Not just cattle. Potatoes too. And I'd wonder how much of that was coming from County Mayo.'

'And little enough of either there are in Mayo.'

'I know.'

'But enough of that,' Murty said. 'Tell me about this Irene woman. What's she like?'

'In one word – tough. That's not to say that Danny isn't, he wouldn't make it as a contractor otherwise. No, Danny is really tough. Works everyone hard, pays them little and makes sure everything is on time. But I thought I'd seen everything until he took up with Irene. I've never seen a woman like that in my life. She tells Danny he's too easy on everyone and paying them all too much. She knows how to deal with the suppliers too, a tough dealer, she is. She leaves the big contractors and the banks to Danny, they don't know anything about her, but she's always there in the background. She knows to the penny what the railways will pay, and she knows how to squeeze the suppliers 'till they squeal. And as for the workers, they're lucky if they get over a shilling a day.'

'A shilling!'

'Tenpence halfpenny when they start.'

'And all of them coming from Mayo?'

'Most all of them. Danny reckons he can get the lowest wages of all from the Mayo men. That's the very reason he won't hire from around Kilduff. He doesn't want paying that kind of wage to our own people.'

'But what about Bernie Lavan? That Roughneen fellow? McManus too?'

'They're different. They're gangers.'

'But surely...'

'They learned early on which side their bread is buttered. It's the fellows from out Erris and the rest of West Mayo, they're the ones who do the navvying for Danny. They eat what they're given and get paid damned near nothing. They don't speak English, so what chance have they? And Bernie and the rest of them, they know where they'd be, if it weren't for Danny. Six shillings a day, they get.'

'Six shillings!' Murty exclaimed. 'And the workers only get tenpence halfpenny. That's one hell of a difference. What will they think of that?'

'I don't think Danny or Irene care much what the navvies think. And that's the reason they don't want navvies from around Kilduff. They don't want stories getting home about that kind of thing.'

'And this is the kind of business Danny is running?'

'It is.'

'And this Irene woman is tougher?'

'A lot. She's one hell of a lot tougher, as Danny is going to find out.'

They took a train from Liverpool to Manchester, changing for Stockport.

'Not a bad looking house,' Murty said when they arrived.

'It is, but we're only renting' Murtybeg said. 'They'll be building a new house for themselves out by Newton. A cottage beside it for yourselves. I don't know when it'll be ready though.'

Danny looked up as they entered.

'Father...Mother...'

He ran across and embraced them both. Irene seemed surprised, but said nothing.

Aileen was weeping. *'My son, my son,'* she whispered in Irish.

Danny stepped back.

'So ye made it.'

'We did,' said Murty. 'Murteen here took good care of us.'

'He kept ye in the best hotels, I'm hoping.'

'Of course,' Murty answered, a touch of sarcasm in his voice. 'Better than we're used to at home.'

'I'd hope so.'

Danny waved them all to sit, and ordered the maid to make tea. But first he poured glasses of whiskey, while they waited for the tea. Murty sipped it.

'What of your news then? You're to be married, the pair of you?'

'For sure,' Danny answered. 'It's a question of timing though.'

'Murtybeg said three weeks.'

'Not a chance. We've far too much work. We want a proper wedding, and that'll take time to organise. So we're putting it off, a few months at least.'

'Yes,' Murty said. 'That would be wise.'

'But enough of that,' Danny said. 'What of Mayo?'

'Worse than ever,' Murty said. 'The potato is back, but there's not enough of it.'

'You're lucky to be out of it so. But what of the others? Michael? Eleanor? Pat?'

'Pat is clerking in the Poor Law Union,' Murty replied. 'Good job, from all we hear. But there's a lot of stories about the Workhouses. Half of them are bankrupt.'

'So what if Pat loses his job?' Danny asked.

'I wouldn't worry. They'll still have enough money once Luke gets to America.'

'Why America?' Irene asked quietly.

'He'd have no chances in Ireland,' Murty said. 'That's why.'

'He could have come over to us.'

'Yes,' Danny said. 'He's a sharp fellow, my cousin. He could have done well here.'

'As a ganger?' Murty asked. 'I don't know that he'd care for that.'

'Didn't he do it on the Relief Works?' Danny said. 'He has the experience.'

'I don't think he liked that experience, neither,' Murty said. 'He'd like it less here. Isn't that it?'

'Oh, I don't know,' Danny said. 'Luke's more than a ganger. I'd have taken him as a partner. He knew that, but he wouldn't have it.'

Irene was watching Aileen closely. She had noticed her quietness. Aileen had only spoken four words since they arrived, and those in Irish.

'So how did you find the journey?' Irene asked her directly.

'Fine,' Aileen replied in English. Silence again.

The maid had brought the tea. Murty waited as she poured it.

'Luke would do well, whether in America, or over here. Murteen was telling us about the railways hereabouts. Seems to be a damned good business.'

'Powerful,' Danny said.

'He says you're employing four hundred men.'

'Near enough. And more to come very soon. Four hundred more perhaps. It'll double our size.'

Murtybeg looked at Danny in astonishment. 'Four hundred more? You never told me that.'

'Yes,' Danny said. 'Things have changed a lot since you left. We're working for Brassey now, you know. Dealing directly with head office.'

'Brassey!'

'No less. The biggest railway builder in England.'

'Damn it, I know who Brassey is,' Murtybeg said. 'But what? Where?'

'A new cutting, down on the North Staffordshire line. It'll be the biggest we've ever done.'

'How much?'

'I'll tell you later. But you know the best thing of all? He came to us. We didn't have to ask. Brassey knows how good we are.'

'Well, that's great. But where will we get four hundred men?'

'That's the question, Murteen. And I'm hoping you'll have the answer.'

That evening, as the light died, Murtybeg helped the maid to bring the luggage up to the refurnished loft, where Murty and Aileen would be staying. She had already lit a coal fire.

Aileen followed, with Murty behind, carrying a candle in a holder.

'There you are,' Murtybeg said. 'Nice and warm. You'll live well here.'

'Indeed we will,' Murty agreed. He stood close by the fire, looking at the distant glow of the lights of Manchester in the night sky. 'But tell me, I thought you said they were getting married soon.'

'That's what I understood,' Murtybeg answered. 'It seems they're going to wait a while though.'

'I wonder why that is? Do you think he's nervous of her?'

'I doubt it. They're two of a kind, that's for sure. No, I think it's the reason they gave. They've too much work. And if you want to worry about anything, I'd worry about that. It might be they're trying to do too much. Taking on a contract with Brassey, that's really something. I'd never have expected that.'

When Murtybeg returned to the dining room, Danny and Irene were having a heated argument.

'I'm sorry,' Murtybeg said, making for the door.

'No,' Danny said, pointing to a chair. 'Let's hear what you've got to say. It's about mother.'

Murtybeg dropped his eyes.

'Come on,' Irene said, 'you can tell us. What's wrong with her?'

'Hard to make out,' Murtybeg said. 'I was surprised too when I first met her back in Carrigard. She'd never been that bad in years gone by.'

'So what caused it?' Irene asked.

'A lot of things,' Murtybeg replied. 'She was upset when Danny left.'

'Me?' Danny protested.

'Yes, you. She'd understood you were only going to England for the summer. Kept your bed warm ever since, waiting for you to return.'

'But that's years ago,' Danny said.

'I know. But it seems me leaving made it even worse. Then Nessa dying. But when father lost the school, she reckoned he was going to leave for England too, leave her all alone. She was frightened of that, I can tell you.'

'But there was no question of that,' Danny said. 'He'd never have left her.'

'I know. But then, even the thought of going to England upset her too. You've no idea.'

'So what are we going to do about it?' Irene asked. 'We can't keep her here.'

Murtybeg looked up in alarm. 'Where would you send her?'

'God only knows,' said Danny. He thought it better not to mention their earlier conversation about Weir Mill. He could never see his mother as a millhand.

'But what...?' Murtybeg asked.

'Let's hire a nurse. Stay with her while father is working.'

'The maid will do, as long as she's here,' Irene said.

Danny held up his hand. 'Well, one thing's certain. We're not going to agree on this tonight. We've other problems.' He glanced at Murtybeg, who nodded.

'Yes. I know what you're going to say. Workers. Isn't that it?'

'That, Murteen, is precisely it.'

'And you're seriously expecting me to find four hundred more?'

'I am, and damned fast.'

'So what now?'

'Liverpool,' Irene replied.

Murtybeg did not respond.

'I'm afraid so, Murteen,' Danny said. 'It's our only way.'

'After me only getting back from Mayo,' Murtybeg said.

'I know. I know.'

Next morning, Murtybeg left Stockport before anyone was awake, and travelled to Liverpool.

As Danny had expected, his father had little difficulty in adjusting to work in the office. Danny had suggested a starting salary of six shillings a day. He gave him a separate office with his own clerk. Murtybeg occupied the same office on the rare occasions he was in Stockport.

For the first few days Murty worked on simple accounts, adding and multiplying long columns of figures. It was he who had trained Danny, Murtybeg, Luke and Pat together with a hundred other pupils every year, pushing them harder and harder until their arithmetic was faster, and more accurate, than almost anyone. Irene had noticed this in Danny and Murtybeg, but she had been surprised to notice it even in Danny's gangers. Their fluency in the English language had surprised her. There were certainly no similar skills in the navvies they recruited from the west coast of Mayo.

Danny was very cautious in the way he approached his father. He knew Murty found it difficult to be working under his son, and Irene had been doubtful when Danny told her of Murty's skills, but within a few hours, she was convinced. She realised then that she had to be more careful in her approach to Murty, and never discussed Aileen in his presence. She understood too that she would have to watch the way she handled the accounts, since Murty might question her on what she was doing.

One evening, Aileen left the table early, and went to bed. The maid followed her.

'She's different to what she used to be,' Danny commented.

'She is,' Murty replied, quietly.

'The hunger must have upset her.'

'Yes. The hunger was one cause. Not in our family though, and all thanks to you for that. Without your money, we'd have starved.'

'Of course, father. But what else would I have done? We're all family.'

'We are,' Murty said, 'but it wasn't that there was hunger in our house. It was what she could see on the road. Starving people, bodies in the ditches. There were frightful sights just outside our front door. But that – even that – would not have been enough to shake her so much.'

'What so?'

'Many things, but Nessa's death was the worst. She was bad before, but Nessa – that was the real shock that broke your mother's heart.'

'I know,' Danny said, 'it was a shock to all of us.'

'Enough of a shock for ye to beat the hell out of Jimmy Corrigan.'

'Who told you that?' Danny asked. 'Murtybeg?'

'I never said a word,' Murtybeg said.

'His brother, that's who told us,' Murty said. 'Owen. Said the two of you beat Jimmy so bad he'll never work again.'

'Well, he was the one who'd killed Nessa,' Danny said, in defence.

'It's up to the law to decide that.'

'They'd never do anything about it. If Corrigan hadn't made the baby with Nessa, she'd still be alive today. Isn't that it?'

'Be that as it may, making a baby with Nessa was hardly a crime. And surely not murder.'

'That's your opinion,' Danny said. He could see that Irene was surprised. 'And anyhow Corrigan would never have left Mayo if he didn't know he was guilty.'

'He'd have stayed at home, if he'd known what you and Murteen were planning for him over here.'

'It wasn't just me,' Murtybeg said, lamely.

'No,' Murty said. 'It was the pair of ye. And, one way or another, we'll have to make some settlement with him.'

'A settlement. You're seriously expecting us to settle with Jimmy Corrigan.'

'I am.'

'But we don't even know where he is.'

'You were well able to find him when ye wanted to beat the living daylights out of him.'

'Yes,' Danny said, 'but that was different.'

'It's not different, Danny. You find him. Just go and do it.'

Danny noted that Irene had said nothing. He wondered what she was thinking.

As they undressed for bed, she turned to Danny.

'You never told me that business about that fellow you beat up. Who was he? What on earth did you do to him?'

'He was the one who got my sister Nessa with child, and the baby killed her.'

'Many women die in childbirth.'

'Who cares about many women? It was Nessa. My own sister. And Corrigan made the baby.'

'So what did you do to him?'

'Myself and Murteen, we'd heard he was in Liverpool. So we found him and beat him. Just like you heard.'

'But your father says he'll never work again.'

'We broke his knees and his fingers. That was all.'

'That was all,' she echoed. 'You know, I thought I was tough enough, but I don't think I'd be up to that kind of thing.'

'Well, I'm not sorry,' Danny said, 'and you know as well as I do that we have to be tough in the contracting business. Very tough.'

He blew out the candle and slipped in beside her.

The matter was never mentioned between them again. But Danny could not get Jimmy Corrigan out of his head. The thought of Corrigan never working again had given him an idea. He and Murtybeg had traced him once before. It might be even easier now. If Corrigan couldn't work, he could well be in Liverpool Workhouse, not as a worker but as an invalid. The more he thought about it, the better he felt that the chances were that this would be where Corrigan had ended up.

The real question was what to do if he found him? Should he, as Murty had suggested, make some sort of restitution to him, or to the family. The very thought of it was galling.

What else? He found it hard to think, when the question of Corrigan's whereabouts was only a guess. The best answer was to find out if Corrigan was in the Workhouse or not.

Danny suggested to Murty that he might like to visit a cutting. He himself wanted to visit McManus' cutting.

When they arrived, Murty took in everything very quickly.

'Good God, Danny, those horses are better fed than the men.'

'Bigger loads to pull, that's why. And hay is cheap.'

'But the men – they're desperately thin.'

'No thinner than they'd be back beyond Belmullet or Louisburgh,' Danny said. 'Up from Tourmakeady too, they're starving in the mountains up there.'

'Don't you care?'

'Of course I care. That's why we feed them so well when they get here. We build them up as quick as we can. We have to.'

McManus came over.

'The Master,' he exclaimed. 'I'd heard you were coming. I never thought I'd see the day.'

'Neither did I,' said Murty, 'but the day came.'

He looked around him, preferring not to mention the health of the navvies again.

'This is a massive undertaking,' he said.

'Indeed it is, Master,' McManus said. 'Bigger than the Relief Works were back at home, I'd wager.'

'It is,' Murty answered.

They went to the shed, which served as McManus' office.

'Still behind schedule?' Danny asked.

'We are,' McManus answered. 'We've a desperate need for more workers. But you know that.'

'We do, and right well,' Danny said. 'I've sent Murtybeg back to Liverpool the very morning after he arrived. Scouring the docks and the Workhouses, he is. We should have men for you very soon, Jamesy.'

The three men walked out again, going back along the lines of navvies.

'There's one other thing I must mention to you,' Danny said. 'We're taking on a new contract. Johnny will be taking it over as a matter of urgency.'

'Is it close by?' McManus asked.

'Fifty or sixty miles. It's on the North Staffordshire Line.'

'Must be a big one if you're asking Johnny to take it over so.'

'You could say that. A Brassey contract,' Danny said.

'Brassey!'

'And we'll be needing three or four hundred men for it.'

McManus stopped. 'My God, Danny, we're short of men already. Do you think we can do all this?'

'It's not a matter of 'can we',' Danny said. 'We must.'

Murty and Danny discussed it all in the train back to Manchester.

'Jamesy got quite a surprise there,' Murty commented.

'Didn't he just?'

'Did you see the alarm on his face when you mentioned four hundred workers?'

Danny laughed.

'Hardly surprising. He's short of workers already, and the thought of another contract competing for that number would put him in a right panic.'

Murty glanced out the window as a train passed in the other direction.

'Wouldn't it be easier if you raised the wages,' Murty asked.

'And lose our profits. There's no way I'd do that.'

They sat in silence for some time. It was clear to Danny that the question of wages was disturbing to Murty, but he did not want to discuss it further. He decided to change the subject.

'Tell me,' he asked, 'do you remember Tim Kearney?'

'Sure didn't I teach him?' Murty replied.

'Of course you did. Well, we're sending Johnny Roughneen down to take over the Brassey contract, and I'm thinking of asking Tim to come and work with us, and take over from Johnny.'

'But where is he?' Murty asked.

'We reckon he's over in Leeds with the gang.'

'Farrelly's crowd?'

'As it was before Farrelly left.'

'Is Tim still there though?' Murty asked. 'Will he come if you ask him? He's not gone to America too.'

'He'll surely come if we find him. Six shillings a day will decide that very quick. And if he isn't there, there's still Joe Gilligan. Good men. Hard workers, and well educated, as you know well.'

'Indeed,' Murty said.

When Murtybeg arrived back from Liverpool, Danny was dismayed to see that he had less than twenty men with him.

'It's getting harder,' he told Danny.

Danny took him aside. 'Listen, Murteen, there's one thing I'd like you to do straight away. Put these lot back on the train, and bring them down to McManus. He has a desperate call for them.'

Murtybeg shook his head. 'We can't go on like this.'

'I know,' Danny said, 'but we'll work it out. Don't worry.'

It was late that evening before Murtybeg arrived back.

'Jamesy was sure delighted to see me,' he said.

'I'm sure he was,' Danny said. 'He's getting behind on the contract. He's the one who needs the men the most.'

'But this Brassey contract! Hundreds more men! What on earth are we going to do about that?'

'Send you back to Liverpool, Murteen.'

'That won't work anymore, Danny,' Murtybeg said. 'Liverpool is getting tougher for finding workers. There's fever in the City. They're terrified of the Irish now. They say we're the cause of the fever. Already the Workhouse is starting to send people back to Ireland. Dublin, Cork, Westport or wherever they came from.'

'They can't do that,' Irene said.

'Oh, but they can,' Murtybeg responded. 'And there's worse. The port is stopping any ships coming in with fever. Already they're using hospital ships on the Mersey. Any ship with fever has to run up a yellow flag and discharge straight into the hospital ships. Quarantine they call it, but the locals call them Death Ships. And it's worse for the Irish ships.'

'Worse,' Danny exclaimed.

'They started by stopping people right off the gangway, checking for fever. Now, if they've got Irish passengers, they often just turn them straight around, send them back to Ireland. Not all of them, mind, but there's very few get through. And any with fever don't stand a chance. No quarantine, they just take the cattle off, and send the passengers straight back to Ireland.'

'And what of the rest of the town?' Irene asked. 'The slums and the like.'

'They'd be a poorer class of person,' Murtybeg answered. 'If they can't get work after months or years in Liverpool, they're not the men we'd want. They're either the sort don't want to work, or they're heading to America.'

'But the Americans won't let them in.'

'Quebec will.'

'And women?' Irene asked. 'Why not use women.

'Women!' Danny exclaimed. 'They wouldn't have the strength.'

Irene laughed. 'And what of the coal mines. The pitbrow girls over at Gatley Pit. They're as tough as any man. Shows the women can do it.'

'Well, we're not doing it,' Danny said.

Danny and Murtybeg discussed it all at length over the next few days. Then Danny wrote a note to each of his gangers. Two days later, they convened in the Stockport office.

'You all know,' Danny said, 'we've a problem with finding navvies. And it's getting worse because of the Brassey contract. Murtybeg. Explain the situation.'

For the next ten minutes, Murtybeg explained the state of affairs in Liverpool. When he finished, there was a silence around the room.

'So what do we do now?' Roughneen asked.

'I think my cousin has the answer,' Danny said. Something Murtybeg heard from him back in Mayo.'

'Luke? He's gone to America.'

'No, not Luke,' Murtybeg said. 'His brother Pat. He's clerking now, Knockanure Workhouse...'

'But that's by Kilduff,' Lavan said. 'A few miles only. You said you wouldn't take men from there.'

'True enough,' said Murtybeg, 'but hear me out. Knockanure is chartering ships to send their inmates to America. Some they're sending from the Mayo ports, mainly Westport or Killala, and straight to America. But it's cheaper sending them over by Liverpool first.'

'Liverpool!' Roughneen exclaimed.

'Yes, Liverpool,' Murtybeg continued. 'The Liverpool passenger trade is only a quarter the price of the Mayo ships. That's because the Mayo ships are passenger ships. The ships leaving Liverpool are all coming from Canada, carrying lumber, with empty holds going back. They pack passengers in, cheap as they like. So the plan is this. Like you say, we don't take inmates from Knockanure. We must contact the west Mayo Workhouses. First, Westport. It covers the sea coast all the way to Louisburgh, and from what we hear, the villages there are in a desperate state, and putting terrible pressure on the Workhouse. Second, Ballinrobe, which covers Partry, and God knows, a more forsaken place you never saw. My reckoning is Ballinrobe and Westport might be able to supply us with enough. If not, we could consider Newport, which stretches all the way out to Achill, which is in a desperate way too. Last of all, Ballina, which goes all the way out to Erris. Erris itself is in a frightful condition. There's talk they might be building a Workhouse in Erris itself, but it might not be ready for some time. So Ballina could certainly supply us with many inmates.

'But are those Workhouses sending their inmates to America?' Roughneen asked. 'I'd heard some of them were.'

'I don't know,' Murtybeg said. 'Pat might have the answer. If they are, we can try stopping them at Liverpool, but if they have tickets for America, they wouldn't want to work with us.'

'Then that doesn't help,' Lavan said.

'No,' Danny said. 'So we make sure they don't have tickets for America.'

'And how would we do that?' McManus asked.

'Bring them straight in from Mayo,' Danny said. 'Direct from the Workhouse. It would save the Workhouse a fortune, and from all we hear, they're half bankrupt already. So we take half their male inmates, and ship them through Westport ourselves.'

'Ship them?' Lavan asked. 'On what?'

'A cattle boat,' Danny said. 'Or a corn ship. Whichever.'

'That would cost money.'

'Not as much as you might think,' Murtybeg said. 'The cattle boats, they'd be cheap enough. The cattlemen pay for the boat, the passengers are the profit on top for the boatmen. And there'd be volunteers enough. The hunger is desperate around the west of the county, and from all we hear the Workhouses are over-crowded. No, I don't think we'll have a problem in getting navvies, nor much cost in getting them over here neither. They're charging a shilling a man on the cattle boats from Dublin. My guess is two shillings a man out of Westport, though we might keep it lower.'

'Little enough, as you say,' Roughneen said. 'But what if they send the boats back without unloading?'

'They might not if there's no fever,' Murtybeg answered. 'So we check them first at Westport. Any showing the slightest signs of fever, we send home. Check them again at Liverpool. Hide the fever cases down the back, behind the cattle or the corn, and send them back to Mayo after we've let the rest off. Sure, it's a risk. They might send the boat home without unloading. Or they might not. A pound or two in the right place could sort it all out.'

'I don't know,' said Roughneen. 'It's all one hell of a gamble.'

'One we must take, though,' Danny said. 'Just look at it this way. If they turn the boat around, what have we lost? The cost of bringing them over, that's all. But we lose an awful lot more if we don't get those contracts. We must at least try it.'

'And who should we send over to arrange all this?' Lavan asked.

'Murtybeg,' Irene answered. 'No choice.'

'So back to Mayo again,' Murtybeg said, wearily.

'Needs must,' Danny said. 'We need workers. And fast. We need hundreds already. And if we get contracts from anyone else, we'll be looking for hundreds more again.'

McManus stayed back as the others left the room.

'A word with you, Danny.'

'I know, I know,' Danny said. 'You want workers.'

'I do,' McManus replied. 'But it's not just that. We might have an answer to the Liverpool problem.'

'You might?' Danny said. 'What kind of answer is 'might'?'

'Better than that,' McManus said. 'I'm pretty well sure.'

'Go on, go on.'

'I don't know if I ever told you, but I've got cousins over in County Cavan. Second cousins more like. A tougher lot you never saw. But one of them, Gene Brady, moved to Liverpool twenty years back. And he's a man you'd want to know. He controls the Irish in Liverpool.'

'Controls who?'

'The gangs.'

'The gangs? Railway gangs?'

'The other sort. The Irish mobs.'

'You're kidding.'

'I couldn't be more serious.'

'So where does that get us?'

'Just think it through, will you? Liverpool is as Irish a city as you can get. How many Irish are there now? Damned near half the city. Might be more. And some of the most violent gangs are Irish.'

'But the police? What are they doing?'

'Nothing much,' McManus said, 'nor do they want to. They know Brady is their one trump card in controlling any Irish gangs that might start up in Liverpool. There's an understanding – nothing stated, nothing written – between the police and Brady.'

'But the Orangemen. They control the police.'

'Not as much as they'd like to think. The police need Brady, more than he needs them.'

Danny shook his head. 'So what are you suggesting?'

'This problem of getting the workers off the boats. If there's one man who can make sure you can do it, it's Gene Brady. His word is law among the Irish in Liverpool. And if we want to make sure our workers get off the boats, he's the one man can make sure of it.'

Danny's mind was in a whirl. He had to be certain that he could get workers, but he was not convinced that this approach would work.

He lit his pipe slowly. 'So what now?'

'I'll write to my cousin. I don't need to tell him what we're thinking. Brady is the one who'll know who needs to be paid. Just as important, who needs a warning? Carrot or stick, it'll work either way. And if I write to Brady, I'd be doing it in my own name. After that, you can decide.'

'My God, Jamesy, it's a hell of a chance.'

'The alternative is worse.'

Danny puffed slowly at his pipe.

'Fine,' he said, 'write to your cousin, and let's see what he says.'

Afterwards, Danny poured himself a whiskey.

He still had concerns about a crash in the market for railway building, but the massive Brassey contract seemed to weigh the balance the other way. Even if there was a downturn in the market, it should not affect Edwardes & Ryan.

Provided, of course, he could get the workers. For a long time, he sat in his office, not noticing that it was getting dark.

McManus's suggestion had unsettled him. He had no idea who Gene Brady was, nor how he might control the Liverpool Irish. He had never thought of working with criminal gangs before, though there was nothing to say that Brady ran a gang. But if not, how did he control them. Best not to know perhaps.

Irene entered. 'What on earth are you doing there?' she asked.

'Just thinking.'

'About what?'

'Getting workers. What else?'

'What did McManus have to say?'

'Something about a cousin of his. It seems he has strong pull with the police in Liverpool. Jamesy reckons he can sort out any problems in getting navvies through Liverpool Port.'

'How could he do that?'

'Damned if I know, Irene. And maybe I don't want to know. But any man who has friends in the Liverpool police is well worth knowing. That's for certain.'

*

After Irene had gone to bed, Danny wrote a letter to Pat.

Mr. Patrick Ryan

Knockanure Workhouse

Knockanure

Co. Mayo

Edwardes & Ryan

c/o Hailey House

Edgeley

Stockport

Lancashire

My Dear Pat,

I hope you are keeping well through these terrible times. I had heard that Luke had gone to America so he at least will no longer be in the middle of a Famine, though I am sure he will still have concerns about his new wife until she joins him.

You will know that my mother and father have joined us here in Stockport. Father's school would have been closed when the new schools are set up around Kilduff. He is presently working on my accounts, and we hope mother may soon have some work of her own. I had explained to father that the only Kilduff men working with me are the gangers – Bernie Lavan, Jamesy McManus and Johnny Roughneen. All the rest at present come from the western part of Mayo.

The market for railway building continues to grow, and we have a growing need for labour, which will increase over the next few months. We are looking for at least four hundred men. Murtybeg will soon be travelling to Mayo again to assess how many workers we might find, and that is why I am writing to you.

I had heard some of the Mayo Workhouses are paying people to go to America. It was then that the question struck me as to why they should be sent so far, especially when there is so much work with Edwardes & Ryan over here.

Surely the Atlantic crossing is expensive. If a few hundred men were to be shipped directly to us instead, it would be much cheaper than sending them to America. We would pay for the shipping, thus saving the Workhouses any expense, and also reducing the cost of running the Workhouse. This is something that might be of interest to the Workhouses in the western part of Mayo, especially those in Ballinrobe, Westport and perhaps Newport and Ballina.

If you think this is all possible, I should certainly be delighted to hear it. If so, perhaps you could drop me a line and we can put the arrangements in train. But let me know either way.

I remain, your affectionate cousin,

Daniel Ryan

Chapter 7

Quebec Gazette, August 1847:
From information recently given to us, the quarantine at Liverpool is not only worse than useless as regards this country, but absolutely murders the emigrants intending to embark hitherward. We are told that from 15 to 16 hulks are stationed off the port for the reception of the refugees from Ireland, who, when sick or doubtful looking, are transferred to them from the Irish steamers and from whence, after a short probation, shipped on board vessels destined for Canada; and that, too, as may be naturally conceived, in a worse state than if allowed to proceed on their voyage at once. The passengers in the Triton were of this class, among whom disease appeared the day they left the docks. Her deaths before reaching Grosse Île numbered 83, including all the officers of the ship and several of the crew; the master, also, being very sick.

The Atlantic was still running wild, as the sun rose higher and reflected from the waves and the ice. Luke blinked in the early morning light. Tyler was beside him.

'Don't often see them so far south this time of the season.'

'I wouldn't know,' Luke said.

'I suppose you wouldn't. Them 'bergs should be all gone by now though. That bastard's a long way from home. Either that, or we're a long way north. We've been running north with the storm. The question is, how far?'

Another wave smashed into the white cliffs, and fell back.

'So where could we be?' Luke asked.

'Hard to say,' Tyler replied. 'Could be that we're running close to Greenland by now, or half way up the Davis Strait. Baffin even, if we're running with the Greenland Current. God knows it's possible.'

'You don't know?'

'I'll take a sighting on the sun at noon, then at least we'll know how far north we are.'

Still Luke could not take his eyes off the iceberg. It was so unyielding with the savagery of the waves, unlike the ship which was still running before the dying storm. He still felt an unreasoning fear. The crew were not worried though. Neither was Tyler. They had missed the 'berg.

'How long will it take then?' Luke asked 'How long 'till we make Quebec?'

'Who knows? Could be three weeks? A lot longer if we're too far north, or the wind is against us. And if we take much longer than that, and the St. Lawrence freezes early, we won't make it at all.'

'What's that you say?'

'Stands to reason. The Centaurus don't sail over ice. Never heard of any ship could.'

'So then what?'

'St. Johns,' Tyler said. 'We might put in at St. Johns. We'll be running out of supplies anyhow. Sailors too. Three of them are down with fever. And there'll be more. Just pray we make Quebec.'

He left Luke and climbed back up the rigging. Luke fetched his bucket, knelt down, and started to scrub the deck.

And if we don't make Quebec, he thought. What then?

An hour passed. Then the hatch opened, and more skeletal corpses were manhandled up the ladder and onto the deck. Luke could tell which had died of hunger, and which of fever. He knew the stink of fever, and the sight of decaying flesh. He knew too the hairy faces of starving children.

The corpses were laid out side by side, women and children wailing alongside.

The priest made the form of a cross on the forehead of a man's corpse.

'Per istam sanctam Unctionem...'

Luke went down on one knee. The corpse was passed over the side of the ship. Then the same prayer was repeated.

When the blessings were finished, he walked over to the priest.

'More dead,' he said.

'Yes,' the priest replied. *'And many more to come before we make land.'*

Another woman's naked corpse was brought up. Another blessing, another dead body thrown to the insatiable sea.

'So *what are you thinking of doing when you get to Quebec?'* the priest asked him.

'*I might work on the forestry a while,'* Luke replied. *'Somewhere around* Quebec, *if I can. But then I'm hoping to travel down to the* United States, *if I can get across the border, that is. I've heard they're stopping us on the border.'*

'Yes, I'd heard that. But what if you get across? What then?'

'*I've friends working the railways in* Pennsylvania. *We worked together in England, and they tell me there's any amount of work on the railways in*

America. So I'll head down to New York, then Philadelphia, then on out to Harrisburg. That's where the railway building is now.'

'It's a long journey,' the priest said

'Long enough,' Luke answered. 'But what of you, Father. That's a big group you're leading. Is it an eviction?'

'A class of an eviction. Most of them are tenants from Viscount Palmerston's Estate over by Classiebawn in County Sligo. Some sort of a Government Minister in London, he is, not that that made much difference. The Viscount wanted the land for sheep, and he saw the hunger as his chance to clear it. His agent bought all the tickets to send us to Canada, and then they evicted everyone. The most of them they sent out through ships they had hired running from Sligo Port to Quebec Town. Two thousand they sent out that way, God knows what's happened to them, we haven't had any word of them since. But there wasn't enough room for them all on the Sligo boats, so they gave me a little money and a letter to Stewart & Kincaid, Palmerston's agents in Dublin. So we walked across Ireland to Dublin, and there they gave me ships tickets, told me I was to take them to Liverpool, find the Centaurus and lead them all off to Quebec. Or America. Anywhere but Ireland, didn't much matter to them where.'

'You're lucky they got you the tickets,' Luke said. 'When Clanowen carried out his evictions at Gort-na-Móna there were no tickets. Nothing. We all had to take people in, but many died and others have disappeared.'

'Clanowen is the spawn of the devil.'

'True, Father. I'm not sure that Palmerston is much better though.'

'No. The end is the same. Now all the cabins are tumbled, and our church is empty. And why? Because Viscount Palmerston wants a sheep run. Sheep are more profitable than men. Those four-legged creatures will ruin Ireland.'

Another corpse had been brought up. A young man walked over to Luke and the priest.

'That's the end of them, Father.'

'Well, thank God for that, Conaire.'

When the priest had returned to the passenger decks, Luke stayed outside, listening to the flapping of the sails and feeling the breeze on his face. Scrubbing the deck had exhausted him. The iceberg was receding into the distance.

The man called Conaire came alongside Luke. He was thin, but not as thin as most. The flesh on his face was drawn over his cheekbones and into the eye-sockets, but his eyes had none of the broken, defeated stare of many. His clothes were ragged.

'They're saying it's ice,' he said.

96

'*Yes,*' said Luke. '*Nothing but ice.*'

He saw the man had lice, and drew away, He had seen enough of lice and fever in the Workhouses and on the Relief Works in the mountains.

The man had been talking again. He nudged Luke.

'*I'm sorry,*' Luke replied. '*I'd been thinking. What did you say?*'

'*I said, you're a quiet man. I've been watching you all this time, and you never talk to any of us.*'

'*Perhaps I've nothing to say.*'

'*Or perhaps it's that you've nothing to say to people like us. You talk enough to the priest – and that officer fellow there. Perhaps we're not good enough for you to talk to. Is that it?*'

'*Believe what you want to believe,*' Luke said. '*You will anyhow.*'

'*So where are you from? Is it Mayo? You have the accent of it.*'

'*Mayo surely. Over by Kilduff. Do you know it?*'

'*Aye, I've heard of it. It was bad there?*'

'*Bad enough.*'

Yes, Luke thought, bad enough. But worse on the Mountain. And worse again in the mountains and wretched mud villages around Brockagh – Ardnagrena, Lisnadee, Burrenabawn, Teenashilla, and Benstreeva. And Croghancoe. The people dying along the Works. The hopelessness in their eyes. And the hate. Hating him because he was the ganger. The government man.

'*You're well fed though,*' the man said.

'*I was working,*' Luke said

'*You were earning enough, I'd say though. Better than the most of us, I'd wager.*'

Yes, Luke thought, gangers earned better than others. Men, women and children on the Works earned anything from eight pennies to as low as two pennies a day. But he himself earned more, and Pat was earning far more as a clerk. His father too, renting out the horse and cart as well as working. There was no need to mention all that.

'*What is it to you?*' he said abruptly.

'*What indeed*' the man replied. '*What is it to me or any of the others?*'

'*They paid what they paid, and they paid little enough in Kilduff, though there were other places that were worse, I can tell you that. The Ox Mountains...*'

'*How would you know that?*'

'*Because I was there.*'

'*You were there? Why were you there?*'

'*Because they sent me,*' Luke replied, realising at once he had made a mistake.

'*They sent you. They wouldn't be sending ordinary people though, would they? They came because they had to. Why would they send you?'*

'*Does it matter?'*

'*Yes it does. They sent you because you were different. Isn't that it? Why else would they send you?'*

'*Because I could read and write.'*

'*So you were a ganger. That's it, isn't it?'*

'*Perhaps it is. Is it any business of yours?'*

'*Yes it is,'* the other man said. '*It most surely is. Over in Torán, we had gangers. Utter brutes they were. The lowest of the low.'*

Abruptly, Luke grabbed him by the shirt, and shoved him back out over the rail.

'*And you might go a lot lower too,'* he said, nodding towards the waves below.

The other man looked at him in fright. Then he relaxed.

'*You wouldn't do it. You're not the murdering type. Are you?'*

'*Just try me,'* Luke said. He let go his grip, but still the other man taunted him.

'*Gangers are worse than animals. Madmen. Mad for power. What else do they understand?*

'*Maddened by power, more like'* Luke answered, '*but you'd not understand that. Having power over people's lives, all it brings is hatred.'*

'*And you can't understand why?'*

'*Yes,'* Luke said, wearily, '*I can understand it well. But you – it's you cannot understand the place of someone like me. I became a ganger because I could read and write. I was told it was my duty to help my people, and few others could. And I believed that. But then came Selection. In a famine, no matter what you do, you never have enough. It doesn't matter whether it's work or food. You think at first it's great, you're helping people, giving them work. But there's never enough, so you have to select those who get the work. And that means selecting those who do not. Those that have to die. And that means hatred.'*

'*It does, it most surely does.'*

'*But what would you have had me do?'* Luke asked. '*Give out no work. That'd be worse. And even when you do give out work, those who receive it will hate you. They hate you because they hate charity. They have their pride. Every man or woman wants to be able to feed their own. When they cannot do that, it breaks their pride, so they have to hate someone. They could hate the blight that brought the hunger, but no, they have to hate the ganger. Isn't that right?'*

'*Even so there are the others who love power. Love the feeling it gives them that they are better than other men or women.'*

'*Love power!*' Luke exclaimed. '*I told you, that's a madness. All I ever wanted to do was to get away from it. Not have to make choices that broke people. But always they told me that if I didn't do it, somebody else would. And if nobody would, then the starvation would be worse. And whether you like it or not, that's true.*'

'*It might be true of you, but it certainly wasn't true of all.*'

'*So you admit that I'm a man. Better than a brute?*'

The other man looked at him, surprised. '*If I were to believe all you're saying, maybe I would believe you were better than a brute. But not much. It's not just the sense of power that some men have. It's the way they do things. The way they drive the people. And* piecework. *The accursed* piecework. *Was that needed?*'

'*I agree,*' Luke said, '*but it is not the ganger that devises things like that. The orders come from the County fellows in Castlebar, or direct from Dublin Castle, and if the orders are not obeyed, then no work, no food. Piecework – that came from Castlebar. And any time the wages were reduced, I can swear that came from Castlebar too. They wanted everything done faster, at a lower cost, no matter what the pain. The men of power, the top men in the Union or in the County, many of them hated the Irish. Many of them were Irish too, they hated their own. Can you understand that?*'

'*I can, I understand it well. There's many people like that. Put them in a place of power and they despise those under them.*'

'*True, too true. But even so, I must tell you something else. Even in the Union and the County, there are good men too. Men who understand suffering and pain. But still the system breaks them. I know it. I've seen it. My own uncle. He was a good man. A Surveyor with much responsibility in the county, but there was not much he could do, and it broke his heart. He's dead now. The fever got him. And don't tell me he was a mad brute. If you do, you really will end up down there.*'

Conaire leant on the railing, looking straight at Luke.

'*You're a strange man so,*' he said. '*I think I might even start to understand you. With time. Who knows?*'

'*Do you think I'm worth understanding?*'

'*I do. By God, I do.*'

'*Understand me or not, there is only one thing I would ask of you. Don't judge me until you know me. And until then, keep your damned mouth shut. Not a word to anyone.*'

'*Would I dare?*'

A man came across from the hatch, and tapped Luke on his shoulder.

'They're asking who's next on the pumps.'

Luke cursed. '*Come on,*' he said to *Conaire*. '*Time to go.*'

'Still the ganger?' Conaire said. 'County Mayo or out on the ocean. You don't change, do you?'

'Go to hell,' Luke replied.

He followed the other man, but Conaire stayed on the outer deck. Luke selected three men to work the bilge pump, and worked alongside them for some hours.

When he returned to the passenger deck, he saw the next line of people waiting to climb up the ladders. He could see the hairy faces of starving children along the line. At the end of the line another corpse was being carried out, the priest following.

'No end,' he whispered to Luke as he passed.

The next day, Luke was lying on his bunk, when Conaire walked past with a pot. He thought to ignore him, but changed his mind.

'Going cooking, are you?' he called out.

'I am. Are you?'

'Hold on.' He took out his pot and flour from his bunk, and followed him down to the line for the kitchen.

'So how do they call you?'

'Luke. Luke Ryan is the name to me. And you? Conaire, isn't it?'

'Conaire Ó Coisteala. Or Costello in the English speech. From Torán, out the far end of Erris.'

'Erris,' Luke echoed.

'Yes, Erris. And what of it?'

'Nothing,' Luke replied. 'Nothing at all.'

'You've been there, have you?'

'Never. I've heard much about it though. You remember I said about my uncle.'

'The Surveyor?'

'Yes. He travelled the county. He spoke of Erris as a wild place on the edge of the ocean. Bitterly cold through the winter, it was. That's what he told me.'

'He was right too,' Conaire said. 'A wild place even in the summer, when the wind came in off the ocean. This last winter, it came off the land, but it was far colder. Many, many people died of cold, those who were not already dead from hunger, and the gangers forced them to work on – work 'till they dropped. And whether you like it or not, your uncle was part of that system.'

Luke bristled, but did not react. He changed the subject.

'And I suppose the Workhouse wasn't able to do much.'

'Workhouse! There is no Workhouse. For years they've been talking about it, but that's all they ever do. Talk, talk, talk. No, the Poor Law fellows never wanted a Workhouse in Erris. The nearest was in Ballina. Many tried

*to walk there, but most dropped on the way in the desperate cold. And
those who reached Ballina Workhouse, they weren't allowed in because they
weren't local. So those with sense, they stayed on the Relief Works in Erris.
We had two gangers there – McHale and Barrett. Irishmen they were. Erris
men what's worse. And they were savages. And when the Works ended, there
was no food, and the hunger killed many more. Then the fever came from the
East, from the rest of Mayo and down the length of Erris. It was almost as if
the Poor Law sent that too.*'

'*That's nonsense*,' Luke said.

'*It surely is, though many believed it. The charitable ladies from Westport
and Castlebar, the Protestant kind, they sent us clothes during the winter.
Many would not wear them. They held that the clothes brought the fever.*'

Yes, Luke thought. Second-hand clothes with lice. No need to say
anything on that though.

'*Go on,*' he said. '*Go on with your story.*'

'*So me and my brother left Erris. Men spoke of ships leaving Ballina
for America, and more spoke of Sligo, though few knew where that was.
So we went for Ballina, but my brother died on the journey and when I got
to Ballina, there were no ships that would take me. So I walked to Dublin,
working on the big farms as I went, for pennies and food. Enough pennies to
cross over to Liverpool. I had to work my own passage from there though,
so here I am, cleaning out the shit buckets with the women and children.
Dark to dark, they work us. That Starkey fellow is a right bastard.*'

'*He is*,' said Luke. '*Even so, it's lucky you are, or at least you will be if
you don't get fever from that class of work. You'd never work your passage
any other way though, the price would be too high.*'

'*It's high enough on this wreck.*'

'*Lower than others though. Dublin, then Liverpool to Quebec. That's
the way we both came, and why? Because it's the cheapest way to America.
All the American ports, Savannah to Bangor, they won't allow most of the
Irish ships. Only those that are designed as passenger ships with few people
in them, and none with fever. That's why we must go to Quebec.*'

Luke wondered whether he had been rooked. The thought had struck
him in Liverpool, but he had dismissed it. No one had told him about
travelling on a lumber ship, and he felt certain that the fare would have been
lower than what he had paid the shipping agent in Kilduff.

They shuffled forward with the queue. The girl in front of him had long
black hair, reminding him of Winnie. It was greasy though, and he could
see the white lice eggs standing out against the black. And there lay the
difference. Winnie with lice? Never.

Many passengers, having run out of their own supplies, no longer used the kitchen. They ate ship biscuits, putrid with maggots. Luke wondered if his own supplies might run out before they reached port, and he would be forced to eat the same.

'*Are you intending staying in* Quebec,' *Conaire* asked him.

'*Not if I can help it. It's America I'm headed for, if I can cross the border.*'

'*So where would you go in America?*'

'Pennsylvania,' Luke said. '*Some place called* Harrisburg. *I never heard of it before, but that's where I'm headed.*'

'*You've family there?*'

'*Friends. I'd worked with them on the railways in England for years. They've gone to America, the half of them. There's good work on the railways there.*'

'*Yes. I've heard that,*' Conaire said.

'*They'd always said I was a fool to go back to Mayo.*'

'*Maybe you were, but who'd have known all this was going to happen. When did you return?*'

'*Last year.*'

'*Last year!*' Conaire exclaimed. '*You left England, and went back to Mayo. You left England then?*'

'*I did.*'

'*Good God, weren't you the right amadán. Couldn't you have seen it coming by then?*'

'*Maybe you're right. I should have.*'

'*And you must have been making good money on the railways.*'

'*I was,*' said Luke.

Yes. Four shillings a day. What a fool he had been to leave it all.

'*So if you were earning such good money in England, why did you go home in a famine?*'

'*It wasn't so bad at the start of '46,*' Luke replied. '*We hadn't heard much of it when I left England. And by the time I got back, the potatoes were only half gone.*'

'*It was bad enough, though. Surely you knew that? And anyhow, the money was better on the rails, isn't that what you said?*'

'*Arra, it wasn't just the money. It was the lease too.*'

'*Yes,*' said Conaire, '*it's always the lease. Or the lack of it for the most of us.*'

They had reached the top of the line. Luke felt his eyes watering in the smoke. He put his pot on the fire, scooped water from the barrel, threw in his flour and placed it on the fire.

Now he had very little smoked beef left, and knew it was not sufficient to last the journey. So there was no beef today.

They moved away from the kitchen, and sat in a quiet corner to eat.

'*You're right about the lease,*' Luke said. '*We had a twenty-one year lease...*'

'*Twenty-one years! Sure no one has that much on a lease.*'

'*I know. It's rare enough. Still we had it, but it had come to an end, and my father was too old. We had a quarry for spreading stone on the roads, and the landlord's agent said father couldn't work that on his own. So there was no argument – he wouldn't let him sign again.*'

'*The bastard.*'

'*They're all bastards. But I've a younger brother, Pat, could've worked the quarry, but the agent said he was too young to sign. So they'd been running two years without a lease, and the agent was insisting that something had to be done, or they'd have to go. And the only way he'd let them have a new lease was if I co-signed it with my father – they'd have been evicted otherwise.*'

'*But they'll be evicted now, with you gone,*' Conaire said.

'*Not now, they won't. The agent is finding it impossible to get rent-paying tenants around Kilduff. So he's happy if we pay the rent, and he knows Pat will be old enough in a year or two. So that was what we agreed with him. No, they're safe enough.*'

'*If they pay the rent.*'

'*Isn't that what we're going to America for? The both of us, our families need the rent. Our agent – he knows that too. He knows where the rent money will be coming from.*'

He was thinking of Carrigard. Eight miserable acres, wet land where you couldn't use a horse for ploughing. Backbreaking labour on the farm and the quarry, year in, year out. Still, they had only eight pounds and ten shillings a year to pay in rent, and it was hard enough to pay even that. But they had taken on another lease on a neighbouring farm, where the other family had emigrated. So how much was the rent now? How many acres? And what would other people think of his father renting another man's land? No need to talk about that either.

'*Yes,*' Conaire said. '*They tell me I've got to send the rent back to Erris. I don't know how to do that, and even if I did, I'm not sure who might be left alive to take it. But you were telling me about Kilduff. Working as a ganger, you were.*'

For a while, Luke did not reply. He screwed his eyes tight, trying to think, trying to remember. Watching people starve. Watching them die of fever, screaming in pain. What of it? Was it just that he was getting used to it? Worse than that. Guilt. Guilt at *Sorcha's* eviction, closing the Relief Works, closing the Kitchens. But that had all been under orders – there was nothing else he could have done. He had killed a starving man too, but that was in defence of his father. Did he want his father dead? But it was more than guilt. The hate in people's eyes, always, always hating him.

'*Why would you want to know about that?*' he asked at length. '*Is it to tell everyone else? Is it to have them kill me?*'

'*You don't believe that,*' Conaire replied. '*If I hadn't told them already I won't tell them now. And now you know the kind of man you're dealing with. Go on, tell me about Kilduff. Tell me about being a ganger man.*'

'*Fine,*' Luke said, '*I'll tell you, and don't say you didn't ask. How would you know the kind of man I am, otherwise? But the first thing I'll tell you is this – my own family lived through it all. Father got fever, but he was always a strong man so he pulled through.*'

'*And the starvation...?*'

'*It wasn't for us. Father had the quarry like I told you, so he had good work in his own quarry, overseeing fellows breaking the stones.*'

'*Overseeing?*'

'*Yes. Me too. It was easy enough to start. They began Relief Works just beside our own farm in Carrigard. At first they just asked me to be a clerk, writing things out and adding things up. But after a few days, came the Selection. Then they asked me to make a line, and decide the men and women on it who would be given tickets for the Works, and those who would not. They had strict rules as to who could be chosen. I had no say in it. And so I began selecting those who would work, and those who would not. And, by the rules, I had to refuse many who could not, and I knew I was condemning them to starvation. Many enough were my own friends, and I was dooming them. It's like that the hatred starts. Your own people, they hate you for it. And, before you say it, I felt in my heart that I could not blame them. But after a few days of this, they told me that the Workhouse in Knockanure was short of clerical workers and sent me there. It was a comfort not to be doing Selection any more. But then they told me they wanted me to work in another part of the Union. Up in a place called Brockagh, where they were expecting me to start the Works in two places. So I did it for them and became a ganger. Then the snows came. Many times I tried to have the Works stopped, but the people themselves, they would not have it. They needed the money for food. So they worked on and died of cold instead, and what could I do about it?*'

He stopped. No need to talk about Winnie. Nor Croghancoe. The mountain still terrified him, and still he did not know why.

'*Go on,*' Conaire said, impatiently.

'*Yes,*' Luke said, '*I had two gangs to start and four by the time it was over. One hundred in each – four hundred men, women and children. Four* hundred when they weren't dying on me. Then they told us the Works had to stop. No mention of Soup Kitchens then, just 'stop the Works'. What choice did I have? They gave me no money so how could I pay anyone. So the Works were stopped, and the hunger worsened, and then the fever came. The Quakers, English Quakers, they came to Brockagh and started opening fever sheds. Soup Kitchens too. They asked me to set up the Soup Kitchens which was hard enough in its own way. When they were running right, I was sent back to Kilduff to set up the Government Kitchens there. So I did that, and when the corn started coming into Westport from America, they asked me to help with that too, bringing the corn on wagons from Westport to Kilduff. The people would attack us for the corn as we brought it across, but we had to defend ourselves and get the corn to Kilduff, to our own people. But then, the Kitchens around Kilduff, they stopped. They said the famine was over. It was then I decided for sure to go to America. So that's my story. You still hate me?'

'A hard question,' Conaire replied. 'You say you did what you had to do?'

'I did,' Luke said. 'I did what I had to do, and believe me, you would have done the same.'

'Perhaps. But I had no letters or numbers. Isn't that the difference?'

'It is. And isn't it damned well time you learned?' He observed Conaire closely. Thin, but at least they were both eating something.

'It's a bit late for the learning,' Conaire said, after a long hesitation.

'Maybe it is,' Luke replied. 'But what of you? Will you stay in Quebec?'

'Quebec!' Conaire said. 'The devil I will. There's fever in Quebec. I'm going to get out of it as fast as I can. New York, that's where I'm headed.'

'Isn't there fever there too?'

'Might be, but it's not as bad as Quebec, that's for sure. And anyhow, I have family there.'

'You have?'

'My brother. His wife and four little ones. At least there were four the last time we heard. Maybe it's more now.'

He pulled a scrap of dirty paper from his pocket 'This is where he's living. Five Points...'

He thrust the scrap into Luke's hand. 'Can you read it?'

Luke peered at it in the light of the ovens' fires, and read out the address.

'Mr. John Costello, Costello's Bar, Orange Street, Five Points, Manhattan, New York City.'

'You read the English well,' Conaire said.

'I was long enough in the learning,' Luke said. 'But forget that, it's New York that concerns me. From all I can work out, if I want to get to

Pennsylvania *I have to get to* New York *first.'*

'*So we should go together? Is that what you're thinking?'*

'*Perhaps,*' Luke said. '*Why not?*'

'*Why not, indeed? And who better than Luke Ryan as a partner for the road. I'll say this for you, Luke. You're one hell of a tough man.'*

When they were finished cooking, they carried their pots and spoons back to *Conaire*'s bunk. He sat, pointing to the space beside him.

'*Here, rest yourself.'* He held the pot on the blanket and spooned the food into his mouth. Luke sat beside him and ate.

'*When do you think we'll see land?' Conaire* asked.

'*God only knows,*' said Luke. '*We should have seen it by now, that's what* Mr. Tyler *is saying. But after that storm, even when we see land, it won't be the land we're searching for. They're reckoning we might be too late for* Quebec, *and might head for* St. John's.'

Luke returned to the bilge pump. One of the men had collapsed. He was dreadfully thin.

'This man can't work,' one of the other men said.

'No, he can't,' Luke replied. He had the man carried up to the lower deck, and for the rest of the shift, he worked the pump himself.

Over time, the sloshers died faster than the rest, and soon there were few left. When Luke said this to Tyler, he found himself appointed to a new task – organising the other passengers to clean out the buckets themselves. As ganger of the bilge pump, this seemed natural, though many resisted it because they were well aware of the death rate among the sloshers. He wondered about *Conaire*'s chances.

The number of dead was over eighty.

Chapter 8

The Times, London, September 1847:
The fact of more than a hundred thousand souls flying from the very midst of the calamity into insufficient vessels, scrambling for a footing on a deck and a berth in a hold, committing themselves to these worse than prisons, while their frames were wasted with ill-fare and their blood infected with disease, fighting for months of unutterable wretchedness against the elements without and pestilence within, giving almost hourly victims to the deep, landing at length on shores already terrified and diseased, consigned to encampments of the dying and of the dead, spreading death wherever they roam, and having no other prospect before them than a long continuance of these horrors in a still farther flight across forests and lakes under a Canadian sun and a Canadian frost – all these are circumstances beyond the experience of the Greek historian or the Latin poet, and such as an Irish pestilence alone could produce.

After two more days sailing the open Atlantic, they saw land. They had been in the hold for those two days. A man and a young orphan had died. Luke had gotten little sleep since then, roused again and again by the screeching of the fever patients, when he was not supervising or working the bilge pump.

That morning he was woken by the screams of a woman in labour. She died, but the baby survived. Luke thought of his cousin, Nessa. She too had given birth, even as she lost her own life. Little Brigid had been born an orphan, a dead mother and a father who had disappeared, but ever since she had been well fed, and cared for by Luke's own mother, together with the other women. Winnie too, since he had brought her to Carrigard.

He was startled when Tyler appeared beside his bunk. 'There's land ahead,' he said, 'would you like to see it?'

'Land?' the man from the next bunk said. *'There's land ahead,'* he shouted.

Tyler returned to the ladder. Seconds later, there was a rush for the ladder, but most stayed lying in their bunks. Luke found *Conaire* at foot of the ladder. The rush had become a fight for a place on the ladder.

'We can take our time,' Conaire said to him. 'You'd near get killed on that ladder now. Let's sit down a while.'

They went back and sat down on an empty bunk. There were lice on the blankets.

'I wonder how near Quebec we are.' Conaire asked.

'God knows,' Luke replied. 'We'll find out soon enough now, as soon as they know what land it is.'

People were clambering back down the ladder now. 'Must be cold up top,' Conaire said.

'Damned sure, it is,' Luke replied. 'Come on. They're all coming back down. There'll be room above.'

'There's nothing there at all,' a woman said as she came down the ladder.

When there was a break in the people coming down, Luke climbed up and ran to the rail. There were only a few people left standing alongside him. The wind was brisk and bitingly cold, but he hardly noticed it. He scanned the horizon, but could see nothing. He ran towards the front, rushing from side to side. Still nothing. A sailor on a spar above them was pointing ahead and to the right. Luke positioned himself on the right hand rail, but still nothing.

Conaire came alongside.

'Where is it?'

'Damned if I know,' said Luke. 'I can't see a thing but it's meant to be over there.'

Conaire gazed at the horizon, searching. 'There's nothing there yet.'

Three more sailors had climbed up the rigging, pointing excitedly.

'Do you think they're kidding us?' Luke asked.

'I'm surprised at you saying something like that. Surely even an amadán like you can work it out. They're up there...'

'Ah yes,' said Luke, 'and we're down here.'

'We'll see it in time.'

More people went down, disappointed. Luke and Conaire stayed above.

'There it is,' said Conaire at length.

'Damn it, you've good eyesight.'

Within minutes there was a crush of people behind them.

'Buíochas le Dia,' an old woman said. Thanks be to God.

She was dressed in rags, a bony pinched face under a tightly wrapped black shawl.

'Thanks be to God' is right,' Luke said. 'We're past the worst of it. We'll make it now.' The old woman made her way back towards the hatch, staggering with a rolling gait as the ship pitched and rolled.

'Did you think we wouldn't make it?' asked Conaire.

'*I wasn't certain,*' Luke answered, looking back to the low white hills on the horizon.

'*But the question is when?*'

'*Yes,*' Luke said. '*We're a long way north.*'

'*I know we are.*'

There was a spout of water from the ocean. Out further, a black tail rose, slapped the water, and disappeared.

'*What the devil was that?*' Luke asked, surprised.

'*Whales,*' Conaire replied, '*and many of them too.*'

'*Whales?*'

A whale breached the surface, jumping high. '*See that one,*' said Conaire. '*He's come from deep down to make a jump like that.*'

'*And the water rising? What's the cause of that?*'

'*That's them breathing out.*'

'*You know a lot about them.*'

'*Why wouldn't I? We'd see them off Torán regular enough, though these fellows are different. There were times they'd come round the land side into Blacksod Bay, and get themselves caught by the tide on the beach. Some of the people would eat them. But only in the years the potato failed. I only tasted it the once myself.*'

The whales were closer now.

'*God, there's enough of them,*' Luke exclaimed.

'*Dozens,*' Conaire said.

Another whale breached, and came crashing down.

'*Tell me about Torán,*' Luke said. '*Like the rest of Erris, was it?*'

'*The same. A miserable place. And isn't that a terrible thing for a man to say about his home. It's down by the Inner Mullet.*'

'*The Inner Mullet?*'

'*Out the furthest end of Erris. It's a sea lake, with a long neck of land stretching well down from Belmullet to the west of it. And Torán is half way down that neck – the Mullet they call it, the land I mean. Ocean on three sides of it.*'

'*So who evicted ye?*' Luke asked.

'*We weren't evicted at all. The landlord – Mr. Walshe – he's a Catholic. He won't evict us. Not for the likes of him to evict. Only Lord Palmerston and scum like that evict. Not that Walshe done much else though. Damned little in the way of soup kitchens or building roads for Relief and, like I said, the nearest Workhouse is in Ballina. I'm praying they build the one in Belmullet. It might give father and mother a chance of living, and the children too – six more of them still at home.*'

'*Will they keep their land though?*' asked Luke.

'Of course. Why wouldn't they?'

'There's some question they mightn't let people into the Workhouse if they're renting land.'

Conaire shuddered. 'Are you certain?'

'I'm certain of nothing, to be honest,' Luke replied. 'Just some story I heard from some fellows at the Workhouse at Knockanure. Maybe it's just a story.'

'I hope to God it is.'

The thin line of white had grown larger on the horizon.

Tyler came over.

'At least it's not Baffin Island. More like the top end of Labrador, Sharkey reckons from our latitude. Close enough to Baffin though.'

'Is that why it's so white?' Luke asked.

'That's the reason right enough. We're a long way north.'

'Are we off course then?'

'Hundreds of miles off course. It could have been worse – we could have been halfway up the Davis Strait by now. But we're not, and we're in the Labrador Current now, heading south. Still it'll be some time before we get to Quebec. There's many of these poor devils will never get to Quebec at all.'

'What's he saying?' Conaire asked.

'He's telling we're not so far north. That's Labrador over there, but it's still some way to Quebec.'

'Can he not talk English?' Tyler asked.

'No,' Luke answered. 'Not all of us can.'

'It'll be tough on him when he gets to Quebec. You'll find people to speak English, and people to speak French, but there's none as would speak like that. Excepting a few of your own, of course.'

'What's he saying?' Conaire asked again.

'Just that you'd better learn English,' Luke replied.

'I'll do that in time. But what about Quebec? Is there no faster way of getting there?'

'A good question he's asking,' Luke said to Tyler. 'Is there no faster way of getting to Quebec?'

Tyler was silent for a moment. 'Aye,' he said then. 'There's a faster way right enough. Mr. Starkey could take the shortcut through the Labrador Strait by Belle Isle. But if he does that, there's a chance none of us might make Quebec.'

'Why's that?'

'The tidal currents in the Labrador Strait are like you'd never believe. Many a good ship's gone down there. No, I reckon he'll have sense, and go for the Cabot Strait. That means going all the way around Newfoundland

110

Island, but it takes another week. Far safer though. Just pray the captain doesn't have a say in it, or we'll all die.'

'*What's he saying now?*' Conaire asked again.

'*Just that there's a fast way and a slow way. The fast way means the ship sinks. The slow way takes an extra week.*'

Two more naked bodies were taken up, blessed and thrown over. No one said a word.

The ship tacked down the coast of Labrador. As they did the snow cover disappeared. The weather had improved too, and the hatches were only brought down twice as rain came over. For the rest of the time, the passengers were allowed up for a few hours every day.

Most of the time the sun shone from the right. Luke could see the ship was sailing east. He was holystoning the deck one afternoon when Tyler appeared beside him with a sailor.

'We're taking you off the scrubbing, Luke,' Tyler said. 'Mr. Starkey reckons you have too many other tasks. Pumping, slopping out and the funerals should be enough for any man.'

Luke stood up, and handed the holystone block to the sailor, with a smile.

'We're heading back the other way,' he said to Tyler. 'Are ye taking us back to Liverpool?'

'Will you stop worrying, you fool. It's just the shape of Labrador. We have to head this way to get around it, that's all.'

'Fine so,' said Luke.

'So forget about all that, there's more important things for you to consider. Have you thought any further about working the forests?'

Luke leant on the railing. Small pieces of ice passed the ship.

'I have,' he said. 'I can't see any better way of getting to New York, except through logging. At least I'd earn some money through the winter.'

Tyler knocked his pipe on the railing. 'Yes,' he said. 'There's good money in the forests. Mind what I say though. The real money is out in the forest, not in the caboose. Felling the lumber, driving the horses.'

'Horses?'

'They use teams of horses for dragging the lumber to the river. Have you worked with horses?'

'I have,' Luke said, thinking of the teams of horses dragging soil and rock on the railways.

'You'll make good money so.'

'I hope so,' said Luke. 'But I've little enough hard facts to be thinking about. What would you say I should do to start?'

'What I'd say is this. The moment you get off this wreck, head straight for Gilmours. They're one of the big saw-mills. They send more lumber from

Quebec than any of them. Shipbuilders too. Most of the ships running to Liverpool were built by Gilmours, this is one of them. Tough bastards, they are. They'll work you hard, but you'll make good money. And there's no complaining about that.'

'There isn't,' Luke agreed.

'I worked with Gilmours years back, but things might have changed since then. They're logging the timberlands at a hell of a rate now, and they've a great need for men, both as millhands and loggers. Last time I was in Quebec, they were still working the Gatineau hard.'

'The Gatineau?' Luke echoed.

'It's a river in Quebec Province. Flows to the Outaouais River, and so to the St. Lawrence. There are big timber lands up there. We'd work there the whole winter, right up to April. So you can do the same. That's provided nothing goes wrong.'

'Like what?'

'Like getting delayed too much on this accursed boat. Even supposing we make the Gulf of St. Lawrence in time, we'll still have problems. If we have to stop off for quarantine at Grosse Île – and we will – we'll be running things very tight. Once the river freezes and the snows come, it'll be damned tough to get up the Gatineau.'

Another whale breached.

'I'm thinking of all you say,' Luke said, 'and it seems a good plan. There's one other question though. What of *Conaire*?'

'Your friend?'

'Well – yes.'

'I don't know, Luke. Gilmours are a damned rough lot. I doubt he'd have the strength for it.'

A few days later, they came to the end of Labrador, but as Tyler had said, they did not take the Labrador Strait.

'*Too dangerous,*' Luke said to *Conaire*. '*And that means another week to run around* Newfoundland *Island.*'

'*We're going to run out of food so. None of us have enough, and even the sea biscuits will run out.*'

'*You're right,*' said Luke.

Next day, they were outside again.

Four more bodies were lying on the deck beside them – two women, one man and a child. All had bloated faces, bloated feet and black and purple sores. Their families stripped the clothes from the corpses.

Again and again, the priest gave the blessing.

'*Per istam sanctam Unctionem...*'

Conaire and Luke threw the bodies over the rail. The bodies were

112

weighted, so as not to float. They were too close to land to risk the bodies drifting onshore. Luke was afraid of getting fever, but he had no choice.

He cut back on his rations again, wondering how much weight he had lost on this voyage already. Whatever he had lost though, *Conaire* had lost more, and it concerned him.

He saw too the effects of starvation around him. At first this had been limited, and he had been more concerned about fever. But now, more and more, he saw the children with the facial hair. The faces of foxes. The faces of hunger.

For some days, the ship was caught in a thick fog. From time to time, Luke could hear the distant sound of bells from fishing trawlers on the Newfoundland Banks. Then the fog disappeared, and it began to rain. That night was dark, and he was concerned that the ship was still sailing fast, but Tyler assured him that Starkey was navigating on dead reckoning. Luke was worried that Starkey might not have the ability to do this, and he was relieved when the ship hove to at St. John's in Newfoundland. Many passengers lined the deck, though fewer than before.

The waterfront of the city was a wasteland of burnt out houses.

'I'd heard about this,' Tyler told him. 'Summer of last year. That's what comes from building in wood, when they're packed too close together.'

Eleven ships were riding at anchor.

'Seems busy,' Luke said. 'I thought St. John's was a small place.'

'And so it is. It'll be a hell of a bigger place when this crowd have all off-loaded. Most'll go into quarantine on the island. Those that don't will be held on the ships. Most of them die there anyhow.'

The passengers on the Centaurus were being herded back down.

It was only as the ship was moving again that they discovered that barrels of fresh ship biscuit had been taken aboard. Luke bought ten pounds weight of biscuit, using it together with his own food so as to spin out his provisions. *Conaire* had no money though, so Luke had to share. He noticed many of the other passengers had no money either.

'*No maggots this time,*' he observed. '*For us with the money. But the rest...?*'

'*Back to starvation for them,*' Conaire said.

'*Aye,*' Luke said. '*Just like Mayo.*'

They sailed into the Gulf of St. Lawrence, entering through the Cabot Strait. St. Paul Island passed to the south, with the coast of Nova Scotia beyond. Then the Magdalen Islands were visible in the distance.

Luke never tired of watching the changing scenery. In some ways it calmed him, so that for some time at least he could forget the brutal horror of the Centaurus, and the uncertainty of his future.

The decision had now been made that, since they were in the Gulf, there would be no further sea burials at all, and all new corpses were bundled in a rick near the bow. Now the outer deck held its own horrors, day and night. Still, Luke spent much of his free time at the rail. One morning, he saw the body of the priest had been added to the pile of the dead.

The ship was becalmed for a day, before sailing up between Anticosti Island and the Gaspé Peninsula. From time to time, the high lands in the south were covered by dense clouds of mist, always in motion, sometimes brilliant white, sometimes red. Then the mist would clear, revealing wooded mountains and bays, and, on one occasion, there were walrus in the water. Not that he knew the name of the animals, but their unfamiliar tusks fascinated him.

One night he stayed out late after most of the others had gone back down. He had been watching the shore to the south of the ship. He went to walk to the starboard rail. He stopped, and stood dead still.

High over the northern horizon, the sky was swirling with yellow and green.

It brought back memories of the first time he had seen the aurora. 1839, just after the Big Wind and before little Alicia's death.

Fever then. Fever now.

Next day.

'So *what do you think of this business of having to speak English?*' Conaire asked.

'*You have to do it, that's all about it.*'

'*But how?*'

'*Not by staying with only Irish speakers, that's for sure. They're the ones that get mistreated. An Irish ganger gets hold of them, and they do what they're told, because they can't understand anything else. They stay together at night too. That's no way to learn.*'

'*So how did you learn?*'

'*First, because my Uncle Murty was a teacher and he taught us. And second, the years working the railways in England. Sure, we had our own ganger, and he was Irish, but we all had to deal with the other fellows on the line, and we even spoke English among ourselves. Martin Farrelly was one of us too, no interest in taking advantage of us. That's why we'd elected him as ganger. The other fellows don't have that kind of choice. They don't elect their gangers, just take who they get.*'

Silence.

'*God, but it's cold,*' Conaire said at length, '*I'm going back down.*'

'*You go on,*' Luke replied. '*I'll stay here a while.*'

He stood at the railing, not noticing that most of the other passengers had gone back down to the warmth of the passenger decks.

On one side, the land ran along to a cape with a lighthouse, a small white cottage beside it. Seals too. On the other side, the land was low, with pine along the water's edge.

It was clear to Luke that Conaire was afraid of trying to live and work in a land and a language he did not know. He depended on Luke. By rights, Luke knew, he shouldn't have been concerned about Conaire in any way. Did Conaire even respect him? He himself believed that he was right in what he had done, acting as a ganger on the Relief Works. Conaire had listened to his excuses, but he surely despised gangers, and Luke was not sure how far he accepted his reasoning. But they spoke together, they ate together, the question was – why? Were they both becoming more accepting of each other? Perhaps. And he might need Conaire and Conaire's contacts when they arrived in New York. But would Conaire have the strength to work in the forests, and survive a Canadian winter?

He tried counting the number of whales, but gave up. Always some were blowing, while others dived. The woods came down to the shore, trees standing right to the edge of the cliffs. From time to time there were breaks in the forest with small wooden houses.

Near a cape was a more substantial wooden village. He could see canoes with men fishing. As the ship came abreast he waved, and one man waved back.

'They're the Innu,' a voice said from behind him.

He turned around. Tyler was there, smoking a pipe.

'The Innu?'

'Innu Indians, that's their settlement. Filthy they are, the scum of the earth. But don't worry. Soon enough, we'll be rid of them. Quebec is opening the Indian lands to settlement. Far too good for them, I reckon. The government should hunt them down, shoot them all, that's what I say.'

Luke was stunned. Hunt the Indians? Why not hunt the Irish? He thought of the Clanowen evictions at *Gort-na-Móna*. Yes – hunt us all down. Why not? Why should I think like this? The devil take it.

'I don't know,' he said, 'they look a lot healthier than we do, that's for sure.'

'Aye,' Tyler said, 'you're right there, but the Irishman and the Englishman aren't that far different, and if we weren't on this ship, there'd be no damned difference at all.'

An Indian stood up in a canoe, holding a fish and pointing at it. Luke waved again, half expecting the Indian to bring the fish over, but he did not.

A pod of whales was following the ship.

'See them there,' Tyler said. 'They're Minke.'

At that precise moment, another whale breached, and crashed back violently.

'And that's the Blue Whale,' Tyler said. 'Giant of the oceans. Biggest living creature. That one could sink a ship, if it tried. Has done, many times.'

Sharkey called out. Tyler swore silently, knocked the ashes from his pipe, and left.

The shore was tree-lined on both sides since they had left the village of tents behind. But Luke was still thinking of the Innu, and Tyler's comments.

To hell with that – just stop thinking about it. Watch the river.

The whales still followed the ship.

A few days later, Luke was at the rail when he spotted a schooner in the distance. Behind him there was activity among the sailors at the stern.

He went down to the passenger deck. *Conaire* was asleep. He shook his shoulders.

'*Come on, there's a boat outside.*'

'*Just like a ganger, always giving orders, eh?*'

'*Arra what. Come on up, and no more of that.*'

Conaire followed him, and they both leant on the rail, watching the schooner.

'*Still hate me?*' Luke asked.

'*Getting less. Anyhow, it was our own people are to blame for the hunger.*'

'*The landlords?*'

'*I wouldn't blame them the most, bad enough as they all were. No, it's our own people, they're the ones to blame. They're the guilty ones. You, me, our own families, and all the rest of them. Never had the guts to stand up and take them on.*'

'*But…what could they do?*' asked Luke, surprised.

'*What could they do? Everything. Stop working for them. Stop paying the rent…*'

'*But they'd only have the police on them, or the army.*'

'*We could fight them.*'

'*Fight them!*' Luke exclaimed. '*The army!*'

'*Yes, the army. And the landlords, their agents, the police and anyone else who as much as spoke to them. Kill them. The priests too, God damn them.*'

Luke was staring *at Conaire*, unsure if he could believe what he was hearing.

'Kill them?'

'Yes, kill them. All of them.'

'And their agents?'

'Their agents, surely, filth that they are. Their servants, and anyone who works for them, just give them one warning. After that, kill them. Everyone goes on and on about who's to blame for the evictions. The truth is simple. We are. We're the guilty ones. We let them ride all over us, and do nothing to stop it.'

'But people are starving. Dying.'

'All the more reason. All them down below – men, women and children – they brought it upon themselves.'

Luke was thoroughly stunned. He tried to think what to say, but then decided to stay silent.

'Have I shocked you?' Conaire asked.

'A lot more than you might think. You're a strange man, that's for sure.'

'You can hardly talk, and you a ganger man.'

There was a loud rattling from the stern. The ship had dropped anchor. The schooner came alongside. A man scrambled on board from the schooner, which then departed. Tyler had come out to meet the man. They spoke for some time, and then the man went into the bridge, where Starkey was waiting.

'I wonder who the devil he is,' Conaire asked.

'Some fellow trying to get up to Quebec? Though I'd guess there are quicker ways than that.'

'He'd know,' Conaire said, pointing to where Tyler was supervising the sailors working the capstan, weighing anchor again. Luke went across, and waited 'till they finished.

'Who's that fellow there, we just took on board, Mr. Tyler?'

'Oh, him. That's the pilot. Wouldn't you have known? You need the local fellows to show the way up river. Otherwise we'd be aground soon enough.'

'I see,' said Luke. 'Help us on our way, like?'

'That's it,' Tyler said. 'But he's bringing bad news from ahead. The quarantine is getting tighter, and the island's a living hell.'

Luke did not have to ask about that. He knew exactly what 'quarantine' meant from his time in the mountains of Mayo during the fever epidemic. But how would they be quarantined here? Forced into cottages with fevered patients? To get this far across the ocean, and die at the end of it. No.

'So what happens now?' he asked.

'We wait 'till we get to Grosse Île, then we anchor, hoist the ensign and wait for the quarantine officer.'

Tyler walked back to the bridge. Luke watched him go, thinking of what

117

he had said about the killing of the Innu. He thought too of *Conaire's* ideas about killing off the landlords, and holding the starving guilty for their own starvation. It struck him now that Tyler and *Conaire* were far stranger than he had thought. More brutal too.

Conaire was there.

'Well?'

'*Seems like we're going to be a good while at* Grosse Île,' Luke said.

'*Yes. I'd guessed that.*'

'*And longer again in* Quebec, *I'd say. Then I'm heading out the forests, and God knows how long it will take to get down to* New York.'

'*So you will go to the forests? You've decided?*'

'*I have,*' Luke said. He hesitated. '*Do you want to come?*'

'*For sure. And then we can both head to New York in the spring.*'

'*We can,*' Luke said.

'*And you get out to your friends on the railways?*'

'*Yes.*'

'*It's far enough.*'

'*Damn it to hell, don't remind me.*'

'*Is it so good, this railway work?*'

'*I hope so. From all I hear, they're paying well.*'

'*Better than England?*'

'*So I believe, though if I'd stayed on longer in England, I'd be making more money than on any railways, American or otherwise, that's for sure.*'

'*How's that?*'

'*Better chances*' Luke said. '*When I was working in England, I was with my cousin. Worked with him for six years, and he seemed like all the rest of us. But he always had this thing about being a contractor, working for himself, employing men and making money out of them. So that's what he did. Left us and set up contracting. Good at it too, he is, and one of the toughest rats in creation, but I couldn't work with a man like that.*'

'*Why not?*'

'*Too rough. He's asked me already. Wanted me to work with him as a ganger. Work men hard. I've had enough of that class of thing.*'

'*Where does he get his men from?*'

'*From all I hear, he sends his brother up to the* Liverpool Docks *and the* Workhouse *to find desperate fellows who'd work for any wage. And by God, he does not believe in paying any kind of decent wage. Himself and his woman, they know well how to keep wages down.*'

'*But English fellows wouldn't put up with that.*'

'*Oh, it's not English fellows. That wouldn't suit him, not at all. It's fellows from the West of Ireland he wants, starving and willing to work for* damned little. *And not speaking English, how can they get by in a foreign land? No, they have to take whatever he gives them. Himself and his woman, they know that, and they know it well.'*

'*The West of Ireland, you say? All of it.'*

'*No, Danny's too smart for that. He wants fellows whose language he'd know and understand, and who'd speak the same language among themselves, but with no knowing of English. Mayo – all along the west of it. Partry, Achill, Erris...Oh God...'*

He stopped.

'*Yes,'* said *Conaire, 'Erris, that's what you said. And you're* Daniel Ryan's *cousin, aren't you?'*

'*I am.'*

'*A brute of a man, well known along the coast of Mayo. And you are of his family.'*

'*I am. And what of it?'*

'*Damned if I know,'* said *Conaire. 'If I met* Daniel Ryan, *I'm not sure if I'd kill him or shake his hand.'*

The death toll had passed a hundred.

Chapter 9

Freemans Journal, Dublin, September 1847:
What are the poor to do at this moment who have no food? Must they not plunder to support life? The Workhouses are not able to support their present inmates, all the Unions are in a state of bankruptcy. Mayo has thousands upon thousands of reclaimable acres of land; why does not the Government commence some process by which they would be brought into cultivation? Labour is cheap in Mayo. The people are most willing to work. Will a Government lavish of fine promises permit their wholesale extermination?
John Coghlan, Parish Priest, Kilmovee

'Letter for you there, Pat,' Sarah said.

'I wonder who this is.' He saw the Stockport postmark.

'Danny, by God. Now what could he want?'

He slit it open and gave a low whistle.

'Well, isn't he the sharp one?'

'What is it?' Sarah asked.

He gave her the letter. She read it slowly, then folded it again.

'So what do you think?' she asked.

'Damned if I know,' Pat said. 'Danny is one of the roughest thugs alive. I'd pity any fellow working for him.'

'Still, it might be better than anything else. What other choice have the poor devils got? We can't even let them all in. You know there aren't enough potatoes planted, and they're going to die if they stay here. And on top of that – look at these figures. You know yourself, the Workhouse is on the edge. But the strange thing is, he's looking for inmates from any Workhouse except Knockanure. Why is that?'

'Oh, well I know the answer to that one,' Pat said. 'Danny doesn't anyone here to know what he's doing. He wants men from out west, where no-one would know him. His gangers though, they all come from Kilduff and around. They won't be complaining, they're doing too damned well out of it. So it's gangers from here, navvies from the west coast.'

'I thought you said his mother and father had gone over to work with him.'

'So they have, and I'm sure there must have been one hell of a row once Uncle Murty worked out what Danny was up to. But it's too late for him now.'

'But – that's horrible.'

'Don't I know it?'

She chewed the top of her pencil, thinking.

'So what will you do?' she asked.

'I could talk to Voisey about it.'

'Yes. You'll have to.'

He pushed his chair back and took his jacket.

An hour later he returned.

'You were long enough with him,' Sarah said.

'A lot to talk about. Trinder was there too. And he couldn't understand why we couldn't take men from this Workhouse, and I didn't feel I could explain Danny's thinking all the way. But in the end he reckoned that even if Knockanure doesn't benefit, there's no reason the other Workhouses shouldn't. Voisey convinced him. So they told me to go to Castlebar.'

'Castlebar?'

'Said I should talk to Gaffney.'

'Gaffney? Who...'

'He's the fellow organised the Relief around Kilduff and Carrigard. Seems he's moved to Castlebar now, working for the County Surveyor.'

'You knew him?' she asked.

'When he set up the Relief Works around Carrigard, I did. Luke knew him better though. One way or the other, he's the man to talk to. So what I'm planning is this. I'll ride over to Castlebar tomorrow, see if Gaffney is there, and see what we do from there.'

Pat left Knockanure Workhouse before dawn. He walked to the stables, where the inmate on duty saddled up a horse for him. The air was still, and he could smell the stink of the death pit, even from that distance. Then the sweetish smell from the fever sheds. There was an inmate on guard at the gate, but no one outside, so he and the horse were let out easy enough.

As he rode past the Workhouse wall, he saw families asleep alongside. Some had blankets, some had not, but it was not raining.

As the sun rose, he saw the potato beds were all empty. He knew the crop had been a good one, but everyone also knew that so little had been planted that it would make little difference to the hunger. Once he saw an old woman scrabbling in one of the potato beds in the distant hope that the harvesters had left one behind, but he knew there was no chance of that. Some miles later, he passed two men saving turf in a bog, clean cut sods being flung out to dry. The men were thin, but they could work well with a *sleán*. He saw the body beside them, and he knew at once there was another purpose.

As he rode, he kept his face down, trying not to see what might be on the side of the road, or look into the eyes of those coming towards him. He had seen enough of that dead look in Knockanure Workhouse.

In Castlebar, the streets were awash with human sewage, manure heaps outside many of the cottages.

He led the horse to the Workhouse Buildings. There was a crowd close to the gates, but there were soldiers of the Inniskilling Dragoons guarding it. He passed through the people easily enough, explained his business to a lieutenant and was admitted.

Gaffney looked up, surprised.

'I know you...'

'Pat Ryan. Luke's brother.'

'Of course, of course. Sit down and tell me what brings you here.'

Pat explained. He told Gaffney about Danny, the work on the railways and the rapid expansion of railways across England. He told him of Danny's request.

Gaffney made an arch of his fingers. 'Yes, yes. It's a strange request, but it makes sense. It could certainly help us, though I still can't understand why he would not start with Knockanure. Still, that's his decision. How many is he looking for?'

'Four hundred.'

'Four hundred! What size of a contractor is he?'

'A big one. It's like I told you, Mr. Gaffney. The railway system is growing very fast in England. Danny has certainly got call for that kind of number. The question is – where should we start?'

'That depends. The easiest answer would be Westport, I understand they've cattle ships running to Liverpool or the other English ports. But as to which would need it – the Workhouse trying to feed the most with the least – that would be Ballinrobe.'

'Ballinrobe?'

'Yes. It's not that bad around the town itself, but the rest of the Union is in a terrible way.'

'What about Erris?'

'They're not organised at all over that way. They're building a Workhouse, but as to when...'

'Fair enough,' Pat said. 'So the decision is yours – the easiest, or those that need it the most.'

'Since you put it that way, Ballinrobe, it has to be. God knows, they'd need to find feeding for two thousand people.'

'Four hundred is what we want.'

'I meant for the families.'

'Danny doesn't want families. Only men to work. The families follow later.'

Gaffney shook his head. 'A sharp fellow, your cousin.'

'He is all that,' Pat said.

'So the next question is – how do we get a message to Ballinrobe?'

Pat looked at him in surprise'

'Write, surely.'

'There might be a better way than that,' Gaffney said. 'I'm thinking if we sent you direct, it might have more force.'

'Send me...? Now why on earth...?'

'Because you know what your cousin wants better than I do, and you'd be better at persuading them. If you're anything like Luke, you'll have no problem. And perhaps you could take Luke with you.'

'Luke's in America.'

Gaffney groaned. 'Another gone. We can't go on losing men like that for ever.'

He hesitated, thinking.

'Right, there's two things I'll have to do,' he said. 'The first is to talk with the fellows here – the County Surveyor and the rest of the County fellows – and once they approve what we're planning, I'll have to write directly to Trinder and Voisey and explain to them we need you more than they do. So there'll be no need for you to go to Ballinrobe 'till then. And oh, I'm assuming you'll do it?'

'Do I have any choice?' Pat said.

Pat left the Workhouse buildings. As he led his horse through the gate, a group of gaunt men and women rushed it, but the soldiers held them back at the point of bayonets.

Sometime later, as he passed the turf bog, he noticed the two men were gone. So was the corpse.

Late in the afternoon he arrived in Knockanure. There was still no difficulty leading his horse through the gates. Men, women and children were sitting around it, but no one stirred.

Sarah was still working by candlelight. 'Well...?'

'They'll do it, I think. Gaffney has to clear it with the Surveyor first, then he'll write to Voisey and Trinder.'

Sarah looked surprised. 'What would they have to do with Westport?'

'Oh, it's not Westport he's thinking about. It's Ballinrobe. And the reason he's writing here is that he wants to borrow me for a week or two.'

'Borrow you...?'

'He wants me to go down to Ballinrobe, persuade them what they have to do.'

A female inmate, dressed in the drab grey dress of the Workhouse, came in carrying a creel of turf. She poked at the logs in the fire until they blazed up, then carefully set the sods of turf on top. She went out again without a word.

'But Ballinrobe...?' Sarah said.

'If he asks, I'll have to do it. There's nothing definite yet. Let's wait and see.'

Sarah leant back in her chair.

'Well, while you're waiting for that, there's something else will surprise you. Mother's leaving.'

'Leaving!' Pat exclaimed.

'Leaving Knockanure...'

'But what...When did she decide on that?'

'She'd already been thinking it. She swore me to secrecy until she was sure of it.'

'Secret from me even?'

'I didn't want worrying you.'

'That was kind of you,' Pat said, sarcastically. 'But why? Why would she want to leave?'

'You know yourself,' Sarah said. 'The Workhouse is close to bankruptcy already. I don't have to tell you that. They're halving her pay. That, and the fever sheds. She's had enough – the cut in her pay was the final straw.'

'But what will she do? Where will she go?'

'Westport. There's a place for a matron in the Workhouse there.'

'I didn't know that.'

'Why would you? It was advertised in all the papers – The Telegraph, The Constitution and The Herald. She wrote, asking to be considered. They wrote back, giving her the post. They didn't even want to meet her, just told her to go on over. Shows you how desperate they must be for good matrons.'

'And what about yourself?'

'Well, what about me? All this time I've been working for the Union for no pay at all. What difference will it make in Westport? And God knows, there might be more chances of getting some kind of paying position.'

'Clerical?'

'Anything. Even working in a shop in the town. They might need somebody with some ability with accounts. Who knows?'

He sat, stunned.

'And before you say it,' Sarah said, 'yes, it means we won't be working together. But we'll meet often enough, we can see to that.'

'But Westport, it's thirty miles if it's a mile.'

'And we can write, can't we? It's not like Winnie and Luke, is it? If I were going to America, then you'd have cause to be complaining.'

Next day, Pat brought Sarah to Carrigard again. He was driving a donkey and cart for comfort. Winnie greeted her warmly, Eleanor standing in the background. Yes, she thought. Sarah is the one. No doubt about it now.

When they had dismounted, Pat tied the donkey to the post by the door.

Eleanor came up to Sarah and hugged her. *'It's good to see you again,'* she whispered.

She led her inside, sat her at the table and placed a mug of buttermilk beside her. She watched as Sarah drank it, trying to appear unhurried. Sarah too was thinner than she had appeared in the summer.

Eleanor was delighted to meet Sarah again, even if she was still not quite sure how it would all turn out. Winnie would be leaving, and Eleanor knew that her own relationship with Sarah was vital. At times she wondered if Sarah would see it the same way. How would she think of her as a mother-in-law? More important, if Pat lost his post in Knockanure, how would Sarah settle in to living and working on a small farm? So many questions. And at a time like this.

A few minutes later, Michael came in. He sat on the bench by the back door, untying his laces.

'Young Sarah, is it?'

'It is, Mr. Ryan.'

'Any news?'

'We've a letter from Danny,' Pat replied.

'Have you, by God?'

He walked across to the fire and sat on the ledge beside the pots. Pat took the letter from his pocket, and passed it to Michael. Michael glanced quickly through it.

'Danny's some lad.'

'Don't I just know it,' Pat said.

'But the real question is – what do we do now?'

'That's what I was wondering too. So I spoke to the Master. He said I should go over and talk to Gaffney about it.'

'Gaffney? The fellow who was over here?'

'Yes,' Pat said' 'that's the man. He's in Castlebar now, working for the County Surveyor. Trinder told me to go over and talk to him. No one else had the time to go to Castlebar. So I went over to see him.'

'And what did he say?' Eleanor asked.

'Well, Gaffney's not against it, that's for sure. He was a bit surprised that

Danny was looking for men only, and they wouldn't be let bring their families along, but I think he saw the sense in that soon enough. He's reckoning Ballinrobe Workhouse might be the best to work through, they've the most call for it.'

'We don't hear much about Ballinrobe over here,' Eleanor said.

Pat was silent. Better not to mention that he might be travelling to Ballinrobe, he thought.

Michael poked at the fire, sending clouds of sparks rising from the turf.

'Well, I don't know,' he said. 'It's good and bad, I'd say. Danny's one tough fellow, from all we hear. Damned if I'd like to work with a fellow like that. But still, what choice do they have? The Soup Kitchens are near all gone. No Relief Works either. So what can a man do? Starve and let his family starve? That or Danny? I can't see they'd have the choice, if they're chosen. At least, working with Danny, they'd be fed, and have some pennies they might be able to send back to Mayo.'

'Yes,' Pat said, 'and have Danny make a fortune for himself while he's at it. But I agree with you, father. If a man is selected, he's no choice, he must go.'

Winnie sat beside Sarah. 'How's Knockanure?'

'Not the same as across the summer,' Sarah said. 'They're not sending them to Quebec anymore. Too late in the season. They might start again come April, but until then, we're just turning people away at the gates. They can't allow the overcrowding like they used to, it kills far too many, and they know that.'

'But the Workhouse?' Eleanor asked. 'How can it go on now?'

'God only knows,' Pat said. 'I'm watching the figures, there's only two ways they can do it. One is pushing the rates collectors, see how much more they can squeeze from the landlords. But that's fine for the likes of Clanowen, it's the smaller landlords, they're the ones in real trouble. The half of them are near bankrupt. The rates are double, and they're not getting the half of their rents in. The collectors are threatening them with court action, bankruptcy, all kinds of things, but you can't squeeze blood from a stone.'

'But what else can they do,' Eleanor asked.

'Cut the running cost of the Workhouse, that's what. The merchants won't extend any credit, so they have to cut back on the food. Half rations the past few weeks…'

'Half rations!' Winnie exclaimed. 'But sure they're half-starved already.'

'That's as may be,' Pat replied. 'But the Workhouse – they're hoping some little bit of food will keep them going until the winter is out.'

Eleanor looked at Pat closely. She had little doubt that he was already thinner. As an officer of the Union, he was hardly starving, but still it worried her. Every weekend she tried to feed him better, but she knew he

126

was reluctant to take it when the family had so little.

'There's other news too,' Pat said. 'Sarah and her mother are leaving Knockanure.'

'Leaving,' Eleanor exclaimed.

'Mrs. Cronin is going across to Westport as a matron in the Workhouse.'

'And you, Sarah?'

'I'll be travelling with her,' Sarah said. 'I can't be staying on at Knockanure with no pay at all, so I wrote to them in Westport. I think they're near bankrupt themselves, but I guessed they might have problems with their accounts, and sure enough they offered me a post. Only a shilling a day, but that's a shilling more than I was earning at Knockanure. I'll be working with the Clerk of Union, so I'll have a good understanding of the Workhouse and the Union. Not that I really want to, given the state of the county.'

'I know what you mean, girl,' Michael said. 'But it won't be like this always. It'll get better, it must get better.'

Eleanor had put out the plates, and was ladling the potatoes.

'It's a long way though, Westport,' she said. 'I'd hoped we see more of you, but it won't be too easy now.'

'It'll be difficult, right enough,' Sarah said,

'It's quite a move for you, too. Westport from Knockanure. A much larger Workhouse, I understand.'

'It is,' Sarah said, 'but what of it? It's work.'

'And what do you hear of the condition of Westport?' Winnie asked. 'How would it compare to Knockanure?'

'I don't really know,' Sarah said. 'We haven't heard so much, and a lot of what we hear is rumour. Militia men, surveyors and the like passing through, they tell us what they've seen, but I reckon some of it is only stories. It seems better in some ways now though. There's more food coming into Westport – no need for carts to bring it inland, and little need for militia men. With the militias being so stretched around the county, Knockanure is harder to supply. No, it's much easier for the Westport Workhouse with them being beside the biggest port in Mayo.'

'Yes,' Eleanor said, 'I can see that.'

'From what I hear though, the over-crowding is worse than Knockanure. And it's not just the Westport Workhouse. Erris is in a terrible way and their nearest Workhouse is Ballina. There's talk of them building a new Workhouse, but God knows when that'll come.'

'So, what do they do?'

'The poor souls come down to Westport, looking for ships to America, but they have no money at all to get there.'

But Eleanor was more concerned about Knockanure.

'What of you,' she asked Pat. 'How long...?'

'A while yet,' Sarah answered, before Pat could speak. 'I don't know what they would have done without Pat. He's very quick with numbers.'

'*Arra*, go on,' Pat said. 'There's others around would be faster than me.'

'No, no, it's no little thing. They must have someone for the accounts, especially now.'

'But they can't afford to pay much,' Pat said. 'They're reducing my wages. Ten pounds a year for as long as the hunger lasts.'

'What's that you say?' Michael exclaimed.

'The Union is hoping they'll be able to pay more next year,' he said. 'But as long as Knockanure Workhouse is in the condition it is, there's little they can do. I've been through the accounts myself, I do it every day. The land rates are far less, and every penny there is to spare goes on food.'

'I'm sure Clanowen could well afford to pay his rates, whatever about the others,' Michael said.

But Eleanor was not thinking of landlords. What would Pat's salary bring in now – it must only be shillings a week? So it all came back to Luke. How long would it be until the letter arrived? Would there be money with it? Was he still alive? Of course he's alive. And the potatoes are good, they'll be better next year. We'll all be able to eat, God willing. Enough of that.

Sarah was talking. 'So tell me about Luke. Have you heard back from him yet?'

'Not a word yet,' Winnie said. 'We're still waiting...'

'What do you expect?' Eleanor interrupted. 'He's not been gone long enough. It takes time to get to Quebec, and time for a letter to get back.'

She noticed that Sarah had winced at the word 'Quebec'.

'It does,' Sarah said. 'It all takes time. But Luke is tough. Running four Relief Works in the mountains – not many could have done that? It was bad enough in the Workhouse, but from all he told us, it was worse in the mountains.'

'Let's not talk of what happened in the mountains,' Pat said.

'You're too easy upset, Pat,' Sarah said. 'What happened in the mountains is part of the story of this county. Someday the story will be told. And believe me, the story of Knockanure Workhouse will be told too. All the people who died for no reason, my own father included. They wanted us all to do the impossible, gave us no money, and expected us to save lives with nothing at all. And you know what the terrible thing is – that the people blame us. Who else is there for them to blame? They don't get to meet the government men back in Dublin or London. So the only ones they can blame are us – the ones who are working day and night, without help or thanks.'

'I know,' Eleanor interrupted. 'I know just what you're talking about.

Luke told us everything. In the end, he was the very same. And wasn't that the real reason he went to America? It wasn't just building the roads in the mountains. He had to do that in Carrigard too. And running the Soup Kitchens – then having to close them. What could he do? He could only carry out the orders he was given, he had no money for anything else. But no one would see it that way. That's why he's gone to America now.'

'Yes,' said Winnie, 'and that's the reason I'll be following him. The ganger's wife. God, how they hate me for it. Carrigard and Brockagh. I've no home here anymore.'

'You'd always have a home with us, child,' Eleanor said, 'no matter what anyone else thinks.'

But what of Pat, she was thinking. How long would that last? And then there was the other question – how long could Michael run the farm? And two quarries? Luke was gone to America, and Eleanor at least did not believe he was going to return. Was he dead already? She thought of all the stories of the coffin ships, and the rumours that were circulating Mayo. And then there was Sarah. If Pat returned to farm Carrigard, what then? Could Sarah adapt to that kind of life?

Soon afterwards Sarah and Pat left Carrigard. Eleanor hugged Sarah. Then they mounted the cart, and Pat whisked the reins.

As soon as they reached Knockanure Workhouse, Pat wrote a letter to Danny telling of his meeting with Gaffney, and advising him to wait until he got more information. Within days he had his answer from Gaffney. He had full agreement for all of Danny's requirements. No one in Castlebar had dissented.

Pat wrote to Danny a second time. Within three days, a response arrived from Stockport.

Pat passed the letter over to Sarah. 'Here, you can read it.'

Sarah scanned it. 'What's this about Murtybeg?' she asked.

'Yes,' Pat said. 'Danny's sending him over. Make sure the job is done right. I didn't expect that.'

'What will you do?'

'I'll take him down to Ballinrobe. Let him see a bit of Mayo, for a change.'

Two weeks later, Sarah and her mother left Knockanure. Pat watched from his window as one of the inmates drove the cart carrying the two women and all their possessions out through the gates. No one tried to force their way in.

He went back across to the office and kicked the logs in the fire until the flames soared.

Chapter 10

Freemans Journal, Dublin, October 1847:
How can I calmly contemplate the number who died of starvation and disease? Alas! There was neither fabrication nor exaggeration – for, since the 5th October 1846 up to the 15th October 1847, thirteen hundred and sixty one deaths have been registered, besides many that occurred in the distant glens and remote shore creeks, of which God and his recording angels alone were cognisant. 1361 of my peaceable, moral and hitherto hospitable and charitable parishioners swept into eternity – and in a few months, too, by famine and its manifold accompaniments.
Patrick MacManus, Parish Priest of Kilgeevor, Louisburgh, County Mayo

The following night, Pat left Knockanure and walked back to Carrigard. He spent the weekend helping his father around the farm. The potatoes no longer had to be guarded, since Michael had ensured that they were all taken inside the house. On the Sunday, he attended Mass with Eleanor and Michael, while Winnie looked after Brigid. That afternoon it was back to hard work, re-building dry-stone walls where they had collapsed.

He stayed overnight in Carrigard again. He left early, and walked out the road to Knockanure.

After a mile, he came across soldiers resting on the side of the road. There must have been hundreds, he thought. All along the other side, horses were tethered to blackthorn bushes and ash trees. From the soldiers' cylindrical tall helmets, he recognised them as dragoons. The helmets were black with bright yellow cords. They wore grey trousers and black jackets, each crossed by white straps. The men were sweating, though it was not warm.

He stopped by a group of three, sitting on the bank

'Where are ye all going to?' he asked.

One of the soldiers stood up. He was tall and young, but even so, had a weather-beaten face.

'Castlebar,' he answered with a half sneer. 'The middle of Mayo.' He waved at the fields around. 'Is it like this all over?'

'Pretty much, if it's the hunger you're speaking of,' Pat replied.

'And worse than that, we hear. Fever?'

'Aye, you'll see enough of that in Castlebar. But what are ye going over there for?'

'Replacing the Inniskillings, that's what we're doing. They're being sent back to Newbridge Barracks.'

'A long way for them,' Pat said.

'It is.'

'And ye?'

'Thirteenth Light Dragoons. Down from Longford.'

By now, a group of soldiers were standing.

'What's he saying?' one asked.

'Telling us of Castlebar, he was.'

'Not that I know much about it now,' Pat said. 'There's stories of fever there now though, and God knows, that's bad enough. But there's one thing you'll like about it – the barracks. Plenty of room for the lot of ye if the others have left. Ye'll have no problem with that anyhow. And from what I hear, the depot has enough corn, at least for the army.'

'But not for the horses,' one of the other soldiers said. 'That may be why they sent the Inniskillings away.'

'Ye've enough horses I'd say,' Pat said.

A lieutenant had joined them. 'Come on you lads, back in line.'

Pat watched as they lined up.

'What have you been telling them?' the lieutenant asked.

'Just about Castlebar,' Pat said. 'Isn't that where you're going.'

'It is,' the lieutenant said, 'but after that who knows? Tell me, what's Belmullet like?'

'Ye're not going there,' Pat said.

'Some of us might. Us or the Forty Ninth. What's it like?'

Pat thought of Belmullet.

'Damned if I know,' he said. 'It's out the far end of Erris, almost. From all we hear it's a forsaken place. And near wiped out by fever, Belmullet was, back in the summer. I don't know what it's like now, but no one would go near the place if they wanted to live. And God knows why they'd want to send the army there. I'll tell you this, you'll have no fighting the locals there, there's few enough of them left, and those that are, sure they're scarce able to stand.'

When Pat arrived in Knockanure he saw another company of the Light Dragoons marching past. He stood by the gates of the Workhouse to watch. On either side of the gate there were families sitting on the ground, leaning up against the Workhouse wall. An old woman was sitting beside where Pat was standing. She was desperately thin.

'*Isn't it well fed they are?*' she said to him.

'*They are,*' Pat answered. '*Damned well fed.*'

'*Sure wouldn't they want to be strong brawny lads to be fighting us,*' she said. '*They must have great fear of us to be sending us the likes of them.*'

A Workhouse inmate walked across the yard, saw Pat, and opened the gate. '*There's some fellow here waiting for you,*' he told Pat. '*Looks like Quality.*'

Pat looked at him in astonishment, wondering who the stranger might be. He went to his office.

'Murteen! Where the devil did you come from?'

'Over from England. Where else would I be coming from?'

'*Arra,* I know. It's just I wasn't expecting you today. Have you been long waiting?'

'Only since last night. The decent people here, they fed me, and gave me a bed. I was a little surprised, mind you, what with the starving outside, but I guess they thought I was on official business.'

'And aren't you?'

'Now what do you think? Danny sent me over, and that wasn't for the good of my health. He's looking for more workers, reckons the country isn't sending enough of the fellows he wants.'

Pat sat down at the desk and waved Murtybeg to a seat.

'I know all that. But I thought you were getting the fellows out of Liverpool Workhouse. Wouldn't there be enough for ye there?'

'Not of the right kind,' Murtybeg answered. 'Sure, they can give us plenty, but the most of them are from the wrong parts of Ireland. We're looking for West Mayo, nowhere else.'

'I know.'

'That, or places like it. Danny wants men who are desperate, men who'll have no way back to Ireland because of the hunger, men who have to earn money to send back to their families if they're to have any chance of bringing them over. He doesn't want any fellows from Dublin or the Midlands, not even the Plains of Mayo.'

'So, what are ye suggesting?'

'Well, that's up to you. Maybe we should head over to Castlebar, and meet this Gaffney fellow you wrote about. Then go on to the other Workhouses along the coast. What do you think?'

'God, Murteen, I always knew Danny was a tough bruiser, but I think you're getting the same. You've changed a lot since I last knew you.'

'Sure I had to. How else would I live?'

Pat had an idea.

'Have you seen much of the Workhouse?'

'I haven't been over there yet. They fed me and put me up here beside the Administration.'

'Fine,' said Pat. 'Let's give you an idea of this place.' He walked out, followed by Murtybeg. They walked across the yard to the Workhouse building. First they went through the refectory, but Pat did not stop. Murtybeg gasped at the scene around him, and held Pat by his shoulder.

'What's this?'

'*Arra*, don't mind this,' Pat said. 'There's more to see than this.'

He led Murtybeg up a flight of stairs where they could see into the women's dormitory, women and girls getting dressed.

'Don't mind that either,' Pat said. 'Come on.'

Up past the men's dormitory. Then up to the top of the Workhouse. Another dormitory.

'This'll interest you,' Pat said. 'We call this the Overflow Ward.'

'The what?'

Pat opened the door and walked in. He saw Murtybeg whip his hand across his nose, his eyes staring. 'Oh, Christ Almighty.'

On one wall, beds were crushed side to side, two men in each. A line of poles with ropes ran down the centre of the ward, blankets and curtains draped over them. On the other side, the women and children. Two bodies lay on the floor just beside the door. Half way down was a chamber pot whose contents has been strewn across the floor, seeping under the hanging curtains. The stench was overpowering.

'It's like I say, it's only the Overflow Ward,' Pat said. 'The fever sheds are full, and we can't leave them out in the rain, now can we?'

'But – how long does it take to cure them?'

Pat looked at him in derision.

'Cure them? Have you any idea what's going on here, Murteen? The most of them will never come out of here alive. They're dying like flies – damned near a hundred a month.'

'A hundred!'

'*Arra* hell, sure that's nothing. Earlier in the year it was nearer two hundred. But sure I wouldn't worry about it, the faster they die, the faster we can take in more, and kill them too.'

'Now, don't be like that,' Murtybeg said. 'You're not like that. You wouldn't mean that.'

'I don't know what I mean or what I don't mean any longer,' Pat said. 'One way or the other, we've no room here for any more. Come on.'

Murtybeg followed him down the three flights of stone stairs. They went out into the yard again. Pat pointed to the line of fever sheds along one wall.

'They're the murder sheds.'

'Stop that,' Murtybeg said, angry now.

'Isn't that all they're doing? The landlords want rid of them, and this is the fastest way. They don't even have to send them out of the country. Liverpool, Manchester, nor America even. No cost to anyone.'

Pat went over to one of the fever sheds. Murtybeg followed, and caught Pat's elbow.

'I don't want to see this.'

'What sort of man are you?' Pat said. 'Fine, fine. I won't show you that. Come on over here.'

He led Murtybeg to the death pit.

Two inmates took a naked corpse off a stretcher by the arms and legs, carried it to the pit and threw it in. Pat pointed down at the heap of bodies. Most were putrescent and many partly eaten. The only sound was the squeaking of the rats.

'There you are, Murteen,' Pat said. 'There's County Mayo, Year of Our Lord 1847.'

Murtybeg said nothing. Pat turned around. Murtybeg was on his knees.

'Are you praying or what?' Pat asked.

Murtybeg was gagging and shaking his head. Pat took his arm and dragged him up.

'Well, Murteen, it seems you're not as tough as you thought you were. Come on, if you can't take it, we won't force it on you. Time for business.'

Murtybeg followed him back to the Administration Block.

When they had sat down across the desk from each other, Pat looked across to Murtybeg whose face was still red. 'Well, Murteen. What do you think of County Mayo now?'

Murtybeg shook his hand. 'Forget that for a minute. I wanted to ask you about Luke, what are you hearing? What's things like in America?'

'How would I know,' Pat answered. 'We haven't had a letter from him – no news at all.'

'How long is it...?'

'Ten or twelve weeks, I'd reckon. We should have news soon. Is he dead? Who knows? Now, enough of that. Let's go over what you're looking for.'

Murtybeg leaned down into a satchel and took out some papers.

'Danny is looking for four hundred men.'

'But would ye have call for all this,' Pat asked.

'Might even be more. He needs ninety for the contracts he has already. Fifty for McManus, twenty each for Roughneen and Lavan. And that's only the start.'

'Only the start! Pat exclaimed. 'You want ninety, and that's only the start. What of the rest?'

'We've just got a new contract, Pat' Murtybeg said. 'Our biggest yet. With Brassey.'

'Who?'

Murtybeg was surprised. 'Who? Have you not heard of Tom Brassey?'

'Never,' Pat answered.

'I'd have thought Luke would have told you about him. Brassey is the biggest railway contractor in the world. Employs well over fifty thousand men. And Danny is subcontracting to him for a cutting down in Staffordshire. He'll be employing three hundred, at least, maybe more. That, with the other ninety, brings you to near four hundred.'

'Now?'

'Not all at once,' Murtybeg answered. 'Two hundred now, for certain. More to follow as we ramp up over the next three months.'

Pat shook his head in bewilderment.

'So what do you want now?' he asked.

'Just this. Can you get them to a port? If it's the west of Mayo I'd guess Westport would be the best way. Otherwise get them across to Dublin, if they have the strength to walk it. One way or the other, Danny will pay the costs, all the way to Stockport.'

'Isn't he very generous?' Pat said, disparagingly.

'Don't be like that,' Murtybeg said. 'We're doing the best we can.'

Pat shoved his chair back and stood, eyes blazing.

'Look, Murteen, don't give me any of that. I know what you're doing, I know the way Danny drives men. But the only reason I'm talking to you is because I have to. These poor devils out in Partry, they've no choice. They're starving, and we have to take whatever you and Danny give them. And so, yes, in answer to what you're looking for, I'll give you what you need. Don't think I like it though, and don't make out that you or Danny are saints.'

'Sit down, for God's sake.'

Pat sat again.

'Now, if you'd refer to my previous correspondence with Danny, you'd see that we've already put this in train. Gaffney has already agreed, got it through the Committee too.'

'Yes, I know,' Murtybeg said.

'Now, all you've got to do is to go over to Castlebar and get it all moving. Then we'll see who else to visit. Gaffney reckons Ballinrobe is best.'

'Why not Westport?'

'The condition of Ballinrobe is worse than Westport.

'Will you come with me?'

'Maybe, I don't know. We'll have to see Voisey first. Follow me.'

Murtybeg followed him down the corridor.

Pat knocked on the door of Voisey's office and entered.

'Remember all I told you about my cousin looking for workers in England,' he said.

'Ah yes,' Voisey answered.

'This is his brother, Murtybeg Ryan. He's over here to organise everything.'

'Yes,' Voisey said. 'We met last night. Seemed too tired to talk then.'

'He'll be going on to Castlebar, and maybe after that to Ballinrobe. I understand it's over-crowded.'

'Just like everywhere,' Voisey answered.

'I'm proposing to go with him, if you can spare me.'

'Spare you? You know we can't spare you, Pat. But if it has to be done, it has to be done.'

Murtybeg raised his hand.

'One other question, do we have to walk or is there any other way?'

'Well, we've no carriages,' Voisey said, 'but there are horses. You could take two of those perhaps.'

'That would be kind of you,' Murtybeg said.

'It would have been kind of us,' Voisey said, 'but that would have been a year ago. We're short of money now, I'm sure you can understand that.'

'Indeed,' Murtybeg said.

'A shilling and sixpence per horse per day. How does that sound?'

'That will do fine,' Murtybeg said. 'Do you need a deposit?'

'No,' Voisey replied, 'we'll be kind with you on that. I've always trusted Pat here, so I know the horses will come home, and the money with them.'

When they returned to Pat's office, he passed an open ledger to Murtybeg.

'Here, Murteen, you might like to see this.'

Murtybeg glanced down the figures.

'I don't know about you,' he said, 'but it looks to me as if the Workhouse is damned near bankrupt.'

'I know,' Pat said.

They left the Workhouse, riding Union horses.

'How did you get here yourself?' Pat asked.

'The Bianconi coach to Ballaghaderreen, and I walked from there. The Bianconi isn't so bad.'

'For those that can afford it. But don't forget, both these horses must come back here.'

'Fine,' Murtybeg said.

They rode on. 'Is this the right road?' Murtybeg asked.

'The road to Castlebar.'

'Aren't we going to visit Carrigard?'

Pat stopped his horse.

'Now, Murteen, do you really think I'm going to bring you there, and tell them what the pair of us are about? It's bad enough as it is, let's just keep going and forget Carrigard.'

They arrived in Castlebar. Again, Murtybeg held his nose against the stink of manure heaps along either side, and human faeces running from an open sewer.

'You get used to it,' Pat told him.

They passed a woman lying on the side of the street.

'Fever, I'd say,' Pat said. 'Don't go near her.'

They saw a company of horse soldiers advancing towards them dressed in bright red jackets with white straps.

'Dragoons,' Murtybeg exclaimed as he dismounted and pulled his horse into the side.

'The Inniskillings, I'd guess,' Pat said.

'How do you know that,' Murtybeg asked.

'Never mind.'

When they arrived at the Workhouse in Castlebar, there were still people along the walls, but soldiers were lined up in front of the gates.

'More dragoons,' Murtybeg exclaimed.

'Thirteenth Light I'd say.'

'You seem to know them well.'

'Sure how wouldn't I? They're crawling all over Mayo. They need them to keep the starving in rein. Eat our corn too.'

He spotted the lieutenant he had spoken to on the Knockanure road. He rode over to him, explained his business, and both he and Murtybeg rode inside.

As an inmate took their horses from them, Pat noticed the sound of hammers on rock.

'*Stone-breaking?*' he asked.

'*Stone-breaking is right,*' the inmate replied. '*They've nothing for us to do, so they put us to breaking stones that might or might not be needed, God knows when or where.*'

When they met Gaffney, Pat introduced Murtybeg quickly. Within minutes, the business between them was finished, with the agreement that Ballinrobe was the best Workhouse to visit.

'Daly is the Clerk of Union,' Gaffney told them. 'There's one other matter you must consider though. You've got to have some way of shipping out of Westport. I'd have recommended you to talk to William McAliskey here – he represents many of the shippers in Westport and Killala. The only problem you'll have though is you don't know the number of men you'll have with you, or even if you'll have any at all.'

'So what can we do then?' Murtybeg asked.

'Wait until you get to Ballinrobe. McGuinness is the passage broker there. The Workhouse will put you in touch with him.'

That night they stayed in the Administration block.

Next morning, they left, holding a letter from Gaffney to the Clerk of Union in Ballinrobe Workhouse.

'If we're lucky we might make Ballinrobe tonight,' Pat said. 'And if we don't, we can sleep in any shack we can find. But don't worry, we'll get there.'

As they rode away, Pat saw the same lieutenant again, mounted this time.

The lieutenant nodded to him in recognition. 'You were right about Castlebar,' he said to Pat.

'It's not the worst,' Pat said. 'Like I told you, if you go to Belmullet, you'll see a lot more famine and fever face to face. More than here, I'll tell you'

'Yes,' the lieutenant replied, 'you'd warned me of that. But thank the Lord, we're not going there. It's the Forty Ninth Regiment – they've just been sent out in that direction. And good luck to them too.'

As they rode through the town, a funeral procession was coming down from Staball Hill. Four men were carrying a corpse by the hands and feet. The corpse was wrapped in rushes from the knees to the top of the head, tightened onto the body with rough cord.

They stopped to allow the procession to pass. There were only five or six mourners following. Even at that distance, they could pick up the stench of decomposition.

'No coffin,' said Murtybeg.

'It's like this all over,' Pat said. 'You don't think anyone can afford coffins, do you?'

For some hours they rode on in silence.

Outside Ballintubber they saw a man lying at the side of a mud cabin twenty yards away from the road.

'What's wrong with him?' Murtybeg asked.

'Let's go and ask him,' said Pat.

They rode up the narrow lane, half overgrown with brambles, and dismounted.

'I think he's dead,' said Pat, as they came closer.

The corpse was thin, dressed in torn rags. Pat knelt down to examine it. The flesh was decaying, giving off a repulsive sweet stench. Murtybeg leaned against the side of the cabin, gagging.

Pat stood up abruptly.

'It's fever.'

'Like hell, it is,' said Murtybeg.

'I'm telling you it is. I know that smell. Gangrene, that's what it is. Comes with fever.'

He turned away. Murtybeg ran after him, and grasped him by the elbow.

'Damn it, Pat, we can't just leave him there.'

'You stay if you like,' said Pat. 'I don't want catching fever.'

'We've got to do something.'

'Like what?'

'We can't just let on we never saw him.'

'Fair enough, so,' said Pat. 'I'll tell you what we'll do. We'll go on into town and find the priest, that's what we'll do. Let him sort it out.'

They rode into Ballintubber, and found the church. When they told the priest, he said nothing at first. Pat repeated their story in Irish, though he felt certain it had been understood the first time.

'*Fine,*' the priest said after another long pause. '*I'll see to it so.*'

'He didn't seem surprised,' said Murtybeg as they rode back out of Ballintubber.

'He didn't, did he?' said Pat. 'Nor very interested neither.'

Beyond Ballintubber the road was being repaired. Cartloads of rock had been dumped at the side, and for a mile along the road, hundreds of men, women and children were smashing the rock into ever smaller stones. The horses slowed as they came to broken parts of the road, and stumbled on the unlevelled stone. Pat and Murtybeg dismounted and led the horses along.

'I'd thought this road building was over?'

'So it is,' Pat replied, 'this is only annual repairs. The Workhouses do most of it.'

'Which Workhouse?'

'Who knows? Castlebar or Ballinrobe I'd say, one or the other.'

As they came towards the end of the roadworks they saw a donkey and cart coming towards them. A man and a woman were sitting inside with a baby and four older children. They were very thin. The cart swayed over the broken road. Pat and Murtybeg held their horses at the side as the family went past.

'I wonder where they're going.' Murtybeg asked.

'Castlebar Workhouse, most likely. We're still nearer Castlebar than Ballinrobe.'

They came to Partry village. Many houses were empty, some with collapsing thatch, others with their doors swinging open.

They went on, Lough Carra to their left, Lough Mask to their right, the Partry Mountains rising above. 'And by all I hear,' Pat said, 'the mountains there are where you'll be getting your people from. We hear stories all the time in Knockanure of starvation in Partry. They're the ones we'll find in Ballinrobe Workhouse.'

'You seem to know all about it.'

'Sure why wouldn't I? Half the county knows. And isn't this what you're looking for? Desperate men, desperate for work. Good for business, eh Murteen?'

'Go to hell.'

Now they were passing small groups of men, women and children walking towards Ballinrobe. They were all thin, dressed in grey shredded clothes.

'The better clothes are auctioned,' Pat explained. 'One way of buying food. A good way of spreading fever too.'

'Just shut up, would you.'

It was nearly dark when they arrived in the town. They rode down a street of thatched cottages, some with decaying roofs. On some the roofs were burnt.

'Evictions?' Murtybeg asked.

'God knows,' Pat replied.

They arrived at Ballinrobe Workhouse. What they saw outside the Workhouse astonished even Pat.

Right along the wall of the Workhouse, fires were burning. Men, women and children crouched around each one. Ghostly black figures flickered against the light of the fires. Further out, hundreds more were sleeping on the open ground, without any fires.

Carefully Pat and Murtybeg led the two horses through the sleeping bodies up to the gate. There was no one there. They shook the rails and shouted, but there was no response.

'It seems like we've no beds for tonight.'

They led the horses back, and found a burnt house on one side. Some half burnt straw lay on the ground.

'Right, Murteen, you can sleep for now. I'll wake you in four hours.'

'Why don't you sleep?'

'And have no one watching the horses. They'd be eaten before morning.'

At sunrise, they led the horses back to the gate. There was still no one there, but then a horse and cart came from behind the Administration building. An inmate came to let it out.

'A heavy load that,' Murtybeg commented, looking at the broken rock it was carrying.

'It is,' Pat said. 'More road repair, I'd guess.'

Pat showed Gaffney's letter to the inmate, but he was unsure whether the

140

man could understand it. He certainly spoke no English.

'Mr. Daly,' Pat said, *'that's who we're looking for.'*

The man led them inside. He shouted in Irish, and a young boy came over to take their horses. Another inmate led them to the Administration building and down a long corridor to an office. He knocked on the door and handed the letter inside.

'Wait here.'

They waited. Sometime later, a man came out and waved them in. Another man was sitting beside a desk, a priest standing alongside him. The priest was holding Gaffney's letter.

'Four hundred men, ye want?' he asked, without waiting for introductions.

Pat glanced across at Murtybeg.

'Three hundred for now,' Murtybeg said, 'though if you can't do it all at once, I'll understand. Two hundred, anyhow.'

'And men only?'

'Men only,' Murtybeg confirmed. 'Twelve years and up.'

'Well,' the other man said, 'we won't have three hundred for you today. Nor tomorrow neither. There's too many in fever in this Workhouse, and those that aren't are too weak from hunger. I'd say we could have near a hundred men together for you though.'

'That'd be good for a start,' Murtybeg said. 'According as you can strengthen them up, then you could send more?'

'That's what we'd plan,' the man said. 'But there's another matter too. Who'd pay for this? We must get them to the ships, then to England.'

'Edwardes & Ryan will pay,' Murtybeg replied without hesitation. 'But the question in my mind is – where could we ship them from?'

The priest answered. 'Dublin's too far, that's for certain. They'd never be able to walk that distance. So that leaves Westport. We could consider Galway or Killala either, but they might be too far too.'

'Westport so,' Murtybeg said.

'Fair enough,' the man at the desk said. 'It shouldn't cost you too much either, a few shillings a head maybe. Hardly cost you two or three sterling for shipping.'

'Fine so,' Murtybeg said. 'McGuinness I understand.'

'That's the man.'

They left.

'I guess we'll have to talk to this McGuinness fellow now,' Murtybeg said.

'Yes,' said Pat. 'We'll find him easy enough.'

'And who's to get these fellows to Westport?'

'We are,' Pat said. 'And you're going to Liverpool with them.'

They left the Workhouse walking, leaving their horses inside. They asked their way to the passage broker. As they went down the street, Pat guessed his location from a group of people at the window.

There were two posters in the window, one advertising a ship from Sligo to Quebec, the second a ship from Galway to Boston.

'I wonder why the Sligo one is so cheap.' Murtybeg asked.

'God knows,' Pat said, as he pushed the door open.

Inside, a paunchy man sat behind the desk, two other men in front. Pat noticed they were all well dressed, too well dressed for Ballinrobe perhaps? A silence descended.

'Well, gentlemen, how can I help you?' the man behind the desk asked at length.

Pat was uncertain, but the two men stood up and gave them the seats.

'I'm sorry...' Pat said.

'Don't worry about us,' one of the men said.

Silence again.

'Mr. McGuinness...?'

'Yes.'

'I was given your name in Castlebar...' Pat said.

'Who?'

'George Gaffney. You know him?'

'Of course.'

'Yes, he said you were the man to talk to in Ballinrobe. We're trying to put together a group of fellows to go to Liverpool out of Westport.'

McGuinness picked up a pen, dipped it in ink, and started to write.

'How many men?'

'Hard to say at the moment. A hundred from Ballinrobe, we're hoping. Probably more from Westport. Or Castlebar even.'

'Could be two hundred or so?'

'Could be,' Murtybeg responded. 'We'll see.'

McGuinness held up his hand and wrote further.

'So what's your price?' Pat said at last.

'A shilling and ninepence a head.'

'That's costly,' Murtybeg said.

The man looked at him in astonishment. 'A shilling and sixpence so, I won't go lower.'

'Fair enough,' Murtybeg said.

'Now there's the question of the deposit.'

'Ten shillings,' Murtybeg said.

'Fifteen shillings.'

'Fine so,' Murtybeg said. 'But when does the next ship go?'

'Wednesday is the next. The Altair. After that – depends on the tides and the winds, but there should be another Friday or Saturday.'

McGuinness took another sheet of paper. Again he wrote.

He handed it to Murtybeg. 'This is a receipt for fifteen shillings. Also an instruction for McDonagh & Wilson in Westport.'

Pat stood to leave as Murtybeg counted out the money. The two men had not said a word.

When Murtybeg came out, he laughed.

'A shilling and sixpence a man. How could we have got it so cheap?'

'I thought you said it was expensive.'

'Ah, that was only bargaining. I was determined to get him down, whatever he said. But still – one and sixpence – I never expected that.'

They returned to the Workhouse building. Next morning, they joined the inmates for breakfast. Pat noticed the activity as men were assembled for the journey.

He nudged Murtybeg. 'I wonder what they're telling them.'

'God knows,' Murtybeg replied, 'and to be honest, I don't care. All I want is workers.'

The Workhouse had assembled eighty four men. Murtybeg counted and signed for them. As they came out, they saw an inmate waiting, holding the reins of both horses, already saddled.

'All ready to go,' he said to them.

Murtybeg smiled and handed him a penny.

They mounted their horses. As they went out, Pat saw the priest, leading a donkey.

'Are you going the same way?' Pat asked.

'As far as Tourmakeady,' the priest answered as he mounted the donkey.

The little procession started to move. Another donkey accompanied them, drawing a bread-cart. The three men rode together behind the cart, followed by the men from the Workhouse.

'Is it like this all over?' Murtybeg asked.

'In Mayo, at least,' the priest answered. 'God knows what the rest of the country is like. And I'll tell you this, I don't want to know either. All I seem to do here is give the Last Rites, again and again and again. It never ends.'

'Sure what else can you do,' Pat said.

'Write letters! And God knows, I've done enough of them. Letters to Lord Lucan, even to the Viceroy. All they can do is shake their heads and say how terrible it is. I've written to the Freeman's Journal, but what good does that do either? The Telegraph in Castlebar, at least they print my letters, let the rest of the county know what's going on in Partry.'

'It wasn't like this when I left last year,' Murtybeg said.

'You've got to understand,' the priest said, 'this is one of the most God-forsaken places on earth. All up the mountains they're dying at an awful rate. Their families are burying them in ditches, turf banks, wherever they can.'

Pat noticed they were being followed by a woman carrying a baby. The priest turned back to her. Pat stopped, watching. He rode down.

'She's following her husband,' the priest said. 'They're from Aghinish, she'd heard he was going.'

'But we can't take her,' Pat said.

'I know,' the priest said. 'But she won't go back. You'll have to take one little family anyhow.'

'God damn it to hell,' Murtybeg said. The priest winced.

'Don't be blasphemous,' Pat said.

'*Arra*, what.'

The woman followed. Pat could see she was very weak. He dismounted. '*Here*,' he said, '*sit up here and rest the baby.*' She sat side-saddle, grasping the saddle with one hand and her baby with the other. They went on, Pat leading the horse.

When they stopped to rest, a man came back from the group and took the woman down. Pat took the baby and handed it back to her. He noticed it was not moving.

He went over to the priest. 'The baby's dead,' he said flatly.

The priest walked over to the huddled group. Gently he took the baby from the mother's arms, and laid it on the bank at the side of the road.

He stood. Raising his right arm, he gave Extreme Unction.

Pat went back to Murtybeg.

'What's happening, Pat?'

'It's dead,' Pat said.

'Dead!'

'Sure how would it not be. It's carrying fever.'

'And what of the mother?'

'She seems fine to me. I think she'll pull through.'

'What if she has fever?'

'She doesn't have fever. Leastwise, no sign of it that I can see. And I'll tell you this, Murteen, I've seen enough fever to know.'

Pat leaned on his horse, watching as the small group walked into a bog. The baby was placed in a bog hole, then the man and the priest went above it and started kicking at the side until the turf and heather started to collapse on top of the child. The mother was keening – a grisly, high-pitched sound.

'Oh God,' Murtybeg said, 'can you not get her to stop it?'

'If you can resurrect the baby...'

'Shut up, God damn you.'

As they travelled, Pat discovered a lot more about the priest. His name was Peter Ward and he was Parish Priest of the enormous Partry parish, stretching right across the mountains from Ballinrobe to the coast and out to Clare Island. He told Pat and Murtybeg much of what had been happening – not only starvation but the ravages of fever, killing thousands.

The unending detail shocked Pat. From time to time, he asked a question, but most of the time there was no need as the priest spoke on. Even with such an enormous parish as Partry was, Pat wondered at how so many people could die in it. But he suspected Father Ward was not exaggerating.

Murtybeg rode alongside, listening, but saying nothing.

They stopped to rest in Partry village.

'Now I'll soon be going off,' the priest said. 'Up towards Tourmakeady and through the hills. What of ye?'

'Well,' Pat replied. 'As you know, Murteen here will be going back to Liverpool. But after Westport, I'll head back to Castlebar, meet Gaffney there and tell him how things have turned out. After that, it's back to the Workhouse at Knockanure.'

'You'll be meeting Gaffney?'

'I will.'

'There's one favour I'd ask of you so. The condition of the Workhouse in the Parish is in a terrible state. You must tell this to the County people as soon as you get to Castlebar.'

'I will,' Pat said, 'I'll make a full report to Mr. Gaffney. I promise you that.'

They watched as a convoy of three donkeys with carts passed by.

'Castlebar Workhouse?' Murtybeg asked.

The priest stood on the road watching as the convoy turned left as the road split.

'No, they're turning off. Heading for Westport, I'd say.'

'Emigrating?'

'Maybe, but God knows how. They won't go to America, that's for sure. They're probably more your type of people. Heading to Liverpool, I'd say. They'll get to Westport, sell the donkeys for meat and head out in the cattle boat to Liverpool.'

They took the left turn out along the Westport road. Shortly after Father Ward went to take the road towards Tourmakeady and the mountains.

'I wish I could take you with me,' he said to Pat and Murtybeg. 'If you thought you'd seen famine or fever, the mountains here would still have the power to shock you.'

Pat thought of Luke's stories of the Ox Mountains. 'I'd believe you,' he said.

'Tell that to the fellows in Castlebar.'

Pat watched the diminishing figure of the priest and donkey, until the next corner.

Murtybeg put his hand on his shoulder. 'Come on, Pat. Time to go.'

Once they saw a body lying in a ditch but they did not stop. Soon after, they passed three men digging turf in a bog.

'Do you know what I'll tell you, Murteen,' Pat said, 'it's got this way with me. Any time I see anyone digging in a bog, I think they're digging a grave.'

'You're just letting it all get to you,' Murtybeg said. 'Now come on, let's get to Westport.'

They rode on.

'Now, there's one other thing I must tell you,' Pat said. 'My girl works in the Union.'

'Your girl? Sarah, isn't it.'

'That's right.'

'Is she breaking stones?'

Pat laughed. '*Arra*, no. Sarah's not for that kind of thing. She's working on accounts with the Clerk of Union, I understand. Her mother is matron in the Workhouse. We'll marry soon.'

'But...? When?'

'God knows, but soon enough.'

'At a time like this?'

'Luke did it too, didn't he? Yes, Murteen, we're getting married. We won't give up. Whatever you and Danny might think of this county, there'll still be men and women living here when this is all over.'

'But what would you live on?'

'Right at the moment, my wages at Knockanure.'

'But you saw it yourself. It's near bankrupt.'

'Sure what of that,' Pat replied. 'If I can't get a job there, I'll get it somewhere else. And if that's not possible, I'll farm.'

'Did you never think of the railways?'

'The railways!'

'Danny's looking for good men.'

'To be worked into the ground?'

'No, not as one of those fellows. We're growing fast. We need good men managing the business – gangers, accounts clerks, everything. And I'm damned sure, being family, Danny would have you high up.'

'Oh the devil take that,' Pat said.

Cloonee. Drumminroe. Kiltarsaghaun.

They stopped in each village. In Drumminroe one of their men could not get up. In Kiltarsaghaun, another was unable to rise. They were both put on the bread cart.

'God,' said Murtybeg, 'are they all like this?'

Killavally. Devleash. Drummin. Knockrooskey. Ballydonnellan.

Now two more men were not walking, and the woman was on the bread cart.

They walked down Altamont Street into Westport. Neither were riding, each carrying a man on his horse.

'So much for these fellows being in good condition,' Murtybeg commented.

'It's only a few,' Pat said, 'and just be thankful it wasn't more.'

They crossed the town, and so to the quays.

As they came closer, they saw people lying along the road in shacks made from weeds, potato tops and little else.

'How can anyone make shelter out of that?' Murtybeg asked.

'And how can anyone live in it either?' Pat replied. 'That's what I'd like to know.

It was drizzling.

'What now?' Murtybeg asked.

'We've got to get these fellows under shelter. But where?'

They left them in the lee of a warehouse wall. Both mounted their horses, and rode down onto one of the warehouses.

'Wait here, Murteen,' Pat said.

He went inside. He saw a clerk at a desk on the other side of a large hall sitting alongside a mound of stacked sacks. Pat went over to him.

'You're looking official,' the man said to him.

'Just over from Castlebar,' Pat said, not wishing to mention Ballinrobe. I've men going to England. We're looking for shelter.'

'Fair enough,' the clerk said. 'You can shelter them in the next shed. Can't risk it here – the corn wouldn't last long.'

'Good to see corn is still coming in,' Pat said.

'Coming in!' the clerk exclaimed. 'That's going out.'

'What? Isn't it needed for feeding the people?'

'It's needed for the landlords to pay their land rates. Not that it'll save the most of them from bankruptcy. The rates are far higher than they were two years back.'

'And what's coming in?' Pat asked. 'Is there nothing coming in at all?'

'Little enough,' the clerk said. 'See the sacks over there?'

'It's not much,' Pat said.

'Not much at all, and the half of it is rotting. It came over from America

147

in barrels, but they sold the barrels, and put all the corn into sacks. What they wanted the barrels for, I've no idea, but once they put the corn into the sacks it started to rot with the damp.'

Pat went outside again, and he and Murtybeg brought the men to the adjoining shed.

'Is that them?' the clerk asked as he unlocked the shed. 'You're not sending them to England like that?'

'How else would you expect them to be?' Pat asked.

They rode further along the quays. There were two boats, one being loaded with cattle. As they spoke, the other started to pull out. They were directed towards the captain of the first ship.

Pat saw the name on the second. The Altair

Murtybeg handed him McGuinness' requisition and receipt.

'For how many?'

'Eighty four, so far. More later, but we'll pay then.'

'Either of you travelling?'

'Just me,' Murtybeg said. 'And I presume, as ganger, I go free.'

A scratched calculation. 'Three pounds nine shillings.'

'Less deposit?'

'Two pounds fourteen.'

'Do you have it?' Pat whispered.

'Of course. But no Bianconi to Dublin now.'

'Might be good for you, Murteen' Pat said.

'That's not funny.'

They rode back along the quays. At the warehouse, a few of the men were smoking clay pipes. Pat stopped and explained the plans for the morning. Then he rode on to the Workhouse with Murtybeg.

The gates were locked, and three soldiers were standing outside in the rain. Quickly they were admitted. A soldier entered with them, and led both their horses towards the Workhouse stables.

'Nice horses,' he said. 'We're short enough of them since the Inniskillings left.'

'Did ye not bring enough?' Pat asked.

'We would have, but they told us there were more here.'

'Well, don't let ye be tempted to take ours.'

At the Administration block, Pat asked for the Clerk of Union. They were ushered into an office.

A man rose to greet them from behind a desk.

'Egan's the name,' he said, extending his hand. 'Clerk of Union for these parts.'

Pat handed him the letter.

'Pat Ryan so, is it?'

'It is,' Pat said.

Sarah was staring at them from the corner.

Quietly, Pat explained their business, but knew Sarah was listening intently.

'I can understand what you're looking for,' the Clerk replied, 'and God knows, the Workhouse here is over-crowded, and bankrupt too.'

'Bankrupt!' Murtybeg exclaimed.

'Aye. And it would be shut long since, if it wasn't for Lord Sligo, paying for it from his own pocket too.'

'I'm surprised by that,' Pat said.

'What choice do you think he has? They're dying all around him.'

'I hadn't thought he was that kind of man though. Why would he care?'

'I won't comment on that,' the Clerk said.

Quickly it was agreed that a hundred and fifty men from Westport Workhouse would be taken to England. The Clerk organised two officials to do the selection.

'You'll stay the night,' the Clerk asked. Pat hesitated. He thought of the men in the warehouse. By rights he should sleep there. He whispered to Murtybeg. He was surprised when Murtybeg agreed to return to the warehouse after dinner.

Sarah was at dinner that evening, together with her mother and the Clerk of Union. Pat sat beside Sarah's mother, and introduced her to Murtybeg. Mrs. Cronin shook his hand gravely.

'I don't know how you do the job you do,' she said.

'Isn't it better than leaving men starving in Mayo,' said Murtybeg.

'Is it? I don't know that it is. Let that be your opinion. Now let's hear what you've been seeing since you left Knockanure.'

'I don't know that you'd want to know,' Pat said.

'You needn't worry about that,' Sarah said, from across the table. 'We're all well used to it. How's Knockanure?'

'Murtybeg will tell you about that.'

'The hell, I will,' Murtybeg said.

'And there's your answer,' Pat said. 'There's a man who knows Liverpool Workhouse, and many others too in England, and he can't even talk about Knockanure. I showed him the overflow ward and the pit, and it gives him nightmares.'

'Not nightmares,' Murtybeg said, 'but close enough. I'll tell you, I don't want to see anything like that again.'

'But what Workhouses have you seen since Knockanure?' the Clerk of Union asked.

'Castlebar, Ballinrobe and now Westport,' Pat said.

'How would ye compare them?'

'We never saw the insides of Castlebar or Ballinrobe,' Pat replied, 'only the Administration.'

'And let's leave them at that,' Murtybeg said. 'Damned if I want to see the inside of any more Workhouses in County Mayo.'

'But ye're no good at all,' Sarah said. 'Here ye are, travelling all over the county, and ye can't tell us a thing.'

Pat held out his hand. 'It's just we've seen so many bodies on the roads and beside them.'

'Sure we've got that here in Westport,' she said.

'You know all about it so,' Pat said. 'But Ballinrobe Workhouse could only get us eighty four men. How many are there – a thousand? More? Who knows? And of the eighty four they gave us, four weren't even able to walk as far as Westport here.'

As Murtybeg left for the Warehouse, Pat stood beside Sarah outside the dining room.

'What do you think of me now, Sarah?' he asked.

'Doing what you have to do. Isn't that it?'

'Ye were hard enough on Murtybeg.'

'True enough,' she said. 'But you're not working them as slaves in England.'

'I'm not sure that it's much better than here.'

'Maybe not,' she answered. 'Fever's killing them in terrible numbers. Not as bad as the spring though.'

'They're still dying,' Pat interrupted. 'The fever is still running.'

'Isn't that the point?' Sarah said. 'If we want them to live, we have to get them out of Mayo. There's no other way.'

'I'd agree with you, but for one thing,' Pat said. 'Danny won't take families. Sure, he wants men with families, but he prefers them to leave the women and children behind. That way he can control them the easier.'

'Yes. I know all about Danny and his ways.'

The following morning, Murtybeg arrived back at the Workhouse, and commenced counting the inmates for England.

'A hundred and fifty, as requested,' one of the junior officials told him.

As Murtybeg was signing, Pat noticed Sarah at the door of the Administration block. He went over and hugged her.

'Till we meet again, my love.'

'When might that be?' she asked.

'God only knows,' Pat said.

'Well, don't let it be worrying you. We can always write, the both of us. And one way or the other, we'll meet again soon, I'm sure of it.'

'I wish I could believe that.'

'Well, you'd better believe it. I'm always here for you, Pat. Don't forget it. And don't be worrying.'

Later, Pat and Murtybeg left the Workhouse. They walked to the post office where Murtybeg bought a stamp, a letter and an envelope.

'What are you writing?' Pat asked.

'A note to Danny. Just telling him the ship we're on, and when it might arrive in Liverpool.'

He sealed it and left it with the clerk. They went back to the docks, and asked for the captain.

'A hundred and fifty more,' Murtybeg said.

The captain looked at him, eyes narrowing.

'Fifteen pounds,' he said.

'Damn it to hell,' Murtybeg said. 'That's two shillings a man.'

'Your choice,' the man said. 'Do you want to go to England or not?'

Murtybeg took out his pack, and found a bag. Very carefully he counted out fifteen sovereigns. The captain nodded.

They returned to the warehouse and gained admission easily enough. Then they made their way out through the gates, leading their horses as the miserable group of inmates followed them to the docks.

'Where's the donkey?' Murtybeg asked.

'I sold it last night. Ten shillings for the donkey, a pound for the cart.'

'I wonder how long the donkey will live.'

'Who cares?' Pat answered.

'But who owned the cart?'

'Ballinrobe Workhouse, I presume,' Pat answered, 'but I wouldn't worry about it. We've taken eighty four men off their hands, and they'll be glad enough for that. No, they won't be concerned about any donkey and cart.'

The Ballinrobe men had already been brought on the ship, and were sheltering under a canvas cover just beside the cattle.

'There you go, Murteen. Not like the ship you came over on, I'd guess?'

'Don't sound so glad of it,' Murtybeg said.

'You'll write to me when you get to England?'

'I will.'

'There's one other thing,' Pat said. 'The hire of the horses.'

'From Knockanure?'

'Yes.'

'Damn it,' said Murtybeg, 'I was hoping you'd forget that.'

'One and sixpence a day by two is three shillings. Five days, I reckon.'

'And you want fifteen shillings now, do you?'

'I do.'

Murtybeg swore. He put his hand in his pocket, and pulled out a half sovereign, followed by two half-crowns.

Pat rode out the Castlebar road from Westport, leading the second horse past the walls of Lord Sligo's estate. He stopped at Castlebar again, and went to see Gaffney.

'Well, Pat, you've seen a lot.'

'I have,' Pat replied. 'Too much at times.'

'Now you know the conditions of four of Mayo's Workhouses.'

'When you look at it like that...'

'I want you to do a report before you go back to Knockanure. Compare the conditions of the four Workhouses, and tell us what else you've seen.'

'Yes,' he said, 'I met the priest down in Ballinrobe. He asked me to do a report too.'

'Father Ward, was it?'

'That's right.'

'Everyone knows Father Ward. He does enough of his own reports too – for the Telegraph and any other paper that'll print them.'

Pat spent the rest of the afternoon writing. He told of what he had seen of the three other Workhouses, comparing them to Castlebar. He described his journey between them. In particular, he described Ballinrobe, and included the priest's descriptions of the Partry Mountains.

'But you weren't in the mountains,' Gaffney said when he saw the report that night.

'Hardly. We couldn't go that way with all the men.'

'You couldn't, but it's a hell of a pity even so. We keep on getting letters from the good Father. I'd visit Partry myself if I could, see the truth of what he's saying. Still, it's an excellent report, Pat. You write well. Very well indeed.'

That night he stayed at the Workhouse. As he left Castlebar the next morning it was raining. He thought of Murtybeg's suggestion of travelling to England and working with Danny. As what? A clerk? A ganger? One way or the other, treating men like slaves, and leaving Sarah too?

No. Not that.

He rode directly to Knockanure, not caring to go by Carrigard. The rain had stopped by the time he had reached Knockanure, but a deep depression settled on him.

Chapter 11

Friedrich Engels, *The Condition of the Working Class in England*:

Heaps of refuse, offal and sickening filth are everywhere interspersed with pools of stagnant liquid. The atmosphere is polluted by the stench and is darkened by the thick smoke of a dozen factory chimneys. A horde of ragged women and children swarm about the streets and they are just as dirty as the pigs which wallow happily on the heaps of garbage and in the pools of filth. In short, this horrid little slum affords as hateful and repulsive a spectacle as the worst courts to be found on the banks of the Irk. The inhabitants live in dilapidated cottages, the windows of which are broken and patched with oilskin. The doors and the door posts are broken and rotten. The creatures who inhabit these dwellings and even their dark, wet cellars, and which live confined amidst all this filth and foul air – which cannot be dissipated because of the surrounding lofty buildings – must surely have sunk to the lowest level of humanity.

Description of Manchester's 'Little Ireland' at the start of the Irish Famine

Pat's letter from Knockanure Workhouse some weeks before had galvanised Danny. Even before Murtybeg had left England, Danny felt there was little doubt that he could get workers directly from the Mayo Workhouses.

Now he wrote a letter directly to Tim Kearney at a site near Leeds. Three days later, a reply arrived. As Danny had anticipated, the offer of six shillings a day had ensured Kearney's interest.

At the ganger meeting that morning, he told everyone that Kearney had accepted his offer, and would be starting over the next week or so.

'Kearney!' Lavan exclaimed.

'None other,' Danny answered. 'One of the old gang.'

'Isn't that great?' Lavan said. 'I always had great respect for Tim. A hard worker.'

For the next hour, the discussions were of a more general nature, covering one contract after another, but always coming back to the key subject of labour shortage, and the risk of bringing workers in through the Port of Liverpool.

As the meeting finished, McManus slipped Danny a blank envelope. No one else noticed.

Danny retired to his office. Inside the envelope was a letter. It read:

'Danny – I wrote to Brady, and he wrote back saying there would be no problem in bringing the navvies through the port. He would like to meet you in Liverpool first, and would prefer that no-one else comes. I have not mentioned you by name, nor Edwardes & Ryan. If you mention me though, you will have no problem. He lives beside McCabe's bar in Vauxhall. McCabe will know him. Just go to the bar, and ask McCabe for him.'

Vauxhall, Danny thought. Just off Scotland Road. A rough area. Many Irish too.

Afterwards, he showed the letter to Irene.

'What do you think?' he asked.

'We've no choice, you'll have to go.'

'I wonder why he wants to meet me alone.'

'These kind of people always do. They like to exercise their influence quietly. The less who know, the better.'

Kearney arrived in Stockport.

That evening, he joined Danny and Irene for dinner.

'Your letter caused some remarks among the other fellows,' he told Danny.

'I'd say it did.'

'You know I'd been elected as ganger after Farrelly left for America.'

Danny laughed. 'I hadn't. But it certainly seems as if we have the ability to pick the very best. So have they elected anyone to replace you?'

'Joe Gilligan.'

Danny smiled. Roughneen had been correct in his assessment of the best men on the gang.

'And how's the gang going?'

'Very well,' Kearney answered. 'We were up to full strength before I left. We'd write home to find out which of the fellows were working the railways here. Chiefly the ones who had book learning from your father's school. There's some hard workers among them, and while most of them were earning well enough, they knew they'd earn better on the gang with us. So we'd find out from their families at home where they were working, then a quick letter would be enough to bring them over. And I'll tell you one thing, Danny, there's many more good Kilduff men out there, all around the country.'

154

'Worth remembering,' Danny said. 'I reckon we're going to need more gangers ourselves here.'

Yes, he thought. There's any number of good gangers out there.

'You can rest here a while,' he told Kearney. 'Tomorrow I'll bring you over to Mrs. O'Brien's. She'll have a room for you. Good food too, as the fellows will tell you.'

Irene had said nothing. He noticed Kearney was looking closely at her. Assessing her, perhaps. And, he reckoned, she was assessing him.

Next day, Danny took Kearney out to meet Roughneen. Three of the old gang together. There was much laughter, and exchanging of stories since they had last met.

'And Farrelly gone to America,' Kearney said.

'Yes,' Roughneen replied. 'Wasn't that the biggest surprise of all?'

They walked the site. Danny could see that Kearney was surprised by the low quality of the labour.

'They'd never make it on the old gang,' he commented to Danny.

'Sure as hell, they wouldn't,' Danny replied. 'They're all from west Mayo. All out that way, the Hunger has them famished. But we'll build them up in time.'

'But their rate of work. It's hardly half of what we'd be doing.'

'Yes,' said Danny, 'but that was working the butty system. Damned good money for hard workers.'

'And these.'

'They just work directly with us. We pay them damned little. A shilling a day if they're lucky.'

'A shilling!' Kearney exclaimed.

'Sure it's all they're worth. And it's better than they'd be getting on the Relief Works in Mayo, and even that's closed. And they'd be getting nothing at all in the Workhouse. But it's not only the pay that's better for them. We feed them up too. Get them used to hard work.'

'But…how easy is it to find these fellows.'

'Getting harder,' Danny said, 'As you might know Murtybeg is in Mayo. We're expecting him back very soon. And don't worry, he'll have workers with him, I'm sure of it. I'm hoping it'll be enough to get the present sites back on course to complete in time. And I'd be disappointed if he didn't have at least a hundred for the North Staffordshire.'

Roughneen nodded. 'I hope to God he does.'

Danny left Kearney with Roughneen. It had been agreed that Roughneen would stay on for another two days until Kearney had a proper grasp of the site. Then Roughneen would leave Kearney, travel to the North Staffordshire to mark out the site, and locate suppliers. Danny told him that Irene would be able to help him with the suppliers.

When Danny arrived back that evening, the letter from Murtybeg was waiting for him.

'An efficient fellow, your brother,' Irene commented.

Danny glanced through it. 'Two hundred and thirty four...' he gasped. 'That should sort us out.'

'There's more,' Irene said.

'I know,' said Danny, reading on. 'Oh my God! Friday?'

'That's not to say it'll arrive on time,' Irene said, 'but it certainly won't be early. But there's one matter that concerns me.'

'I know,' Danny said. 'The ship. Disembarking them.'

'Exactly,' she said. 'And we'll have to have someone waiting there too. And it's going to have to be you.'

'It will,' he said. 'With a pound or two to grease some palms. After I meet this Brady fellow.'

'I hope it'll work,' Irene said.

'It'll have to.'

Next morning, Danny left for Liverpool. He went directly to the Docks, and found the harbour master's office.

'Not arrived yet,' he was told. 'There's been no storms though, and the winds have been good. I'm guessing later this evening perhaps. Or sometime tomorrow.'

He walked across to Vauxhall. He knew what he was going to see, but even so, it shocked him. The 'courts' behind the buildings, the low cellars, the gaunt faces, the stink of poverty. And the white crosses on doors. Fever! Murtybeg was right. There was fever here.

When he found the street, he saw it was lined with Irish beggars. Many were not even able to beg in English, others had only a few words. Half were mothers, babies clasped close, begging for money for the child.

He found McCabe's, and went in. The bar was full, with a loud buzz of conversation. There were many men, most dressed in the rough clothes of the navvy. A sharp smell too, mixing beer and cabbage with the smell of raw sewage.

The moment Danny entered, the noise died away. There was a deep hush, as dozens of men turned around to look right at him. He walked towards the bar, the crowd opening for him, and closing behind, still silent.

'Mr. McCabe?' he asked the barman.

'Yes.'

'I'm looking for Mr. Brady.'

'We're all looking for Mr. Brady.'

156

There was a sound of raucous laughter, and the hum of talk started again. McCabe indicated Danny should come to the end of the bar, and let him in.

'In the name of God, what did you come in like that for?'

'How else could I come in?' Danny asked. 'I was told to come to McCabe's and ask for Brady. Am I right or am I wrong?'

McCabe muttered a curse under his breath. 'It's still a damned dangerous thing to do,' he said to Danny. 'Now, how do I know you're looking for Brady, or who you are?'

'Ryan is the name. I'm a friend of Jamesy McManus. Mr. Brady knows him, and is expecting me.'

'Today?'

'No. But the matter is urgent.'

'Follow me.'

Danny followed down a long corridor, crates and barrels of beer on the sides. McCabe knocked on a door and opened it. There was a whispered exchange. Then he led Danny further down the corridor, and brought him into a dark room, without windows. There was a chair, a table and a candle which McCabe lit. He told Danny to sit, and left.

Danny sat, staring at the candle. He was far away from the bar now and could scarcely hear the talk and laughter. As the minutes dragged, he began to have misgivings. He had surely taken a risk coming here. He only had the word of McManus that Brady was reliable. After a while, Danny realised he was only panicking himself. For a long time he tried to think of nothing at all.

The door opened, and a woman entered. Too well dressed for Vauxhall, Danny thought.

'This way,' she said.

She led him along another corridor, and ushered him through a door. He saw at once this was nothing like the rest of Vauxhall.

The room he entered was well appointed. He could see the carpets were expensive. The back of the house had wide sash windows, looking into a high-walled garden.

A man strode across to him. He was tall, and elderly.

'Mr. Ryan.'

'Daniel Ryan,' Danny said. 'And Mr. Brady, I presume.'

'Indeed, Mr. Ryan. Sit here, and relax yourself.'

'Thank you,' Danny said, still on his guard.

'So you know Jamesy McManus, do you?'

'For many years. He comes from the same part of Mayo as I do. We studied together, we worked together, now Jamesy works for me as a ganger.'

157

'A ganger?'

'On the railways.'

'I see,' Brady said. 'You're a labour contractor, Mr. Ryan?'

'I am. Being from Mayo, we've many Mayo gangs.'

'Ah yes, Mayo. As you might know, I'm from Cavan myself. Jamesy's grandmother and my grandfather were sister and brother. She married into County Mayo.'

Tea had been prepared. The woman handed Danny a cup.

'Milk or sugar?' she asked.

'Both,' Danny said with a smile.

'So what can I do to help you?' Brady asked. 'Jamesy mentioned something about a ship.'

'Indeed,' Danny said. 'The Altair she's called. A cattle ship, for the most part. We've a load of men coming from Westport on the Altair. Two or three hundred, all told. We've work ready for them on a number of cuttings we're constructing around Manchester.'

'Of course,' Brady said. 'A lot of work around Manchester, I believe.'

'Indeed. That's why I have so much call for labour. But I believe a possible problem has arisen, in that many of the ships from Ireland are being turned around without unloading. With the contracts we hold, we couldn't possibly let that happen.'

'So that's why you come here.'

'Exactly. Jamesy is running a cutting for us. He has a sizeable call for labour, and it was he who said that his cousin might be able to help. And that's why I'm here.'

'Yes,' Brady said, 'I can see your problem. Nothing to fear though, something can surely be organised.'

'I was hoping you'd say that,' Danny said. 'This is a vital matter for us.'

'So when is the ship due?'

'Today was the date I'd been given, but the fellow in the harbourmaster's office says it might be this afternoon, this evening or tomorrow.'

'That's short notice.'

'It's all the notice I got.'

'Which dock?'

'The Clarence.'

'Well, no need worrying about that. I'll send one of the runners down, keep an eye on the dock. He should spot it when it's a good two hours out. He'll stay all night, if need be.'

'Fine so.'

'Where will you be?'

'I have some business over the next hour or so,' Danny said. 'After that

I'll rest in the Adelphi hotel. I'll stay there overnight if I have to.'

'Good,' Brady said. 'No need worrying yourself. We'll meet the ship, I guarantee it. And the Adelphi to the Clarence Dock is no more than twenty minutes.'

Brady sipped his tea.

'There will be a charge for services.'

'Of course,' Danny said. 'How much?'

'Ten pounds. You should also allow for a pound at the top end for greasing one or two palms at the dock.'

'That would be fine,' Danny said. 'Cash on delivery?'

'Of course. We only charge when the goods have been delivered. There is one other point I must stress. Even with greased palms, the goods must leave Liverpool at once. They will be accompanied to the station, and must be loaded on the wagons, and be seen to leave the city.'

'I understand,' Danny said.

When Danny left the house in Vauxhall, he walked directly to Liverpool Workhouse.

There was a guard on the gate, where many people were trying to gain admission. The guard spotted the quality of his coat, and let him through a side gate, where he was directed to a small office.

'Daniel Ryan,' he explained to the man inside. 'Brother of Murtybeg Ryan.'

The man looked at him in some bewilderment.

'What's that?' he asked. 'You mean Martin Ryan? The Irish fellow.'

'Martin', Danny thought. Smart move that, Murteen.

'Of course,' he said, 'it's just in the family we call him by a class of a nickname.'

'This way, please.'

A few minutes later he found himself sitting with one of the Workhouse clerks.

'Daniel Ryan,' the clerk said. 'Martin has told me a lot about you.'

'Yes,' Danny said, 'so there's no need to introduce Edwardes & Ryan, I'd say.'

'Of course not. You're well known in Liverpool Workhouse.'

'We've done a lot of business together,' Danny said

'And we'll do more in the future, no doubt. Things are a little slow at the moment though. I don't have to tell you about the fever around Liverpool, and it's creating havoc in the Workhouse. Typhus and dysentery. It's hard enough finding young fellows not coming down with one illness or the other. Also, Liverpool Corporation is trying to limit the numbers of Irish coming in through the port. The people are terrified of fever. The last time Martin came by, we gave him – what was it? – twenty two young lads, though I understand he needed much more.'

'He did. And we still do.'

'Well, we'll have to be patient. If you send him back, let's say in two weeks, we should have more for him. I don't know how many, but whatever we have, we'll give you.'

'Fine so,' Danny said.

As he went to the door he stopped.

'Oh, one other thing I almost forgot. There's a friend of ours came over to Liverpool, and we haven't heard from him since. I just thought he might be in the Workhouse.'

'And his name?'

'James Corrigan.'

'Come this way.'

He brought Danny into another office, where he pulled down a large volume.

'Any idea when he might have come in?'

Danny thought back to that day when he and Murtybeg had given Corrigan a beating.

'About eight or nine months back.'

The clerk ran his fingers down the columns.

'Ah yes,' he said. 'James Corrigan. Kilduff, is it? County Mayo.'

'That's the man,' Danny said.

'I'm very sorry to inform you, Mr. Ryan, Mr. Corrigan died last month.'

'What! How?'

'Typhus.'

Danny left the Workhouse. The news of Corrigan's death had surprised him. He had not expected that. Now, at least, there was no requirement for restitution.

He stayed in the Adelphi that night. He woke early, and checked with the hotel staff, but no one had been looking for him.

He had a good breakfast, then he sat in the lounge, near the entrance, sipping a coffee, thrumming his fingers impatiently.

Then the runner arrived. The doorman pointed him across to Danny.

'Mr. Ryan.'

'Yes.'

'She'll be docking very soon, Mr. Ryan.'

Danny paid his bill, leaving his valise with the porter. He followed the boy down to the dock. Brady was waiting. The ship was still in the Mersey, coming closer. There were many dock workers, waiting to tie up the ship.

There were nine other men, one in the uniform of the Port of Liverpool, and eight policemen.

'Ye needn't worry about them,' Brady told him, nodding to the police. 'Thirty shillings extra for special services, though. A little more than I thought. They're reckoning they'll need eight police to accompany your goods to the station. They're not used to such high numbers.'

'I understand,' Danny said.

When the ship had docked, Murtybeg was the first off.

'Danny. I wasn't expecting to see you here.'

'I thought it better to be sure than sorry,' Danny said. 'We had to make sure that you'd be able to land your cargo. There's far too much depending on it.'

Murtybeg looked at the group of police.

'Is this what you call making sure? I doubt this lot are going to let us through.'

'Oh, but they are,' Danny said. 'The peelers are here to help us. They'll protect us on the way to the trains.'

Murtybeg returned to the ship, as the mass of men started coming down the gangway. Under his instructions, they formed six lines.

Brady came alongside. Danny counted out eleven sovereigns, together with four half-crowns. 'As agreed, then?'

'Indeed,' said Brady. He strode away from the dock, being watched closely by the official and the police.

'Who was that?' Murtybeg asked.

'Never mind.'

The unloading went on.

'How many?' Danny asked, when all was complete.

'Started out as two hundred and thirty four. Lost two dead on the voyage.'

'I knew you could do it, Murteen.'

'Did I have any choice?' Murtybeg asked.

Danny smiled. 'Not much.'

He accompanied Murtybeg, as the police led the group of men towards Lime Street Station. When they arrived, Danny stood alongside the wagons, counting as the men were loaded.

'Exact as always,' he said to Murtybeg. 'Two hundred and thirty two.'

'Of course.'

'Now, what I'd like you to do is bring them over to Lavan's site for the night. Tell Bernie to sort out whatever is needed for all the Anderson sites, including Ancoats, and tell him to take them there. I'm sure Bernie can be spared for a day or two, seeing as it's the weekend. They shouldn't need too many, certainly less than a hundred between the four sites. Then take the rest straight down to the North Staffordshire railway. Johnny Roughneen has taken over, and I understand he's got some shacks for this lot. Go down as far as Stoke, and you should be able to get instructions for our site easy enough.'

'Fair enough,' said Murtybeg.

Danny returned to the Adelphi, collected his valise, and took a cab to the station.

That evening, he told Murty about Corrigan's death. As he anticipated, his father was furious. He blamed Danny and Murtybeg for Corrigan's death. Danny protested that Corrigan could have gotten typhus anywhere in Liverpool, but Murty did not accept that. He was angry too that it was impossible to make any restitution directly to Corrigan. He demanded it should be made to the Corrigan family in any case, but Danny refused to accept this.

He visited the Brassey site again. This was far more important to Edwardes & Ryan than Ancoats would ever be. The light rain had stopped. It was warm for autumn. He arrived, and stood outside the work area, watching. The edges of the cutting had been marked off with stakes driven into the ground. Throughout the site, the topsoil was being removed. It was soft enough. Danny knew the real work would begin once they hit shale. Or even worse, rock.

He saw the site hut a hundred yards away. He walked across. Roughneen stood outside, a chart in his hand. He scowled at it, looking up occasionally at the site.

'Doing well, Johnny?'

'My God, Danny, don't sneak up on me like that.'

'Anything wrong?'

'Nothing so far. I'm just trying to see it all in my own mind, what it's like now and what it's going to be.'

'You got the new fellows from Murtybeg, did you?'

'That's them. A hundred and forty he brought, that's all. They've only just started.'

'They're working very slowly.'

'You always say that Danny. Don't worry. We'll have them working faster in a week or two.'

'And the shacks?'

'Just behind the hedge over there.'

'Let's have a look.'

They crossed the site to the hedge. When they went behind, Danny drew back in surprise.

'Is this it? Mud cabins.'

'It's what we're doing for now,' Roughneen replied. 'We got some bits and pieces of crates around for the roofs. Keeps the rain off and the wind out. I'm intending on having something better before winter, but that will cost money.'

Danny shook his head. 'My God, Johnny, they're tighter than we've done before.'

'No tighter than the *sceilps* back home, from all I hear. But you're right, Danny, we've got to get better shacks before the winter.'

Danny walked towards a hut, standing a hundred yards off.

'No need to go nearer,' Roughneen shouted after him. Danny turned back. 'Why?'

'Fever. Three only, but we've got to keep them apart.'

Danny swore softly. They walked back towards Roughneen's office.

'We'll have to do something about those huts,' Danny said.

'I know. I've it underway already. I've managed to find some timber – offcuts from some of the local saw-mills and some rafters from demolitions. That way, we won't be needing mud cabins. We'll need more timber though. Sewage pipes too. No doubting that.'

'This'll all cost money.'

'It will,' Roughneen said. 'It'll cost more if we lose the contract though.'

'Any other problems, Johnny?'

'Not so much with the site itself. It's the locals, that's where the problem is. Them and the other navvies. They're all convinced the Irish are bringing fever across, and if it don't kill them, they reckon the Irish are taking their jobs anyhow.'

Danny laughed. 'I wouldn't blame them for that,' he said. 'We are taking their jobs from them. But we better make sure not to be giving them fever.'

When they reached Roughneen's office, they spent some time going through maps, distances, measurements, cubic yards to be removed, estimated wage costs, requirements for implements, carts and horses, and many other things.

After quite some time, they finished and stepped outside. Roughneen glanced up, and then looked more closely.

'I wonder who that is over there.'

A coach had drawn up on the other side of the site. Already, the coachman had dismounted and opened the door, as two men stepped out.

Danny knew, even from that distance, that the coach was an expensive one.

'Let's see what this is all about,' he said to Roughneen. They strode across the site, as the two men came towards them.

'Good God,' Danny gasped, as they drew closer. 'It's Brassey!'

He went across and held out his hand.

'Mr. Brassey. I'm Daniel Ryan.'

Brassey smiled.

'Ah yes, Mr. Ryan, delighted to meet you. And this is Edwin Kane. One of my senior managers.'

Danny introduced Roughneen as his site manager. Brassey eyed him closely, assessing him perhaps.

'I'd like a general look round,' he said. 'Perhaps you'd both be so good as to accompany us.'

As he walked, Brassey watched the working lines of men very closely.

'They're very slow, Mr. Ryan. Do you think you can make our deadlines?'

'We always complete on time, Mr. Brassey...'

'Yes,' Brassey interrupted, 'I'd heard that. But at this rate, and this number of workers?'

'I can understand your concerns, Mr. Brassey,' Danny said, 'but you have to remember two key points. First, these men have just been brought over from Ireland. They're not like men who have been working for years on the railways. Some of them had been strong enough before...'

'Yes,' Brassey interjected, 'but now the Famine...'

'Just so,' Danny said. 'As soon as we get them here we feed them well. Very well. Two pounds weight of beef or mutton a day, and ten pounds of potatoes.'

No need to mention that 'beef or mutton' was chiefly offal. It all came from cattle or sheep.

'Yes,' Roughneen added, 'if we feed them well, and exercise them well, within weeks we will have them up to a good rate of work. But there is a second factor. We have only started on the contract, so we don't have a full labour force as yet. Our plans are to double or treble that. Perhaps four hundred men in total. It might take three or four weeks yet, but we will do it.'

The four men walked to Roughneen's shed. Now Brassey interrogated them far more closely. For the next hour, they went through all the maps, figures and calculations that Danny and Roughneen had been working on earlier.

Then he shook hands with both Danny and Roughneen.

'I'm afraid we both have to go now,' he said. 'But I can assure you, if you complete on budget and in time, there will be more contracts for you. Should you have any problems though, Mr. Kane here is based at our main office for the North Staffordshire at Stoke. Equally, he will drop by from time to time.'

After Brassey and Kane had left, Danny walked with Roughneen down to the site entrance.

'My God,' Roughneen said, 'it felt like I was in school again. Even your father, he'd never throw questions at us that fast.'

'Damned right, he wouldn't,' Danny responded 'I feel all wrung out myself. Still, Johnny, I think we passed our first examination. And thank God he didn't come by the other road. If he'd seen the mud cabins we'd have failed, there and then. It's like you said, we'll need more timber to replace them.'

'I'll get on to it.'

'Do that. Still, Johnny. More Brassey contracts ahead. Did you hear that? Did you?'

'Loud and clear, Danny. Now all you got to do is get the workers for me. These lot are fine to start with, but we'll need more.'

'Ah yes, I was thinking of that,' Danny said. 'And I noticed how quick you were to commit me to four hundred men, you bastard.'

That evening, as Danny prepared for bed, he could see that Irene was angry.

'What's wrong, my dear?'

'Having your parents here. This is not going to work.'

'Why not?'

'There's a lot of reasons. But let's start with your mother. Have you seen the condition of her?'

'Oh, don't worry about it. She's had a hard time.'

'Hard or not, she should have more respect for the people she's staying with. Do you know what she told me this morning? She said we were living in sin, the two of us. Sleeping together and not even married. Is the woman mad or what?'

'You're worrying too much,' Danny said. 'You must realise, she comes from a Catholic country and the priests control her. That's the way they think now. When they're over here long enough, they'll think different.'

'I don't believe that.'

Danny blew out the candle and got into bed.

'But it's not just that,' Irene said in the darkness. 'She's in a terrible state, whatever the causes. She hardly talks, and when she does it's only to criticise. If it's not our morals, it's the amount of money we're spending, and if it's not that, it's the way we're dressing. I can't stand that day in, day out.'

'You've got to understand that she's a frightened woman. She's been years worrying about the school closing, and that they'd have nothing to live on. Nothing at all, and you know what that means in County Mayo.'

'Weren't you sending them money? And Murteen, couldn't he send them some?'

'True enough, but that's charity. All the pride of being a teacher's wife,

165

reduced to charity. No, I can understand it well enough.'

'She's just like you so. Worried to death, isn't that it?'

'I'm not worried,' Danny said.

'Even so, your mother is,' Irene said. 'Or maybe it's just a form of madness. One way or another, she can't live on her own. Have you ever thought of what she might do when there's no one around? She's so wretched, she could well kill herself.'

'Don't be silly. She'd never go that far. Don't forget she's a Catholic.'

'What's that got to do with it?'

'Catholics never kill themselves.'

'Do you believe that?' Irene asked.

Danny did not reply.

Chapter 12

The Tablet, Kent, October 1847:
The commercial crisis under which England is suffering is becoming more intense every week that passes over our heads, nor does there appear any present symptom of its cessation. Having indulged itself with a sweep through the commercial world, as if to prove by experiment how many failures for above half a million it would be possible to bring about in a quarter of a year; having performed a terrific dance through every department of commerce with every part of the world — at length the Monster-Crisis makes an inroad into the world of Banking, and at one blow levels the most powerful establishment of the second city of the empire. How far this dire calamity may reach; what may be its direct results; what the effect of its example; what panic-terrors may spring from its roots, and how many neighbour trees of the forest it may tear down in the violence of its fall, no man can possibly predict. The general solvency of the great Banks appears to be no adequate defence against such a wide-spread catastrophe.

All through September, Danny's requirement for workers was extreme. Sourcing them was getting more difficult too. He had been concerned about dealing with Brady, but he was beginning to feel that this was the only way he could get sufficient workers at low wages. Liverpool Workhouse could continue to supply them, but this would be nothing like the numbers they had given him in the past. From letters received from Mayo over the past weeks, his gangers were able to tell him what was happening. The massive death toll in the Famine and the enormous emigration to both England and America were both reducing the number of labourers in Ireland itself. The big farmers in Ireland were now becoming desperate for workers. They too were hiring poor men from the west of Ireland. They had been paying ten pennies a day plus board and lodging, but, through the harvest, this had jumped to two shillings. The Mayo Workhouses were no longer as overcrowded as they had been. Even on the west coast of Mayo, men were not as desperate as before.

One night, Danny wrote a letter to Pat, asking if he could source labour directly from the Workhouses in Ballina and Newport, as well as whatever might still be possible from Ballinrobe and Westport.

As he expected, Pat's reply was ambiguous. Many men had left Knockanure Workhouse to work in Tipperary, Kilkenny, Kildare, Meath and other counties in the Irish Midlands. From what he had heard, other Mayo Workhouses were the same. Pat felt he could get a limited number of workers in the west of Mayo, but far, far fewer than before.

Then, the floods came.

For days, there was torrential rain. At first this did not concern Danny unduly. Wet or dry, work would continue on the railways.

He became more concerned though as the rain went on. He watched as the Mersey rushed through Stockport, becoming deeper every day. A number of the roads around were flooded, as the river burst its banks.

He decided to visit the sites. He travelled, first by train, then by stagecoach.

When he arrived at McManus' site, he was relieved to see that the Works were still proceeding. The men were drenched through, but still they were shovelling wet mud into barrows and wheeling it away, or shovelling it directly onto railway carriages. He spotted McManus in a heavy mackintosh and sou'wester.

'Well, Jamesy. Still working.'

'Trying to make up time, Danny.'

'Will we make it?'

'We will now.'

Danny left.

At Kearney's site, he saw the fields around were all flooded. The Works were stopped. The flood had not reached any of the site, but there were no men working. He walked to the site office. Kearney looked up.

'All stopped, Danny.'

'I know,' Danny said. 'I'd noticed. Where are all the workers?'

'In the shacks, God help them.'

'Why so?' Danny asked.

'Most of the shacks out the fields have flooded. They're all squeezing into the higher ones, and even there, the rain is coming in through the roofs.'

'Might be as well to have them out working. What do you think?'

'I tried that. They just won't do it.'

'Damn them to hell.'

He travelled on to see Lavan. He went to the site office. Lavan was stretched out on a truckle bed. He looked up as Danny entered.

'Not a thing we can do about it, Danny,' he said. 'Not in mud that deep.'

'I know,' Danny said.

He was thoroughly drenched when he reached Stockport late that night.

Irene was already asleep. He stripped, and rubbed himself down well.

He left before she woke, and travelled down to the North Staffordshire Line. At the site, the Works were flooded. Roughneen was not in the office but he found him in an inn nearby, where he had rented a room.

'All stopped?' he said to Roughneen.

'Worse than that, Danny,' Roughneen answered. One of the puddle banks has collapsed. It'll be a while 'till we dry this one out, and even then we'll have to re-build the bank.'

Danny travelled back to Manchester, and out to Ancoats. He almost felt he was dreading this, but if he was tougher than most, he would have to brave it out. He had a hard reputation, and that reputation had to be maintained. Even so, he was shocked by what he saw when he reached Ancoats.

The site was fully flooded. Broken furniture and dead pigs floated in the water, a dead dog on one bank. There were no workers, though that was hardly surprising. Where the railway was being built, he could see a few dozen mud cabins. Across Oxford Road itself, there were more cabins, if they could even be called that. They reminded him of the famine *sceilps* that he had seen in County Mayo.

He went to Steele's office. Steele was there, playing cards with three constables. He stood up at once.

'We can't work today, Mr. Ryan.'

'I know,' Danny said, indicating him to sit. He pulled up a crate, and joined them at the table.

'They're in a desperate way,' Steele said. 'Fever and worse. Two pigs were drowned in one of the cellars, and the family ate them raw. Passed a few hams across to some of our fellows, and now they're doubled up with the shits too. I'd say a few might have fever, and I'm just hoping it doesn't spread.'

'Nothing much we can do about it, until things dry out,' Danny said. 'What are ye playing?'

'Pontoon.'

'Deal me a hand.'

Over the subsequent days, he and Irene went through figures again and again, trying to calculate the cost of the storms. Irene suggested that for as long as the workers were not working, they should not get paid.

'But we can't do that,' Danny responded.

'Why not? We can feed them, and they should be glad of that.'

He considered that.

'Fine so, half wages, and I'm not going lower.'

Afterwards, Danny discussed the matter, first with Roy Anderson, who,

169

he was surprised to hear, had built in contingency and allowed Danny for excess costs and wages.

Danny thought of asking Edwin Kane whether Tom Brassey would consider the same, but then decided not to. The Brassey contract was far too important, and if Edwardes & Ryan could take the hit from the floods, it would prove the quality of contractor they were.

He was surprised when Irene accepted this point at once.

'So how much will the puddle bank at on the Brassey cost to build again?' she asked.

'About a hundred pounds, I'm estimating,' Danny said. 'We'll probably lose another fifty on all the extra wages we'll have to pay, just to catch up. Say two hundred at the most.'

'So that's that then,' Irene said. 'Lucky we built in such an amount of contingency, isn't it?'

'Yes, it is,' Danny said. 'You're always right.'

But floods were not the only problem that Edwardes & Ryan had to deal with. In spite of his demand for labour, Danny had been getting more edgy about business prospects in the long term. At first, he had been able to hide it from Irene, but that was no longer easy.

Share prices in the London and North Western Exchanges had been dropping. He watched the Manchester and Liverpool exchanges avidly. Manchester – the commercial and trading centre for the industrial west of England – was the centre of his business. Liverpool – the largest port on earth and second city of England – was the source of his cheap Irish labour. Only forty miles separated them.

The drop in the share prices of the railway companies was more disturbing. If any of his customers went bankrupt, his contracts could disappear. Every day, he watched for news of the North Staffordshire Line, or the other lines, but there was no dramatic news on any.

Equally disquieting though, a bankruptcy of one of the major banks could have a knock-on effect on other banks, and if the Manchester & Salford suspended trading, then Edwardes & Ryan would have no source of credit.

But more than the Manchester banks, it was the Liverpool banks that worried him. There were sudden bankruptcies among many Liverpool trading houses and importers, and Danny feared this could spread to the banks who were lending to them. Any collapse in Liverpool could certainly spread to Manchester. In Liverpool, the top bank was the Royal Bank of Liverpool which was seen as one of the strongest in the country. But for weeks now, its shares had been dropping. Then, one day, Danny was startled to see that its share price had dropped by a third in just two days. He read the Liverpool papers, trying to deduce what was happening, but while they detailed the drops, none of them gave any cause. And the shares of the Royal Bank went on dropping.

But what of Irene? Danny knew she was not worried.

She had a different approach to hiring labour. In spite of Danny's concerns, she reckoned too that their strategy of employing desperate men from the west of Mayo was working well, and would continue to do so. The men they already employed had little alternative. Few of the other contractors were taking on labour.

She was totally ruthless. She reasoned that if they wanted to increase profits, wages would have to be reduced. The other contractors were taking on far fewer navvies, at any wage. The men on the gangs were trapped. No work anywhere else, and no way home. Only death by starvation or fever awaited them in Mayo. If they could even get that far. Edwardes & Ryan was the only contractor that needed new workers.

But Danny would not reduce wages. They were already the lowest in the North West, and he would not be moved on this.

Food was the one area they agreed on. Irene did not want to cut back on feeding the men. The business had to maintain the strength of their workers. Building railways was hard work. Still Edwardes & Ryan paid less for meat than other contractors. No prime cuts of beef here. All the Edwardes & Ryan workers ever got was sheep heads and offal stews. Irene knew that this was just as nutritious as prime beef, but far cheaper.

Now though, her respect for Danny was lessening, and Danny knew this. She had seen him as a powerful and ruthless man, reflecting her own strength. Now, seeing how he was worried by every move in the stock market, she was no longer as sure as she had been. The first hint of softness she had detected in him was bringing his own parents over from Mayo, but she had accepted this. She had little respect for Murty, but kept him in the office working on accounts, or out inspecting the sites. At least he could add, subtract, multiply and divide, and he had known most of the gangers since childhood.

But Danny's mother, Aileen? Terrified of everything. Working in a mill – that was all she was good for. But the mills were closing. Perhaps Danny had inherited his unknown fears from her.

She wondered if she could bring him back to what he had been before he started reading the Manchester Times. Could she bring back his old ruthlessness? She knew Edwardes & Ryan could survive any crash and come out of it far stronger as all their competitors went bankrupt. But could she convince Danny of that?

She crossed to his desk.

'What's frightening you?'

'I'm not frightened,' Danny said.

'Not frightened! There you are, reading the Manchester Times every day, looking for the worst.'

'But it is bad,' Danny said angrily, 'and getting worse. You know it yourself. The banks are just not lending.'

'The Manchester & Salford are lending to us. They've given us a lending facility, and they can't withdraw it. They might cut back their new lending, but they can't – and they won't – cut back on us.'

'Fine,' Danny said, 'Even so, the railways might pull out of some of their contracts.'

'And what if they do?' Irene said. 'We've got the Brassey contract, and he knows what he's doing. And just remember this, the ones who go to the wall are the ones who can't handle tough times. But we can. One way or the other, we'll come through, and when we do, when times get better, there'll be less fools of competitors to compete with. No, this is a time of opportunity, and I don't want you to wreck it all by being terrified when opportunity is staring you in the face.'

Next morning, a letter arrived from Manchester & Salford Bank. Danny opened it, but said nothing.

'What now?' Irene asked.

'It's Winrow. He wants to meet me, Tuesday next.'

'I'm sure he does,' Irene said, dispassionately. 'It doesn't worry you, surely?'

'Damned right it does,' Danny said.

Irene sat on the side of his desk.

'It's not you that should be worried, Danny,' she said. 'It's the bank. Think of it this way. We owe them money. We have the whip hand.'

'But what if they close our facility?'

'We refuse to pay them what we've borrowed already. If they end the facility, they're in breach of contract, and they know it.'

The day before the meeting with the Manchester & Salford, Danny and Irene spent much time in the office, with instructions that they were not to be interrupted. They went through accounts again, and again. Sometimes they checked newspapers, mostly they didn't.

For the most part though, Irene insisted on her own approaches to minimising any crisis Edwardes & Ryan might face. By Sunday evening, she was confident that Danny understood exactly how the crisis could be turned to their own advantage.

Winrow rose to meet him, when he was ushered in.

'Mr. Ryan. Good to meet you again. I hope you won't mind the inconvenience.'

'Of course not,' Danny said. 'We had agreed to meet regularly, so it was no surprise to me. All in the course of normal business.'

And I know damned well that's not what's on your mind, he thought. There's other reasons for this meeting. No need to say that. He waited.

'Indeed,' Winrow went on, 'though it's not just normal business that I was thinking about.'

'The floods, then?'

'And more, Mr. Ryan. I think I can say, the last week has been among the most remarkable in the history of British banking. You may have noticed the turmoil on the Stock Markets.'

'Yes,' Danny answered. 'The drop in the shares of the Royal Bank. They had the highest reputation possible. I couldn't understand how that could go down so far, and so suddenly.'

Let's see how he handles this one, he thought. If the Royal Bank can go so low, the Manchester & Salford can do the same.

'Too true,' Winrow said. 'It turns out though that their position was not as strong as they thought. They had massive amounts of lending to three customers, and that makes any bank vulnerable. It is rumoured that one of the three is not in a position to honour their commitments. It is not our policy to lend as recklessly as that. The Manchester & Salford will never allow itself to be so exposed. Don't misunderstand me though, Mr. Ryan. I have no reason to think Edwardes & Ryan will not honour their obligations. Having said that, you are a substantial customer now, and it is the policy of the board that we should have a good understanding of our top borrowers. Particularly, those in the railway sector.'

So that's it, Danny thought. Railways.

'I know,' he said. 'And I can understand your concern. I am here to help.'

'Excellent,' Winrow said 'Perhaps you better give me a quick run-through of the financial position of Edwardes & Ryan.'

Danny laid a number of sheets of paper on the desk.

'This is a quick summary of our position,' he said. 'As you can see, we continue to be very profitable. We would have been more so, except for costs associated with the floods.'

'Ah yes, the floods.'

'We had to suspend the worksite on the North Staffordshire line, and on two of the other sites. Only for a few days in each case. But we also had to carry out a lot of additional work to minimise the floods. All of this cost money.'

173

'Which you have passed on to your customers no doubt?'

'Roy Anderson was most understanding, so we had no problem there. He allowed for cost over-runs on wages. Tom Brassey though? I wouldn't even ask. Not that I'm a fool. You must understand this, Mr. Winrow, we have a strong reputation for delivering on budget and on time. We are being very closely watched on our Brassey contract. Our competitors on the North Staffordshire feel that we could not possibly carry it out on those terms, but I intend to prove them wrong. It's not just a matter of protecting our good name. Once we have completed the North Staffordshire contract, we will have a reputation far above what anyone would think possible, both with Brassey and with the other big contractors. That is absolutely vital to the future of Edwardes & Ryan. So, while the profit we are showing is excellent, it would be even better if not for the exceptional circumstances of the floods.'

For some time further they continued through the accounts. Then, there was a knock on the door. 'The Credit Committee is ready for you now, Mr. Winrow.'

Winrow left the room. Danny followed. The Credit Committee, he was thinking. Now we'll see what's really on their mind.

When they entered, Winrow joined eight men at one side of the table and Danny sat facing them. The man in the centre, the Chairman, Danny guessed, got down to business straight away.

'Thank you for coming, Mr. Ryan. We're now reviewing our loans outstanding, and that is the reason for your presence.'

'I can understand that, given present circumstances,' Danny replied.

Might as well get that out of the way, he thought. Present circumstances. I know, as well as he knows, that the Manchester & Salford is exposed, no matter what Winrow thinks.

'Indeed,' the Chairman said, uneasily. 'We need to understand that our top borrowers can continue to repay their loans, as and when agreed.'

'Of course,' Danny said.

'So, first we have to understand your accounts. I believe Mr. Winrow has been checking that.'

'Yes,' Winrow said. 'In spite of the floods, the accounts are satisfactory.'

'Excellent,' the Chairman said. 'We've given you an additional facility. Do you feel that will be satisfactory for your commitments?'

'Absolutely,' Danny said. 'The first reason is the contract we hold with Brasseys on the North Staffordshire Line.'

'An excellent endorsement,' one of the other men said. 'You're probably aware that the Manchester & Salford are acting for the North Staffordshire on its next share issue.'

'I wasn't,' Danny said, 'but I know Mr. Brassey would only deal with the best.'

'That's true,' the Chairman said. 'So of this latest facility, how much have you borrowed to date?'

Winrow responded. 'Just a little over two thousand pounds,' he said. 'And from what I see, Mr. Ryan is on time with his contracts. And with his general borrowing facility, though there seems to be no likelihood of that being overdrawn.'

'Why is that?' the Chairman asked.

'Cash control,' Danny answered. 'An important part of our overall cash policy is to extend the payment terms we demand from our suppliers. That is only a minor factor in our cash position though.'

'I see,' the Chairman said. 'So tell me, Mr. Ryan. What is your credit control policy with your clients?'

Danny hesitated. He thought of Irene. What would she say? He might not agree with her on everything, but he was beginning to believe that Edwardes & Ryan was in a stronger position than he had thought.

'Our policy is not so much through enforced credit control. More through the quality of our clients. Brassey already makes staged payments to us as the contract proceeds, and we have every confidence in Brassey. Then there's Roy Anderson. Roy is a good friend and a good client, and we would certainly extend him credit.'

'Yes,' the Chairman said, 'we know Roy very well. Most reliable.'

'He is,' Danny said.

'But that could leave you very vulnerable, having so few customers.'

'I doubt it,' Danny said. 'In any case, the ultimate customers are the railway companies that our direct customers work for, and they are more diversified. Also our intention is to gain more large contracts, with large contractors such as Mackenzie or Peto. Mackenzie has already shown interest in working with Edwardes & Ryan, as Mr. Winrow knows. That is the reason why Brassey's North Staffordshire contract is so vital. We must prove to the entire market that we can handle major contracts, and deliver on budget and on time.'

THE WEEK OF TERROR. Murtybeg travelled to Liverpool to meet with the Workhouse administration. He was more optimistic now about the labour situation. The financial downturn meant that unemployment was increasing. More and more desperate men were entering the Workhouse.

As he reached it, he saw it was just as he had anticipated. There was a crowd outside the gate, larger than before. A number of police were keeping order. When he made his business known, he was admitted at once though.

'Mr. Ryan, you're most welcome,' the clerk said, extending his hand. 'You know we met your brother?'

'I know. I'd heard.'

'As you can see, there's increasing pressure on the resources of the Workhouse, and anything you can do to reduce that would be most welcome.'

'I'd be delighted, of course,' Murtybeg said, 'particularly if you have workers from the west coast of Mayo.'

'Ah yes, Mayo,' the clerk said. 'I think I might have just the man to help you with that.'

He went to the door and opened it.

'Could you tell Mr. Solan to join us now?'

Murtybeg was surprised. Solan! A common enough name in Mayo.

A young man entered. 'This is Dominic Solan,' the clerk said.' This is Mr. Ryan, Dominic. I've told you about him.'

'Yes indeed,' Solan said. 'I'm delighted to meet you, Mr. Ryan.'

Murtybeg recognised the accent at once. 'You're Mayo, I'd say,' he said.

'Right first time. Castlebar to be quite exact.'

'Dominic is highly educated,' the clerk said. 'He only joined us a few months ago, but I can assure you, he knows his business. Perhaps you could explain your specific requirements.'

'Of course,' Murtybeg said. 'We're looking for Mayo men, but only from the far west. In particular, we don't want to hire from East Mayo, where our own people are, and that applies even to Castlebar. We presently have arrangements in train with two of the Workhouses – Westport and Ballinrobe – though they have little enough just now. Hence our interest in the Mayo men you might have in the Workhouse already, or even those trying to get in.'

'But a lot of them are very weak.'

'That's why we feed them well,' Murtybeg said. 'Toughens them up in no time.'

Solan had sat down, and was scribbling fast. 'So how many would you need?'

'A hundred straight away.'

'I'm not sure that we'd have that many West Mayo men, but we might. What about the rest of the West Coast? I'm thinking of Donegal in particular.'

Murtybeg was taken aback by the question.

'In principle, Donegal could work well. The only problem there is that the Irish, as they speak it, is very different to Mayo. We might have difficulties in speaking.'

Solan nodded. 'Yes,' he said, 'I know what you mean.'

The clerk took over again.

'It'll take some hours to organise all this,' he said. 'Could you come back tomorrow morning, say about ten o'clock, and we will have it all ready then. A hundred if we can, we'll see what we can do. Could be two hundred with the women and children.'

Murtybeg looked up in surprise.

'Women and children! We don't have them on the Works.'

'Not as workers,' the clerk said. 'They won't leave their men though. It'd be cruel to separate them.'

'But…that's impossible.'

'Not so hard as you might think. We work them hard enough here. And you don't have to pay them a man's wage.'

Murtybeg shook his head.

'If you say so.'

When Murtybeg left the Workhouse, he walked down towards the Adelphi Hotel. He saw a small crowd outside. A newsboy was shouting –

'Read all about it. Collapse of the Royal Bank.'

Disbelieving, Murtybeg joined the crowd and pushed his way through. He bought a copy of the Liverpool Albion, and pushed back out again. Under the guttering light of a gas lamp, he read the headline – Stoppage of the Royal Bank of Liverpool.

He made his way to the hotel, and booked a room.

'Yes,' the clerk said to him, spotting his newspaper. 'All Liverpool is talking about it.'

'Stopped, they say.' Murtybeg said.

'Stopped, sir? Bankrupt is the real word.'

Murtybeg went to his bedroom and read the article. Suddenly, he stood up. He went down to the front of the hotel, and hired a cab.

'Royal Bank of Liverpool. Do you know where it is?'

'All Liverpool knows where it is now,' the cabbie said. 'Can't tell you how many fares I've had there tonight.'

When they reached Dale Street, he got off and paid the cabbie. Outside the Royal Bank of Liverpool, hundreds of people were milling. Hundreds more were sleeping against the walls, or simply lying down in blankets. It reminded him of a Workhouse, but this was no Workhouse. All along the wall and the windows, notices were pasted up –

'All Payments Suspended'.

Attached to the inside of one of the windows of the bank was a notice.

'The Directors of the Royal Bank of Liverpool regret to have to announce that, owing to the extraordinary pressure of the times, they conceive it to be in the interest of all concerned to suspend the operations of the Bank until the result of the proceedings of a deputation now in London has been ascertained, which will be immediately announced. Monday, 18 October 1847.'

A man in a top hat was reading it closely.

'Can you imagine it?' he said to Murtybeg. 'The Royal Bank. The safest in England, that's what they told us. If the Royal goes, everything will go.'

'I know,' Murtybeg said. He turned away. The cab was gone, and there were no others. He walked all the way back to the Adelphi.

Yes, he thought. Everything can go. What will be next?

Next morning, he walked to the Workhouse. Solan met him.

'We've fulfilled what you requested,' he told Murtybeg.

Murtybeg led the ragged group to the station and loaded them on open wagons. That afternoon, they arrived at the North Staffordshire Railway.

'And amn't I delighted to see you,' Roughneen exclaimed. 'We could do with these fellows.'

'Should I bring them to their shacks?'

'We've not enough yet, so we'll have to squeeze them in tight. We're building more as fast as we can, but, damn it, I never expected, women and children too.'

'The Workhouse insisted we take them.'

'I know. Just tell Danny we'll need a lot more money for timber. I'm using offcuts, but one way or another we'll need well-built shacks before another Brassey inspection.'

It was late when Murtybeg arrived in Stockport. He joined Danny and Irene for dinner.

'You heard about the Royal Bank?' he asked.

'Heard about it,' Danny said, morosely. 'That's yesterday's news. It's worse now.'

'Worse?'

'There's another one followed it. The Liverpool Banking Company have closed their doors.'

'What! Two banks in two days.'

'Yes,' Danny said. 'Two banks. Two Liverpool banks. And now I'm wondering about the Manchester banks. What if it spreads?'

Irene laughed. 'I've been telling him not to worry about it. Just think about it. There was a run on every one of the Liverpool banks and all the others pulled through. So don't worry.'

'But what about the Manchester & Salford?' Murtybeg asked.

'They're far too strong,' she replied.

'They said the same about the Royal. It was supposed to be one of the best in the country, and look what happened.'

'Fine,' Irene said. 'Suppose they collapse. Then they refuse to lend us anymore. What then? We just don't repay what we owe them already. And there's no way they can come after us, since they'll be in breach of contract if they don't lend us on our present facility. I've explained this to Danny already, but I'm not sure he believes it.'

But if Danny was concerned about banks and stock markets, the newspapers shocked him more, as the crisis spread to the railways.

He was reading the Manchester papers next morning.

'My God, Irene,' he exclaimed, 'see this?'

'I told you, you should stop reading papers. What is it this time?'

'The Lancashire & Yorkshire. They've suspended their Works!'

'They've what?'

'Stopped construction. Closed down.'

'So what?'

'Damn it, Irene, Brassey is the leading contractor on the L & Y.'

She grabbed the paper from him. For a while she said nothing. Then she sat down, calmer than before.

'You know, Danny, this could be a great chance for us.'

'What on earth do you mean?'

'Think of it,' she said. 'How far is Burnley from here?'

'Thirty miles.'

'Thirty miles up that road, there's hundreds – thousands – of men, desperate for work. Thrown off the Works, no warning, no nothing.'

'So what are you suggesting?'

'Send Murtybeg to Burnley. Right now.'

'Why on earth would we do that? Can't you see? If the L & Y have suspended their Works, who's next? The North Staffordshire? Then we'd be firing men, not hiring.'

'You're worrying too much, as usual,' she said. 'Just because one line has suspended, that doesn't mean anyone else is going to. Just keep calm, will you?'

Danny slept uneasily that night. Perhaps Irene was right. A single suspension meant nothing.

The next day brought more shocks. More railway lines around Manchester suspended construction.

'Including the London & North Western,' Danny said. 'The biggest of them all. But even worse, the Birkenhead & Cheshire. That's another Brassey contract. They're all far too close for comfort. At this rate there'll soon be no work within a hundred miles of Manchester at all.'

'So what do you suggest?' Irene asked. 'Give up?'

'We can't do that.'

'Look at it this way, so. We've two main clients, Brassey and Andersons.

The North Staffordshire isn't suspended. And Anderson hasn't suspended any of his sites'

'Not yet,' Danny said.

'And maybe not ever.'

'So what are you suggesting?'

'We just keep working,' Irene said. 'With Anderson, we work as normal. Roy is good with payments, and there's nothing to suggest he'll be any different now. Brassey is the key though. We should finish the Brassey contract as soon as we possibly can. He's good on staged payments, Brassey is, so we've nothing to worry about that way. The more we get done, the more cash we get in. It also gives us the chance of finishing well ahead of schedule. And anyhow, if there are closures, we just fire all the men at once. That way we lose nothing.'

'Yes,' Danny said, thoughtfully. 'We just hope we don't get suspended. But in the meantime...'

'In the meantime,' Irene interrupted, 'we take on as many workers as we possibly can. All around us, there's thousands of them, desperate to work for any wage.'

'I doubt they'd work for a shilling a day though.'

'Who knows?'

Danny sent Murtybeg to Burnley.

A few days later, he arrived back.

'How did it go?' Danny asked.

'Pretty well. I got eighty seven. Took them all down to McManus. He seems happy enough now.'

'Fine so, Murteen,' Danny said. 'But from now on, I want you to bring men down to Roughneen, down on the North Staffordshire. It's the Brassey contract that's important now. We've got to get that finished as soon as we can.'

'I'm not sure I can get much more in Burnley.'

Irene interrupted. 'And it's not necessarily Burnley we should be looking at. There's railways suspending operations all around us. It's a matter of going where the navvies are. They're desperate enough right now.'

Murtybeg agreed. 'But there's just one thing I don't understand,' he said. 'What on earth is causing all this?'

'A shortage of cash, pure and simple,' Danny said. 'And from all I can see, there's two main reasons. The first, as it happens, is the Famine back home. I told Irene that. The Government has lent huge sums to the landlords and to Dublin Castle. God knows if they'll get any of it back, but they sure as hell don't have it now. But the Railway Mania only added to that. Thirty million pounds in new investment. Where the devil did they think it was going to come from? Now, when you look back at it, this was bound to happen.'

Danny was stunned at the speed at which the railway market had turned. Still, as Irene said, Edwardes & Ryan were making money. But now they were hiring Irish navvies from all over the country, and at higher wages too. Once again though, it did not worry Irene. The new navvies were not starving, and they were used to hard work on the railways. They were still paying more overall, but Edwardes & Ryan's profits were holding up very well.

The Works suspensions continued on different railways. But still their luck held. There were suspensions on other Brassey sites, but not on the North Staffordshire. There were suspensions on the Manchester South Junction line, but, even here, construction went on at Little Ireland without interruption.

Chapter 13

The Quebec Gazette, September 1847:
The emigrants arrived at this place during the past week have been very numerous. The tales they tell of sorrow, suffering and death are heart-rending and in many cases, less than half the number of individuals constituting a family when they left Ireland, have lived to complete the migration thus far. It is computed – and we fear there are too many good grounds for believing the computation a close approach to truth – that of the immense numbers that left Ireland for Canada during the current season, not one-fourth will be alive at the beginning of the New Year. What a dreadful sacrifice of human life! And for what? Why, that the Irish landlords may escape the payment of Poor Rates!

Daniel Ryan's cousin?

Yes, Luke had admitted it. He looked closely into *Conaire*'s eyes, searching for a reaction. It had already struck him that *Conaire* was a more complex person than he had thought. Did he despise him for being a cousin to such a bitterly ruthless man as Danny? Or did he admire what that kind of ruthlessness could bring?

'Yes,' he said, *'I'm Danny's cousin, and there's damned little I can do about that. Neither of us could choose our parents, could we? But it's not as easy as that. Six years, I worked with Danny on the railways when we were both simple navvies. Even then he was tough, but the other fellows got on with him, and I liked him well enough. No, it was more than that. He was friend as well as family. But then I had to go home to Mayo, and Danny set up as a contractor. As you say, he became a ruthless bastard, hiring men to make money for himself. He's despised for that, and I can see why. I hate him for that myself. But, as his own brother once said to me, Danny feeds people. Pays them too. Damned little, but a hell of a lot more than they'd get in Mayo, that's for sure. Would you prefer to have him or not to have him? If he wasn't hiring men, they'd only be dying in Mayo instead. At least Danny's men had money to send back to Mayo. Not enough, for sure, but it made a difference to those with nothing at all. But still I hate him for all he's done.'*

Conaire observed the sea for some time. Then he said:

'*There was a time I'd agree with you. I'd hate a bastard like that, hate him with all my heart and soul. But not now. Do you know, I've come to the understanding that the only damned thing we Irish are any good at is whining? We bring it on ourselves, wallowing like pigs in a sty, waiting to die. What we need is men with the spirit to go out in the world and make the chances for themselves, and the work for others. Isn't that it?*'

'*I don't know,*' Luke said. '*You're being very hard on people. There was nothing they could do about the Hunger, nothing at all.*'

'*And that's where you're wrong,*' Conaire said.

Luke said nothing more. Again, he leant on the rail, thinking. Why was he so surprised by *Conaire*? He had thought of *Conaire* as a victim, but now he was seeing the exact opposite. A man who no longer cared about Mayo. A man who might go far in life. Who knew?

But what did he think himself? His mother? His father? And most of all, Winnie? Could he see them as nothing but whiners?

And the death pit in Knockanure? Were the dead guilty of their own deaths? He could never think that way. Could he?

Conaire had scorned him when he found out that Luke himself had been a ganger on the Relief Works in the mountains. Should he feel guilty or proud of what he had done there? A hard question. Still it did not mean that he would have to despise his own people for their own weaknesses.

So was *Conaire* a friend? Luke knew they were committed to being together, for the next months at any rate. Best try to get on with him in that time. Could he persuade him he was wrong though?

Or was he right?

He rose early. It had been impossible to sleep because of the groaning of an old man, all through the night. He made his way to the stern. It was still dark, with a hint of light in the east as it came to dawn. He could just see a group of rocks, at the end of which there was a revolving light. As the sun slowly rose, he could see a chain of hills to the south. By the time it was fully light, they were passing a village of white houses around a small church. A saw-mill stood next to a pier, where ships were being loaded with lumber.

The Centaurus passed through the channel between the light-buoys and the rocks. There was an island on the north, a chain of hills visible to the south. Then small islets. Then they saw vessels lying at anchor. At last, they anchored alongside another ship. Luke squinted against the sun to see the name and port painted on the stern.

The Robert Peel. Liverpool.

Behind it he could see a larger island.

Grosse Île.

As they passed the Robert Peel, Luke saw three boats being rowed away from it. Two of them were crushed tight with people sitting and standing. The third was piled with corpses.

'And there's a real coffin ship,' Tyler said. 'The poor fellows alive are going to the hospital, or to quarantine, God knows how many will get out of either. And the other boat – it's going straight to the graveyard. There'll be more left inside the ship too.'

The first two boats had reached the island. Luke could see sailors carrying the patients over the rocks, as others scrambled to follow them.

The boat with the corpses went to the far end of the island where it joined a queue of boats waiting to offload. At the head of the queue, there were men manhandling the corpses into horse drawn wagons.

Where the corpses were being brought ashore, fir trees grew in profusion. The grey of the rock, the green of the trees and the blue of the sky formed a picture of tender beauty. Luke thought of Mayo on another sun-drenched day – the day of the Lucan evictions. Misery then, misery now.

He heard the rattle of chains as the anchor dropped. Within moments, the sailors were swarming over the rigging, rolling the sails under the yards, from the masts out to the yardarms.

He went below. All was activity. Water was being sluiced over the floor between the bunks, even as some passengers still lay on their beds in fever.

Tyler spotted him.

'Luke, in the name of God, where have you been? I can't look after everything. Will you take over here? Make sure they clean it well, we've a medical inspection coming. I'll be upside if you want me, we've got to swab down the decks.'

Now the people looked to Luke for direction. The mess, mixed in with straw put him in mind of the Workhouses and quarantine sheds back in Mayo. No time to think of that.

Conaire came over.

'Ever the ganger, eh?'

Luke was angry. 'What the hell else do you expect me to do? There's medical fellows coming, and this place has to be clean. Otherwise we'll never get into Quebec, let alone the rest of Canada.'

'Fine so,' Conaire said, with derision in his voice. 'What should I do?'

'It would be useful if you could find more buckets. Shovels too. When they've swept this into piles, we need to start taking the mess up, and throwing it overboard.'

When the buckets and shovels arrived, he himself started shovelling. He felt better working. How many years had he shovelled like this back on the

184

railways? Yes, earning money then, not risking his health and life on a fever ridden ship.

He followed some of the passengers up the ladder, carrying stinking buckets of muck. He tipped it over the edge of the ship which was already streaked with the trail of the many bucket loads which had already been thrown over.

When the muck and shit had been cleared, the decks, inside and out, were swabbed down with lye.

Many of the sails had been rolled. The lower parts of the rigging were already draped with bed linen and clothes hanging out to dry.

A small boat came out from the island, four oarsmen working it. At the back, a man in a leather coat steered the boat. Within a few minutes it was alongside. The man boarded. Then all the passengers were told to return to the lower decks. They waited in the semi-darkness.

At length a sailor came down, carrying a whale oil hurricane lamp. He was followed by the man from the boat.

'God, how this place stinks.'

He walked around the passenger decks, examining each of the patients closely. He stopped at one bunk, and opened a man's eyelid.

'This one is dead. Take him out.'

Then the passengers were instructed to go up the ladder. When Luke and *Conaire* came back into the open air, they joined a growing crowd of passengers, and stood waiting on the deck.

'*Must be a doctor, that fellow,*' *Conaire* commented.

'*I'm sure you've the right of it.*'

After some time, the doctor came up, and the passengers were asked to form a line. Now he examined each passenger more closely. He looked closely at Luke, and then waved him past. He stopped *Conaire*, asked him to hold out his tongue, looked at it closely and then waved him past too.

They were both directed to a group of passengers close to the mainmast. Others were being sent to a smaller group towards the stern. Some in the second group might have been feverish, though Luke could not be certain. He could see all in their own group were healthy, even if many of them were thin.

They were standing close to the six corpses, which smelt strongly of gangrene and corruption.

A man in the other group collapsed. The doctor returned, and opened his eyelids. 'Take him back down,' he said. Two sailors went to lift him. The woman beside him threw her arms around him.

'*No, no, no. Wake up, Eoin. In the name of God, wake up, wake up.*'

The sailors separated them, and held the woman back, still screaming, as the man's limp body was taken below.

The doctor filled in two forms, and signed each. Tyler took the forms and handed them separately to two sailors, who were instructed to lead each group.

Then, the procedure was finished. The doctor returned to the boat, and the oarsmen started to pull away.

Luke saw that three other boats had come alongside. Cautiously, the group at the stern were sent down into the boats, which pulled away in the direction of the island. Still, the woman screamed.

After landing on the island, the boats came back to the ship again, and the process was repeated. When they came back a third time, they began to load the group at the mainmast, but Tyler held Luke back.

'I'll still need you,' he said. 'And you too,' to *Conaire*.

For the next hour, Luke watched as the boats passed between the ship and the island. At length, the group was gone, but still Tyler held Luke and *Conaire* back.

'*And I know why you and I are being held,*' *Conaire* said, nodding to the rick of corpses.

'*Right again,*' Luke said.

Now only one boat returned from the shore, two men rowing. An officer and a passenger sat at the front. When it arrived alongside, only the passenger boarded the ship. A priest.

'Luke,' Tyler said. 'Will you take this gentleman below?'

'*Good luck,*' *Conaire* said.

The priest shook Luke's hand. 'Bernard McGauran.'

'Luke Ryan, Father.'

'Well, come on, Luke. We'd best get this job done.'

Luke descended the ladder, the priest following. Luke was horrified to see there were still many men, women and children lying on the bunks, some clearly in fever.

As they reached the bottom, the priest gagged.

'I'm sorry, Luke,' he said. 'No matter how often I do this, I can never get used to it.'

'I'm well used to it, Father, after all this time aboard.'

The priest took his bag and pulled out his vestments. Luke helped him to dress.

Beside them, an old woman was mumbling incoherently. Fr. McGauran handed Luke a small jar.

'Here, hold this.'

He made the sign of the cross over her. Then he dabbed the chrism on her forehead.

He absolved her.

'*Per istam sanctam Unctionem...*'

Through this Holy Unction, may the Lord free you from sin, and raise you up on the Last Day.

At the next bunk was a young woman. She was conscious but desperately thin.

'Father...' she said.

'My child.'

'To come all this way...'

'I know. I know.'

Luke recognised her accent.

'County Mayo?' he asked.

'Kilmeena,' she said. 'Just beside Westport. And wasn't I the right eejit, not to travel from Westport?'

The priest and Luke made their way on around the bunks. Many of the patients were unconscious. Where they were fully conscious, Luke and the priest spent a few minutes with each, talking gently, sometimes in English, most often in Irish. For some, the priest heard their confession.

Luke realised he was seeing the outline of the west of Ireland, from Donegal, through Sligo, Mayo, Roscommon, Galway, Clare and on down to Kerry and Cork.

'And you'd wonder why they didn't come out through Cork,' the priest said. 'Not so far as walking to Dublin and crossing to Liverpool. But the Cork ships had a terrible name as coffin ships.'

'They could hardly have been worse than Liverpool,' Luke observed.

They went on.

'*Per istam sanctam Unctionem...*'

Repeated again and again and again.

Luke thought of Croghancoe and another priest absolving the dying and the dead. Then he was trembling violently as the terror gripped him.

The priest looked up in alarm.

'Are you all right, Luke?'

Luke shook himself.

'Yes, I'm fine,' he said. The trembling stopped.

At length, the absolutions were finished. The priest disrobed himself, and Luke followed him up the ladder. Tyler came over.

'How many now, Luke?'

'A hundred and thirty one.'

Tyler organised two sailors and a stretcher. The sailors swore vociferously in French, but went down with the stretcher, and brought the corpses topside to join those outside. Then all were loaded into the waiting boat.

Tyler handed Luke an envelope. 'Your wages. Four pounds, six shillings Canadian.'

Luke's eyes lit up.

'And you don't have to worry,' Tyler said. 'I've worked it out exactly, right to the penny. Made sure to give you the full amount. Not that the captain liked it, but he'd only spend it on rum. Now I'll give you one word of advice. Get it into a bank as soon as you can. The best one is the Bank of British North America. Anyone in Quebec will direct you to it.'

He shook hands with Luke.

'And I'll see the pair you in a week or two.'

'Are you not going straight to Quebec?' Luke asked.

'With this lot!' Tyler said, nodding towards the hatch. 'No, we won't be let out of quarantine that fast.'

Luke, *Conaire* and the priest scrambled down to the boat.

The boat was heavy now. Luke and *Conaire* were put to a pair or oars. They pulled away from the Centaurus.

'County Mayo, is it, Luke?' the priest asked.

'You're quick, Father. Mayo right enough. Close to Kilduff. And *Conaire* here is a Mayo man too. And yourself?'

'Cavan, for my sins. At the edge of Corglass Lough.'

'Been over long?'

'Twenty years at least. And I've never seen anything like this. Not even when the cholera came to Quebec in '32.'

They reached the island.

The officer instructed Luke and *Conaire* to assist in carrying the corpses ashore, where a driver waited with a horse and cart.

'*Light enough too,*' Luke commented, as they lifted a corpse.

'*He's still got enough fever to pass on and kill a man,*' Conaire said.

'*Or two men,*' Luke added, scathingly.

They carried it to the cart and piled the corpse up, as the priest gave it absolution. Then Luke and *Conaire* went back to the boat for more of the dead. Again and again.

At last, they finished, and followed the priest and the cart. They went on a rough track, and then through a group of buildings, passing the hospital, still under construction. Beyond the buildings was a graveyard.

'This is the Western Cemetery,' the priest told them. 'They call it the Irish Graveyard. Only the doctors and the clergy get buried beside the churchyards.'

Luke saw the pile of roughly-cut coffins. Beside them was a mass grave, Luke reckoned. He could see the side of coffins already buried, three deep, with no more than a few inches of clay on top. And always, the rats. He was trembling again, but no-one noticed. Soon, it died away.

They loaded the bodies into the coffins and helped lower them into the grave. Luke looked at the trees around him. He recognised them all, from the time his father had pointed them out to him in Carrigard, Fir, birch, beech, and ash. No oak.

Fungi grew on decayed stumps, between carpets of wild flowers.

When all the coffins had been put into the ground, Luke, *Conaire* and the priest left the others shovelling clay on top.

'It's terrible here,' Luke said.

'It is,' the priest replied, 'but it was worse a few months back. May, June, July, that was the nightmare. See the pile of canvas over there? They were the tents, we've taken them down now, there's no more call for them. The fever sheds are shut too. All the patients were sent into the hospital. That's nearly complete now. There's many patients in there. And the healthy ones held in quarantine – like yourselves – you go into the sheds at the eastern end.'

Again, they went past the buildings, but this time continued through the woods up through the island, passing the military barracks, where soldiers marched and wheeled in formation.

Through the woods again. Then there were rows of sheds, a dozen perhaps, Luke reckoned. They were timber built, windows along the front, with smaller gables with louvers projecting in places from the roof.

'And where will we be staying?' Luke asked.

'In here.'

Luke stopped. 'A fever shed? It looks well built for that.'

'Come, come. Don't be alarming yourself. These aren't fever sheds. These are for the healthy passengers.'

'So there's no fever here?'

'None,' the priest said. 'Or not much anyhow. Nothing like what you've been used to shipboard.'

Luke and *Conaire* were allocated beds beside each other.

'*And a bit better than the bunks on the* Centaurus,' *Conaire* commented.

'*That wouldn't be hard*,' Luke said. '*Now I've need of a needle and thread.*'

'*Don't we all?*'

Luke walked away. A few minutes later, he came back, with a needle and a spool of thread.

'A decent woman gave it to me. I promised her a farthing for the thread.'

He sat on the other side of the bunk, and removed his trousers. Carefully, he checked that the money was still inside his pocket. Then he stitched up the pocket, and over-stitched it. No one had noticed.

Conaire borrowed the needle and thread. When he was finished, Luke returned them to their owner.

Afterwards, he took the pillow off his bunk, replaced it with his pack, and slept through the rest of the afternoon, evening and the night until he was woken up by a call of 'breakfast'.

'Bread and oatmeal,' Conaire noted.

'Better than on the Centaurus,' Luke answered. *'At least there's no weevils.'*

As they ate, one of the servers came and sat with them.

'Well lads, ye're looking healthy enough. Strong too.'

'I don't know about that,' Luke said.

'Don't worry. If ye're not, we'll soon strengthen you up. They're looking for workers for erecting tents.'

'Tents!' Luke echoed. 'I thought you were finished with tents.'

'So we were. Have ye seen the number of ships just come in. Must be dozens of them. End of season, all rushing to make it in in time.'

'Are they that bad?' Luke asked.

'Worse than bad. There's two just in – one from Glasgow, one from Liverpool – and they're among the worst we've seen. We've had to take some of the poor wretches into the sheds here, and them not even being able to stand up.'

'Hold on,' Luke said. 'I thought these weren't fever sheds.'

'They weren't. They are now.'

Luke thought of what the priest had said only the previous day. It seemed his comments on everything getting better were a little hasty.

'So how long is it since the tents were all pulled down?'

'About a week. We thought it was over.'

Luke made to speak, but *Conaire* put a hand on his arm.

'What's he been saying?' he asked Luke.

'They're looking for men for erecting the tents again.'

'And how much are they paying?' Conaire asked. *'Or had you not thought of asking that.'*

'I hadn't. I'll ask him.'

During the conversation with *Conaire*, Luke had noticed that the other man did not seem to understand Irish.

'My friend here was asking how much we'd get paid for working on the tents.'

'God, he's quick, isn't he. A shilling a day Canadian, that's what they're paying. The same as we're getting here. Are ye interested or not?'

'We are,' said Luke. 'But tell me this. Would we earn enough for the cost of a letter back to Ireland?'

'Ye might.'

'And what of a post office?'

'There's plenty of them in Quebec.'

'What of the Island?'

'I don't know,' the man said. 'They've some class of postal service here for the medical fellows and the officers. I wouldn't risk it though. If you put cash in a letter, it most certainly would not arrive in Ireland. And even without the cash, the post would be expensive enough, and I wouldn't be sure that they wouldn't take your money, and have the letter disappear before it even gets to Quebec. No, best to wait 'till you get to the city, then write your letter as soon as you find a post office.'

'Fine so,' Luke said.

'Good. Now when you're finished your breakfast, I'll take you over to your ganger.'

'*I understood that word,*' *Conaire* said to him.

'*I thought you might,*' Luke said.

Sometime later, another man came to their table.

'Bob tells me you're interested in working.'

'We are,' Luke said.

'Well, come with me so.'

Again, they walked most of the length of the island back to the Irish burial ground.

'So where have ye lads come from?' the ganger asked.

'We're both Mayo. We came by way of Liverpool on the Centaurus.

The ganger stopped, and grabbed Luke by the arm.

'A Mayo man! And you came by Liverpool!'

'What else could I do?'

'Go through Westport.'

Luke laughed.

'Westport? That would have been pricier. Only the rich go through Westport.'

'And what of that? You wouldn't be here if you had, that's for certain. Nor would you have been on a floating charnel house like the Centaurus. Good Christ, I had to go through Liverpool, no choice, but you – you had a choice.'

'So what's so special about Westport?' Luke asked.

'Clean ships. Proper ships. The Dewdrop earlier in the summer, everyone talked about that. Crossed the Atlantic and through quarantine without losing a soul. And I saw the Grace out of Westport too after I'd arrived. That wasn't even stopped at quarantine, straight through to Quebec. Or Montreal perhaps. But a man like you, you had the choice and you risked your life on a coffin ship instead.'

191

Luke thought back to when he had been leaving Mayo.

'Not as much of a choice as you might think. Like I say, the Westport ships were expensive. Killala too. I thought it better to go to Liverpool, and leave the money with my family. God knows, they'll need it enough with the shortage of potatoes.'

When they arrived, Luke was surprised at the size of the tents. Many had already been erected. They were put in with three other men, and quickly learnt the system. They worked for some hours, until a break was called for food. Bread and water. They sat with the other three.

'*So where have you come from?*' one of the men asked.

'*Mayo. We came over on the* Centaurus *by way of Liverpool, and our ganger friend doesn't seem to think much of that.*

'*I wouldn't blame him. We just heard tell of that. Bad, was it?*'

'*Damned bad,*' said Luke. '*There's worse, I hear. Not many I'd say.*'

'*Ours was one. Myself and my brothers, we came over with the* Virginius, *and a more accursed ship you never saw. Left* Liverpool *with five hundred men, women and children in May. Two months on the Great Ocean, and a hundred dead every month. What do you think of that?*'

'*I'd heard things were bad,*' Luke said. 'The Robert Peel...'

'*Another* Liverpool *ship. But by Christ I'll tell you, the* Virginius *was worse, a living Hell. Hardly anyone able to get off the ship without being carried, that's how bad it was. And another hundred dead in Grosse Île. My brothers and myself, we were the lucky ones.*'

'*Ye're looking well enough,*' Luke said.

'*We're only a short time off that god damned ship. But we're recovered well, and fed better.*'

'*So what part of Ireland...?*'

'*County Roscommon. Town of* Strokestown. Denis Mahon, *he was our landlord. Cleared the whole lot of us out. Thousands of people, I've no idea how many. Then we had to march across Ireland, and take the cattle boat to* Liverpool. The Virginius *was waiting, do you see.* Mahon *had paid our passage on it and all, he did. All the way to* Quebec. *Decent fellow, you might say, but it shows how desperate he was to get rid of the lot of us. And on a hellhole of a ship like that. Someone should kill that son-of-a-bitch.*'

Abruptly, *Conaire* stood.

'*I'm sick of hearing this,*' he said, voice raised. '*Ye'll be going on about it to the end of time. Can you not leave it rest?*'

The three brothers looked at him in astonishment.

'*I'm sorry,*' the first said. '*I didn't mean to be upsetting you. Would you not think we should kill* Mahon, *is that it?*'

'*It's not that at all,*' Conaire replied. '*Look at this,*' he said, gesturing across the river. 'Quebec. *Or the rest of* Canada. *Whatever ye suffered, the landlord has given you all that.*'

Luke had stood. He put his hand on *Conaire*'s shoulders.

'*Hold it there,*' he said.

Conaire stood away, angry.

'*No, I will not hold it. It's what none of us Irish will ever understand. No one's interested in all this nonsense.*'

One of the brothers stood. '*Nonsense…?*'

'*Yes,*' said *Conaire*, '*and you can hit me if you like, but I'm still right. That's the trouble about the Irish, we go on suffering, and griping about our suffering to the end of time. Look, you're in a new country, in a few weeks you'll be in* Quebec. *A man must take his chances and stop looking to the past and whimpering like an infant.*'

The other man sat.

'*By God, you're a strange fellow.*'

On Sunday, Luke and *Conaire* attended Mass with the others. They both stood up for communion, as the priest gave out the communion wafer to the long line of communicants.

'*Corpus Christi.*' Body of Christ.

'*Corpus Christi.*'

'*Corpus Christi.*'

After Mass, they stood outside smoking pipes.

'*You're a religious man anyhow,*' Luke said to *Conaire*.

'*I don't have to leave everything behind.*'

After a while, the priest came over to them.

'Luke, isn't it?'

'Yes Father.'

'All well?'

'Good and bad,' Luke replied. 'We're sleeping and eating down at the healthy sheds. Yesterday we were setting up tents down by the Irish cemetery. I'd not expected that.'

'Ah yes,' the priest said. 'I'd heard of that. We've big numbers coming in again. Sometimes I think it will never end. The ships are making a desperate dash out of Cork, Liverpool, Glasgow and everywhere to try to get up the river in time. God knows, some of them are in a dreadful state, and there's dozens of them, as you can well see. There's desperate pressure on us all. The most heart-breaking are the orphans and it's hard to find anyone to mind them. But our brethren in Quebec are trying to sort that problem. The churches are offering the people in Quebec twenty shillings a month and a clothing allowance for each orphan they take into their care. An excellent idea, you might think, but the chief problem is to find relatives or friends of the children in Quebec, and, God knows, that's not easy.'

Sunday or not, Luke and *Conaire* had to work that afternoon. The ganger brought them back down the east end of the island again, where they were put to work, cleaning the ditch beside the cemetery, which stank. After some hours, they were brought up and into the cemetery to dig mass graves and bury more coffins, shovelling more clay on top. As they walked back to the other end of the island that night, Luke saw the tents were already full.

After a few days, they were transferred to the wharf, where rock-filling was being carried out to extend the dock. It was backbreaking labour, which put Luke in mind of English railways. He noted that *Conaire* was becoming stronger, and working harder than he had before. He thought of the lumber mills and the forests. Perhaps it would all be possible for both of them.

One morning, the doctors came to the sheds and started checking the people. Luke and *Conaire* stood in line, and were asked which ship they had been on. When they indicated the Centaurus, they were sent back in. Most of the rest of the people in the sheds joined a growing crowd outside. Looking through the windows, Luke estimated it at hundreds strong. After a few hours they started moving down to the sea, where boats were waiting to take them off to a steamer.

Luke could see Fr. McGauran at the boats, blessing each group as they pulled away. After some hours, the loading was completed and the steamer pulled away up river. The Centaurus people were allowed out. As the priest came back up the track, Luke went over to him.

'What was that, Father? Where are they going?'

'Montreal, God help them. They're supposed to be the healthy ones. And enough of them are, perhaps, but I reckon there are some there with fever. But we haven't room enough here for everyone, so they have to go. All we're doing is sending fever up river. They'll be dying before they even reach Montreal, poor devils, and once they bring them into the Emigrant Hospital, they'll be dying even faster.'

'Where's that?' Luke asked.

'*Pointe St. Charles*. It's a class of an infirmary in Montreal. And it's in a desperate state, I can tell you. I've been hearing stories of it all summer. It's not a place I'd want to go. Sheds, that's all they are. They say there's hundreds dying. The nurses and the nuns, they've been dying at a terrible rate. Doctors too. Just like here. And it's not just the Irish, neither. Everywhere the emigrants go – Quebec, Montreal and further – they bring fever with them. The local people don't like it very much. There's strong feeling against the Irish in many towns in the Canadas.'

Next morning, Luke and *Conaire* were brought out to the Centaurus, together with most of the rest of the Centaurus passengers on Grosse Île. They were paid five shillings each as they left.

When they arrived, Tyler greeted Luke on the deck.

'I wasn't sure I'd see you again,' he told him.

'I wasn't sure either. We didn't know if the ship would wait.'

'Oh, they wouldn't let us out that fast. Had to wait for most of them to die. We're a clean ship now.'

Minutes later he heard the sound of the anchor being weighed. He walked back along the side to the capstan. Then the anchor was aboard.

'What now?' Luke asked.

'That's it' Tyler said. 'That's the end of Grosse Île for us, we're heading to Quebec.'

Luke and *Conaire* glanced at each other. 'That's it?' Luke echoed.

'Didn't I tell you we're a clean ship now? Just give thanks to the Almighty, and we'll have you in Quebec in no time. But you'd better shave first.'

Luke and *Conaire* went down, and shaved in cold seawater. Later they were back on the outer deck.

The Centaurus sailed on, passing between more ships. Many boats were going forward and back from shore to ship. Then Grosse Île lay behind them.

They passed churches surrounded by cottages and fields. At another village there were houses painted white, with red roofs and yellow doors. More islands and villages followed, until they dropped anchor as darkness came.

After only a few hours, the Centaurus was moving again. As a red dawn brightened over the St. Lawrence, they dropped anchor again.

Quebec.

Chapter 14

Morning Post Correspondent in Montreal, October 1847:
The number of emigrants arrived in this country during the past summer has probably exceeded 100,000; but owing to the awful visitation of disease and death amongst them, that number has been already, and is likely to be still further, fearfully reduced before the closing of the approaching winter. It is supposed that, at least 10,000 deaths have occurred on the passage out, at Grosse Île and at Quebec; while the deaths at Montreal and other places in Lower Canada have probably averaged 500 a week, or 2,000 a month, and may be fairly stated in round numbers at 8,000 souls. If 18,000 human beings have fallen victims to the fearful malady of typhus before reaching the Upper Province, it is not unlikely that the deaths in Western Canada have not fallen much below, if indeed they have not exceeded, the average numbers that have perished in the Eastern section of the province, so that we may safely estimate the total amount of mortality at from 35,000 to 45,000 souls – a frightful picture of disease, death and destitution to be presented by a colony like this.

Luke found it impossible to count the number of ships in the harbour. Quebec sparkled in the early morning sun – the domes and spires of its churches standing high above the city. He could see many docks, similar to Liverpool. He could also see ponds with floating timber. He watched closely, wondering which forests they might have come from.

A six oar rowing boat came alongside, a union jack at the stern. Two men scrambled up to the deck. Luke and *Conaire* watched from a distance.

Tyler came on deck with the captain, holding his arm. One of the men presented them with a sheaf of documents. The captain signed where Tyler indicated. The second man examined a few of the passengers, went down the hatch to examine the passenger decks, and came back. More papers were taken out and signed.

Tyler dragged the captain back towards his cabin. Within moments the rowing boat pulled away, and the anchor on the Centaurus was weighed once more. For another hour the ship tacked into the wind, and at last it edged into dock. A gangplank was lowered.

'*Quick, let's get back, and get our packs before they disappear,*' Conaire said.

'*A good idea that.*'

They fought their way down to the passenger deck against the flow of passengers. They slung their packs over their shoulders, scrambled up again, and joined the queue edging towards the gangplank.

Tyler came alongside.

'Well, this is goodbye, Luke. I hope you get on well in Canada.'

'You too,' Luke said. 'I'll think of you every time I see whales.'

Tyler laughed. He shook hands with both Luke and *Conaire*, and returned to the sails.

Luke could see many men milling on the dock.

'*Looks a bit like* Liverpool,' he said to *Conaire*.

'*How's that?*'

'*See all the runners. Watch out for the scum. They know well – a fool and his money are soon parted.*'

'*But how…*'

'*They'll tell you of their brother who runs a boarding-house. Then they pick up your bags, and you have to follow them. If you're lucky you end up with lodgings twice the going rate.*'

'*And if you're not?*'

'*You get a knock on your head down some back alleyway, and your pack and money disappear.*'

They were at the bottom of the gangplank.

'*Now, just hold your sack tight and follow me.*'

They pushed through the crowd and walked a good hundred yards away.

Among the passengers disembarking was a woman with two children. She balanced a trunk on one shoulder, staggering as she descended the gangway. Her two children carried another trunk between them. All three were hollow-cheeked. Luke noticed that the girl was almost bald on the top of her head except for the growth of hair on the side of her face, clear evidence of starvation.

As the woman came to the bottom of the gangplank, she tottered and fell. At once, two men came to assist her, and stood her up. There was a hurried discussion, then the two men took the two trunks, leading the woman and her two children along.

'*Runners, for sure,*' Luke said. '*I wonder what'll happen now.*'

'*Depends on what's in the trunks, I suppose,*' Conaire said. '*God protect her.*'

More people had disembarked and a mêlée developed as the runners tried to get closest to those with trunks.

'No sign of fever anyhow,' Luke said.

'No. I'd guess most of those would be dead on the island. I'll tell you though, this lot look thin enough.'

An argument had developed between some of the passengers and the runners. A fight started.

'Come on,' Luke said. 'Let's get to hell out of here.'

'So what do we do now?' Conaire asked. 'Last night was bitter cold. Another night like that, and we'll wake up dead.'

'Don't you be worrying about it,' Luke said. 'By this evening we'll be wrapped up in warm blankets in good beds.'

'I'm not sure I believe you, but even if I did, the question is – whose beds?'

'We'll work that out as we go along,' Luke said, hefting the strap of his pack onto his shoulder. 'Come on, let's have a look at this town. It's one way of keeping warm.'

Further along the docks, they passed many stacks of squared timber, more being erected.

'Good looking timber, I'd say,' Luke said. 'And a lot of it too.'

'Them fellows would know about working the forests so. Maybe we should talk to them.'

Luke walked up to the gang of men at the timber stacks.

'We're just wondering where we'd find boarding houses in this town?'

One of the men replied angrily in a language that Luke did not recognise, but guessed was French.

They walked on.

'What now?' Conaire asked.

'Let's see if we can find our way into the centre of the town.'

They left the docks, and continued towards the buildings in the distance. The weight of their packs began to tell on them.

Conaire stopped.

'Maybe we should ask someone now?'

'There may be a better way than that,' Luke said.

'What's that?'

'Somewhere in this town we've got friends.'

'Have we?'

'We have. The only thing is, they don't know it yet. All we've got to do is tell them.'

'So how the devil...?'

'Look, think it through, will you. We're Irish. How many Irish are there in this town?'

'Thousands.'

'The first question is – where do all these Irish people live? The second is – where do they drink? Look over. See the bar there? Do you see the name over the door?'

'I do, but if you're a decent man you might read it to me.'

'Thomas Ruane.'

'Ruane?'

'Aye. A rare enough name, but common enough in the east part of Mayo. What say you there's Mayo men here?'

'Sure there's Mayo men everywhere.'

'Come on, let's try it.'

Inside there was a thick, stinking fug of tobacco smoke. He waited a few seconds while his eyes adjusted to the darkness. He saw a long bar, groups of men leaning against it or standing beside it. A few tables lined the wall. Silence fell as they entered, but the hum of conversation and laughter started again soon enough.

They walked down the length of the bar. Luke looked to right and left, as if searching for someone. He listened intently to the voices, trying hard to place the accents. He stopped beside a group of four men with tankards of beer in front of them. Mayo – he was certain of it. He listened more closely. It was centre or east, certainly not west. He pushed behind one of them, waiting as the barman came over.

'Two pints of beer,' he said, placing a coin on the counter. The barman looked at him cautiously, then took the coin, and went to pour the beer. The group had gone silent.

Then one of them spoke. 'Well, what part are you from?'

'Ireland,' Luke replied, feigning innocence.

'Damn it, I know that. What part of Ireland?'

'The same as yourselves, I'm guessing,' said Luke. 'County Mayo, where else?'

One of the men snorted. 'By God, he's a sharp one too.'

'Well, come on,' another said. 'What part of Mayo?'

'Kilduff.'

'Kilduff!' one of the men exclaimed. 'Hey Tommy. We've a Kilduff fellow here.'

The barman returned with the beer.

'Kilduff! Well by God...'

'You're Kilduff yourself, are you?' Luke asked.

'Not quite. Turlough, but I've cousins in Kilduff, or I used to, more like. You know the Roughneens?'

'Didn't I work with them in England,' Luke replied.

'You're better informed than I am so. I haven't heard tell of them in twenty years now. How are they doing, do you know?'

'Not so badly,' Luke replied. 'Johnny Roughneen. Would you know him?'

'He'd be some kind of cousin to me, though how close I don't know.'

'Johnny is working over in England, some class of ganger on the railways. Keeps sending his money back to Kilduff, or so I understand.'

'Enough for them to keep body and soul together?'

'Enough to keep the hunger off anyhow,' Luke replied, 'though I don't know about the fever. It's the real killer.'

'Fever and famine, they always go well together.'

'So what about yourselves?' Luke asked. 'Where are ye from?'

'Turlough too,' the first man answered. 'All of us are from Turlough.'

'Just beside Castlebar, isn't it?'

'It is. You know it?'

'No, though I've passed through it often enough.'

'What're they saying,' Conaire asked.

'Just telling me where they're from,' Luke replied. 'Turlough, they're saying, just next to Castlebar.'

'Be careful,' the barman said. 'We don't allow Irish to be spoken in this bar.'

'You don't!' Luke said, astounded.

'Causes too much trouble. There are Quebec fellows drink in this bar. French speakers, the most of them. Dockers, woodcutters and the like. They reckon the Irish have caused all the fever. Blame us for everyone who dies. Speaking Irish only annoys them. God knows, there's enough fighting between the Irish and the Quebecers as it is. And if we call the peelers too often, they'll close us down.'

'What's he saying?' Conaire asked.

'I'll tell you later,' Luke said. He switched back to English. 'So ye must have been Irish speakers though.'

'It's long enough since we spoke it, and glad enough not to,' one of the men said. 'Remember that, lads? Couldn't stop speaking it fast enough, could we?'

'Dead right, Jack,' the barman said. 'There's no need speaking Irish in this town. French maybe, but there's no thought for Irish. It's English this fellow should be speaking.'

'What's he saying?' Conaire asked.

'He's saying you must speak English,' Luke replied in English.

Conaire looked at him, slightly puzzled.

'Speak…English?' he said, uncertainly.

'Yes,' Luke said. 'English.'

'That's right,' the man called Jack said. 'Keep trying, and you'll learn it soon enough.' He raised a glass. 'Here's to English,' he said.

Conaire raised his glass. Luke could see the fury in his eyes, but held his finger to his own lips. *Conaire* said nothing.

'So how was your own journey?' the barman asked.

'Bloody hell,' Luke said. 'A hundred and thirty dead on the journey, and more in Grosse Île.'

'And a damned awful place that is,' Jack said. 'Wasn't even there when we came over.'

'So what ship were you on, in the name of Christ?' the barman asked.

'The Centaurus, sailing out of Liverpool.'

'Never heard of it,' the barman said.

'I have,' Jack said. 'Bad condition, right enough, from all I hear. How long did you spend in quarantine?'

'Two weeks, I'm guessing,' Luke answered. 'It's easy to lose track of time, though. And any of us who were healthy, we were put to work on the island.'

'You saw the cemeteries, did you?' Jack asked. 'They're pretty rough, from all accounts.'

'Not as bad as you might think,' Luke replied. 'Mayo's worse.'

He thought of the mass grave at Knockanure Workhouse, but he knew if he mentioned it, the trembling might start again.

The barman was washing tankards. He turned back to Luke.

'We've heard Liverpool is a rough town.'

'Yes' Luke said. 'Liverpool is a damned rough town.'

'An Irish town too,' Jack said.

'And a fever town,' Luke said. 'And not just in the docks either.'

Yes. We've heard stories of that.'

'So what of Quebec?' Luke asked.

'There's fever here, right enough,' Jack told him. 'They keep them in the Emigrant Hospital. Hundreds dead, mainly Irish, but many local people, and that's where the hatred springs from. But from all we hear, nothing like Montreal. Our countrymen, most don't stay around Quebec, they head up to Montreal, by boat, or walking, any which way they can, spreading fever as they go. Montreal doesn't want them, but what can they do? They can't keep them out, but they don't like it, I can tell you. They've another Emigrant Hospital there. Dreadful place, I believe. They hate the Irish in Montreal.'

'I can understand that,' Luke said. 'Fever alarms everyone. I've heard of the hospital in Montreal. There was a priest out at Grosse Île told us about it.'

'And he should know,' the other man said. 'There's been an awful lot of them fellows died too. Priests, nuns, medical people, the lot.'

Conaire had said nothing. Luke could still see the anger in his eyes.

'*Later*,' he whispered in Irish. '*I'll tell you later.*'

'But enough of that,' Jack said. 'What about you fellows? Have ye work yet?'

'I was reckoning on asking ye that,' Luke said. 'Where can a man get work in this town? Are there many openings along the docks?'

'This isn't the place you should be looking,' the barman replied. 'This is the first place everyone comes looking as soon as they get off the boat. The gangers, they have the pick of anyone they want. It's further up you'll find work. Along the river in the logging ponds and the saw-mills. That's where ye'd go. There's not many hiring right now, what with the money troubles in England. There's the Gilmour place along at Wolfe's Cove.'

'Gilmours!' Luke exclaimed. 'The Centaurus was a Gilmours' ship.'

'Yes,' Jack said, 'we all know about their ships. There's many who'd describe them as floating hells. It's not so bad working for them though. They work you hard enough in the mills, but you won't die of fever. And they're one of the few places hiring. I warn you – they take only the best though. Have to be strong, and able to work.'

He glanced at *Conaire,* but *Conaire* said nothing.

Luke decided to change the subject.

'And what of lodgings,' he asked. 'We need a place to rest our heads. Where do ye stay yourselves?'

The men whispered among themselves.

'Are you sure you're not carrying fever?'

'Now what do you think?'

'You'd better not. For ourselves, we bunk at McGowan's – Mary McGowan. She's cheap enough, good breakfast and dinner too.'

'Fine so,' said Luke.

'Will ye go there then?'

'We've nowhere else to go. And if ye say it's good, it's surely worth the visit.'

'It is. And when ye get there, ye can tell her one of the Kilgallons sent you. Jack Kilgallon, to be exact. We all work at the Gilmours' shipyard. Her husband, Larry McGowan, he works at Gilmours' saw-mills up in Wolfe's Cove. Some kind of clerk there. He'd be able to get you in if anyone could.'

'He'd be a good fellow to know.'

'He would.'

'And where would we find this Mary McGowan.'

'Come on, I'll show you,' Jack said. 'You lot, too,' he shouted at the others. 'Enough of the talk. Time for work.'

They left the bar. Jack gave Luke instructions, and then followed the others back towards the docks.

'Sorry about that,' Luke said to Conaire. 'They wouldn't speak in Irish. But they gave us enough information to be going on with.'

'Are they ashamed of their own language?' Conaire asked.

'In one word, yes. They're saying the locals here hate us. They reckon the Irish brought the plague over the ocean. It causes trouble speaking it, if others hear you.'

'Yes,' Conaire said. 'I can understand that only too well. And here I am, the poor amadán, who can't even speak English.'

'You will,' Luke said. 'You will.'

They followed the directions Luke had been given, and soon found the McGowan house. It was a well-built stone building with mullioned windows, a heavy wooden door and dormer windows jutting out from the slate roof. They knocked, and waited.

The woman who opened the door was well-dressed, wearing a red blouse and a muslin skirt. Her hair was tied back behind her shoulders, and Luke noticed at once the strong face and eyes.

'We're looking for lodgings,' he said. 'We met some of your lodgers. They recommended you.'

'Which were they?'

'The Kilgallons.'

'Them lot, eh?'

'They said the meals were good,' Luke added.

'Did they, now?' she said, with a touch of sarcasm. 'There's more important things than that.'

'Like...?'

'Ye have money?'

'Enough, and we'll have more. We came to work.'

'Ye have fever?'

'We were quarantined. We're clean. Never a touch of fever between the two of us.'

'Ye'd better not.' She looked closely at both of them, appraising them. 'Come on in so,' she said suddenly.

She explained that she had four rooms in the house, each sleeping ten, men only. She was able to offer cheap lodgings, but she kept everything clean. She named a price. Luke agreed.

'Ye've had breakfast?'

'Not yet,' Luke said.

'What about this fellow?' she said, indicating Conaire. 'Has he been struck dumb or what?'

'He doesn't speak English yet.' Luke said.

'He'd better learn.'

She led them to a dining room and sat them down at the table. She went away but returned almost at once.

'You'll have your breakfast soon,' she said. 'Now you were saying about working. What are your intentions?'

'Work here a while, then go for America. *Conaire* here has a brother owns a bar in New York. I've friends working the railways out in Pennsylvania. That's what we're intending anyhow.'

'Do ye know about the way there?'

'I'd heard a little,' Luke said, 'but I'm sure ye know better.'

'You should go down by Lake Champlain, through the canal and down the Hudson to New York. It's not a bad way to go, if you have money. You'll get to New York fast enough. But what will you work at while you're here?'

'We were told the logging was good,' Luke said.

'It is, but not here. The best logging is up the Rideau River on the north side of the St. Lawrence, though I hear that the Gatineau is even better. It's tough work. They were crying out for good men, last year. It's a lot tougher now.'

'I'm surprised what you say,' Luke said. 'With thousands coming through here every month, surely they'd have the pick of any workers they wanted?'

'That's not true at all. There's a great need for men, but that's in the forests, and most of the men who come through Quebec and Montreal aren't able for it. The Quebecers, they're fine, but there's never enough of them. The Irish are too sick, or too weakened from fever, or just from travel. And most of them just want to stay in Quebec. Or Montreal. The forests are hard on such men.'

'Is it well paid, this forest work?' Luke asked.

'It's good, but not great. I've heard about working on the rails in England, it's not as good as that. Or New York, that's why everyone goes there.'

'But we'll need money for that,' said Luke.

'You'll save enough to get down to New York without any trouble. There's not much to spend your wages on in the woods.'

'How do we get to the woods?' asked Luke.

'First, you have to have patience. They don't start gathering the men for the logging until early November and then they work all winter.'

'Winter! Why winter?'

'Because it's easier getting the timber out. There's too much brushwood in summer. During the winter they slide the logs down on the snow.'

'I hadn't thought of that,' said Luke. 'But November, that's two months away. There's no logging here, is there?'

'Not much, but there's other work. The rafts of logs are still coming down, and there's plenty of work sorting them out, cutting them and loading them on ships.'

'How would we find this work?'

'My husband, he works in Gilmours. He'll tell you.'

'Jack Kilgallon, he mentioned your husband to me.'

'Yes,' she said, 'but the Kilgallons are in the shipyard, and Larry works up by the saw-mill. Gilmours are a big business. They bring the logs down from up river before they ship them to England. Sometimes they look here for men for the camps, if they can't find enough in Montreal. So you might be able to find work in the woods for yourselves, before you even leave Quebec. One way or the other, Larry will be able to put you in the right direction, if it's work you want.'

A young girl placed two plates on the table. Chops and fried potatoes.

'A good looking breakfast, this.'

'Ye'll need it every morning, if ye'll be working in the timber yards.'

She left.

'*What was she saying,*' Conaire asked.

'*A lot about how to get work. Her husband knows. We'll find out more tonight.*'

'*Good breakfast too.*'

'Yes, a very good breakfast,' Luke said, 'and you're going to learn English.'

They went to their bunks and dropped their packs on the floor. *Conaire* lay down, and within minutes he was asleep.

Luke lay down, but could not sleep. After a while, he got up and shook *Conaire.*

'*Come on, boy. We've lots to do yet.*'

'*I'm too damned tired.*'

'*Let's see this city, now we're here.*'

'*What's the hurry, we've only just arrived.*'

'*I've a letter to write.*'

'*Well write it.*'

'*Can't do that without a post office.*'

'*Well, find one.*'

'*Come on, no more excuses out of you.*'

They slipped out of the house and walked towards what seemed to be the centre of the city.

They found no post office.

'*We'd better ask,*' said Luke. He went to approach an elderly woman, but when he tried to speak to her, she scurried away. He tried approaching a younger man, but he only growled at Luke and passed by.

'*Seems he didn't like us,*' Conaire said.

'*Indeed not,*' said Luke.

'*Maybe they think we have fever.*'

'*Maybe they do,*' said Luke. '*Or maybe being Irish is cause enough. We'll go back, and ask Mrs. McGowan.*

As they turned for home, Luke saw a building marked 'Bureau de Poste'. Guessing the meaning of the last word, he spotted a post box.

'*Lucky chance, that,*' he said to *Conaire*. '*Wait here until I get a stamp.*'

He came out and they went on. '*By Christ! The post here is not cheap. We won't be sending many letters home with these prices.*'

'*Did you get one?*'

'*Not a chance. They don't sell stamps in Canada. I'll have to wait until I have written the letter and then bring it back for them to frank it.*'

The next stop was the Bank of British North America, which they found easily. Luke opened an account in his own name, with no difficulty. He left the bank, and took a knife out of his pack. Carefully, he slit the thread along the edge of his pocket, and took the cash out, before returning to deposit the money

'*That was damned dangerous,*' *Conaire* said afterwards.

'*What?*'

'*Carrying that amount of money around the streets. You could have been robbed.*'

'*Arra, no. Sure no one would know I was carrying it.*'

In the next street two men approached them, and stopped on the sidewalk, not letting them pass. One was staggering. He came up to Luke, face to face, and snarled at him in French. As Luke was distracted, the second man punched *Conaire* in the stomach. *Conaire* staggered back, and fell. The man went to kick *Conaire* on the ground, but Luke moved fast, and swung his fist hard under the man's jaw. He dropped to the ground without a sound. The other ran at Luke, but Luke grasped him by the buttocks, drew him in, and kneed him hard in the groin. He doubled over, retching.

Conaire was standing again.

'*Come on,*' Luke said, gripping him by the shoulders. '*Time to go.*'

Conaire staggered, then released himself and followed Luke.

'*By God, you can fight.*'

'*A man has to be able to defend himself.*'

'*Where did you learn to fight like that?*'

'*Oh, all along the railways. Those Welsh fellows, they never gave up on us.*'

Yes, Luke thought. And more than that. He thought of starving people attacking the cart convoy bringing food back to Kilduff. It was not just the

Quebecers and the Welsh. Starving Irishmen and Irishwomen – they had to be fought too.

They walked on until they found the St. Lawrence again, and followed it until they found the lumber terminals. There were long lines of men, waiting to be selected for work. Slowly, they discovered each terminal and saw-mill, and then the rest of the city, until they had a better knowledge of Quebec. At last, they found the side street leading to the McGowan house.

There were six men at the table, playing cards. Luke recognised three of the men from the bar. Jack was dealing.

'Well?' he asked. 'What do you think of it here?'

'It's as you said,' Luke said. 'Good food and good beds.'

'Didn't I tell you it would be so?' He was looking at them, puzzled. 'Ye both look a bit shook.'

'We were attacked,' Luke said.

'I hope ye were able to defend yourselves.'

'We were, well enough,' Luke replied. 'We knocked one over and gave the other fellow such a kick he'll never make children!'

'I wouldn't be telling that to Mrs. McGowan. She prides herself on not having brawlers in this house.'

After dinner that evening, Luke sat by Mrs. McGowan and her husband, while the Kilgallons and two others played cards on the other table.

Luke questioned the McGowans about the logging trade in Quebec. McGowan himself worked as a clerk in Gilmours. Most of his work consisted of writing out letters and contracts for the Gilmours' agents in London, Liverpool, Bristol, New York and Boston.

'I heard you crossed on one of Gilmours' ships,' he said to Luke, at length.

'The Centaurus,' Luke replied.

'Yes. Everyone's talking about it. Pretty rough, I believe.'

'It was,' Luke said.

'The Gilmours are rough too. As Mary might have told you, they do everything from beginning to end. They own the logging camps up the Gatineau, them and the Wrights. They float the logs down to the St. Lawrence, some of them they send up the Champlain and down to New York.'

'New York?'

'That's right. That's where you're intending travelling, I understand.'

'It is,' Luke replied.

'I'll tell ye more about that some other time, we can go over the route with ye, see if we can find anyone else that's travelling that way.'

'Surely the lads here are staying with the saw-mills?'

'Not always. Some of them go with the logs down as far as the Champlain, or the Hudson, and come back up again to work in the mills, or out in the forest, whatever they feel like.'

'Know any going to the forest?' Luke asked.

'Here's one,' Jack said from the other table.

McGowan looked across in surprise. 'You never said that before.'

'I didn't,' Jack said. 'I did now.'

McGowan laughed. 'So there you are, Luke. There's your answer.'

Jack started dealing the cards on the other table, five to each man. He looked across to Luke.

'Well, what do you think of that?'

'I'm with you,' Luke said. '*Conaire* too, I'd say. Four or five months in the Gatineau, that's what I'm thinking.'

Jack picked up his five cards, looked closely, and threw his coins to the centre of the table.

'Then down with the logs to New York?'

'New York, for sure,' Luke answered. 'But you'd know better than us how to get there.'

Jack quickly threw three cards down, waited for the others to discard, and dealt to their discards.

'It's a long way from the Gatineau,' he said. 'But the logs are the best way – you can earn money while you're travelling. Get fed too. It's hard to beat that.'

'It is,' Luke said, and waited as the betting began. But all interest had switched to the cards. After a few moments, he turned back to McGowan.

'Do all the logs go to New York then?' he asked.

'Not all,' McGowan answered. 'The most of them, they bring down here to Quebec, square them off in the saw-mills, and send them over to Glasgow and Liverpool in their own ships that they build here and in Glasgow. And when they're finished, they bring the immigrants back in the ships, as you well know. Scottish immigrants too – it's not just the Irish. And if you think the Centaurus was bad, it wasn't by any means the worst. The Argo back in May time – that was one of theirs. By the time that one put in to Grosse Île, it was in a terrible state. God knows how many died. There was a report sent to Parliament in London, the Quebec Gazette carried the whole story. Not that any of it seemed to worry the Gilmours very much.'

'So why do you work for them?' asked Luke

'Two reasons' said McGowan. 'First, you have to work for somebody. Second, they're not the worst, provided you're not one of their passengers.'

The betting had finished.

'Two pairs, aces high.'

'Three kings.'

'Full house, tens on top.'

'Full house, aces on the roof,' Jack said, as he swept the kitty across to his side. 'By God, Luke, you're bringing me luck already.'

That night, Luke lay in his bunk, staring at the ceiling. *'Are you awake, Conaire?'*

'I am.'

'Sounds like we might be a long time in Canada.'

'A lot longer than we thought.'

The next morning, they went with McGowan to the saw-mill. He brought them directly to the office of the senior manager. After he had explained everything, the manager offered them work on the timber piers, half a crown a day, three pence per hour for a ten hour day. He took their names and asked McGowan to bring them down to the ganger on one of the docks.

They turned to go.

'Hold it!'

They turned back.

'That fellow won't have the strength for this kind of work,' he said, looking at *Conaire*.

There was a stunned silence. Then Luke spoke.

'He's my brother.'

The man looked doubtfully at McGowan.

'The other one is powerful enough,' McGowan said. 'He'll work enough for two men.'

The man nodded. "You'd better be right, McGowan."

"I am. I know these fellows."

They left.

'I understood that 'brother' *bit, easy enough,' Conaire* said. *'It was good of you to say it.'*

'And why not,' Luke said. 'We *wouldn't want you out on the street, begging. Would we?'*

They followed McGowan, along by the side of the saw-mill.

'That wasn't as good as I'd hoped,' said Luke. 'Half a Canadian crown a day is only half what we were earning on the Great Western Railway.'

'That's as may be,' said McGowan, 'but work is hard to get this season. There's many a man would take your place.'

They reached the dock. There seemed to be thousands of logs. Up river, there were thousands more, lashed together in enormous rafts of hundreds of logs, at least a dozen rafts that Luke could see. McGowan brought them to the ganger, a burly Quebecer.

'I've brought you a few more Irishmen, Carlier.'

'More Irish, McGowan! They can work, yes?'

'They'll work as hard as you want,' McGowan said. 'No fever, neither, before you ask.'

'For how much time they want work?'

'Until it's time to go up the forests. Either the Rideau or the Gatineau, I was telling them.'

'I take them so. I do not do but for a friend.'

McGowan turned to go. 'I'll see you fellows tonight.'

Carlier brought them down to his office in a tiny shack to sign them on.

'You want to work? You better know well how to work, or by God, I'll want to know why not.'

He led them down the timber yard, in and out between stacks of sawn lumber. They came to where a stack was being erected. They were given rapid instruction by a ganger in a language that mixed French and English. They joined two other men who spoke French between themselves. They started working at the bottom, hefting planks and beams up to the two Quebecers above. If they slowed down, there was a shout from the ganger. They carried on.

It was tough work. Soon, *Conaire* was sweating heavily. Luke began to take more of the load, lifting more weight so as to give *Conaire* less of the load each time the beam went up. After some hours, they stopped for lunch. Neither Luke nor *Conaire* had anything with them, and the two other men offered them rolls and cheese. Afterwards, Luke lay back in the warm sun, his muscles aching. Then back to work for more long hours, only stopping for water.

At the end, they sat on a squared-off log, gasping heavily.

'I wasn't sure you'd be able for it for this length of time,' Luke said.

'And I surely wouldn't have, but for your strength added to my own.'

'Arra, what. Come on, let's go home.'

They left, joining a long mass of men streaming out of the mills.

'That fellow is a right hoor,' Conaire said suddenly.

'The ganger fellow?'

'Whatever.'

'No less than the rest of the bastards here it would seem,' Luke said.

'The two fellows we're working with seem decent enough, though.'

'That's true, though I doubt there's many like them.'

'But the gangers. Are they like that all over, do you think?' Conaire asked.

'Sure wasn't it the same on the English railways. The Welsh, the English and the rest of them. Work you into the ground if they got half a chance.'

'It must have been hard on ye.'

'Not so hard in that we had our own gang, and ran things our own way. We chose our own ganger, one of our own. But for the rest of the fellows it was rough, and it wasn't just the Welsh gangers. The Irish gangers, they were just the same.'

'Like Daniel Ryan, are you saying?'

Luke flinched. 'Yes' he said, 'just like Daniel Ryan. But Danny's no ganger, as well you know. Like all contractors, he knows well how to squeeze the last penny out of his workers. I told you Danny once wrote to me, asking me to join him as a partner. Told me before that I was a fool going back to Carrigard. He reckoned working as a contractor would make him a rich man, and he offered me a share in it. Can you think of it? But I turned him down, told him I had no interest in that kind of thing.'

'What kind of fool are you, turning down a chance like that.'

Yes, Luke thought. What kind of fool had he been?

He was drained when they arrived back in McGowan's, but he knew the time had come to write to Winnie.

When dinner was over, he stayed at one end the table, as the card game started at the other. *Conaire* sat watching the game.

'Come on and join us,' McGowan said.

'I've a letter to write,' Luke answered. 'They'll be waiting for it at home.'

'They will, I'm sure,' McGowan said.

'I doubt I'll be writing many of them though.'

'Why's that?'

'I never knew postage was going to be as much as that. One hell of a shock it gave me in the post office there.'

'What did you expect? It's a long way to Ireland.'

'It must be, by God. Do you know you'd have to take a whole day on the railways to earn that kind of money, even in England?'

He set down a sheet and an envelope. 'Could ye lend me a pen and ink?'

Mrs. McGowan fetched them from the dresser.

'There's another problem I've got too' Luke said. 'It was hard enough trying to ask about postage – they only spoke French. At least they didn't understand my English. I asked them about the St. Lawrence, but either they knew nothing, or did not want to understand me.'

'What about the St. Lawrence?' McGowan asked.

'Well it's just this. If the St. Lawrence is freezing, how long does it take for the letters to get to Ireland, or England for that matter?'

'Oh, I wouldn't worry about that' McGowan said. 'It's quick enough. Even in the winter, they go overland to Halifax. It's ice-free year round.'

'Well, I'm happy to hear that' Luke said. 'So how long do you reckon on?'

211

'Depends on the storms, of course, but from here, it could be six or eight weeks to Liverpool.'

Luke dipped the pen in the ink.

Ryan Family	Quebec
Carrigard	Canada
Kilduff	
County Mayo	
Ireland	26 September 1847

My Dear Winnie, Dear Father and Mother,

This is to let you know that I have landed in Quebec and I have good health. The journey was not great, but I was not troubled by fever. The ship was blown a long way north, and this added to our journey. I was lucky enough to get work on the ship out, and then the First Mate asked me to act as a ganger over some of the others. I was paid four pounds and six shillings Canadian, though it is less than the British pound by a little. When we arrived close to Quebec, we had to stay some weeks in quarantine on an island in the St. Lawrence River. I was not sick, but they would not let us travel further until they could be certain. There was no bank on the island, and I had no chance of writing to ye. I now enclose three British pounds for you. You should be able to cash it at the Hibernian Bank in Knockanure. It is little enough, but it is most of what I have, and I will send more later.

I met a man from Erris on the ship, *Conaire* Costello is his name, and we intend to travel together. We found work today in the city at a saw-mill where they cut and stack the timber logs. God knows, it is hard work, but I must strengthen myself for the railways in Harrisburg, or wherever. We will be working some time here in Quebec before spending the winter working in the forests. In the spring we intend on travelling from the forests, following the rivers and canals from Canada down to the Hudson River in the United States. From there I may go with *Conaire* to his brother, John Costello, in New York, if I do not go direct to Harrisburg. Either way, I expect to arrive in May or June. God willing, I may then be able to send more money to you, and in time, enough for the American ticket.

When I have a fixed address in New York, or Harrisburg, or wherever I may be, I will write again and await your reply, so you will give me news of our friends and relatives. I hope ye are all in good health, and that the potato crop continues fine.

I have no more to say but remain your loving husband and son,

Luke Ryan

He folded the letter, and put it into the envelope.

'*Can you write a letter for me when we have the money for the post?*' *Conaire* asked.

'*Of course. What would you want to say?*'

'*That I am well, and travelling to my brother in New York.*'

'*What else.*'

'*Nothing. What else would they need to know?*'

Luke took the letter out of the envelope again.

'*Right,*' Luke said, '*let's write.*'

'*Write?*'

'*Why not?*' Luke said. '*You needn't worry about the postage. What we'll do is write it on this letter, and ask them to send information to your family in Torán. It'll only cost them a penny stamp to send it from Kilduff to Torán. Save the cost of postage here.*'

'*But you've no room there, front or back,*' *Conaire* said.

'*Don't let you be worrying about that,*' Luke said. He started writing vertically up the page across what he had already written.

'*Conaire* wants me to send a message to his people in *Torán*, which is down from Belmullet in Erris, but in view of the high price for winter letters from Canada, I would consider it a favour if ye would write a short note to his people instead.'

'*You're destroying it.*'

'*No, I'm not, they'll read it easy enough. I'm just telling them what we want them to do. Now you tell me what you want to say.*'

'*You know, as well as I do. Write whatever is needed.*'

'*Fine so,*' Luke said. Again he wrote –

'You will address it to his father, *Tomás Ó Coisteala*, care of the Parish Priest in Belmullet, and you will write it in the Irish language. You may instruct the good Father to have the letter carried down to the Ó Coisteala family in *Torán* when anyone is going down that way. The letter should tell the family that *Conaire* is alive and well. He has little enough money, but hopes to send some later. The rest of his news is the same as mine, except he will surely go to New York, and stay with his brother at Costello's Bar, Orange Street, Five Points, Manhattan, New York City.'

Luke read the letter out in Irish.

'*You're good at giving them orders,*'

'*Arra, pay no mind to that,*' Luke said. '*They're well accustomed to getting orders from me. Every time I'd send back money from the railways, I'd be giving them orders as to how it was to be given out or spent. No, they won't complain.*'

They went to the Bureau de Poste again, and Luke paid them the cost of franking the letter for Ireland.

They were transferred to the logging ponds. As it got colder, more Irish immigrants poured into the area, but most of them were unable to get work in Gilmours, since fewer rafts were coming down the river, and the final ships were being loaded to clear the St. Lawrence before it froze.

Every morning now, they saw Irish and Quebecers at the gates, asking for work.

'*Hungry looking fellows,*' *Conaire* said one day.

'*They are,*' said Luke, '*and not just the Irish. I don't know where these Quebecer fellows are coming from, but they all look as if they could do with a damned good meal.*'

One evening Luke wrote a letter to Farrelly in Pennsylvania, also describing their experiences, and explaining that he could be very late arriving in Harrisburg.

'*At least the letter will be a lot cheaper to send than the Irish ones,*' he said to *Conaire*. '*And I hope it arrives.*'

'*Why wouldn't it?*'

'*The building of the railway may have moved on from there. The letter may not be delivered.*'

That evening, McGowan had more news for them.

'Times are getting worse,' he told them. 'The mills are shutting.'

'What!'

'Two of them closed yesterday, I hear. There's talk of more closings, and many of those still open might close yet.'

'But why?'

'Some kind of money crash in England, I understand. They're not taking our lumber. Not very much anyhow.'

'So now what?'

'God only knows. I just hope you hold on to your jobs, that's all.'

Their luck held, as thousands of men were thrown out of work right across Quebec, Then Gilmours started firing men. Soon, Luke and *Conaire* were on short-time working, three days a week.

'I wonder how long this will last,' Luke said.

'*God only knows,*' *Conaire* said. '*Just be thankful we have a job, any job, and they can still afford to pay anything, so we get food and shelter.*'

'*True enough,*' Luke said, '*though God knows what our prospects are for winter in the forests if they've no call for timber here.*'

As word of the slump spread across the city, there were fewer men outside Gilmours looking for work, but Luke noticed many women and children begging on the streets.

'*Spare a farthing, sir?*'

As if he had a farthing to spare. He wondered how long it would be 'till he and *Conaire* joined them on the street.

It was bitterly cold.

But still their luck held. One day, Carlier came over to them.

'Time for the logging, if you still want to go.'

Luke and *Conaire* looked at each other.

'We'll be lucky yet,' Conaire said.

They followed Carlier to the office. There was a man writing at the desk.

'We're taking on men for the Gatineau' he said, without looking up. 'You'll be there all winter. The wages are four shillings a day.'

'Four shillings!' Luke said. 'It was five.'

'Ah yes, but that was last year. Do you want it or not?'

'We don't have much choice, do we?'

'Not much. You want to get to New York after?'

'That's our intention, anyways,' Luke said. 'We're trying to save money for it. This won't help.'

'You'll save plenty on the Gatineau. There's nothing to spend your money on. If you want to work twenty hours a day, that's your decision. It's still four shillings a day. Most men work seven days a week, except for Sunday morning, when the priest comes out. They work all winter and then come back to Bytown or Montreal for a few days, and raise hell. Still want it?'

'We do.'

'Good. There's a boat leaving from the timber piers on Wednesday.'

That evening they were paid. The next morning, he went to the bank for a bank draft, and cashed the remainder. He wrote his second letter to Carrigard.

Ryan Family	Quebec
Carrigard	Canada
Kilduff	
County Mayo	
Ireland	5 November 1847

Dear Winnie, Dear Father and Mother,

Ye may be surprised to hear from me so soon again, but now, I can send more money for ye. God knows, ye have been waiting long enough for it, and I am sorry I could not send more earlier, nor more now. Still another three pounds might help ye through the rest of the winter, please God.

We've been working at Gilmours saw-mill, and it's heavy work. But we're earned more money, and what I am now sending is most of what I have with me right now.

Tomorrow, we will travel to the Gatineau Forests, We will be working there for the rest of the winter and perhaps as far as April. The snows in this country are very deep in the winter, so I might not have another chance to write until then, nor will I be paid until our time in the forests is finished. So if you do not hear from me for that length of time, let it not worry ye. I hope to have a lot more money that I can send to ye at that time, and then we may be able to plan for Winnie's arrival in the United States.

I hope ye are all well and have no more to say but remain your loving husband and son,

Luke Ryan

If it would not be asking too much of you, it would be good if you could pass another message to *Conaire* Costello's people in Erris that he continues well. He will be travelling with me to the Gatineau Forests.

Luke woke in the early hours of the morning. The other men were snoring. He got up, and walked to the window. Outside, a wan sun was rising over the timber yards of Quebec.

Yes, he thought, it will be a long time 'till I get to Pennsylvania, or even New York. And when can I ask Winnie to come over? I can't do that until I'm certain where I'll be. I'll probably write to her again after the winter, when I'm sure we are on our way down there. But then, where should I ask her to go to? It would be hard for a woman with a little baby to make her way to Harrisburg. Impossible maybe. So should I stay in New York? Would that be better? Then I might never get to Harrisburg. So? They're not building railways in New York, they're all built. Or should I tell Winnie to wait a year or so 'till I get back to Ireland. If I ever get back to Ireland? No, don't be silly, Ireland's in the past now. Pat will have the farm. He'll settle with it. There'll be no place for me. I'm not going home.

Oh God, Winnie, will I ever see you again?

Chapter 15

Telegraph & Connaught Ranger, October 1847:
Poverty in Mayo is now so great that in the town we live
– the capital of Mayo – dead bodies remain unburied for
days for want of coffins – and this is a time when the agent
and drivers of the landlord are busily engaged in driving and
seizing whatever has remained with the tenant after the last
hard season.

One day, Eleanor insisted on going into Kilduff to buy corn, in spite of
Winnie's protests.

She met a family walking the other way.

'Dublin,' they told her, though Eleanor doubted they had the strength for
six days walking. And where would they get food on the journey?

She joined the long line outside Dillon's shop. Some of the women ahead
of her seemed healthy, but most were thin and gaunt. It seemed to take
forever, but at last she reached the counter. She ordered her corn, but when
she heard the price, she was shocked.

'That's the price' the attendant told her. 'Take it or leave it.'

Eleanor realised that she did not have enough money for what she
wanted, but she took all the corn she could afford.

She walked back to McKinnon's bar, unlatched the front door and
walked in. It took her a moment to adjust to the semi-darkness. At the far
end of the bar, three men were hunched around a candle. They stopped
talking as she came in, gazing at her silently.

The bar was no different to what she always remembered it, except it
was emptier. It had the same long bar, made from a trunk of bog oak, sawn
transversely with the planed side up. The floorboards were well worn after
many years of heavy use. Sawdust was sprinkled all over it to soak up spilt
beer.

Sabina had been seated behind the bar, knitting. She stood up to serve
her.

'No, no,' Eleanor said, 'I've nothing left, just been to Dillon's.' She placed
her sack of corn on the counter.

'Yes,' Sabina said, 'it's a terrible price. I know.'

'The devil take it' Eleanor said, 'and Dillon too. But enough of that. I wanted to know if we're seeing you soon.'

'I'll be up later, so.'

Eleanor left the bar. The street outside was almost empty, and silent. Three women stood by the bar window. They were very thin with pinched faces. One held out her hand to Eleanor, but she brushed past her. As she went on down the street, she wondered if that had been the right thing to do. Perhaps she should have given her a farthing. But if she did that, they would always be following her.

Outside the town, she saw a dog standing in the centre of the road. It too was very thin. As she came closer it growled in a low, threatening way. Eleanor stopped. She went back, and cut up one of the side roads along the back boreens to Carrigard.

Sabina arrived that evening. 'God with ye all.'

Michael looked up in surprise. 'My little sister!'

'Little to some,' Sabina said. 'Though, at my age, there's not many would think me little. Or young.'

'You're early,' Eleanor said.

'And why shouldn't I be. It's not worth keeping the bar open for two fellows drinking so slow.'

'I'm surprised there's anyone with the money to drink at all.'

'A drover and a dealer, who else would have money? When they were finished their beer, I told them it was time to shut up for the night.'

'They didn't like that?' Eleanor asked.

'Maybe they didn't,' Sabina replied, 'but the next time they pass through these parts they'll have forgotten about it.'

She slipped a half bottle of whiskey from under her cloak. 'There's little enough call for it. We might as well drink some of it here.'

Eleanor fetched four cups. Michael took one and waited as Sabina poured.

'Well, tell us this,' he said, 'what are you hearing in the bar? You must be hearing more than any others.'

'I don't know about that,' Sabina said. 'I'm only getting half the story. The ones who are dying, they don't come in at all. The drovers and the cart men, you have to drag it out of them, but they've seen enough on the roads and roadsides. One of the cart men, he's working for the Poor Law all around the county, been delivering corn from Westport to all the Workhouses. Ballinrobe, Westport itself, Castlebar, Ballina, Knockanure...'

'We've heard enough about Knockanure already,' Michael said.

Sabina went on.

'Ballinrobe was the worst he'd seen, the fellow said. All up the Partry

Mountains, they're dying at an awful rate. And the stories of Louisburgh, the fever near wiped them out. Out the Killaries was dreadful. But no one seems to know anything about Erris. It's so frightful, no-one talks about it.'

'God, Mayo is finished,' Michael exclaimed.

'No it's not,' Sabina replied. 'As long as we've got Brigid, it's not.'

'*Arra* hell, are you still on about that?'

'Yes, we are,' Eleanor said sharply. 'We will educate her. You, even you believe it.'

'I surely did. But look at what's happening around us, woman. What chance have any of us got?'

'Give it time, 'Eleanor said. 'We will do it.'

'We will,' Sabina said. 'There's no doubting that. But it's Luke we should be thinking of.'

'And we've no news there,' Eleanor said quickly. 'But it's not late yet. We should hear within the next few weeks. Early October, that would be the time.'

'I don't know,' Sabina said. 'There's bad news coming from Canada. One of the drovers passing by, he was reading the Telegraph. They say there's sickness in Quebec, brought over by the Irish ships.'

Winnie dropped her head to the table. Eleanor walked around the table, and placed her hand on Winnie's shoulder.

'I'm sorry…' Sabina said.

'For nothing,' Eleanor replied. 'It's as well to know. What else were they saying?'

'They're saying it's hard to get work in Quebec. The timber trade is in a bad way.

'So what do you think?' Eleanor asked at length.

'It's clear as water,' Winnie said. 'Luke's gone to a country with no work, but plenty enough of hunger and fever.'

'But we never knew…' Eleanor exclaimed.

'We do now.'

Winnie had been badly shaken by Sabina's news. Over the next days, she tried to hide it, but Eleanor knew well the pain it was causing her.

'But that news is six weeks old at least,' she said to Winnie. 'Anything could have happened since then.'

'It could,' Winnie answered. 'And it could be worse. Even if he lives through the fever, where will he get work, if there's none to be had?'

'I don't rightly know the answer to that,' Eleanor replied, 'but one way or another, I'm thinking we'll know very soon. We'll be hearing from Luke in the next week or two. It's no surprise we haven't heard from him yet. The ships aren't that fast, as you well know.'

In Carrigard tension increased all through October as no letter arrived from Luke. Eleanor still consoled Winnie, but her own voice showed that she too was concerned. She was coming to accept that Luke was dead.

Still the two women fed Brigid, cleaned her and played with her. Eleanor thought it was odd how they both depended on a little baby to keep them amused and bring back laughter. Sometimes Kitty dropped by, and at times like that, Brigid became even more important to them. But Kitty too was concerned about Luke. She had accepted, for more than a year, that her own relationship with Luke was over, but even so, the thought of him dying in fever or drowning in the Atlantic was more than she could bear.

Strangely, there were no bad feelings between Winnie and Kitty. Now that they were convinced that Luke was dead, there was an equality between them.

'Isn't it strange,' Kitty said. 'Only a few weeks back, I was so jealous of you.'

'I know,' Winnie said quickly. 'First you lost him. Now we both have.'

'And in a way neither of us would ever have wished.'

As time went on, their certainty increased. It was late October now.

'We won't hear from him now,' Winnie said.

'It's all this talk of Canada,' Kitty said. 'Quebec, Montreal, and this Bytown place. Everything we hear is nothing but sickness and death. Now, we must accept it, and prepare for living our lives with the knowing that that's the way it is.'

Eleanor could see that Kitty was thinner than ever. Eleanor and Winnie still tried to feed her whenever she came around, but Kitty was beginning to feel that in a famine situation, she could not continue taking food from the Ryans. She told them she was not hungry, but the other women knew better.

They also noticed the bruises on Kitty's face. The beatings had never stopped. Fergus was a brute, and nothing would ever change.

'She's much thinner,' Eleanor said one night, after Kitty had left.

'More beatings too,' Winnie answered.

Then Kitty did not visit at all. After ten days, Eleanor decided she had to find out what was happening. She could put Luke to the back of her mind. That just had to be accepted.

She resolved to visit Kitty. She told Winnie, who wanted to go in her place, but Eleanor wanted to see for herself, and insisted that Winnie stay and mind the child.

She left early the next morning, taking a small bag of corn with her.

The well was quiet in the early dawn. Four women in black shawls were drawing water, but there was none of the chatter and gossip that was common before. Eleanor could hear the distant howling of a dog on the

Mountain. She went on and came face to face with another dog, a scrawny, mangy animal. He growled at her. She picked a stick, and walked on. He ran at her. She lashed hard as he jumped at her. He fell back and ran, howling, through a hedge and into a field.

She walked on. In the distance, she could see the line of villages running across the Mountain.

Abhann-an-Rí, Lios Cregain, Cnoc rua, Currach-an-Dúin, Áth-na-mBó, Craobhaín.

She could see the smoke of the turf in some of the houses. In others, none. Some already had the thatch pulled off the roof, evidence of evictions. And the others? Abandoned? All the signs of never-ending emigration and death. How many houses still contained dead bodies? Most would have been buried in the bog. At *Gort-na-Móna*, she could just make out the burnt out remains of the village, remembering all too well the horrific day of the evictions.

Árd-na-gCaiseal, Sliabh Meán and *Baile-a-Cnoic* stretched further up the Mountain. She looked away, and continued on her own road.

She came to the cluster of houses where Kitty lived. She greeted an elderly woman, but got no answer.

'*God and Mary,*' she said to two children. They ran. She greeted two more women, but still no-one responded.

Grey faces watched her. Grey clothes, frayed shifts and trousers, broken shoes. Broken men and women. Thin, gaunt, dying people.

At length, an old man directed her to Kitty's house.

The half door was open.

'*Kitty,*' she shouted.

Kitty came to the door. Eleanor saw fresh bruising on her face and a gash above one eye. She heard the sound of snoring from inside.

Kitty stepped outside, and embraced her.

'*He's drunk, as usual,*' she said. '*At least it gives me peace.*'

'*I know.*'

'*I wasn't expecting you.*'

'*Sure I had to come, we hadn't seen you for so long.*'

'*Did you have difficulty finding the house?*'

'*Enough.*' Eleanor said. '*But sure I'm here now. And I brought you some corn.*'

'*May God bless you,*' Kitty said. '*You're a true friend. And it's not that I want taking it, but I've little choice in the matter.*'

There was a roar from within. 'Where are you woman?'

Fergus stood up and came to the door, bleary eyed. He stared at Eleanor, unrecognising.

'Who's this?' he roared. 'I know,' he said, before either could answer. 'Luke Ryan's mammy, that's who it is. Am I right?'

'If you want to put it that way,' Eleanor responded.

'Well isn't it as well he got a hold of that other bitch. Won't be rutting with other men's wives now, will he? Or maybe he will.'

Eleanor looked away. He grabbed her, and spun her around to face Kitty.

'Look at her,' he shouted. 'He didn't tell you about this, did he? Only last year, he couldn't keep his hands off her. But, by God, I gave him a beating he'll never forget.'

'I know,' Eleanor said.

'And still you make friends with this one here.'

'I do,' Eleanor said.

'*Arra*, what kind of eejit are you. Where is he anyhow, the brave Luke? Over in England, is he? They've more married women over there to be rutting, that's for sure.'

'He's gone to America,' Eleanor said quietly.

'Well, that's one more bastard out of the country.'

He went into the house and sat at the kitchen table. 'Where's my breakfast, woman?'

'I'm coming,' Kitty said. She turned to Eleanor.

'*You see how it is, my friend?*'

'*I do,*' Eleanor said.

'*You'd better leave now.*'

Eleanor embraced her. '*We'll see you later,*' she whispered. '*We've all been missing you.*'

'*This evening, for sure,*' Kitty said.

As Eleanor returned towards Carrigard, she saw two men harvesting turf in the bog. She walked across, then realised that they were digging a grave in the turf. At the edge, there were two corpses, a woman and a young child. She asked the road to Carrigard. One of the men directed her.

He saw her looking at the corpses.

'*Isn't it as well for them, they don't have to feel the pain anymore. And leave enough food for the rest of us too.*'

'*True for you,*' Eleanor responded.

Without thinking, she dropped to her knees and blessed herself. The two men knelt beside her. The older man started to pray.

'*Our Father, who art in heaven, hallowed be thy name...*'

All three continued the Lord's Prayer to the end.

Then they stood. The men gravely shook hands with Eleanor.

She continued her journey.

'*Now why did I do that?*' she thought. '*I'm not even that sort of person.*

I'm not sure if I believe in it. Our Father! Is there any way to believe in God anymore? Any god? Still, it might have given them some comfort. Who knows? Oh God, I must get a grip on myself.'

She reached Carrigard.

'So how is she?' Winnie asked.

'It's a tough life she has,' Eleanor responded. 'Fergus is nothing but drunk. On the poitín, day and night, and he's still beating her. Getting worse, perhaps. She had a cruel gash over her eye. It wasn't there last time we saw her. But I asked her down this evening. She said she'd come.'

'Please God, she will,' Winnie said. 'But how was your journey?'

'Dreadful. But sure you've seen it all already. Across on the Mountain, it's in a frightful way. Empty houses in all the villages. And Gort-na-Móna, all burnt out. Do you remember that day?'

'I do, full well,' Winnie replied.

'God, and the people. Even around here, they're so thin and wasted. All they do is look at you. It's so hard to get them to talk. Burying corpses in the bogs now, they are.'

'I know,' Winnie said. 'I'd heard tell of that. Seen it too.'

'How long can it go on like this? What kind of god does things like this? I don't know that I believe in him anymore. Isn't that a terrible thing to say?'

'It is,' Winnie said, 'though often I'm not too sure myself.'

Sabina arrived down that afternoon. At dusk, Kitty arrived too.

'Do you have a bed for the night?' she asked.

'Of course, child,' Eleanor said.

'Just for the one night. I'll go in the morning, I promise. I'll still have to feed him, the swine. He was insulting about Luke too.'

'Arra, pay no mind to that,' Winnie said.

'Oh, but I do,' Kitty replied. 'And still no word of him?'

'Nothing, in the wide world,' Eleanor said. 'It's Sabina here you should be asking. She sees the papers.'

'Indeed I do,' Sabina replied. 'Quebec is in a terrible way with the fever. Not much talk of hunger though, which is one good thing.'

'He'll be hungry enough if he can't get a job,' Winnie said.

'That's not likely, though,' Sabina said. 'Luke is sharp and hard-working. He'd get a job ahead of any man.'

'If he's alive,' Winnie said.

Next night, the aurora blazed over Mayo.

Michael was the first to see it as he returned from milking the cow. High over the Mountain, the sky swirled with colour. Pat, who had been spending the weekend in Carrigard, stood beside him.

'Go and tell the rest of them,' Michael said.

Pat went in, and told the women. Brigid was awake, and Winnie took her in her arms before following Eleanor outside.

She pointed to the sky. '*Look Brigid. See the lights.*' Brigid looked, but whether the Lights meant anything to her, Winnie could not say.

'They'll all be going on about this down by the well tomorrow,' Eleanor said. 'Just wait and see.'

'I know they will,' Winnie said, 'and they'll see things in the Lights that aren't there at all. They'll all be frightened of dying.'

'*Arra,* nonsense,' Michael said. 'That's all *piseógs* and fairy tales. Anyone with a *trawneen* of sense would know they're nothing but lights.'

'Be that as it may,' Eleanor said, 'it's not whether it's true or not, it's the believing that's the thing. And it'll terrify many people. And in one way, they'd be right. There's enough death all around, though it doesn't take coloured lights to tell us that.'

Eleanor most certainly was not superstitious. She did not believe that the aurora affected people's destiny in any way. But still, she remembered the aurora of January 1839 on the Night of the Big Wind, and hundreds of people had died that night. Weeks later, the aurora had returned as Alicia sickened with fever, and died. She knew these events were not connected, but still she felt a certain dread when she saw the Northern Lights.

It brought Luke to mind again. How long now? Over three months, and still no word. She knew that Luke might well be dead, but she was powerless to do anything.

With Brigid it was different. Eleanor was determined Brigid would not die. Alicia had died. But even if everyone else starved, Brigid would be fed. She was the future.

But only silence from Luke. Now she was frightened.

Oh God, my son, where are you?

Chapter 16

Freeman's Journal, Dublin, November 1847:
We have been informed that in the neighbourhood of Belmullet, and within the Mullet, instantaneous death from starvation can only be expected – that the people are already sinking into premature graves from lack of food – and that disease is rapid in its ravages. We regret to say that Belmullet is not the only district where destitution exists. In the populous islands in the Clew Bay and along the sea coasts, the peasantry are in the most dreadful condition. Hundreds are at this moment solely dependent for support on turnip leaves boiled, with a sprinkling of raw meal, which in a very few days will be consumed. And we have been assured, by an official who visited Clare Island and Innisturk that he saw several emaciated wretches expiring in agonies from utter want.

Luke's letter arrived.

Eleanor had been feeding the hens when she saw the postman riding out from Kilduff. She was too frightened to hope. Many times she had watched him ride past with no letter. This time he stopped. She held her breath, as he dismounted and walked across.

'Where's it from?'

The postman peered at the postmark. 'Quebec, by the looks of it.'

Eleanor took the letter, her hands trembling.

'Good news, I hope,' the postman said, but Eleanor had already seen the handwriting.

'It can only be good news,' she said.

She went into the kitchen where Winnie was still washing the crockery and pots. Without a word, she placed the letter on the table.

Winnie glanced across to her. *'You're quick feeding the hens.'*

She saw the letter.

'Oh God!'

She ran over and tore the letter open, then she broke down crying.

'What's wrong, alanna?' Eleanor asked, alarmed.

'Alive. He's alive.'

'*Sure I'd worked that out. He wouldn't be writing letters, and he dead. But what does he say? What's wrong?*'

Winnie took a quick look through the rest of the letter, gulping and trying to draw her breath.

'*He's in* Quebec, *in good health.*'

'*Thank God for that. Sure it's like I always told you, he's a tough fellow.*'

'*He had no fever. He's working in a saw-mill. He'll go logging in the forest, and then head towards* New York.'

She stopped.

'*What else does he have to say? What's upsetting you?*' Eleanor asked.

'*He'll write again when he has a fixed address.*'

She gazed up at Eleanor.

'*But I won't be able to travel to America until has an address and he tells me to,*' she said. '*Isn't that the way of it?*'

The two women walked up the back fields to where Michael was re-building a stone wall. Eleanor handed him the letter, wordlessly. He glanced through it.

'He's alive,' he said.

'He is,' Eleanor replied.

'Three pounds!'

'Yes,' Eleanor said. 'For food.'

Late that night, Pat arrived from Knockanure. Shyly, Winnie handed him the letter before he had taken off his greatcoat. He looked through it rapidly and then read it a second time.

'Well, that's wonderful,' he said. 'I'd feared the worst.'

'As had we all,' Eleanor said.

'Aye, but none of ye mentioned it, did ye?'

'We didn't want worrying you,' Eleanor said.

'*Arra*, wasn't I worried enough already,' Pat said. 'We read newspapers in Knockanure too. Trinder leaves them lying around, just to frighten us, I'm thinking. The accounts of the crossings from Liverpool to Quebec are terrible, and that was what I was most worried about. One way or another though, Luke is in Canada now, and that's healthier than being on the ocean, or here in County Mayo.'

'So what are you hearing of Mayo?' Winnie asked.

'The same thing all over. And it's what I see with my own eyes in Knockanure. When you get away from the Workhouse, you see the bodies lying for days unburied. No coffins. But the only ones that are busy are the landlords' agents, demanding the rent, or evicting. Their drivers too, driving the poor man's cattle for payment of rent.'

Pat stayed two nights in Carrigard. Early next morning. Eleanor gave him a breakfast of porridge and buttermilk.

'That'll keep you going for the day.'

'Thanks, mother.'

She handed him the bank draft.

'Can you cash this in the Hibernian Bank when you get to Knockanure?'

'Of course. I'll drop the money into you next weekend.'

He walked out the road to Knockanure. It was a bright morning, but bitterly cold. A thick hoarfrost clung to the branches of the trees and bushes.

Halfway to Knockanure, he saw soldiers. He recognised the uniforms of the Thirteenth Light Dragoons again. He wondered if they had been moved to Knockanure permanently.

He heard a woman scream. As he came abreast of the soldiers, he saw they were driving a cow ahead of them. It was a scrawny beast, but Pat guessed it was the only one the family might have owned. It was followed by two horses drawing a cart, which he guessed was military. It was loaded with grain. Behind it, two soldiers were holding the woman back as her husband stood powerless beside them. He walked on.

When he arrived at Knockanure Workhouse, there were the usual crowds outside.

There were fires burning along the Workhouse wall, dragoons mixing in with starving people, all trying to get closest to the flames.

A lieutenant strode over when he saw Pat.

'Yes sir.'

'I'm a clerk with the Union.'

'Very well, sir. This way.'

Pat followed him towards the gate.

'I thought you fellows were more often in Castlebar?' he said.

'And wish to God we were, too,' the lieutenant replied.' Our lodgings here are no more than mud cabins. Six of the men down with fever too.'

'I saw your fellows out the Kilduff road,' Pat said.

The lieutenant groaned. 'I know,' he said. 'Collecting Lord Lucan's rent for him.'

'The Exterminator!' Pat exclaimed. 'A right bloody bastard too. Won't do his own dirty work.'

'No way. If the people can't pay it, His Lordship demands we bring it in for him.'

'You know those people will starve.'

'They will. But orders are orders.'

An inmate had opened the gate. The soldiers lined up, holding the crowd back, as Pat made his way through.

He spent the rest of the morning working on accounts. The figures told a tough story. If the Workhouse was not bankrupt already, it was certainly close to it. When he finished with the accounts, he started writing letters. This was a new responsibility that Trinder had given him. Trinder himself signed all the letters when Pat was finished writing them. He was grateful for that. At least his name did not have to appear on them.

He wrote three letters to merchants in Knockanure and Castlebar, who had been demanding payment. Trinder left it to Pat's own judgement as to which had to be paid at once, and which could be deferred further. Those demands accompanied by solicitor's demands, Pat paid first, though he noticed more and more solicitors' demands as time went on.

That afternoon, Voisey called Pat in to attend at the Guardians Meeting. For an hour, he was interrogated about accounts, most of all by Lord Clanowen. Pat sat beside Voisey, who examined the figures as Clanowen went through them.

That night, when Pat returned to his bedroom, he saw one of the female inmates was there, lighting a turf fire.

'*And that will be most welcome,*' Pat said. He gave her a farthing. She left without a word.

Just the sight of her had put him thinking of Sarah. He missed her intensely.

The bed was still cold. He stood at the fire, trying to heat himself. At length he sat at his table and began to write.

Miss Sarah Cronin   Knockanure Union
Administration Block
Westport Workhouse
Westport

My Dear Sarah,
Not having seen you for so long, I thought it well to write.

The great news is that a letter from Luke has now arrived. All at home are pleased. It took so long everyone was worried sick, Winnie and mother most of all. When he wrote, he was working in a saw-mill in Quebec. He sent a bank draft with his letter, which will surely be spent well in Carrigard. He tells us he will be working the winter in the Canadian Forests, so we may not hear from him for quite a time again.

Here at Knockanure, we still have no Matron. I am told it is difficult to find anyone for the post, but I think the real reason is lack of money. In the meantime, Mrs. Trinder has taken the position. So once again, we have a man and wife running Knockanure Workhouse. Since you left, they have given me no-one to assist me, and so I am working longer hours than I ever thought possible. I still manage to have a day every week or two in Carrigard, but most of that is helping father out around the farm. I don't know how much longer this can go on, but I must do it.

I fear for you all the time, working in the fever sheds, as you do. Your mother too. Surely there are others who could take the same duties, or even inmates who could be trained to it.

We must meet again, my love, and the sooner the better. It would be great to have a reason to travel to Westport, but I do not think Murtybeg will be coming back over for more workers. I would walk over to Westport myself if I had the time, but I know Mr. Trinder will not allow it.

I have nothing more to say, but remain, your faithful friend,

Patrick Ryan

When Pat went to the Hibernian Bank in Knockanure, he was accompanied by the lieutenant, and six soldiers. He checked the Workhouse's account. Twenty seven pounds.

'But we've more due in,' he told the clerk. 'Rates from the landlords.'

'If you get them,' the clerk answered.

'I just wanted to let you know Mr. Trinder will be sending out two cheques over the next day or two. For oatmeal, the both of them.'

'You have to keep feeding them.'

'We do.'

'And we'll need seven pounds in cash for the Workhouse, and perhaps you'd be good enough to cash this as well.'

He passed over Luke's bank draft.

'From Quebec?' the clerk said.

'Your correspondent bank over there, I believe,' Pat said.

'Indeed. We used to see a lot more of these. Seem to be drying up now.'

'I know. The timber trade isn't doing as well as it did.'

He took the cash and re-joined the soldiers.

'At least you fellows get paid,' the lieutenant said.

'Not much,' Pat answered.

He left the soldiers at the Workhouse gate and entered. As he walked to the Administration Building, he could smell the stink of the death pit. Four corpses were laid at the edge, as the inmates extended the pit.

Nauseated, he walked quickly to the back door of the building and climbed the stairs to his office.

He sat at his desk, hands trembling. He was angry that he could not control his own emotions. He'd lived with the death pit for long enough, why should it keep affecting him like this.

He noticed a slight improvement in the Workhouse. The number of inmates had dropped. As the harvesters returned from the eastern counties, and from the big English farms, they brought money with them, but Pat knew that that would not last, and in a month or so, they would be at the Workhouse gates again.

He wondered whether Danny still needed men. Even if he did though, he would take no workers from East Mayo, so there would be no respite for Knockanure Workhouse.

As Pat went to the dining room that night, he could hear the sound of argument. There was a silence as he entered the room.

Trinder was at the table, together with his wife. Voisey was there too.

'Don't worry about Pat,' Voisey said. 'Everyone will know soon. And in any case, Pat is most reliable. Aren't you?'

'I hope I am,' Pat said with a half laugh.

'It's just we've had news from Strokestown. Mahon has been shot dead.'

'Mahon?'

'Denis Mahon. Owner of the Strokestown Estate. Some fellow stood out in front of his horse and shot him. Dead.'

Pat felt he was expected to feel something, but felt no sense of shock, though it was evident that others around the table did.

'It's a desperate thing when men can't ride around without being shot,' Trinder said.

'Indeed,' Voisey added, looking to Pat. Their glances locked. Trinder was talking again, but Pat was not listening. Finally he interrupted.

'Why don't you say it, Mr. Voisey? Why don't you tell us what you're thinking?'

Voisey looked at Pat, half shocked.

'I don't know what to say,' Voisey said. I've always considered myself a Christian, and this kind of killing was not what I ever believed in. But to me it's a strange thing. The whole country – the papers, the Government and the rest – are shocked when a man like Mahon is killed. But thousands – tens of thousands – die, and who cares?'

'That's unfair,' Trinder interrupted. 'We're all doing what we can. All of us, yourself included. But we don't go on about it, we don't write to papers, we just do our work. Isn't that it?'

Voisey looked at him, pityingly.

'Fine so,' he said. 'Let me go further, Cecil. Remember Mahon's evictions. Did the people want to go? No. He forced them out. Thousands of them. And we all said he was a generous man, giving them free passage to America.

What did we know then of the ships he sent them on. The Virginius, that ship was a disgrace. The victims cry out to Heaven.'

'Cry out for what?' Trinder asked.

'Never mind.'

'Vengeance, is it?'

'Your word, Cecil. Not mine.'

Later that night, Voisey came to Pat's room. Pat was still working on accounts.

'I don't know that I was right in what I said, Pat,' Voisey said. 'It's a terrible thing for any man to say, especially a man in my position. '

Pat hardly knew what to say. He'd always regarded Voisey as a man to respect, a man who was senior to him in every way. He thought the pressure of the past years was beginning to tell on him.

'Perhaps I shouldn't say it,' Pat said, 'but I'll say it anyhow. I think you were right. Mahon paid for his crimes. Penance, I'd call it.'

'Perhaps,' Voisey said. 'Though that kind of punishment should be reserved to the Lord.'

'And not to man?'

'Maybe not,' Voisey said. 'Or do I know?' He shook his head in open doubt.

'But who shot him?' Pat asked, anxious to change the subject.

'Who knows?' Voisey answered. 'The Molly Maguire gang, that's what people are saying.'

'Do they know, though?'

'They don't, Pat. But I'll tell you this, men will hang for this. And it doesn't matter whether they shot him or not, they'll be hanged. The Government needs a hanging, and they will not care who they are.'

In Carrigard, Eleanor was becoming more concerned. The price of corn was rising. Apart from the quarry, their main source of income now was from Pat, and she felt this was unfair. And what would happen if he lost his position in Knockanure?

The work on the farm was much less during the winter months. The quarry though involved very heavy labour, as the roads around Carrigard became more furrowed. Pat was doing what he could to help, but now that was only every second weekend. One way or the other, Michael had to have more food than either of the women. Slowly, Eleanor began to cut back for herself and Michael, but because of her pregnancy, she did not cut back Winnie's food. Nor Brigid's.

Winnie knew what Eleanor was doing, but did not comment on it. As the winter went on, Eleanor and Michael were losing weight. Winnie thought

Eleanor's face was becoming gaunt, but she reckoned, apart from hunger, Eleanor was also worrying about the future. So was she herself, but she was younger.

And what of Luke? Yes, he was safe and well and that had been a huge relief to everyone. But now it was winter. How many ships did the winter crossing? Where would Luke's next letters come from? The forest? How long would the next letter take to arrive from there?

She knew though that, however hungry they were, the area around was worse. Very few seed potatoes had been planted early in the year, and the starvation went on. Fever too. Walking to the well for drinking water had become a nightmare, for her or for Winnie. Going up to the town for corn was even worse.

At the well and in the lines outside Dillon's shop, people were thinner and more ragged than they had been in the summer and autumn. There were fewer of them too. She wondered about that, but she knew the cause. Added to all, there was a silence which she found totally un-nerving.

Then Luke's second letter arrived.

'*Another letter from Luke*,' Eleanor exclaimed.

'*Another?*' Winnie said. '*Sure it's no time since we got the last one. What's he doing writing so often?*'

Eleanor opened it, her hands trembling. She gave the letter to Winnie, while she took out the bank draft.

'*We'll live a while yet, Winnie girl.*'

But Winnie was not listening.

'*He's still working in a saw-mill, but going to the forest until April, and he might not be able to write for that length of time. After April though he hopes to send us a lot more money.*'

Carefully, Eleanor took the letter and put it in the drawer in the dresser, with the bank draft on top.

When Pat arrived to work with Michael. Eleanor placed Luke's letter on the table.

'Here's something for you to see,' she said.

'Isn't he fast writing again,' Pat said.

He glanced through it quickly. 'He'll be working hard now, that's for sure.'

'What else can he do, poor fellow?'

Eleanor placed the bank draft beside him.

'Well, this will keep ye going for a while,' he said.

'Yes,' Eleanor said, 'and it might take some of the strain off you, and thank God for that.'

'*Arra*, don't be worrying about me.'

'Oh, but I do, and I worry about your clerking too. How long will it last?'

'God knows, mother, but it's fine for now, and let's be thankful for that.'

When Pat had left to join Michael, Winnie took the inkwell from the cupboard, and set it on the table.

'*What are you doing, alanna?*' Eleanor asked.

'*Writing a letter.*'

She took a pen from the drawer, and sat. Eleanor put a hand on her shoulder.

'*To Luke?*'

'*Who else?*'

'*But we don't have an address. We need an address to send a letter.*'

'*We've address enough,*' Winnie said. '*He's in* Quebec, *isn't he?*'

Chapter 17

Salisbury & Winchester Journal, November 1847:
Railways. It has been stated in a letter received from Messrs.
Brassey's office, the great railroad contractors, that since
the pressure on the railroad interests, those gentlemen have
discharged 12,000 labourers, with a proportionate number
of officials.

There came the day of the riot.

It was at McManus' site. The Irishmen had been working alongside a Baxendale gang. English and Welsh men traded insults with the Irish. Many Irish did not respond, since they did not know English, but enough did, and some evenings there were fist fights. The shebeens on both sites made matters worse. McManus himself had been concerned about the Irish shebeen. By late afternoon, men were already a little drunk, but the man at the shebeen stated that he was legal, only selling spirits with all excise duty paid, and only accepting the Queen's currency.

But one evening matters went further. A few fist fights, a few traded insults, and within minutes it had developed into a full-scale brawl, involving a hundred men. McManus sent one of his foremen on a horse to Stockport to notify Danny, while he tried to have the riot stopped. But a Welsh navvy knocked him unconscious. When the police arrived, McManus was conscious again – just in time to see a constable go down. By now there were twenty police. They lined up. An order was shouted and the police charged with batons. The navvies scattered.

When Danny arrived, he was shocked by what he saw. Men were lying on the gravel and in the mud. Others were sitting, some being helped by their mates to retreat from the battleground. The police were still standing guard. Danny saw McManus talking to a police sergeant.

'Jamesy, what in the name of...'

'Yes, Danny,' McManus replied, 'a riot. With the Baxendale crowd.'

'We'd been expecting it,' the sergeant interrupted 'There's been fights for long enough. It was bound to grow into a riot sooner or later.'

'Any dead?' Danny asked.

'Thankfully not,' the sergeant replied. 'Mind you, there's some with skull gashes, and a few skulls broken, I wouldn't wonder. Some might die later, but right now the situation is under control.'

'And your men?'

'No problem, thank the Lord.'

Danny stayed in the office with McManus that night. McManus slept on a bunk in a corner, while Danny slept slumped over the desk, his greatcoat wrapped around him.

It was well past midnight when he realised there was a smell of smoke. He could see flickers of flame through the window.

'Jamesy...'

McManus leapt up. 'What, in the name of God?'

'The shacks are on fire.'

Already they could hear the screaming. The two men ran across, but there was little that they, or anyone else could do. The shacks were too far from the stream. Danny watched as they burnt to the ground.

'*Anyone burnt?*'

'*No one,*' a navvy replied. '*We all got out in time.*'

'*No idea who did it?*'

'*Sure how could we see? They were gone well before we could get out. But they weren't speaking English. Irish neither.*'

'*Welshmen,*' another navvy said. '*That's what they were.*'

The next morning, Danny had a visitor in Stockport.

'Inspector James Crawford,' he introduced himself. 'Delighted to meet you, Mr. Ryan.'

Danny shook his hand, and indicated to a chair across from his desk.

'Happy to see you too, Inspector. We haven't met?'

'Not yet. I'm with the Detective Police, working for the City of Manchester.'

'The Detective Police, you say.' Danny said. 'I'd heard of you, but I hadn't met anyone in your line of business.'

'We're unknown to most people,' Crawford said. 'I'm here for one specific reason though. It seems there was a fight yesterday. Anyone killed?'

'Not as I understand it,' Danny replied. 'I was out on the site within an hour of it starting. Some cracked skulls right enough, but nothing serious.'

'Yes,' Crawford said. 'That was my understanding. Nothing more than a navvy riot. The Baxendale fellows hate the Irish. I was disturbed though by what followed. Burning the shacks. That's very dangerous. Have you any idea of the culprits?'

'I'm not sure,' Danny said. 'My information is that they were Welsh. I can't say for certain. Only a few heard their voices. Said they couldn't understand the words, so the language wasn't English or Irish. One man said he recognised the accent.'

Crawford nodded.

'Well, they're probably right, but I doubt we'll ever find the perpetrators. Most disturbing, I'd say. I'm sorry that events like this happen. The Constabulary pride themselves on keeping the peace. So any way we can help you, I'd be delighted.'

Danny considered the matter.

'There is one thing. We have a shebeen on site. Not by my request, I can assure you.'

'Ah yes, we know about that one. Like you, I wish we could get rid of him. It appears he's legal though. Nothing either of us can do about it. There's many like him on the Railway Works.'

After Crawford had left, Danny went over to Irene's desk.

'Seems a friendly fellow.'

'Friendly?' Irene echoed. 'You just watch Inspector Crawford. I reckon he's very dangerous.'

That Saturday, Danny met with his gangers. Irene, Murtybeg and Murty were there too.

'What now?' Kearney asked. 'It's dangerous mixing Irish navvies with English or Welsh.'

'One thing it shows,' Irene answered. 'We're losing control of our navvies.'

McManus made to speak, but Danny held his hand up. 'And before anyone says it, it wasn't Jamesy's fault. A riot could happen on any of our sites. We must put a stop to it. And by God, we will.'

'But how the devil can we do that?' Roughneen asked. 'It's not that I'm afraid, but there will be men killed soon. We've all families to be supporting back in Mayo, and we can't afford to be leaving the sites just because we're afraid of the Welsh and English fellows.'

'And It's costing us money too,' Murty said.

'And how!' McManus said. 'We've men laid up, some won't work for weeks. Four shacks to rebuild. And it's not just that. I've now got navvies on guard duty at night. Can't work them all day, without sleep.'

'So whose fault was it?' Murty asked.

'Everyone says it was the Welsh started it,' McManus answered, 'but that's only from the men I ask. I'm sure if you ask the Welsh, you'd get a different story. But I'll tell you right enough what started it. Drink. And not just among our fellows, I'd say the other gangs – English and Welsh, all have the same problem.'

Irene looked to Danny. 'Yes,' he said. 'Drink is a curse when you're got so many men together. I'd been thinking we'll have to put a stop to it, but, as

Jamesy already knows, the fellow is legal, and we have confirmation of that now. We had an Inspector around yesterday. Like us, he'd love to get rid of the shebeen, but he says it's legal too. He's been checking shebeens all over, not just on our sites. Every one of them, they're too smart to be selling *poitín* or any other kind of moonshine. Whiskey and gin only. 'Duty paid' – that's what they tell us every time. The Excise people are happy, and Inspector Crawford says he just cannot touch them.

'So what else can we do?' Lavan asked. 'Fire fellows for drinking.'

'What would you do then?' Murtybeg asked with a laugh. 'Fire the whole damn lot, ourselves included.'

'But we don't go brawling, do we?' Murty commented. 'But there is one other thing we can do. Let it be well known that anyone involved in a riot will be fired at once.'

'Fair enough,' Danny said. 'Take note of that, every one of you. No questions, no excuses, fire them.'

'And what if we're attacked?' McManus asked. 'We have to defend ourselves.'

'It will be up to you fellows on the sites to decide whether a defence is needed or not. Not easy, I know, but it's the only way we can do it.'

'And what about the shebeens?' Murty asked.

'I don't know,' Danny said, 'I'm thinking about it.'

That evening he discussed it all with Irene.

'What about that Brady fellow?' Irene asked. 'Would he be able to sort it out?'

'Hard to say,' Danny replied. 'Liverpool is a bit far. Still, he might have contacts nearer at hand.'

'If he knows the police in Liverpool, he'd surely be able to find out who to talk to in Manchester. Grease a few palms over here.'

'You're right,' Danny said. 'A few pounds in the right place, and the police will move them on.'

'Maybe,' Irene said. 'Or maybe not. It's worth trying though.'

After Irene had retired, Danny wrote a letter to Brady.

Brady replied, suggesting another meeting.

Two days later, Danny was in Liverpool again, supposedly to visit the Workhouse. After a desultory discussion with Solan, he walked to McCabe's in Vauxhall. He was ushered into the back room.

'Another shipment, is it?' Brady asked.

'Not yet,' Danny answered. 'It's not as easy getting workers from Ireland as it had been. Also, the crash in the markets. I want to wait a little before looking for more men.'

'That's understandable.'

'Yes, it's a different matter I wanted to talk to you about. We had a riot on one of our Works. Irish and Welsh, the usual sort of thing. A lot of skulls cracked, and there were shacks burnt out that night. I had Inspector Crawford around the following day.'

'Ah yes,' Brady said. 'Crawford.'

Danny thought of what Irene had said.

'Came across as a nice enough fellow, but I had my suspicions.'

'You might be right. But we're on your side, remember that. We can help you.'

'How?'

'We've done it already. There's other things we can do. Make sure you never have another riot, for example.'

'How on earth do we do that?'

'Pass the message back to your sites. I can do it through the bodymaster in Manchester. Aidan Sheridan is his name. A good man.'

'And how will he do it?'

'A few words in one or two ears. They'll make damned sure all the fellows understand.'

'Fine,' Danny said. 'But one thing that might help is to stop the drunkenness on site. It's the main cause of violence. And it's not that the men want to drink, but having a shebeen on site is a great temptation for any man.'

'A shebeen?'

'Yes,' Danny said. 'There's one on each of our sites. And the most vexing thing is that they're all legal. They pay their excise, so the police aren't interested. The exception is Oxford Road, but that's in Ancoats, and all the shebeens there are illegal. There's nothing we can do about drinking in a place like that, and I wouldn't even suggest that we try.'

'I see,' Brady said. He took out a pencil, and made some notes. 'And where are your other sites?'

Danny gave him details of each of the other sites.

'One would be enough, I imagine,' Brady said. 'One single example, and you'll find the others will scarper damned quick.'

'What sort of example?'

'A little encouragement, perhaps. That's all.'

'That would be excellent,' Danny said, not wishing to know more.

'All part of the service.'

'So how much would this all cost?'

'Hard to say how much would be involved, but I can understand that a man like you would want a definite answer. Ten pounds. Would that be satisfactory?'

'Certainly.'

For a week, nothing happened. Then, Danny had a visitor. He went to meet him at the door.

'Mr. Ryan.'

'Yes?'

'Mr. Brady sent me.'

'Come in,' Danny said, still suspicious.

Irene and Murtybeg were in the office. The man looked doubtfully at Irene. Danny followed his gaze.

'You may rest easy. She's my wife-to-be. And this is my brother here. No word leaves this room.'

The man still looked doubtful, but went on.

'Our friend in Liverpool just wants you to know that he's sorting out the shebeen problem. First though, it will be necessary for you to talk to our local contact. He'll want full information from you. And payment, of course.'

'And how will I find this contact.'

'You know Forkan's Bar? Not too far from Piccadilly Station. You'll be expected there. Just ask for Forkan. He knows Sheridan.'

There was a silence after the man had left.

'So Brady has his contacts in Manchester after all,' Irene said. 'Didn't I tell you so?'

'It'll be interesting to see what we get for our ten pounds,' Murtybeg said.

'Might quieten the men down a little anyhow,' Danny said.

Murtybeg laughed. 'It isn't the men you should be worrying about,' he said. 'It's them shebeen fellows. So long as they're selling liquor, there'll be men to buy it. You know that as well as I do.'

'They'll get a word from Sheridan too,' Danny said. 'They'll sure as hell know who he is. Either that, or the police will sort them. Now just trust me and stop worrying.'

Irene shook her head.

'We'll have to be very careful though, Danny.'

'I know.'

As Danny travelled into Manchester, he thought about Brady, and now, Sheridan. Did Brady and his associates hold all meetings behind bars? McCabe's and now Forkan's. He wondered what they had in common.

When he entered the bar, he found Forkan, who immediately brought him into a back room. He left Danny there, but this time it was only a few moments until the door opened again.

The man who entered the room was tall, and well built. Even in the poor light Danny could see a long weal across his right cheek. He wondered where that came from.

'Mr. Ryan, I believe.'

Danny held out his hand. 'The same.' His hand was not taken. Both men sat.

'Mr. Brady told me you've been having problems.'

Straight to the point, Danny thought. No small talk here.

'That would be putting it mildly. These damned navvy riots – they're hurting men and they're costing money.'

'I can understand that.'

'And it's not just that. It's the cause of them. While fights can happen at any time, one of the main causes is drinking. Even decent men get violent when they've too much.'

'I can understand that too.'

Forkan entered, placed two glasses of whiskey on the table, and left.

'You're not a temperance man, are you Mr. Ryan?' Sheridan asked.

'Not to the extreme. A glass or two never hurt anyone.'

He sipped the whiskey slowly. Irish, no doubt about it. It had the rough edge which Scotch never had. West of Ireland too. He wondered what distillery had produced this. Legal or not? Excise paid or not? To hell with that.

'So you want us to clear out the shebeens?' Sheridan asked him.

'We do. Whatever the cause of these riots, we must stop them. The question is how?'

Sheridan leant back in his seat. Danny could see the scar more clearly now.

'Gentle persuasion, we call it, Mr. Ryan. A few words in the right ears. A few shillings in the right palms. More than that, you don't need to know.'

'I see,' said Danny. He looked deep into Sheridan's eyes. A tough man. He had the eyes of a man well used to getting his way, and not caring how he got it. He wondered what 'gentle persuasion' would mean with a man like this. Paying off the police perhaps.

'So what next?'

'You'll see in time. And as you can imagine, there are costs to all this.'

'No doubt,' Danny said.

'Ten pounds. I believe that is what you agreed with Mr. Brady.'

'That would be perfectly satisfactory,' Danny said. 'I'll have the money sent to you.'

'You can drop it in here to Forkan if you prefer. He's reliable. He'll give you a receipt. We must make all this business-like.'

'Of course.'

Sheridan took notes of the sites and shebeens. Then he rose to shake Danny's hand. 'And don't worry about the next few weeks. It may take some time to get everything organised. But I can assure you, it will be.'

Danny left, and walked back the corridor. He made his way through the crowded bar, looking neither left nor right.

He walked across Peter's Square, and down to Mosley Street. At the Manchester & Salford Bank, he took out ten pounds in cash and returned to Forkan's bar. Forkan was waiting.

'You're most welcome, Mr. Ryan,' he said, placing a whiskey on the counter.

Danny handed him the envelope. Forkan checked it and placed it carefully behind the bar. Then he took out a piece of paper, wrote across it 'for the receipt of ten pounds' and signed it with an illegible signature. He passed it across to Danny.

Danny threw back the whiskey in a single gulp.

'*A thousand times, thanks,*' he said, and left the bar.

One day, Danny travelled to McManus' site. He could see the Works were proceeding well.

'Enough navvies now?' he asked McManus.

'We surely have. I'm catching up for all the delays we've had. We should make it on time.'

'Any fighting?'

'They're brawling all the time. No real riot since though. But there will be.'

They walked past the shebeen.

'Excise paid,' the man said.

'I didn't say a word,' Danny said.

'Damned bastard,' McManus whispered.

They went back between the lines of working men.

'We'll have to do something about him, McManus said. 'There's trouble brewing. I can smell it.'

'I think we'll have him sorted out soon enough.'

'You've spoken to Brady, have you?'

'I have. There's one of their fellows in Manchester. He'll sort it, don't you worry. But before they do, I think we should give them fair warning.'

'I'd leave that to Brady, Danny. He'll know what to do.'

'Fair enough so. In the meantime, I'd like you to let it be known that no whiskey is allowed on site. Nor nothing else neither. No intoxicating liquor. Anyone found drinking or drunk will be fired. The men have got to understand, this has to stop.'

241

Some days later again, Danny went to Kearney's site. He could see that these Works too were continuing satisfactorily. Kearney met him.

'Everything proceeding well?'

'Better than well,' Kearney replied. He pointed to the road above the site. 'See that?'

Danny looked. He could see nothing strange. 'See what?' he asked. 'I don't see anything.'

'That's just it,' Kearney replied. 'The shebeen. It's empty.'

'But what...?'

'I've no idea. I just came in this morning, and he was packing. He took all his stock, thank God.'

After the inspection, Danny walked back down the line. He had not expected this so rapidly. Brady surely had his ways of helping. Gentle persuasion was certainly working. Totally painless, with no problems whatsoever.

It would not be long until he discovered how wrong he was.

He was startled when Inspector Crawford appeared that evening. Danny and Irene met with him.

'And you can guess why I'm here,' he said to Danny.

'I can,' Danny said. 'The violence we've been having. We'll have to stop this kind of thing.'

'Indeed we will. And not just the rioting. You know about the attack on Eckersley?'

'Who?'

'The fellow in the shebeen.'

'But...what attack? Which shebeen?'

'At Mr. McManus' Works. You know those shebeens are legal.'

'I know,' said Danny. 'Excise paid.'

'A savage attack it was too. Five masked men, with hammers. They shattered both of his knees. He'll never walk again, that's for certain. No. Eckersley's for the Workhouse. It's all he's fit for.'

Danny grimaced. 'Oh, God.'

'I questioned him myself in the Workhouse infirmary earlier. How any man could have lived through that beating, I've no idea.'

'But...but...I don't understand.'

'What's not to understand?'

'I was out there myself just last week. The fellow was still there. I saw it with my own eyes.'

'That was then. Last night was when Eckersley was attacked. They burnt out the shebeen too. Did you not know?'

'No.'

'Strange. I'd have thought Mr. McManus would have told you by now.'

'I've been travelling all day.'

'I see.' He took out his notebook, and scribbled in it.

Danny leaned back in his chair, thinking rapidly.

'I'm very sorry to hear all this, Inspector. But the question is, who did it?'

'I was hoping you might know the answer.'

Danny was surprised at Crawford's insinuation, but quickly recovered his composure.

'I don't,' he said. 'I'd been concerned about the shebeens myself, as you know.'

'Certainly. And it's not that we'd think that you did it, but the question remains – who did?'

The same insinuation again. Again Danny stayed calm.

'Other distillers fighting for territory?' he said. 'Or it might have been organised through the Welsh foremen. They're well into temperance with their chapel ways.'

'Indeed they are,' Crawford said. 'I'd have thought it myself, except for a few things. There were three more attacks on your shebeens during the night...'

'Three more!' Danny gasped.

'Not as vicious as the first attack. No burnings. They beat them with sticks – that was all. More in the line of a warning, I'd say. And each of them was given one of these. The same as Eckersley got.'

He handed Danny a sheet of paper. On it was scrawled a rough outline of a coffin with a cross on it. Beneath the cross were the words – 'Simon Worsley. RIP'.

'Yes,' Crawford said. 'All four got one. They're all gone now, and I doubt any will return. Eckersley can't, and the others won't when they hear what happened to Eckersley. And I can assure you, Mr. Ryan, this has nothing to do with Welsh temperance preachers. It has all the hallmarks of the Molly Maguire gang.'

Chapter 18

Manchester Courier, England, December 1847:
According to the Nation, there are 168 estates in Ireland for sale. No wonder. Of the 265,509 navvies who are at work in this country in May last, it is believed that 128,000 are now unemployed.

Crawford left. Through the entire meeting, Irene had said nothing. Now, she spoke.

'This is getting dangerous, Danny.'

'I know.'

'You heard what he said? 'It's not that we think you did it.' Why would he say something like that?'

'I'd been thinking that myself.'

She pulled over a chair and sat in front of him.

'He clearly does think that you organised the attack. Otherwise he wouldn't have said it.'

'Yes,' Danny said, 'and he'd be right, except I didn't know I was organising something like this. For God's sake, Irene, we were talking about 'gentle persuasion'. A little bribery perhaps. And a few words in the right ears.'

'Yes. A few words. But no one's going to stop anything for that, are they? A few words are only effective with the threat of force behind it.'

'Yes,' Danny said. 'I should have thought of that.'

'We should all have thought of it. Brady and Sheridan fooled you and fooled all of us. We should always remember – if something is too good to be true, it isn't true. We're going to have to be more careful from here on.'

'We are.'

'But tell me one thing, Danny. I've heard of this Molly Maguire gang, but I know very little about them.'

'And I'd never have thought you'd have to either,' Danny said. 'I never knew they were over here, either in Liverpool or Manchester. They're a gang of bandits in the west of Ireland. They say they're standing up for poor people, but most of what they do is shooting landlords' agents, stealing cattle and the like. I would never have thought that Brady was the type. Sheridan neither.'

*

244

Danny was concerned. Crawford's visit had shaken him more than he had let on. Eckersley had been so violently attacked that he would never work again? He had not allowed for that. He thought of Jimmy Corrigan and the time he and Murtybeg had beaten him so badly in revenge for Nessa's death. Corrigan had died in Liverpool Workhouse. But that had been different.

He wondered if he had done the right thing in approaching Brady.

Perhaps not. But McManus had been so persuasive. He wondered about McManus' involvement. Was McManus himself in the Molly Maguires? He would have thought that most unlikely. He had known McManus since they were both children, and the subject had never been mentioned. On the other hand, the Molly Maguires were a secretive, oath-bound organisation. He knew, from stories he had heard in the past that men had been killed for breaking their oath of silence. But McManus as one of them? No. He could not believe that.

But there was worse. Now he himself was getting a reputation for brutality. Did that worry him? Certainly he was tough enough on his workers, but that never extended to that kind of savagery.

What worried him even more was Crawford's suspicion. How far could this go? He guessed Sheridan was careful enough, and the beatings would not be traced back to him or to Brady, nor even to Danny himself. He resolved to have no more dealings with the gang. He would have to explain that to McManus, and probably also to Sheridan and Brady, but that could come later.

At the next ganger meeting, the question of shebeens was the first item to be discussed. All of the gangers declared ignorance as to who had carried out the beatings, though Danny knew McManus was lying, and McManus knew that Danny knew that.

'I'm damned if I'd agree with something like that,' Roughneen said, 'but I won't complain about the results. I'm damned glad to be rid of them. Bad cess to the lot of them.'

'I think we'd all agree with that,' Danny said. 'We'll have less fighting on the sites, especially on pay days.'

Quickly, Irene moved on to the next item on the agenda.

'From what I can see, you're all well on target, timewise.'

'No problems there,' McManus agreed. 'The only question in my mind is – how long will the contracts last? There's contracts being suspended all around us. Everyone says it's only for a short time, but God knows what that means. A week? A month? A year?'

Danny decided it was time to intervene.

'We've no need to worry as yet,' he said. 'There's no suspensions on any of our contracts as yet.'

'There's rumours...' Lavan interjected.

'Rumours only,' Irene said.

'I don't know,' Lavan said. 'The contract with Brassey, that's damned near half of all of our business from what I understand.'

'Less than that,' Danny said. 'But what's your point?'

'Brassey mightn't have suspended any of the contracts on the North Staffordshire yet, but he's sure as hell doing it everywhere else. Already he's discharged twelve thousand navvies around England.'

'Twelve thousand?' Irene asked. 'Where did they get a figure like that from? It's all rumour.'

'No rumour,' Lavan said. 'It's official. A statement from Brassey's own office, no less. It's in all the papers.'

There was a silence around the room. Danny said nothing. He was surprised when Murty spoke.

'I'm beginning to think you're all scared of your own shadows. Brassey might be firing thousands of his fellows, but it's not on the North Staffordshire. And do you know why not? Because they're desperate to finish it. Right at the moment it's a bottleneck between the South of England to the whole North West. They've spent hundreds of thousands – millions – on it and they won't see a proper return on their investment until it's complete. No, I'm reckoning the reverse is what's going to happen. They'll suspend it right enough. On the day it's finished, not a moment sooner.'

Irene looked over to Murty, surprised. She had not expected this. Danny made to speak, but she held her hand up.

'Thank you,' she said. 'That's the most sensible thing I've heard today. It's blindingly obvious, so much so I can't think why I hadn't seen it before. Danny neither, though he mightn't admit it. Suspending the North Staffordshire at this stage would be financial suicide for the Railway. The directors, they know that, they must know it. And if I were a Railway director, the question I'd be asking is – can you finish even faster than you contracted for? What do you think?'

'We could,' Roughneen replied. 'Given the workers, we can do anything.'

Danny arched his fingers, thinking. 'Yes,' he said. 'And there's two ways we can do that. The first is this. If there's any suspension on any of our other sites, we can quickly transfer the navvies down to the North Staffordshire. But even if we keep all our other contracts, there's no shortage of labour now. And it's not just Brassey neither. They're saying that there's at least a hundred thousand Irish navvies out of work around England.'

'Not hard to see either,' Kearney said. 'On every street corner, you see them. It's amazing how quick it changed in a few months, isn't it? Then, we were desperate for men. Now, if we only give the word, we'll have lines of men begging for work.'

'And no need for high wages either,' Irene said.

'I'm not so sure about that any longer,' Murty said. 'The kind of wages we've been paying, that's fine for fellows coming straight off the boat from Achill or Erris. Fellows who've been working a year or two in England already, they'll need something more.'

'Not much more though,' Irene said.

'No, not much,' Danny said. 'Being out of work tames their demands. We'll see.'

As the men made to leave after the meeting, Danny tapped McManus on the shoulder.

'A word, Jamesy.'

'Yes, Danny.'

They stepped into the corridor.

'What on earth happened to that fellow in the shebeen? Why didn't you tell me?'

'I thought you knew. You were the one who organised it.'

'Me? I spoke to Brady, and I spoke to Sheridan. They were talking about 'gentle persuasion'. But damn it, that attack was vicious.'

'I'm surprised at you, Danny,' McManus said. 'You should know what 'gentle persuasion' means by now. And anyhow, it was hardly more than the kind of brawl we have here every day. You're lucky they didn't go all out.'

'All out,' Danny exclaimed. 'Like what?'

McManus drew his finger across his own throat. Danny looked at him horrified.

'In the name of God, Jamesy, we can't have that. The police are watching us as it is. If anyone dies, they'll be down on us like a ton of bricks. Worse than that, they'll be looking for someone to hang.'

'You're worrying too much,' McManus said.

'Like hell, I am. You just get a message through to Brady. Sheridan too. Tell them to go easy. I'm damned if I want to hang.'

'But you know Brady better than I do.'

'I might. But damn it, I'm running Edwardes & Ryan. I can't be drawn into something like this. And in any case, Gene Brady is your cousin, not mine.'

McManus shook his head. 'Fine so, Danny. I'll write to Gene, though I reckon it's all over already. The shebeens are gone, and they're not coming back.'

When Danny returned, Irene was on her own in the office.

'You know, Danny,' she said, 'these figures are very good. And I think your father was right. They're not going to suspend the Brassey contract, but

247

I reckon the faster we finish it, the more money we make.'

'But then half our business will be gone.'

'So what. We'll have made the money, and we can afford to sit on our hands and wait for the next contracts to come along. And they'll come.'

'I wish I had your confidence.'

'Of course they'll come. You know why? Because half the other labour contractors are bankrupt. All they need is a little encouragement, and they'll be gone.'

'I don't know what you mean.'

'You'll see.'

A timber supplier came to the office, looking for a Mr. Miller. Danny waved him across to Irene.

'I'm looking for Mr. Miller,' he said.

'You can call me that if you like,' Irene said, 'though most people call me Miss.'

The man looked bewildered, but then decided to accept the situation.

'It's about our last contract. We invoiced you for three hundred pounds. Payment within two weeks.'

'Three months,' Irene interrupted.

'Three months! Never. I never agreed to that.'

'We never agreed to anything.'

'You can't pay so.'

'Oh, I can pay right enough,' Irene said. 'It's you who can't stand waiting. Bankrupt already?'

'Me? Not I.'

'That's what you all say, but I know you are. And I intend to tell everyone. Three months are the terms, take it or leave it.'

The man looked at her in horror.

'I know who your suppliers are,' Irene went on. 'All I need is to drop them a note. Let them all know you're bankrupt. Three months is what I said.'

'Three months,' the man said. 'That's criminal.'

'Call it what you like,' Irene said. 'They're my terms. Take them, or take the consequences.'

'I...I can't.'

'So you really are bankrupt. Why don't you admit it?'

The man was sweating heavily. He stared at Irene in the eyes, but then dropped his eyes.

'Well, supposing I am.'

For fully half a minute, Irene said nothing, pretending she was thinking. Danny was going to speak, but he felt it was better to leave it to her. When she spoke again, she sounded almost reasonable.

'Fine,' she said, 'I'll help you. If you're that desperate for cash, I'll offer you COD – Cash on Delivery. Would that help?'

'It would.'

'Three hundred pounds, you said. I can pay you straight away. There will, of course, be a matter of a small commission.'

'Commission?'

'Let's say thirty pounds. I can give you £270. All paid.'

'But...'

'Your choice.'

Silence again.

'I'll take it.'

'Thank you,' Irene said. 'Now let's discuss how we go forward. We're looking for timber for shoring. As it happens, we also have a new contract for laying sleepers. I understand you have over three thousand tons in stock. You need cash on all of that. We'll need them delivered – shoring timbers and sleepers cut to length. That way, we can clear out your entire stock for you.'

'You can take my entire stock?'

'That's what I said. It's your only chance of avoiding bankruptcy. You should be grateful. Now how many tons do you have exactly?'

The negotiations continued, on Irene's terms. All this time, Danny had said nothing. He waited until the man had gone.

'How did you know he was bankrupt?' he asked.

'Know it!' Irene said. 'Read the papers. They're all bankrupt. If he wasn't, he wouldn't have been so frightened. He could have proven it quick enough – letters of credit through his bank, or whatever. And if he had stood up to me, I'd have given in – given him his two weeks, at the full price. But he didn't have the guts, did he?'

'I read the papers too, but I still wouldn't have guessed he was bankrupt. You've other sources of information, haven't you?'

'One only. Would you like to meet him?'

'I would. And the sooner the better.'

A few days later, they had a visitor. The maid showed him into the office.

He took Irene's hand. 'Irene, how nice to see you again.'

'You too, Nick.' She sat him at the table. 'And I'd like you to meet my husband-to-be, Daniel Ryan. Danny, meet Nick Roscoe.'

Danny shook his hand, observing him closely. Intelligent, no doubt about that. Tough too? Perhaps.

'Mr. Roscoe. I haven't heard of you.'

'No?'

'My fault,' Irene interjected. 'I wasn't expecting you this morning, Nick. I haven't had a chance of explaining anything to Danny.'

'No, you haven't,' Danny said.

'So…I've known Nick here for ten years at least. Ever since I was a junior legal secretary working with Rothwells. Nick used to work for the Liverpool Detective Police, though that was some time ago, wasn't it Nick?'

'Indeed it was.'

'In Rothwells we used to use Nick for private investigations, ever since he left the police. Family cases mostly, following wayward husbands around, working to see if their wives suspicions were right.'

Danny laughed.

'And how would you do that?'

'Oh, many different ways,' Roscoe replied. 'Everyone says I know every whorehouse in Manchester, though those stories might be a little embellished. It was a long time ago anyhow. Ever since then, I've been moving more into business and industrial investigation, gathering commercial intelligence on suppliers and competitors on behalf of various Rothwell clients. Much more the kind of thing you'd be interested in, I think.'

The maid had arrived with the tea. Carefully she poured it out.

When she had left, Roscoe slipped an envelope across the table to Irene. She took the contents out. At first she was puzzled. All she could see were small, rough pieces of paper. Then she realised she was looking at two paper sheets which had been torn up. Each of them had been carefully re-assembled and glued onto whole sheets.

'What are these?' she asked.

'Two documents that might interest you.' he said. 'Took me all night. They really tore them up small.'

'So I see.'

'Nearly a hundred scraps each. I had to sort them all, get them in order, and then glue them onto the two backing sheets.'

She peered closer. 'You've done a great job, Nick.

'I hope so,' he said. 'As you can see, one is Baxendales Balance Sheet…'

'Baxendales!' Danny exclaimed.

'Yes, Mr. Ryan. It's current from two weeks ago. The other document is a letter addressed to Mr. Baxendale by a Mr. Halliwell. He's the man in charge of accounts at the company.'

Danny pulled his seat around to Irene's side. Quickly, they both glanced through the figures on the Balance Sheet. Assets against Liabilities. Danny saw the balancing figure was positive, showing that Baxendales was solvent, if barely so.

But slowly he began to realise that all was not as it seemed. The assets showed the usual items – Baxendales' head office building, their various yards, machinery, stocks of timber and stone, as well as their cash holdings. But on the bottom of the assets, there were five outside investments, and the figures were considerable.

'And these are the interesting ones,' Roscoe said. 'Second down is Tetlow & Royle. They're a timber importer, specialising in the Quebec trade. Bankrupted four weeks ago. Goodfellows here is in the India trade. Went down about the same time. But the last one is the most interesting.'

Danny followed where his finger was pointing.

'Oh my God. The Royal Bank...'

'Yes,' Roscoe said, 'The Royal Bank of Liverpool. Once the safest bank in the country. Their shares are worthless now. And if you take these three out, the remaining outside investments are worth very little.'

'Yes,' Danny said, 'I can see that.'

'But if the assets are worth much less than you might think, the liabilities are even more interesting.'

'I can see they're borrowing from the Manchester & Salford,' Irene said. 'You told me that. And...what? Three more?'

'Exactly, Irene. Three more banks. And I'll guarantee you, none of them know about the others. And the yards and the buildings are mortgaged four times over. It's a serious fraud. The directors could be jailed for that alone.'

She flicked through the account manager's letter. 'And Mr. Halliwell knows all this?'

'Yes, and now the Baxendale family do too. All of them. By law, the directors have to inform the Detective Police here in Manchester.'

'I doubt they'd do that.'

'No. But I'll tell you one thing, Irene, if any of their creditors were to know, Baxendales would be in trouble. And if the Manchester & Salford knew about this – that would be the end of Baxendales.'

Danny considered the matter. Many questions ran through his mind.

'How did you manage to get this?' he asked.

'Very easy, Mr. Ryan. There's a bar just beside Baxendales' offices. Their staff drink in there. I sat in there on occasional nights, listening to the conversation. One evening, when all the clerks had gone home, two elderly women came in. They were Irish.'

'Irish!'

'Yes. Two charladies. They were complaining about the way they were treated. Real angry, they were. So I waited until one had left the bar and began to talk to the second. She was very bitter. She was being treated with utter contempt, and paid in pennies. I arranged to meet her in another bar, and when I finally gained her confidence, I offered her five shillings for the contents of the directors' waste paper baskets, particularly of Mr. Baxendale's office. You know, it's amazing how these kind of people treat their staff, and how they assume they have no ears. I must admit, a lot of what she gave me was worthless, but as you can see, these two documents are pure gold.'

Danny nodded. 'So what do we do now?'

'Very simple, Mr. Ryan. First, I've got two copies of each, for your records and mine. Then the originals go to the Manchester & Salford. Board level. The other banks too, we'll send them copies.'

'What...?'

'Don't worry. I'll not involve you. I'll get my secretary to write out a letter, ostensibly coming from an embittered creditor, who is terrified he will not be paid anything, and wants to know what the Manchester & Salford intend to do about it.'

'And then?'

'Then they're finished. Baxendales are finished. The Manchester & Salford and the others will demand accurate accounts. When they realise what's happening, they'll close in on them like vultures. Not that you should feel bad about it. If we didn't do this, Baxendales would try to trade their way out of it, but I doubt they'd succeed. It's going to happen sooner or later, but no reason not to do it now.'

Danny grinned.

'This is all possible?'

'Why not? It's one way of getting rid of one of your major competitors.'

Danny was stunned at the idea. What would happen if Baxendales went down? They had already taken business from Edwardes & Ryan. What now? Could Edwardes & Ryan bid again for what they had already lost?

'Yes,' he said. 'That could be very interesting. There's a second point though. We lost a bid at Ormskirk to Baxendales because the Manchester & Salford would not lend to us on it.'

'Yes, I know about that contract. But I've visited the site, and I can tell you they've only just started working on it.'

'After all this time!'

'Yes. And if the bank pull their lending, Baxendales won't be able to proceed at all.'

'Which might mean the bank would lend to us instead,' Irene asked.

'They might, Irene. In fact they might have to. If they don't lend to Baxendales, the East Lancashire might sue the bank for stopping the contracts. And that could cost the Manchester & Salford a lot of money. So they might have to lend to Edwardes & Ryan, whether they want to or not.'

Danny was thinking rapidly now. Could they have the Manchester & Salford lend to them after all? There were certainly other bidders, but he was confident they could under-bid any of them. Baxendales had been the second lowest bidder before. There was another point though. The McManus site.

Irene had been thinking the same.

'That would be excellent, Nick,' she said. 'But it could advantage us in other ways too.'

'Like how?'

'I told you about the trouble we had with a full-scale riot between our men and Baxendales. They are on a site beside one of ours. If they go bankrupt, we would be the obvious contractor to work that site.'

'You might. And I remember what you told me about the riot. You mentioned you met Inspector Crawford afterwards.'

'Yes,' she said, 'and that's the downside to all this. I thought he was a dangerous man, and you confirmed it. He's getting a little more dangerous now. He's been to see us again.'

'He has? But…why?'

'I'll explain this, Irene,' Danny said, abruptly.

Roscoe looked at him in surprise.

'You see, Mr. Roscoe,' Danny went on, 'we'd been having problems trying to get enough workers through the Liverpool Docks. There was a fellow who we'd been using in Liverpool to help get Irish workers into the country, paying the local police to look the other way.'

'Does Crawford know about this?'

'I doubt it, but that's not the problem. The real difficulty is that we decided to use this fellow again to sort out the shebeens on some of the sites. Drunkenness is one of the key reasons for the riots. Regrettably, he and his Manchester associates went too far. One of the shebeen owners was beaten extremely badly. There's some question he might not work again. And the very next day we had another visit from Inspector Crawford.'

'This is getting risky, Mr. Ryan.'

'More than risky,' Irene interjected. 'He definitely suspects Danny of having some involvement, but he's got no proof, and I don't even think he's certain. Still, it's a dangerous situation.'

'It is.'

Danny rose.

'I doubt there's much we can do about it today, though. Let's just concentrate on Baxendales for now.'

'Fair enough, Mr. Ryan. But will you let me know if there are any developments with Crawford?'

'Of course,' Danny said.

Irene went to the dresser, and opened a drawer.

'Now, Nick, how much?'

'As agreed. Ten pounds for the month. Another one pound and seventeen shillings for the out-of-pocket expenses.' He passed an invoice across the table. 'As detailed.'

She smiled. 'No need, Nick. I trust you.' She counted out the exact amount.

They waited until Roscoe had left.

'So that's where you all get your information?' Danny asked.

'It is. And I'll tell you this, Danny, he's the best. He knows exactly how the Detective Police work, both in Liverpool and Manchester. I've been using him for years, all the time I was with Rothwells. And ever since too.'

That evening, the family was at dinner when the maid came over to Danny. She whispered in his ear. 'Inspector Crawford to see you.'

'Show him into the office.'

He walked down, Irene following.

'What the hell does he want now?' Danny said angrily.

'God only knows.'

The inspector was sitting at the office table. His visit was brief.

'Mr. Ryan. Miss Miller. I just wanted to let you know that Mr. Eckersley has died.'

'Died!' Danny exclaimed.

'The blow to his head. It seems it caused some kind of clot in his brain. He died this morning.'

'Oh God.'

'Yes, and now this is a full-blown murder investigation. And I know you will help.'

'Of course, inspector. I'll do what I can.'

'I'm sure you will. One thing in particular, do you know if any of your men are members of the Molly Maguire gang?'

'Not that I'm aware of, Inspector. I will say though, we've hundreds of men, and I cannot speak for them all.'

The inspector nodded. 'Of course not. Even so, can I ask you to keep your eyes and ears open? Any members of the gang, we would like to question them.'

'Certainly, Inspector.'

After Crawford had gone, Irene stood up from the table.

'I'm sure of one thing, Danny. It's you he's after. He reckons you've some involvement with the gang.'

'But I'm not a member,' Danny said. 'Let's leave it at that, shall we?'

Chapter 19

Quebec Morning Chronicle, November 1847:
Scarcely more than half the usual number of mills are working full time; the diminution in the week having been no less than fifteen. The number of unemployed hands is upward of ten thousand, and there are more than twelve thousand working short time. The total number at full work is only about fifteen thousand, no less than five thousand having been placed on short time, or thrown altogether out of employment during the course of last week.

On a bitterly cold morning in November, Luke and *Conaire* set out for the forests. They boarded a steamboat in Quebec, along with many other Irish and Quebec lumbermen.

Luke leaned on the rail, watching the loading of the ship. Ice was forming in sheets on the edge of the St. Lawrence. He felt a hand on his shoulder. He spun around, and saw Jack Kilgallon.

'Christ, don't frighten me like that.'

'A man with a guilty conscience, eh?'

Luke laughed. 'Not that, but fear enough from watching all this ice. If it's cold here, what'll it be in the forests?'

'*Arra*, what are you on about? If it's cold that's worrying you, 'tisn't the forests you should be working.'

Luke looked around.

'Where are your brothers?'

'Oh, they didn't come. Thought it would be too cold out in the forests across the winter.'

'Maybe they were right.'

'Said they'd be better off working in the mills for a while. If they keep working, that is. Damned fools, if you ask me.'

'To be honest, I never thought you'd come either. You never mentioned it again.'

'I didn't want shouting about it. But the shipyards are on short time, so...'

'And what about New York? You still heading that way in the spring?'

'I am,' Jack said. 'I'm not sure the others will come though. If they don't go to the Gatineau, I doubt they'll go to New York. We'll see.'

'I doubt they'll make the Gatineau now,' Luke said. 'This'll be the last boat up the river, that's what they're saying. After this, it's horse wagons, and I reckon that'll be a lot slower, and a hell of a lot colder. And, from all I hear, the Gatineau is going to be damned cold.'

'Cold isn't the word for it. Freeze you, it would, right to the bone.'

They had begun to move.

During the journey Luke, *Conaire* and Jack leaned on the rail of the ship, watching villages go by.

Neuville. Portneuf. Deschambault.

The Quebec loggers stayed on one side of the boat, the Irish on the other. From time to time, insults were traded.

As they travelled, the weather got warmer. Soon there was no ice.

'Bit odd, that,' Jack said. 'You don't see the St. Lawrence clear, this time of the year.'

'Maybe it'll be summer, when we get to the forest,' Luke said.

'We'll have none of your joking,' Jack replied. 'When you get to the Gatineau, you'll learn what real cold is.'

Grondines. Sainte-Anne. Batiscan.

Trois Rivières.

The boat was stopping. Luke was puzzled. He tapped a man on the shoulder.

'What's this?' he asked. 'Why are we stopping?'

The man looked at him in puzzlement, then he pointed at a river and said simply '*St. Maurice*', and went on.

'What did he say?' Jack asked.

'Something about St. Maurice. Must be saying his prayers.'

'I've heard of it. It's another logging river.'

Some of the other Irishmen began to disembark. Then a man came up beside them.

'Time to get off,' he said, in a clear Donegal accent.

'What's this? Where...?'

'*Trois Rivières*. We walk from here. The ship's going up the *St. Maurice* with the Frenchies. So we got to walk the St. Lawrence to Montreal. They say there'll be another ship there.'

'The devil take it,' Jack said. They went down to the lower deck, packed their packs, and raced after the other men. Behind the column, a horse and wagon creaked along.

'Grub wagon,' Jack said.

As they walked towards Montreal, they started to overtake other groups

– men, women and children. One group was carrying a rough rope-made stretcher with a man on it. Luke recognised the reek of gangrene. He noticed too the group were speaking – whispering almost – in Irish.

The St. Lawrence widened. They sat down to rest, close to the edge.

'How long to Montreal?' Luke asked one of the other men.

'Three days total, they're reckoning,' the man replied. 'Seventy-seven miles the last time I walked it. Think you can keep it up?'

'Six days for crossing Ireland, that's normal,' Luke said. 'I'd guess they'd be more or less the same.'

That evening they stopped alongside Gilmour shanties, just off the road.

'Are these like the shanties on the Gatineau?' Luke asked, concerned.

'Not a chance,' the other man replied, 'these are only for resting. No bunks. The Gatineau shanties will be better than these wrecks.'

They stood around the grub wagon. It was only as he caught the smell of cooking that Luke realised just how hungry he was. After a long wait, he was handed a tin bowl and joined a queue behind the other men. The first man ladled out veal glue which had been boiled into soup. The second handed him cold salted pork with sourdough bread.

Luke, *Conaire* and Jack took their bowls across the road and sat by the river.

'A grand looking sight,' Luke said, 'or it would be, if we could forget some of those poor beggars we're seeing on the road. Half-starved they are, and fever too. Will we never get away from it?'

That night they wrapped their greatcoats and blankets around themselves and lay down on the hard wooden floor.

'Bit rotten, I'd say,' Jack said.

'Who cares?' Luke answered.

Next day, they passed many more family groups on the road. Some spoke Irish, or sometimes English with Irish accents. Most were silent. Once Luke noticed a clear Mayo accent, but he did not stop.

They passed a family group sheltering under waste timber and bark. There was a man inside, groaning in pain. A woman knelt beside him, holding his hand. Two children sat alongside, whimpering. Another woman was outside, trying to start a fire.

Luke hesitated.

'Come on,' Jack said. 'He's in fever. You don't want to get it, do you?'

They walked on.

That evening they were passing a river flowing into the other side of the St. Lawrence.

'That's the way up to Lake Champlain,' Jack said. 'The way to New York. Come April, that's the way we'll all be going.'

'Ever gone that route yourself.'

'Not all the way,' Jack replied. 'As far as Fort Edward on the Hudson.'

'And the American border?'

'They let us across easy enough. We were strong. Nothing like the poor devils they were turning back.'

'Irish, were they?'

'Most were. And a few Quebecers. But they're terrified of fever in the United States.

'So when did you arrive in Fort Edward?'

'May, June time. It would have taken a month longer to get to New York. But we reckoned then there were better wages to be had back in Quebec. We kept hearing these stories. They still couldn't get enough men, even off the boats from Liverpool. Nor Ireland neither. No way could they get enough. No, it was a good time in the mills and the shipyards in Quebec. And like yourself, we had to send money back to Ireland. Even last year there was call enough for it. So we said 'forget New York' and went back to Quebec.'

Luke was thinking rapidly. How long to get down to New York? Depends on when we leave. April perhaps. Arrive when? June or even July? No fixed address until then. So if he wrote back to Carrigard, it could be August, or even into September before Winnie could leave. Or later? Getting into the winter season. What then?

They arrived at Montreal. More ragged families, some walking, some begging.

'It's like I told you,' Jack said. 'Montreal is worse than Quebec.'

At last, they arrived at the docks.

'So where do we sleep now?' *Conaire* asked.

'Seems we make our own way.'

They were directed to the Gilmours' agent. Luke knocked on the door of a small shack.

'Enter.'

Luke went in. 'We're looking for Gilmours.'

'We're Gilmours.'

'There's a crowd of us outside, travelling from Quebec up the Gatineau.'

'Ah, yes, we've been waiting for you. We're expecting the ship to leave tomorrow, probably about the middle of the day. You'll have to wait over until then.'

'Fine so,' Luke said. 'Do we sleep on the ship or where?'

'If the ship were here, there'd be no problem, but it's not arrived. You'll have to seek your own sleeping quarters.'

They left.

'So *where do we go now?*' *Conaire* asked.

'*God only knows,*' Luke said, '*but I don't want to stay outside.*'

Jack pointed to some timber sheds further along the docks. 'Let's try these,' he said. 'Perhaps we could force one of them.'

Jack and *Conaire* went ahead. As Luke saw, there was no need to force any door. Jack opened one and stepped inside. Within a moment he was out. 'Oh Christ Almighty,' he gasped.

'What's wrong,' Luke asked.

'Fever, that's what's wrong. They're fever sheds. Oh God, the stench of them.'

'Well we can't stay here, that's for certain.'

Just as they started to walk away, one of the other men shouted. 'This one's empty.'

Luke went over and went into the shed, sniffing carefully. *Conaire* was behind him. '*Was there fever here?*' he asked.

'*Not lately,*' Luke answered. '*I reckon it's safe enough.*'

'*Beds too.*'

'If that's what you'd call them,' Jack said. 'The half of them are in a state of collapse.'

'Well, ye may use them,' Luke said. 'I'm going to sleep on the floor.'

'A bit early for that,' Jack said.

'You're right,' Luke answered, 'and I'm hungry too.'

Two of the other men had lifted one of the broken beds, and were carrying it outside.

'What are ye doing?' Luke asked.

'Making dinner.'

'With a bed?'

Luke, *Conaire* and Jack followed them. The bed was quickly smashed by jumping on it until the boards cracked. Rough straw that had been used in place of a mattress was placed underneath, a match produced and within minutes there was a roaring fire, as more shattered beds were thrown on top. The wagon men began to collect water to boil the dried veal glue into soup. Luke took sourdough bread from the wagon, and, holding it on his fork, he held it as close to the flames as he could. By the time it was toasted, the soup was ready.

'*Pocket soup only,*' *Conaire* commented. '*No salted ham.*'

'*Be thankful to have it,*' Luke said. '*There's others have nothing. What do you think, Jack?*'

'*To be honest, there's only one thing wrong.*' Jack said. '*The front of me is roasting hot, the back is freezing.*'

'*He's got the Irish after all,*' *Conaire* said.

259

'I have,' Jack said. 'And the English. As will you.'

Luke stood up, stamping his feet. In the distance, he saw two robed figures approaching across the snow.

Nuns.

'What the devil…?' Jack said.

One came up to where Luke was standing. 'Irish?' she asked, uncertainly.

'Yes,' Luke said, more intrigued than ever.

'*Vous ecrivez?*'

'I don't understand.'

She repeated the words. Then, with a look of frustration she put her hand into her robes, and drew out a blank piece of paper. Using her index finger, she imitated writing.

'Yes…?' Luke said. 'I don't know…'

'*She wants to know if you can write,*' Conaire said, '*and you can't deny that you can. One way or the other, there's no way I can.*'

'And what about the rest of ye?' Luke said.

'Well, I wouldn't say I could,' Jack said. 'I've written right enough but I can't spell a thing. So it's over to you.'

He pointed at Luke. The nun beckoned him.

'Damn it to hell,' Luke said, 'why should I go?'

'Because you won't know what she wants unless you do,' Jack said.

'Well come on then,' Luke said, 'let's go.'

Jack made as if to get up, but the second nun pointed to Luke.

'You write?'

'Yes,' he said, 'I write.'

'You write?' she asked Jack.

'No.'

Jack sat again.

'Well damn the whole bloody lot of ye,' Luke said.

He followed the two women, who spoke French among themselves, ignoring him.

'Where are we going?' Luke asked at length. No response.

He pointed ahead of him saying 'where' again.

'Hôpital. *Pointe St. Charles.*'

When they arrived. Luke was overwhelmed by what he saw. Laid out in front of him were dozens of sheds. He had no need to ask what was inside.

He followed the two sisters, until they stopped at one of the sheds and brought him in. The stench was murderous. From County Mayo, he could well recognise the sickly smell of gangrene from typhus. The stink of diarrhoea too. Something else?

'Typhus?' he asked.

'*Oui. La fièvre typhoïde, la dysenterie et la diarrhée.*'

Luke was surprised he could understand everything. The smell of dysentery – that was the one he had not recognised.

'*Scorbut,*' she added. This he did not understand.

He looked down the hut. The endless rows of beds, the gaunt appearance of the patients, these were all too familiar to him. The fever sheds in Knockanure Workhouse were much the same.

In the centre, another nun sat at a desk, writing. She looked up as the two sisters brought him over. A discussion in French followed, but Luke could not follow any of it, and waited. Then one of the sisters, picked up a square wooden board, and placed a pen and an inkwell on top. She beckoned to Luke. The second sister followed, carrying a chair.

Some room was made between two of the beds, and the chair placed between them. Luke sat, with the board on his knees. A gaunt face looked up at him. Toothless gums.

Of course. *Scorbut.* Scurvy. And typhus.

'You speak English?' Luke asked.

The man shook his head.

At first, Luke thought that he had been taken to a French speaker, until the truth dawned on him.

'*You speak Irish?*' he asked.

'*I do,*' the man said weakly.

'*Fine so,*' Luke said.

He began to write the letter as the man spoke.

'*Dear Father and Mother, Dear Katie and Dick,*

This is to tell you that I have arrived well in America and am now living in the city of Montreal.'

Luke stared at him, incredulous. Would the man survive typhus? He was already desperately thin. Luke had seen enough of that on the Ox Mountains and in Knockanure Workhouse. He knew it was close to a certainty that the man would die, but he was whispering again.

Once more Luke wrote –

'*I have not any money with me now, but hope over the next few months to send you some as soon as I get work. I hear the potatoes are good, so I have no fear for ye, right now. By early next year it should be possible to send the money to ye, to bring Katie and Dick out to America.*'

Luke wrote for some time yet – more details of travel, of friends and many other things.

At last it was finished.

'*You can now finish it off whichever way is best,*' the man said.

Luke wrote '*I remain, your loving son and brother,*'

'*Your name?*'

'*Éamonn McSuibhne.*'

The nun took the letter, and waved it gently to dry the ink. She gave Luke an envelope. Again, he bent over the man, and wrote as the man told him.

Séamus & Máire McSuibhne.

Boireanach Bán.

Luke looked up in astonishment. *Boireanach Bán* – The White Lady. Burrenabawn.

He wrote Burrenabawn in English, and continued –

Above Knocklenagh

County Mayo

Ireland

Burrenabawn. The name of a mountain, no more. Two, or was it three, mud villages across the side of it. No names, all just known by the mountain's name. And what had happened in Burrenabawn?

He thought back to the savage winter. How many had survived the hunger and cold? Damned few. And even if they had, what of the fever that had followed?

Were the McSuibhnes still alive or dead? Even if they were, they might have left Burrenabawn. He knew the chances of the letter being delivered were slight, but then, he reflected, the chances of the sender living were slight too.

He folded the letter. When he was finished, the nun tapped his shoulder. He picked up his board, pen and inkwell and followed her to another bed. And then another.

There were six more men and two women from Burrenabawn and the mountains around it.

Lisnadee. Teenashilla, Benstreeva.

And Croghancoe.

All the memories of the horrors of the Famine Relief Works in the mountains came flooding back as he wrote. He had come to Canada to escape all that, but even here it followed him. So many in fever, so many dying. What was different?

As he moved towards the far end of the shed, the accents and addresses were from the south west of Ireland – Clare, Kerry, but especially West Cork. He no longer knew the names of the small villages.

By the end, he had written over twenty letters, he no longer bothered to count.

Some of the men and women described their sickness, but even they seemed to believe they would recover. In a few cases, the patients were too far gone to speak. Sometimes Luke guessed what they were saying, sometimes not. He wrote something anyhow.

Many times he noticed patients who had lost most of their teeth. He saw too the rotten gums. Scurvy? Yes, no doubt about it. Though with all the other fevers, it hardly mattered.

At last, he followed the two nuns out. It was almost totally dark. They walked along between a number of the sheds until one of the nuns stopped. She said something in French, and went into the shed beside her.

'Oh God, no,' Luke said. 'Not more.'

The first nun shook her head, and indicated for him to wait. The door opened again, the nun came out, accompanied by another in a grey robe. They were talking in French, but as they came up to Luke, the grey nun put out her hand.

'*Well, what have we here?*' she said in Irish. '*You're a long way from home.*'

He stared at her, astounded.

'*You could say that again,*' he said. '*Luke Ryan, they call me. From the County Mayo.*'

'*As if you needed to tell me where you're from.*'

More discussions followed in French with the other two sisters, then they both shook Luke's hand gravely, and left.

'*Are you lost now, Luke?*'

'*I am. I just followed the good sisters here, and now I've no idea where the devil I am, nor where I started from.*'

'*You're in the* Emigrant Hospital *at Pointe St. Charles.*'

'*I should have guessed.*'

'*Well, come on,*' she said, '*Just follow me. They told me where they got you.*'

As they walked, he discovered many things about Sister Benedict. She was from Skibbereen, in the west of County Cork. She was a member of the Grey Nuns, who had been the first group of sisters to go into *Pointe St. Charles* the previous June.

'*And a dreadful summer it was too,*' she told him. '*Calcutta heat, they called it. Mother McMullen and Sister Sainte-Croix, they were the first of ours to see the sheds, and when they came back, Mother McMullen told us that in asking us to minister for the sick she was sending us to our deaths.*'

'*But you lived,*' Luke said.

'*I did,*' she said, '*and probably shouldn't have. I got the fever right enough* – typhus – *but I'd had it before as a child, and, with God's blessing, I was strong enough to live this time too. But so many of our sisters died in Pointe St. Charles.*'

'*Oh God.*'

'*Yes, I don't know what we would have done without the other Orders too. The Sisters of Providence. The sisters from the Hotel Dieu. The Anglican ministers too, their people died. So many, so, so many. They spent their time like the rest of us, trying to feed the people, cleaning up after them, you know what's it's like.'*

'I do. I saw enough of it back in Mayo.'

'But when we've all these things to do, there's no time for writing letters. If I even gave them the idea of writing letters, there'd be no time to clean up. And of course in the sheds where the Quebec nuns are working, none of them can speak English, let alone Irish. That's why they went for you.'

'Yes,' Luke said, *'they had it very well organised. All the letters I had to write – Mayo, Clare, Kerry. Cork too. It'll cost you a fortune to post though.'*

'You didn't think we'd send them all separately, did you?'

'What then?'

'They all go in one package to the Archbishop of Tuam. He has them re-posted at local rates – a penny a letter. Much cheaper, and paid for by the Archdiocese. So don't worry. The letters will arrive, and you'll have done a great service.'

'Perhaps,' Luke said. *'But even so, I felt bad about the lying.'*

'Lying?'

'Telling their families they were alive and well. Many of them will never live to see the rest of Canada, let alone Ireland.'

'I know, Luke. I know.'

They had arrived at the docks. Jack and a few of the men still stood around the embers of the fire.

'God bless you, Luke,' Sister Benedict said, making the sign of the cross. To Luke's surprise all the other men knelt.

She made the sign of the cross again.

'Ye and your families, wherever ye go.'

Luke stood apart, smoking his pipe. What a fool he had been. The sheds put him in mind of Knockanure Workhouse, but that was to be expected. He had taken a great risk. He could have contracted typhus. And how would he know? He knew typhus took many days to show itself. How long would it be before he might be confident he had not gotten the disease? And what about dysentery? That had been a big killer in the Workhouses too.

He thought of Winnie back home in Mayo, with the baby coming. No, it was not just his own health. He had been careless with his own family. So why him? There must have been other men who could write. He did not have to follow the sisters. Why should he have been the one to go?

Jack stood beside him. 'What's biting you?'

'Just thinking what a fool I've been.'

'I could have told you that,' Jack said. 'You could have got fever.'

'And could yet.'

'Sure let's wait and see. 'Tis all we can do, the any of us.'

'You know what it is,' Luke said, 'I'm sick and tired of famine and fever. I'm sick of Ireland and the Irish. Will it ever change? All I want to do now is get away from it all. Bring my wife and baby over, get work on the railways, and forget Ireland.'

At dawn, they walked to the docks and embarked for the Gatineau.

'And thank God for that,' Jack said.

The magnificent buildings in the centre of Montreal put Luke in mind of London, and even parts of Liverpool or Dublin. But the fever formed an awful contrast in his mind.

Soon after Montreal they left the St. Lawrence, turning into the Outaouais River. It snowed lightly, then stopped. The sun came out, but now it was bitterly cold. And so to Bytown.

'A busy place,' Luke commented.

'Sure why wouldn't it,' Jack said. 'That's the Rideau River there. They're building some kind of dam up there, run the saw-mills off water, they will.'

The ship stopped to take on provisions. '*A small class of a place,*' Conaire said.

'It's growing though,' Jack said in English.

Luke spotted more Grey Nuns on the dock.

'*Better hide out of the way,*' Conaire said.

'*That's not funny.*'

The ship pulled away and crossed the Outaouais, heading north into another river.

'The Gatineau,' Jack said.

On the banks, they saw tiny groups of houses, but they could hardly be described as villages.

Chelsea, Wakefield, Low, Kazabazua, Gracefield.

Luke thought of the villages he had seen coming up the St. Lawrence, but they were nothing like that. The ship stopped at Gracefield, and close up Luke could see it was little more than some kind of depot, with constant movement of horses, wagons and sleighs. Luke and Jack were ordered down to assist in off-loading wagons, and reloading some on the ship.

'*Hard work,*' Conaire said.

'*And it'll be a lot harder in the forest,*' Jack commented.

Early one morning, the ship berthed at a rough-cut timber pier. The snow was deeper now. It was very cold.

As soon as they had disembarked, they were put to work, off-loading barrels and sacks under the supervision of an Irish ganger.

'Pork and flour,' Jack said. 'You'll get plenty of pork and bread on the Gatineau, I can tell you.'

After offloading, they spent more hours lifting barrels into wagons. Last of all, their own packs.

They sat down, gasping. *'Tough gangers here too,'* Conaire said.

'Aye,' said Luke, *'Another Donegal fellow, by the accent.'*

'I don't think we're going to get away from the bastards,' said Conaire. 'Mayo or Donegal. Irish or Quebecer. They're all the same.'

They did not rest for long. Soon they were ordered up.

'What now?' Conaire asked.

'We walk,' Luke said. They started to follow a line of horse-drawn wagons.

'Here you,' the ganger said, grasping Luke by the arm. 'You're a horse man aren't you?'

'I can...'

'You're a teamster now. Get in there with the other fellows.'

'What? Where...'

Luke spent the rest of the day with the horse teams, almost dragging the horses along, across streams and rivers and up through rough tracks scarcely hacked out of the bush and forest. Conaire and the other Mayo men followed behind. At last one team of horses stopped on a slope.

'Come on, offload the sacks,' the ganger shouted. Conaire and the rest were shoved forward and each loaded with a sack of flour.

'Nice to see you fellows do a bit of work for a change,' Luke said, as the others struggled up the slope with the heavy sacks. He went back to the horses, prodding, driving and goading the animals up the slope with the half empty wagon. He waited on the top as it was being reloaded.

'Maybe we should have stayed in Quebec,' Conaire said.

'Arra what,' Jack said, *'it's well time we strengthened you up anyhow. Wait until we get to the shanties, then you'll have cause to be complaining of hard work.'*

But after that, the others went on, while Luke stayed behind with the horses.

That night, Luke slept with the animals, wrapped in his coat and a blanket, and nestled up to a horse for warmth. It was another two days before he arrived in the shanty camp. It was already getting dark.

He asked his way to where the other Mayo men were staying. As he entered the shanty there was a strong warm fug, smelling of smoke, pork, grease and sweat. It took some time for his eyes to get used to the half-darkness, and he tripped on the rubbish on the wooden floor. There was a fire at the far end of the shanty. Beside it he could see sparks flying from a grindstone where axes were being sharpened. On one side of the shanty, men were washing. The other side was mostly taken up by bunk beds, three high.

'*By God, it's great to see you,*' a voice said from a table in the corner.

'*Conaire!*'

'*I thought we'd lost you forever.*'

'*There were times I thought that myself*' Luke said. '*Now show me my bunk.*'

'*Would you not play a hand of cards?*'

'*I wouldn't be able to see the cards with the sleep.*'

Conaire led him to a bunk. Luke pulled a blanket over himself, without undressing. Within seconds he was asleep.

They were roused early by an Irish voice.

'Roarty,' the man beside them muttered. 'Another Donegal caveman, wouldn't you know it.'

Roarty led them up alongside a trail, more stumps showing through in places. Much of the trail was covered with frozen manure. Twice they stood to the side to let men pass, each guiding two horses, pulling a single log to a team.

'*Did you see the size of those logs,*' Luke said. '*The horses back home would never be able for that kind of thing.*'

'*If there were horses,*' Conaire said.

As they reached the standing forest, they could hear the sound of axes far inside. They were shown how to link the chains to the logs.

There was an enormous stack of logs on one side. Slowly they were prised out and rolled across to the three men. They linked the chains onto the logs as they had been shown, under Roarty's direction.

Then they guided the horses down the trails to the assembly station just below the shanties.

Each morning now, they rose well before dawn and worked until they could no longer see the trail. Even then, they worked with the horses when they came back to the camp before returning to the shanty – unhitching them, rubbing them down, feeding them and leading them to their stables.

After a few days, Roarty came alongside as they started the horses down the trail.

'Your friend there. He's never worked with horses?' he asked Luke.

'*What did he say?*' Conaire asked.

'*He says you've never worked with horses.*'

'*Little chance I ever got of that in Torán. Horses were only for gentlemen.*'

'What's that?' Roarty asked.

'He says he's never worked with horses. Didn't have them out his part of Mayo.'

Luke wondered how a Donegal man could not understand Irish. Perhaps Erris was too far from Donegal, and the accent was too different. Or perhaps Roarty simply did not want to show he spoke the language.

'We'll send him down to the river so,' Roarty said. 'He'll be better employed unloading at the dock.'

Conaire left that afternoon for the dock on the Gatineau River.

Chapter 20

Quebec Gazette, January 1848:
The temperature on the 10th and 11th inst., was the coldest of the season, and indeed in no season is the thermometer usually so low in Canada. It has been down for two days at sunrise according to position and thermometers to from twenty five degrees to thirty degrees below zero.

For the winter Luke worked with horses. There were thousands of horses working in the forests. In Mayo he had been used to working with horses on ploughing, and carrying hay and turf. But that was only one at a time. Here the work was far tougher.

But he found it more fascinating too. The enormous logs, the long lines of them being hauled down the trail – this was a vastly greater operation than he had ever seen in Mayo. In many ways, it compared to building English railways. There too, horses were used, pulling carts or rail wagons of spoil from the cuttings to the embankments.

Around the cambooses in the shanties, Luke heard many stories of logging along the Outaouais. Stories of working in the logging ponds, the timber storage yards and the shipyards in Quebec and Montreal. Stories too of working in the lumber camps along the Gatineau River, as well as the Rideau, the Schuyan, the Quio and the Bonnechere. Working the sawmills along the rivers and canals – Brewer's Mills, Davis' Mills, Chaffey's Mills, Kingston Mills and many more.

Floating logs down the river, clearing log jams, floating enormous rafts of logs down the St. Lawrence. He thought again of what Jack had told him. The journey to New York after the rivers thawed. How long 'till he got there? Was it possible for Winnie to reach America in 1848?

Luke noticed that there was one man who spoke little of lumber and forests. His name was Jim O'Neill, a Tyrone man as Luke discovered. But from all Luke could determine, the reason for his silence was that he had no interest in forests. Nor, it appeared, did he have much interest in travelling up and down the rivers and canals to New York. At times, Luke wondered what he was doing in Canada.

O'Neill could have been in the Molly Maguire Gang. Certainly, he spoke enough about it. Luke remembered the night when he had been beaten by three men in the Ox Mountains for destroying an illicit shebeen on the Famine Relief Works. He was almost sure they had been Molly Maguires.

He was certain though, that they had shot Clanowen's agent in County Mayo. He felt the agent deserved what he got. Still, it had resulted in evictions right across the Clanowen estates, including the one he had witnessed just outside of Kilduff. Was it better to resist and take the consequences, or lie down and do nothing?

Late one night, Luke returned to the shanty. He sat at the table by the camboose, and held his head in his hands.

'By Christ, Roarty is a tough son-of-a-bitch to work for. Where did we get the likes of him?'

'They're all the same,' O'Neill said. 'Gilmours drive them hard, and they drive us like animals.'

One of the older men, who had been lying in a bunk closest to the camboose, drew himself up and walked over to the table.

'What are ye fellows going on about? You don't know what tough work is. I'll tell you this, if you had been working on the Rideau Canal back in the '30s, then you wouldn't be whinging about tough work now.'

'That was Gilmours?' Jack asked.

'Or the Wrights? Damned if I can remember. But I'll tell you, it was the hardest work on God's earth. So don't you fellows be moaning and complaining.' He walked back to his bunk.

'What was that all about?' Luke asked.

'Oh, the Rideau Canal,' O'Neill said. 'That was heading back to the St. Lawrence, but the other direction, so as to be sending timber up to Lake Ontario to supply the Americans that way.'

'The Gilmours and the Wrights. All good English names. No Quebecers?'

'I don't know about that,' O'Neill said, 'but at least we got one Irish.'

'That crook,' one of the other men grunted. 'He's worse than the Gilmours.'

'Who's that?' Luke asked.

'Egan,' O'Neill answered. 'John Egan. A Galway man, wouldn't you know it.'

'A tough breed, too,' the other man said. 'Galway fellows are worse than the Quebecers for fighting.'

'*Arra*, go on,' Luke said, 'Mayo can beat Galway any time. But enough of that, tell us more about this Egan fellow.'

'He's the one that's opening up the Bonnechere,' O'Neill replied. 'Said to be the richest man in Canada. And I'll tell ye this, men like that don't get rich by being easy on their workers. No, he's a right son-of-a-whore, may God damn him to Hell.'

'There's one thing I can't understand here,' Luke said. 'These Irish fellows, like Egan, and the gangers, nearly all Irish. I'd have thought you'd have more Quebecer and English fellows up this way to keep us in order.'

'Ah now, that's a little hard to understand, right enough,' O'Neill said. 'Right now, we're working for Gilmours, and they're sure as hell not Irish, even if they're good friends with that Egan bloodsucker. But it all goes back, twenty years damn near, to the time of the Shiners.'

'The Shiners?'

'Aylen and his gang. He'd only hire Irish fellows for his shanties, all here up in the Gatineau. And when he had a good number of them, he reckoned he had an army. Enough to scare the devil out of the Quebecers. Wrecked their rafts too, he did. Same in Bytown, the Shiners damn near wrecked the place. Don't hear much of Aylen now though. Made his money, sold out, and now he's as respectable a fellow as you can get. They all get respectable in the end, and then they're part of the club.'

'Like Egan?' Luke asked.

'Yes, just like Egan.'

Luke found he was becoming accustomed to the shanty and shanty life. Because it was winter, the men spent all their time after work within the shanty. It was warm, and after hours working in the snow, Luke was thankful for that. They were very dark though, with the only light coming from the camboose and the odd guttering candle. It would have been impossible to read, but since they had no books or newspapers, this made very little difference. At first, Luke found it disgusting to wash in the same trough as the other men, and use the same towel, but this too, he grew accustomed to. His blankets were almost black with soot and grease, and the unceasing stink of smoke, soot and grease permeated the shanty.

The stink of human bodies was even worse. Many of the men never removed their clothes, sleeping in them until they were close to disintegrating. Luke made sure to wash his clothes regularly, though since this was in the common trough, he wondered how much difference it made. At least there was some soap alongside, which might have had some effect, he thought. But, unlike Luke, most of the men never washed their feet. They were quick enough to take off their boots and socks though, and very few seemed to worry about the effect this might have had on anyone else.

In ways, the stink reminded Luke of the appalling sweet stink of gangrene in the mud cabins around the mountains in Mayo. Benstreeva, Teenashilla, Burrenabawn. And Croghancoe. But here at least, there was no fever. The men were well fed too, and Luke was thankful for that. Death was one thing which no longer upset him as it once might have. The savagery of famine and fever in Mayo had hardened him long since.

On one occasion, he had seen an axe-man with a broken leg. On that occasion he had been asked to take the man back down to the shanty. He was loaded up on top of the log that Luke was taking down, two of his workmates at each end of him and a greatcoat underneath. The axe-man screamed at every bump and jolt as Luke led the horses along. One of the men tried to tourniquet the leg, and staunch the flow of blood, but it was impossible, and drip by drip the blood stained the snow. When they came to the shanty, he was carefully brought inside. A second tourniquet was applied, which stopped the flow of blood at last, but it was too late. That night, the axe-man died.

When Luke awoke the following morning, the body was gone. He did not ask what had happened to it, nor did he have any wish to know.

In spite of tough conditions, the work fascinated him. The fellers were the most experienced, and many worked year round with the lumber companies, not part-time like most of the shanty men. Luke wondered at their expertise in bringing trees down precisely as they wanted. It was vital that they not hang up on other trees, or sustain damage falling on rocks. Also, they had to be in the best possible position for squaring the log and for hauling. They were all axe-men, the sawyers being regarded as a lesser breed. The sawyer's job was to saw off the branches, and this was regarded as unskilled work. Then it was back to specialist axe-men to square off the log. Sometimes this was done at the edge of the forest, more often alongside the shanty.

Then the logs had to be hauled to the nearest available water. This was easier where Luke and Jack were working, as compared to other shanties further inland. Here the nearest available stream was the Gatineau itself, and there was no need to bring the logs down by smaller streams, where log jams grew.

All through November, it had been snowing, but there were many clear periods, and the snow was not heavy. Each time, Luke found it easy enough to lead his horses back up from the shanty to the logs at the edge of the uncut forest. Because of the weight of the logs, there was little problem in bringing them down, and most times the other teamsters had already flattened the snow on the trail to an icy consistency.

But January was when the real snow came. For two days, they stayed inside the shanty, as the blizzard went on. The third morning dawned bright, and gangs of men were set to digging trails through the snow. Luke and the other teamsters were spared this work, and it was only the next morning they started to lead their horses back up the slope to the forest edge.

One morning, Luke had dragged his logs down to the assembly point. He unhitched the chains, threw them over the horses' backs and started leading them back up the slope. The area alongside, and stretching to the distance, had already been clear-felled. There had been a fresh fall of snow during the night, and most of the landscape was covered with it, stumps of cut trees poking through. In the distance, on top of a slight rise, men were burning branches and shavings in a bonfire. The smoke swirled up against a vivid blue sky.

Like white smoke over a white mountain.

Images flashed through his mind in quick succession. Frozen people building frozen roads in ragged shifts and straw-filled boots. The mud houses on Croghancoe – the screams, the gangrene, the rat-eaten faces. The stink of the fever sheds at Knockanure. The death pit.

His hands were trembling. He grasped the chains, and clung on to the side of a horse, waiting until the trembling stopped. Then he pushed himself back, shook his head, and went on.

One Sunday came the battle.

It started easily enough. One of the Quebecers came over from where they were working, turned around and walked back.

'My axe,' one of the Irish axe men shouted. He's got my axe.' He ran after the Quebecer who raised the axe, and swung it at the axe-man, who jumped aside and came back with a swinging fist. The Quebecer fell on the ground, but jumped up, and came back, swinging the axe again.

Dozens of Irish and Quebecers came out of the shanties to watch. Then the fight became general. Within minutes the whole clearing was a mass of brawling men, with axes and horse chains swinging. Through it all, there was the constant shrieking of the gangers' whistles.

'We'll stay back here,' Jack said.

'Dead right we will,' Luke said. 'No need to get caught up with that bloody lot.'

'What kind of cowards are ye?' one of the Irishmen said.

'No cowards,' Jack said, 'it's just that we have a *trawneen* of sense, that's all.'

Luke watched in horror as one of the Quebecers brought an axe down on the shoulder of one of the Irishmen.

'Lucky he missed the head too,' Jack said.

Now there was blood on the snow. One of the Quebec fighters was hit by a chain across the face, and fell screeching. It got worse.

Two men came close to them, grappling a knife. At last it jerked down, slithering across a ribcage. The knife fell. As the other man went to pick it up, he was hit a blow on the head from behind with an axe handle, and fell onto the man he had come so close to killing.

By the time it was over, many men lay on bloodied snow, as the gangers re-established control.

Men staggered back to their shanties, some walking, some limping and carried by other men. Luke and Jack were ordered in to help. They tried to pick up one of the Irishmen, but he fell back screaming.

'His collarbone's gone,' Luke said.

'Well come along then,' Roarty shouted, 'get a mattress.'

When they had carried the mattress out, they carefully tried to put the man on it, though he screamed all the time. Then four men carried him back to his own shanty.

'He won't be doing too much work now,' Luke commented.

'Not a chance,' Jack said. 'Not with a broken collarbone. Won't be swinging axes anymore.'

That evening the news went around the shanties, that one of the Quebecers was dead.

'And three day's wages deducted too,' Jack said. 'From every single one of us.'

'What class of eejits were ye?' an old man asked from his bunk.

'But we were no part of it,' Luke said.

'Don't matter to Roarty, he ain't going to go around the shanties asking who was there and who wasn't. We're all going to pay the price, and that's an end of it.'

One evening they sat close to the camboose, talking of their future plans.

'Well, Luke, going building rails, are you?' O'Neill asked.

'What if he is?' Jack asked. 'He won't be the only one.'

'Well, I think you're all fools,' O'Neill said. 'All this good land here, and ours for the taking. Are ye mad or what?'

'*Arra* what? Everyone knows there's better chances in the United States. Luke's going to the railways, he knows the chances there. Don't you, Luke?'

'Of course,' Luke said. 'I've worked the rails in England and by God, it was tough there…'

'And what makes you think it will be any easier here,' O'Neill asked.

'Nothing at all,' said Luke. 'In fact I'm hoping it might be even worse. The harder the work, the more the money we make, and the faster we build up a stake for anything else we might want.'

'But that's saying nothing about what you might have to send home either?' said O'Neill. 'You'd have a stake right enough, if your family don't take it all from right under your nose.'

Look peered at the flames in the camboose.

'Maybe you're right' he said, 'but as long as the hunger is running, we can't stop sending the money home. We can't starve them, can we?'

'You wouldn't be starving anyone on a Canadian farm,' O'Neill said. 'Damn well you know it too. Your own food, and not potatoes either. And look at the land, they're charging almost nothing for it. No landlords, cheap land, lots of food. And you want to stay on the railways.'

Yes, Luke thought, the railways. More and more he was coming to accept that he would never return to Ireland.

'So what would you suggest then' he asked. 'Go out bush? I'd still need my stake money, wouldn't I?'

'Isn't that what you're here for?'

'It wouldn't be enough. Food, tools and the down-payment. You'd never make enough here in one year.'

'Perhaps that's why O'Neill has been here twenty,' Jack said. 'Still trying to get the grub stake. That right, Jim?'

'*Arra* whisht, what would you know about it?' O'Neill said. He knocked his pipe on his boot. 'Don't be a fool, Luke, you should consider it. Once you go working on the railways, you'll never stop, and you know that well enough yourself. It'll be just another year, a new line here, a new line there, and by the time you're half ready, you'll be an old man, not able for farming bush, nor nothing.'

'You're too glum,' Jack said. 'Luke's right, and you know it. You've as good a chance of earning your stake working the American railways, better even. They pay higher wages than here, that's for sure.'

'But he'd never stop working the railways, would you, Luke?'

'Of course he would,' O'Neill said. 'You've more sense than that, Luke, haven't you?'

Luke stared into the flames. 'What you're forgetting, Jim, is that there's cheap land in the United States too. Once the railways are built, the land on either side comes up for sale.'

'That's if you get there. Any which way you look at it, getting into the United States is not going to be easy. Don't seem to like Her Majesty's subjects, do they? A cousin of mine, he was caught on the border and sent all the way back to Quebec.'

'*Arra*, will ye stop your worrying,' said Jack 'It's easy enough, just get off the boat at the lake, walk a few miles, pick up the boat again, and no one asks any questions.'

'I doubt it's that easy, Jack,' Luke said.

'You worry too much, Luke. And anyhow, there's talk they're going to end all that nonsense, and then a man can sail or walk into the United States whatever which way he pleases.'

As Luke unhitched his horse one night, Roarty came up to him. 'You're going down to the river tomorrow.'

'The river?'

'The Gatineau. We've got too many logs in this station. Got to start taking them down. Two days down with the logs, sleep at the dock, then pork and flour back.'

'Fine so,' said Luke.

Before dawn, Luke was working on assembling a sleigh load of smaller logs, then they hitched four horses. Luke climbed on top of the logs.

'Just follow Breslin here,' Roarty said, 'and you'll see how to do it.'

Luke flicked the reins, and fell in behind another sleigh, gliding effortlessly over the compacted snow.

It was easy enough at first, but it did not last. As the downward slope steepened, the sleigh in front started to accelerate. Luke reined in his horses at the top and watched as the other sleigh went faster and faster to the bottom of the slope, and was then reined in.

He flicked the reins and started forward. He was horrified to see the gap between the sleigh and horses shortening, and knew within seconds their legs would be crushed. He heard a scream from Breslin.

'Faster, for Christ's sake, faster. You'll wreck it all.'

Faster on a downward slope? He could not believe it, but he flicked the reins hard, and the horses galloped. He felt terrified, and tried to hold the reins at the same time so as to hold the horses in from the side. He was at the bottom of the slope and started to rein the horses in, careful that it did not catch up with the horses legs. He brought the sleigh to a stop behind the other.

'That's mad,' he shouted at Breslin.

'Mad? How else would ye get them down?'

Luke shook his head. 'Damned if I know, but not like that.'

'*Arra*, don't you be worrying about it. Just give the horses their head. They're well used to it, they know what to do.'

'They'd surely need to, because I didn't. You should have warned me.'

'Well, now you know. Come on, let's move.'

When they arrived at the dock, Luke worked at unloading the logs. When he was finished, he unhitched the horses.

'And they deserve their rest,' Breslin said to him.

'They surely do,' Luke said.

He followed Breslin towards a shanty, but one of the gangers stopped him. 'Where do ye think ye're going?'

'Get a bite to eat. We're hungry enough.'

'Right so, but you've got fifteen minutes.'

They went into a shanty and ate near the camboose.

'Good pork, anyhow.'

'It is.'

Then they went down to the dock, unloading and reloading barrels. Luke saw his own sleigh go back up the trail.

'Don't worry about it,' the ganger said. 'We'll have another one down for you by tomorrow.'

He worked on. There was a shout, 'Luke.'

'*Conaire! Where the hell...*'

Conaire came over.

'*Where? I'll tell you where. I've been working here for the past months. They still won't let me near the horses.*'

There was a scream from the boat. 'No slacking...'

'Damn it to hell,' Luke swore and went back working.

That evening they sat in the shanty, listening to the singing and fiddle-playing. Then the buck-dancing began. Because there were no women, some of the men wore blankets around their waists and kerchiefs over their heads, playing the part of the women in the dances.

The jigs and reels went faster as the night went on. There was a thick fug of tobacco and men's sweat. It was hot.

Luke went outside. He always enjoyed the dancing, but to him there was always an under-current of fear. He remembered the night he had been attacked by the Molly Maguires gang in Brockagh. Men dressed as women! The beating had been savage. Still, here it was all innocent with no violence.

The river was frozen, the trees black against a starry sky on the opposite bank. Far to the north, he could barely see the flickering lights of the aurora, shimmering in green and blue.

He heard voices and went around the corner. *Conaire* was there with four other men, speaking quietly. He saw the four were newcomers, and recognised their accents as Mayo.

'*I haven't met these fellows yet,*' he said to *Conaire*. '*Mayo I'd guess.*'

'*All over the county,*' *Conaire* said. '*All excepting Donohoe here, a Roscommon fellow, but there's none of them lads around here, so he stops with us.*'

'*So which way did ye all come?*' Luke asked.

'*The most of us came through Killala,*' one answered. '*And maybe we shouldn't have. From all accounts, the Westport ships were better.*'

'*They were,*' said Luke. '*I'd half thought of going out through Westport myself. But like the eejit I am, I went by Liverpool instead. The* Centaurus *into* Quebec.'

'The Centaurus!'

'No less. Over a hundred dead before we reached Quebec.'

'By Christ!'

'So which were ye?' Luke asked.

'The Yorkshire Lass. Five dead on the crossing. And while five is bad enough, it's nothing like what ye had. A hundred, by God.'

'More. Much more.'

'As bad as the Ashburton so?'

'I don't know,' Luke said. 'That one arrived in Quebec just as we were leaving for the forests.'

'Some big land-owning fellow up in Sligo sent it over. Palmerston was the name to him.'

'I've heard his name before,' Luke said. 'Supposed to be something in the Government in London.'

'That's right. He chartered the Ashburton, and sent them all off on it. They say he promised them five pounds for clothes on their landing. Anyone's seen them will tell you, they've no clothes at all. And there sure wasn't five pounds waiting for any of them. And it wasn't the first from that son-of-a-bitch either. The Carrick of Whitehaven. That was a Palmerston ship too.'

'I didn't hear of that one,' Luke said.

'A wreck, a total wreck. Most all of them drowned. Weren't many got through to Quebec.'

The dancing had ceased. They returned to the shanty. Already a sound of snoring was coming from some of the bunks.

One of the men took a bottle of whiskey from his bunk. 'You'll join us,' he said to Luke.

'You're very generous.'

Carefully, he tasted the whiskey. Good quality. American. 'But what of yourselves?' he asked. 'Were ye evicted?'

'Now what do you think?' the man answered. 'Of course we were. Clanowen, he's a right brute. A bitter man.'

'Clanowen!'

'You know of him?'

'Dead right, I do' Luke said. 'After they shot his agent, I reckon he went half mad for vengeance. There were evictions enough around our area too. Clanowen got his revenge, that's for certain.'

'Where's that you were?'

'Kilduff. You know it?'

'I've heard of it. So you were evicted too?'

'Not me,' Luke said. 'I'd worked with fellows on the railways in England before all this started. A number of them moved over to Pennsylvania,

278

working on the railways there. When they heard I was still in Mayo, they told me the chances were better on the American railways. And after the past two years, I was inclined to believe them.'

'You're just like Conaire, then,' said one of the men. 'He wasn't evicted neither.'

'Not by the landlord,' Conaire said. 'It was hunger that evicted me.'

'Arra, they're all evictors, them landlords,' said another. 'Out west, wasn't that where Lord Lucan evicted any number of them?'

'Ah, yes,' Conaire said, 'but our landlord is Catholic. Wouldn't evict people, Mr. Walshe wouldn't. That's for sure.'

'That's what you think,' the man replied. 'They're all evictors, the whole damned lot of them.'

'You may hold your opinion,' Conaire said, 'but not all men are the same, even landlords.'

'So he's a better class of a man, aye? What did he feed you during the hunger? You tell me that.'

Conaire did not respond.

'I'll tell you what he fed you, if you can't,' the other man continued. 'Nothing. And what were ye left to feed on? Grass? Seaweed? Whales even...?'

'There were no whales then,' Conaire responded.

'There you are so. Grass and seaweed. Isn't that it?'

Again, Conaire did not respond.

'I may not be from Erris,' the other said, 'but I've met men who were. And the stories they told of men, women and children starving to death, eaten by rats, their little tigíns pulled down over them. Or buried in the sand for later generations to find them.'

'Arra,' Luke said, 'would you stop being at him like this.'

'Fair enough,' the man said. 'There were good things too, down Torán and Blacksod. Men who had fire in their bellies, enough to go after the corn ships on the ocean. And not just corn coming in either. Corn that was being sent out from Ireland over to Scotland, they took that too. How did the Scots need it more there than we did? No, for me the Erris men had courage. They had the courage to empty the ships on the ocean and the courage to defy the Royal Navy, or anyone else Her Majesty's Government could send against them. And they had the courage to die.'

Silence.

A pack of cards was taken out.

Another man came over. 'Deal me a hand,' he said.

'Fair enough.'

He sat across from Luke, watching him closely. At the end of a deal, he put his cards down sharply.

'Luke Ryan, *I'm sure of it.*'

Luke was startled. '*What if I am?*'

'*A murderer, a bloody murderer. Lisnadee. I remember you well. By Christ, the gangers here are bad, but you were the worst.*'

'*I was only doing what I had to,*' Luke said. '*If you didn't have gangers, you wouldn't have eaten, and you know that as well as I do.*'

'*Forcing people to work, even when they were starving. Freezing to death too. It didn't have to be like that.*'

'*They wouldn't have it any other way,*' Luke said. '*Castlebar...*'

'*And the piece-work. Who brought in the piecework? You did, you bastard.*'

'*It wasn't me ordered it. You know that too.*'

'*This man is a murderer,*' the other man said. '*Men, women and children, forced us all on the Works to freeze to death.*'

'*There was no forcing...*'

'*You're a liar.*'

'*Leave him be,*' *Conaire* said abruptly.

'*You knew this fellow,*' the other man said. '*You knew he was a ganger?*' He stood up, and left the table.

Conaire said nothing as the man stalked off. The cards were dealt again, one hand less.

Next morning, Luke and *Conaire* were loading sleighs.

'*I'm sorry about that last night,*' Luke said.

'*Arra, pay them no mind,*' *Conaire* said. '*Ganger or not, sure it's all in the past now.*'

'*It is, but there's many men won't forget it. And now I've got you in trouble too. There's men here won't talk to you now.*'

'*Sure leave them be. They will in time.*'

Chapter 21

Mayo Constitution, January 1848:
Death from Starvation. Last week a poor man dropped dead, from hunger, at Antigua, near this town. For want of a coffin his body lay for some days, we are told, in the open air, when decomposition having nearly exhausted itself, Mr. William McAdam got a coffin and had what remained of the wretched victim, interred. Thus within a mile of the town, with Relieving and Deputy Relieving Officer, and two Workhouses within musket shot of each other, has a human being been allowed to die of starvation – and afterwards let to manure the earth and impregnate the air with the odour issuing from the putrefied corpse.

All across Ireland, corn was running low.

'*We'll need corn, mother,*' Winnie said. '*I'll go up to the town.*'

'*I'll go with you,*' Eleanor said.

'*Indeed, you will not. And don't say otherwise.*' She took the purse from the cupboard and left.

When she arrived back, Eleanor was washing potatoes, softly singing.

'*You got enough,*' she said.

'*I did,*' said Winnie, putting the sack of corn on the table. She began to cry. Eleanor came over and sat beside her, her arm around Winnie's shoulders.

'*What's wrong, alanna? Why are you crying?*'

'*Well, I've no need for laughing,*' Winnie said.

'*But what...?*'

'*Oh, nothing. It's a body I saw on the road.*'

'*That's not nothing.*'

'*And there were dogs. They were fighting over, tearing parts off it, and fighting each other at the same time. It was so badly destroyed, I couldn't tell if it was a man or a woman. I took a stick and tried to drive them off, but they only growled at me. Then one jumped me, and...Oh, God, I don't want to talk about it.*'

'*No, alanna.*'

'*It's just...can't you see what's going on all around us?*'

'I know. Sure can't I see it with my own eyes, anytime I go to town? And even staying here, the carts going past with the dead bodies, and the state of them too. So hush there, alanna.'

Winnie said nothing.

'There's other things too then,' Eleanor said. 'That's not the only thing that's worrying you.'

'You're right,' Winnie said. 'The fever worries me too. They say there's fever in Quebec.'

'He's a strong fellow, Luke is,' Eleanor said. 'You've got to remember that. He's had fever as a child, and if it didn't get him then, it won't get him now. You know that.'

'But it's not just the fever. It's what's inside his head too. He broke once...'

'No he didn't,' Eleanor said, sharply. 'It's like the fever. He came close to breaking right enough but if that didn't break him, nothing will.'

'The hatred they had for him...'

'Yes. But he lived through it all. He would never give in. He won't now.'

Winnie poured water into the skillet pot. She placed it on the crane by the fire, swung it over the flames, and began to carry potatoes across.

'Maybe you've the right of it,' she said. 'You're always right...'

'Musha, go on out of that.'

'No, it's not just that. I come back, and there you are, singing, and not a care in the world.'

'No,' Eleanor said, 'it's not that. It only looks that way.'

'All the pain and the dying. Doesn't it get to you in the end?'

'I don't let it.'

'So what's your secret?'

'Between us women, there's no secret,' Eleanor said. 'It's only a secret from the men because they don't understand it, they can't understand it. It's a secret I learnt from my own mother many years ago, when I saw my little brothers and sisters on the Mountain, dying. All through the desperate pain of watching that, and you know what fever is like yourself. You've seen it in your own family, I'm certain of it. And I've seen it twice in this family. The last time was when Alicia died, the screaming pain in my own daughter. I told you that. But it's at times like that you cannot let yourself break. All a mother can do, all she must do, is stay with the child, hold her hand even when she no longer knows her, watch her face going black and mop the fever with cooling water, and sing. Soft songs, lullabies, old laments. Whether the babies hear you or not, it doesn't matter, but the rest of the family hears, and it quietens them too. Yes, they think you're singing for the child, that's what they would think. And Alicia wasn't the first – my first son, he died *too. Half my children, I buried half my children. And then what did I do? I came back home each time, fed the chickens, milked the cows, they don't understand a woman's pain. Or maybe they do, maybe they could sense it. I don't know. But one way or another, the pain is always there, it lessens a little with time perhaps, but it never stops. A woman needs strength for that, a strength a man will never have. That's what my mother taught me on the Mountain, and by all that's holy, we needed strength on the Mountain. The famine, twenty, thirty years ago, back in the 1820s, that was a terrible thing. Another little brother died, and they threw his body on the cart along with all the others going down from the Mountain to the graveyard in Kilduff. But they never got there. They were all buried in a bog. Better than many others though. Hundreds had their houses pulled down around them, never got a chance of burial, in a bog or elsewhere. And when you think – that was only the Mountain. It was like that all over. All around Baile-a-Cnoic and Árd-na-gCaiseal was nothing but the stink of death. Yes, we saw all that, Winnie. We saw death all across the Mountain, the same then as it is now. But my mother taught us the women must have strength, and more important, they must hide it. Never let on we're stronger than the men. Gentle, loving and kind, that's what we must be. Stop the terrors of the children. And the men too, though they'd always deny it. They don't know we're the stronger, and we always will be. 'Soft power', that's what my mother called it. Always gets your way in the end, in such a way that the men thought that they had won. Look at Michael now. He thinks the idea of educating Brigid was his idea. It takes time, but slowly he forgets how strong he was against it. He didn't want us to adopt Brigid either after Nessa's death, but now he thinks it was his idea too. They think we just accept our fate, but never understand how we shape it, for them and for us. Love and kindness that hides our strength. And singing. As long as we sing, they think we're happy. And you, Winnie, you'll learn to sing. Hide your strength, and believe me, you are strong. Yes, you'll have your baby. You'll take it across the Great Ocean. Then you'll meet Luke and set up a new home in America. That takes strength, it all takes strength. But you have it, I know it.'*

On the Friday, Eleanor was feeding Brigid at the table, as Winnie and Michael were eating. The door opened.

'Pat!' Eleanor exclaimed. 'We weren't expecting you so soon again.'

'And it's just as well you weren't,' Pat answered. ''Tisn't ye I'm visiting at all.'

'Well who else would you be visiting?' Michael asked.

'Who else indeed,' Winnie said. 'Surely ye can all work that out.'

Pat smiled. ''Tis quick you are, Winnie.'

Eleanor slapped her forehead. 'Of course, why didn't I think of it?'

'What are ye all on about?' Michael asked.

'You tell him,' Eleanor said to Winnie.

'Westport,' Winnie replied. 'Isn't that it, Pat? A visit to young Sarah?'

Pat leant on the table. 'It is. And I'd have thought you'd have worked that one out, father.'

'*Arra,* hell,' said Michael.

'Now if ye'd all excuse me, I've got a horse to put away.'

'A horse?' Michael asked.

'The Union lent it to me. Sure they knew I wouldn't get to Westport otherwise. I've still got to be back Monday morning.'

When he was finished with the horse, he came in again, carrying corn in his pack. He sat with the family, just finishing their meal of potatoes and yellow meal, but no meat.

'Where did you get this?' he asked.

'Winnie got it up at Dillon's,' Eleanor said. 'Will I cook you some?'

'No, I've eaten already.' He took a pinch of meal from Michael's plate, and sniffed it.

'We've had a lot of trouble with this in the Workhouse. It gets rotten quick. Not that the merchants seem to mind.'

'You needn't worry about that,' Winnie said, 'I smelt it before I bought it. It's fine.'

Next morning, he rose very early. Only Winnie was awake. She prepared him a breakfast of yellow meal.

'Isn't it great about Luke,' Pat said.

'It is,' Winnie said, 'but I'm wondering how long it will be 'till I get to America?'

'Yes,' Pat answered, 'it could be a long time yet.'

As he rose to go, Winnie kissed him on the cheek. 'Now, you're to tell Sarah we were all asking for her. And don't forget.'

'Would I ever?'

He rode through Kilduff and reached Castlebar just before sunrise.

Ballymacrath. Pheasanthill. Islandeady.

At Keeloges three men rushed from a boreen beside the road. One tried to grasp the reins, but Pat pulled away. Another grabbed at his leg, but he kicked back hard. He whipped the horse into a gallop. The men ran after him, trying to catch him. One took up a stone and threw it after him. It hit the horse on the withers. The horse whinnied, but did not stop.

Kilbree. Knockbrack. Sheeane.

When he reached Westport Workhouse there was a big crowd around the gate. It was drizzling. He saw mounted soldiers.

284

Once again, he recognised the uniform of the Thirteenth Light Dragoons, but the lieutenant was not there. The crowd did not move. He kept edging the horse forward, shouting 'clear the way, clear the way.'

At length he reached the dragoons.

'Union business,' he said to one of them. He nodded and let Pat forward. The gate was opened.

Leaving his horse with one of the inmates, he passed through the breakers yard. There were hundreds of men breaking stones. He stood by as two carts trundled past. On the other side he saw the fever sheds and he thought of Sarah's mother. And what of Sarah? Did she ever work in the sheds?

He went to the offices of the Clerk of Union. The Clerk looked up at him.

'Mr. Ryan, isn't it?'

'That's right.'

Sarah spun around, and ran over to him.

'Pat! You're drenched.'

'*Arra*, what of it. Only a little.'

'Come over here and sit by the fire at least.' She hugged him.

The Clerk walked over. 'Well, what business brings you here? Looking for more men for England, are you?'

'Not yet,' Pat replied. 'I don't know they've call for men in England just now. It's Sarah I came over to see.'

The Clerk laughed. 'Yes, yes' he said, 'I'd thought she was spoken for right enough.'

Sarah excused herself and brought Pat down to the refectory. It was still half full, but they sat at the other end from the crowd at a table close to a large open fire. One of the inmates brought them two cups of buttermilk.

'We can't afford tea in the Workhouse anymore,' Sarah said.

Pat drank a good part of it. 'Sure wasn't I brought up on this, I've no complaints. But enough of that. We hardly got a chance to talk to each other the last time.'

'Not with your cousin around that time,' Sarah said.

'No,' Pat said, 'I'm sorry I had to come with Murtybeg. This thing of taking inmates from the Workhouses to England, I don't know that we should be doing it.'

'Is there any other way?' Sarah asked.

'I don't know that there is,' Pat said. 'But I'll tell you this, Danny's a rough employer. Sure, he feeds them, but ye're doing that here.'

'No, we're not,' Sarah said. 'We're hardly feeding a tenth of the people that need it around Westport. Sending men to England lets us take more in, lets us feed more.'

'Yes' Pat said, 'but even so, I wouldn't like to be working with Danny. Oh

God, if it wasn't for the potatoes…'

'Sure wasn't the last harvest a good one…'

'If they'd planted enough it would have been.'

'But this year's harvest, they'll plant enough and there'll be plenty for everyone.'

'Will there? I hope you're right. But enough of that, tell me about yourself. How are you finding things here?'

'Well enough,' Sarah replied. 'Dougal's not bad to work for, I'll say that. He's a hard worker too, and he has me working all the hours God sends. Not that I'm complaining.'

'I'll help with the figures after so,' Pat said.

'That would be good of you.'

He thought of the sheds.

'What of your mother?' He saw the fright in her eyes.

'I'd hoped you wouldn't ask me that,' she replied. 'Every time she goes to the sheds, I worry about her. At least the fever is less than last year, we've none in the dormitories now. Even so, what happens if she catches it? I just don't know.'

'Surely she had it as a child…?'

'No, and that's the thing. If she catches it now she could well die.'

Pat put his hand on hers. 'I'm sorry,' he said, 'but what of you?'

'I had it as a child,' she said. 'I'm one of the ones who lived. But even so, don't you be worrying about it. Mother won't let me near the fever sheds any longer.'

There were tears in her eyes.

Now he put both hands on hers. 'Sarah…'

For some time, she said nothing, then she took her hands away and wiped her eyes.

'Do you know, Pat, when I first met you, you were such a young gossoon, and you trying to court me. The cheek of it! But I'll tell you one thing, you've changed.'

'Sure why not,' Pat said, 'that was a year ago if it was a day.'

'No,' she said, 'it's not just a matter of time. We've been through hard times, all of us have. It's enough to make a man out of any young fellow. I could see it in the way you dealt with your cousin, well able for him, you are, and anything hard times might throw at you.'

They went back to the office.

Pat spent the remainder of the afternoon and evening working alongside Sarah by the light of a candle.

'These figures are terrible,' he said.

'Don't I know it?'

'There must be great hunger around here?'

'And evictions too,' Sarah said. 'It was a dreadful time they had out in *Torán*.'

'*Torán*?'

'No one's heard of it,' Sarah said. 'It's out the far end of Erris, down by Blacksod Bay. On the edge of the Atlantic. Some fellow called Walshe, evicted the lot of them.'

'Walshe!'

'I know what you're about to say,' Sarah said. 'Yes, a good Catholic name. Evicting his own. And then what did he expect of them? To walk all the way to Ballina, that's what. The nearest Workhouse for Erris, and it miles away. Some came here, the rest kept walking. God knows where they thought they were going.'

'But…a Catholic!'

'That doesn't mean he should be holier than anyone else. I'm sure he couldn't have been thinking of the Lord Jesus when he gave them a Christmas surprise like that, throwing them out in the cold and rain.'

'Did they not fight back?'

'Sure what point was there in that, when they had the soldiers guarding the depot?'

'Yes,' Pat said, 'I'd heard about the soldiers. Though God alone knows what they'd need an army for out in Erris. Army or no army, no one out that way would be able to attack a depot.'

The Clerk looked up from his papers.

'They might be better able than you think. When men are desperate, they'll do desperate things. Sure isn't there piracy out at Blacksod now?'

'Piracy?'

'It's been going on around Erris this long time, well before the evictions even. There was a ship going from Limerick to Glasgow there before Christmas carrying oats, boarded off Blacksod Bay. They say fifty or a hundred fellows jumped the ship off *Torán*, and took twenty tonnes of grain. And that wasn't the first attempt either.'

'What in the name of God were they carrying grain for?' Pat asked. 'Didn't the fellows in Limerick need it? What kind of people are they that send grain out at a time like this?'

'You don't seem to be too worried about the piracy?' the Clerk said.

'*Arra* what,' Pat replied. 'If they weren't sending the grain out, there'd be no need to be jumping ships like that.'

'I don't know I should agree with you there. I very well might, but I wouldn't go around giving out opinions like that.'

'Fair enough,' Pat said, 'but what are they going to do about it?'

'Naval cutters, that's what,' the Clerk replied. 'They're bringing in the Navy to protect our merchant marine from the starving people of Erris. Where's Admiral Nelson now we need him? No heroes today, eh?'

He pushed his chair back and stood. 'Time for dinner,' he said, 'and don't tell anyone I said all of that.'

At dinner, Pat met with Sarah's mother.

'What business brings you over this way?' she asked.

'Just visiting, Mrs. Cronin,' Pat said quickly.

'And he expects us to believe that too,' the Clerk said. 'The question is, who?'

'Ah yes,' she said, 'that is the question.'

She went on eating. Mostly corn, Pat noticed. Only one potato each. No meat.

'So how's Knockanure now?' Mrs. Cronin asked him.

'Just the same as all the Unions in Mayo, I'd guess.' Pat said. 'Pushed to the limit, never enough money, never enough room in the Workhouse. And the merchants don't help.'

'Yes,' she said, 'it's the same all over.'

After dinner, Pat stood with Sarah in the hallway, talking quietly.

'So what does your mother think now?'

'She thinks well of you now. But like your own mother, I think, she's worried about the future of the Workhouses.'

'Do you think she thinks I might lose my job?'

'She does,' said Sarah. 'And let's be honest, it might happen. And I could lose mine too.'

'But at least your mother won't lose hers?'

'Not in the same way,' she said. 'But there's other ways someone can lose a job. Do you know why she got this position in Westport? Well I'll tell you – it was because the last matron died. Died of fever. And they couldn't get anyone wanting to replace her.'

'Oh God…'

'And she wasn't the only one. Dr. Flaherty, he died. Four of the inmates nursing in the sheds, they died too. And as for the patients, the dying never stops.'

Chapter 22

Telegraph & Connaught Ranger, February 1848:
Bryan Solan, Mary Solan and Eileen Stanton died of starvation in Ballintubber this week. Their bodies are still unburied for want of coffins. There are three others in the same village whose deaths are hourly expected from hunger. These creatures were on the relief list, but being unable to attend the calling of the roll, as they lived some miles from the work, they were struck off, and were thus left a whole week without a morsel of food.

Pat left Westport and rode directly to Carrigard. He stabled the horse and entered the house. Michael was sitting by the fire, poking at the turf.

'Well, Pat, what news?'

'The Workhouses are desperate,' Pat replied. 'Little food, and less cash, but they seem to be spending enough on the military, that's for sure. All the big towns, especially Castlebar, and now they've dragoons out in Erris...'

'Erris?' Eleanor exclaimed. 'Sure Erris is in a terrible way, from all accounts. They're all starving out that way. Why should they want soldiers?'

'They're pirating the ships, and that worries the Government. That's why.'

'Pirating?' Winnie asked.

'There's terrible hunger out there. When they see ships with corn going from Ireland, what do you think they'd do? What in the name of God can they do, except steal it?'

He stayed overnight. He was up early the next morning.

'Where's father?' he asked Eleanor.

'Up the quarry, I think.'

'On a Sunday!'

'It's no differ to him what day it is,' Eleanor said.

Pat left the house, and went up the fields looking. He heard the rhythmic crash of the sledgehammer in the quarry. He went to the edge and looked down. It looked very different to the previous year. It was far deeper than it had been two years previous. But now the Famine Relief Works were over, and the quarry was empty except for his father. Last year there had been dozens of men, women and children working slowly with picks, hammers and shovels. No more. He wondered where they had all gone. Emigrated? Or dead?

Already, there were many heaps of broken stone, and Pat wondered if more were necessary. Perhaps his father was working off his frustration of the times. Pat knew the family had enough potatoes, but even so, there might have been doubt. They could still rot, even inside the house.

His father had spotted him.

Pat joined him beside the heap of larger stones. He noticed a scar on one side of his father's face, running down from just above his eye to under his chin. He said nothing. Without a word he took the hammer from Michael and started to swing it. Michael smiled at him.

'Still able for it, I see.'

'I don't know,' Pat said, 'I might need some practice yet. Swinging a pen isn't quite the same.'

It had begun to rain. A fine drizzling rain, penetrating. Pat could still see the Mountain, with Nephin in the distance, but they too had clouds of grey rain moving across them. Michael took his arm, and they walked over to the whin bush at the side of the quarry, where they sheltered under Michael's greatcoat.

'You're working hard,' Pat said.

'And why not?'

'I don't know,' Pat said. 'I just thought with the Relief Works being over, there wouldn't have been such call for it.'

'Damned if I know,' Michael answered. 'But now with Bensons gone, we've two quarries.'

'Of course.'

'And that means we're sharing two contracts with Burke.'

'Good takings so?'

'Not now. With the way things are, they're stopping everything. And it's not just the Relief Works. They're all gone this long time. But the County can't even afford road maintenance. The Barony neither.'

'But the contract...?'

'Sure what's the use of a contract if there's no money?'

Pat pulled the greatcoat further over his head.

'I don't know,' he said. 'I haven't heard any of this.'

'No? I thought you might have.'

Neither Nephin nor the Mountain were visible now.

Pat looked around to Michael, hunched close beside him under the greatcoat. 'You should be more careful of yourself,' he said.

'Why's that?' Michael asked.

'That scar. What were you doing that brought that upon you?'

'I was hoping you wouldn't ask me that. Didn't your mother tell you?'

'Not yet, she didn't. Maybe she didn't want to, is that it?'

Michael fingered the scar. 'It wasn't myself that caused it,' he said. 'It was the Molly Maguire gang.'

'The Molly Maguires...?'

'Isn't that what I'm saying?'

Pat was thinking. He knew a lot about the Molly Maguires, or rather, on reflection, he thought he did. A criminal gang, that was certain. Or was it? They claimed to be rebels, fighting for the Irish cause. Not that Pat had ever believed that. He had always reckoned that was only a cover for robbery and murder. But anything else he knew was uncertain.

The landlords and the gentry certainly feared the Molly Maguire gang because they claimed to be a revolutionary organisation dedicated to overthrowing the landlords and anyone else they saw as being too wealthy.

But Pat felt that too was only a bluff. Their activities hit the small farmers harder. They demanded that no rent should be paid to the landlords, but for most that would only result in eviction. What was worse, Pat thought, was the demand for the Molly Maguires' rent. Since the farmers were not to pay rent to the landlords, the Molly Maguires demanded it instead. Now, in the middle of a famine and fever epidemic, the poor were expected to pay two rents, when they could not pay anything at all. Was that fair?

The consequences of non-payment, Pat knew, could be worse than eviction. There were many stories of men being killed by the Molly Maguires when they resisted payment. Not potatoes or vegetables or turf – these were too hard to carry. Cash was always demanded. Families without cash lost their livestock instead. Cattle from the better-off farmers, and pigs from those who did not have cattle. These were sold at livestock fairs by men who were law-abiding by day and masked criminals by night.

'So what happened?' Pat asked again. 'What did they take?'

'One of the cattle, the bastards. They tried to take the second, but I stopped them. Then one of them ran at me with a knife.'

Pat examined the scar closely, passing his finger along the length of it. 'You're a damned fool, father. They could have taken your eye out. Or killed you.'

'*Arra,* what.'

'No, it's no little thing. What would we have done then, and you dead?'

'What would we have done without both cattle? Aren't we close enough to hunger as it is?'

'And you thought you could take on three men? You're not a young fellow now, father.'

'Don't you be worrying about me, young lad. I'm tough enough yet.'

Pat fingered the scar again, wondering how much blood Michael might have lost.

'So they didn't come into the house?' he asked.

'I think they wanted to. Check out for sovereigns perhaps. Gold rings either. But between the shouting and the cattle kicking up hell, they were scared that others might hear it, so they skedaddled off with just the one cow.'

The drizzle had eased. Nephin stood out in sunshine, but grey mists still clung to the Mountain.

Winnie was always in Eleanor's thoughts. The baby was coming in March, if only the fever didn't come first. Stop thinking like that. But what of the baby? What of the birth? She thought back on the times she had given birth herself. Painful, but not over-much. One born dead, but that was normal. No, Winnie was strong. She would not, could not, die in childbirth.

But what of Nessa? She had died. Remember that nightmare day? Now, stop this, she told herself. But still, there were other odd things. Danny's reaction. She had never expected that. Yes, he was Nessa's brother, but even so. What had it been then? Love of his sister? Or the savage desire for revenge against the man who had fathered the baby, and tried to disappear. With Danny, it was hard to know. Perhaps a bit of both.

One afternoon Sabina and Kitty arrived.

'*Well how are ye now, acushla?*' Kitty said, taking Brigid on her lap.

'*She's well fed, at least,*' Sabina said.

'*Isn't it what we have to do,*' Eleanor said. '*We're fine, we can be a thin as we like. But little Brigid, we wouldn't want to stunt her growth.*'

'*Nor her brains neither,*' Winnie said from the fireside.

But the baby was already asleep on her lap.

'*What age is she now?*' Kitty asked. '*Must be near two.*'

'*Near enough,*' Eleanor said.

'*So, when does she start school?*'

'*It will be more than a year to that,*' Sabina answered. '*They won't take her under three years of age. After the summer of 1849, that'll be the time.*'

'*And what then?*' Eleanor asked. '*Seven years of schooling, then the secondary school in Castlebar. But she'll only be ten. Would they take her so young?*'

'*Sure we won't tell them her age,*' Kitty answered.

'*And fifteen years old for teacher training in Galway or wherever?*' Eleanor said. '*Are we expecting too much of the child?*'

'*Maybe we are, and maybe we're not,*' Kitty answered, '*but sure we can only try.*'

Yes, Eleanor thought, we can only try. She knew she would always miss Brigid, even if she was not her own daughter. Perhaps she will become a teacher, perhaps she'll come back to Kilduff. Do I believe that? Who knows?

Kitty was talking about money.

'*Isn't it the right cheek we all have,*' she said. '*We've not enough money to feed ourselves, and here we are making grand plans as to how we'd spend it.*'

'*True for you,*' Winnie answered, '*but Luke is sending money already. Not enough yet, but there'll be more when he settles. And then, maybe I'll be earning too, who knows.*'

'*With a baby?*' Sabina asked.

'*He'll be going to school soon enough too,*' Winnie answered. '*And anyhow, there's Danny...*'

'*Danny!*' Sabina exclaimed. '*You're expecting Danny to send money? I'll tell you, I'll give the little I can, but I wouldn't expect much from Danny.*'

'*Oh, I don't know,*' Eleanor said, '*we haven't asked him yet. And there's one thing about Danny you shouldn't forget. He's a pride in himself, and there's Nessa too. His own sister, dying in childbirth like that. That shook him. No, I reckon Danny will do anything for Nessa's daughter, anything we ask him.*'

After Sabina and Kitty had left, Eleanor and Winnie started cleaning the table and the floor.

'*I wonder which of us had the right of it.*' Eleanor asked.

For a moment, Winnie was puzzled, then slowly it dawned on her.

'*You mean about Brigid? And Danny?*'

'*Exactly,*' Eleanor said.

'*You seem to be expecting a lot of him.*'

Eleanor stopped rubbing down the table. '*Maybe we are, Winnie girl, but there again, maybe we're not. He's a strange fellow, Danny is, there's no doubting that. A tough man, you've heard all about that. He'll be marrying a tough woman too, and they're both doing well in a very tough business. There's not many men with his ability, nor his cruelty, but still, there's something about Danny I don't understand. You heard about him beating Corrigan?*'

'*I did,*' Winnie said. '*Savage too from all accounts.*'

'*Indeed. But just think of this. Why did he do it? He did it because he held Corrigan responsible for killing Nessa. He held that if Corrigan had not put her in the way of a child, she would have lived. It was a matter that upset him greatly. There's more love in Danny than many people can see.*'

'*'Tis hard for me to say,*' Winnie said. '*I know all you say is true, but there is another way of looking at it. Danny might consider that Corrigan*

293

caused the baby, but it was the baby that killed Nessa in the birthing.'

'Perhaps,' Eleanor said. 'Another way though is that Danny might have a deep fondness for Nessa's child. Deeper than any might think.'

'He might,' Winnie admitted. 'The question is – how can we find out?'

'Write to him.'

'Write!'

'There's no other way. You and me, we'll write him a letter, and not breathe a word to anyone else.'

They waited until the next morning when Michael was working in the quarry. Eleanor took the pen, ink and a single sheet of paper from atop the dresser.

'Now, I'm not too good at writing,' she said to Winnie, 'so it's best if you do that. But perhaps we should both sign it. Do you agree?'

'I do,' Winnie said. 'You know we'll have to tell Sabina, though'

'Why?'

'Secrecy. We'll have to use her bar as the address. If Danny refuses, I wouldn't like anyone here to know what we've done.'

The two women spent an hour in writing the letter. They requested total secrecy from Danny. Then they explained about Brigid, continuing with their plans for Brigid's education in detail.

When Winnie had finished writing, and they had both signed the letter, Eleanor picked it up.

'He'll think we're senseless, won't he?'

'I think your own man thought we were senseless too, but he's come around now. Hasn't he?'

'Indeed he has. It took us long enough though, and we had the benefit of having him close to hand. I don't know if we'll succeed with Danny. We'll only have the one chance. A single minute, and he'll decide.'

That afternoon, Winnie brought the letter up to town. She showed it in confidence to Sabina. Then, with her permission, she added a postscript, requesting that Danny should reply directly to her at Sabina's address.

Pat was on guard at the potato field one night, when he heard a bellowing from the cowshed. He ran down, but his father was already inside, holding a lantern.

'What's wrong, father?'

'They've hocked her.'

'Hocked her? What? Where?'

Michael held the lantern behind the cow. The light was very dim, but Pat could see the blood oozing from the tendons at the lower part of the cow's hind leg.

'Hocked her well and truly,' Michael said. 'She'll never walk again.'

'The bastards. Did you see them?'

'See them? They ran like the devil.'

'In the name of God, where are they now?'

Michael realised the danger. He rushed to the door. 'Quick. The potatoes.'

They ran to the potato field. In the moonlight, they could see shadowy figures at the top end of it. One of the intruders whistled sharply. At the signal, the remaining potatoes were piled into three sacks, and the men ran. Pat ran after them. As he gained on them, the men panicked and, one by one, they dropped their sacks. Pat stopped running, and gathered up the sacks with the potatoes. Michael arrived, gasping.

'At least we kept the potatoes,' Pat said.

'Yes,' Michael answered. 'Now let's get them into the house, and see about the cow.'

Pat spent the night at the potato field, while his father stayed in the cowshed.

Next morning, Michael killed the cow with a rapid blow to the head from the back of an axe. The cow sank to her knees, let out a single bellow and rolled on her side.

Then the hard work of butchering began. Using sharp knives, Michael and Pat skinned the cow.

Eleanor brought out basins to collect the blood, to make into black pudding. She could see that Winnie was queasy, but said nothing. Best to let her get used to it. She had seen enough stomach-turning sights already. This was only one more.

Using the axe again, Michael split the cow down the middle. They began to take out the offal, separating out the waste and retaining the edible parts, including the liver, heart, kidneys and more. Then it was time to cut the cow into its primal parts of beef, a process carried out by Michael and Pat. These were brought into the house, and the women began to salt them.

Sabina arrived at Carrigard. The other three women were there with the baby.

'*A letter for ye,*' she said.

'*From Danny?*' Eleanor asked.

'*Now you don't think I'd be opening your post, do you? It's clearly addressed to the pair of ye only.*'

Impatiently, Eleanor snatched the letter. She saw the Manchester postmark.

She slit it open. A bank note fluttered out.

'*Five pounds,*' Winnie gasped. She picked it up. '*Why on earth would he* send money in the post? A bank draft would have been safer.'

'Maybe he wanted it kept secret,' Kitty said.

'But five pounds!'

'Didn't I tell you he'd be generous,' Eleanor said. 'Here, you read it.'
She handed it to Winnie.

'Well, here's one man doesn't think we're crazy,' Winnie said. 'He reckons with a mother as bright as Nessa, Brigid should go all the way to training college.'

'College!' Sabina exclaimed. 'Starvation all around, and he talks of college. Is he mad too?'

'No more than the rest of us,' Kitty said, 'but with this class of madman backing us, we can do anything.'

Winnie looked closely at the banknote.

'So what now?'

'What now?' Eleanor echoed. 'Tomorrow morning, I'll go straight over to the Hibernian Bank in Knockanure. I'll open an account for Brigid.'

'Can you open an account for a baby?'

'I can ask.'

Chapter 23

Staffordshire Advertiser, January 1848:
On Messrs Brassey & Co.'s contract, which comprises the Pottery line from Macclesfield to Colwich and the Norton Bridge and Newcastle branches, a length of 40 miles, 1,950,800 cubic yards of earthwork had been removed; considerable progress has been made with the heavy Works at Macclesfield, by arching over the river Bollin, and building the retaining walls through the town. The viaducts over the river Dove, and at Congleton, may be considered as each half finished. At Congleton some of the centres are erected for turning the arches.
Report of the Engineers to the Directors of the North Staffordshire Railway

In England the letter from Eleanor and Winnie had stunned Danny. Until the moment he received it, he had not thought of the baby in anything but abstract terms. Now she had a name.

Nor had he thought about the fact that Eleanor had been fostering her. From the time of Nessa's death, he had not cared any more about the baby, but now she had been presented to him in very real terms. Brigid. Nessa's daughter. The only sliver of Nessa left on earth.

What had astonished him too, was the sheer ambition of the women. He could well remember Eleanor from so many years ago. His first memories were of playing with Luke in Eleanor's house. She was a strong woman, and, to some degree, had reared Danny almost as her own son. Even before he had left Mayo, Aileen had begun to withdraw into herself.

Teacher training! He knew that Eleanor had all the strength to achieve her aim. Would the child be able for it though? He thought of Nessa's bright intelligence, and his own father's ability as a respected and capable teacher. Of course Brigid could become a teacher. What other outcome was possible?

Cash was not an immediate worry for Danny. He was more concerned about future contracts.

That morning he had received a letter from the Brassey head office. It stated bluntly, that the North Staffordshire contract was to be finished by the first of May.

'And that causes two problems,' he told Irene. 'First, that we need even more labour than we expected. And second, we'll need new contracts. Brassey represents damned near half of what we're doing. How do we replace that?'

'I wouldn't worry,' she said. 'I'm reckoning we'll pick up the Baxendale contracts.'

'We might, alright.'

'We will. They're going bankrupt, and if we play our cards right, we'll take much of their business. The one by McManus' site for certain, and with a little luck, we might be able to take that Ormskirk contract too.'

'Assuming the bank lends to us on Ormskirk.'

'They will when Baxendales have gone bankrupt. It's like Nick Roscoe said. They'll have no choice.'

'I wish I had Roscoe's confidence.'

'There's no question of Baxendales not going bankrupt. This is a time of great opportunity for us.'

'And a time of great risk.'

'What risk?'

'For God's sake, will you look around you, Irene? The country's in a desperate state.'

'What's that to do with the railways?'

'They're the worst. Look at all the suspensions. Deferments. Postponements. Whatever you want to call them. And outright cancellations too.'

'And none of them affect us. Nor will they, if we complete our contracts fast enough. You say Brassey want us to finish quickly. Fine, let's give them what they want. It's as your father said. The North Staffordshire will have wasted huge sums of money if they can't complete the line. Their outlay is only worthwhile on a railway with trains running all the way through. Isn't that so?'

'It is,' Danny admitted.

'So any railway will only suspend those Works that are not necessary. And we've got them there on all Andersons' contracts too. They have to be finished. They're worthless unless they are. The railways know that.'

'And the Manchester South Junction? They're already suspending Works.'

'Not ours. The Ancoats Works are more than a railway. The Council in Manchester is desperate to clear the slums. The whole world knows about Little Ireland. No, they won't stop that one. Not until they're all evicted.'

Danny was more puzzled than ever.

'And if we finish all these contracts, what then?'

'Then we've cash in the bank. Nothing to worry about for a long time.

But even there, I don't believe it will happen that way. By that time, they'll be giving us contracts.'

'Giving us!'

'Look at all the bankrupt contractors. Sooner or later, those lines will have to be completed, and we're the ones that can complete them cheapest. The railways know that. And so do the banks.'

'I know. Low wages…'

'And more than that, Danny. Much more. Low timber prices. The merchants are near bankrupt too. We can buy timber for whatever we like. Cash on delivery gives them the only chance they have to avoid bankruptcy. We string them out, just keeping them in business, and take all their profit for ourselves.'

'But…what of the workers? What do we do when we finish the North Staffordshire? It's huge.'

'Just fire them. Remember this. There's thousands of navvies out of work, up and down the country. Wherever we've contracts, we hire. Where we don't, we fire them.'

'Have you no conscience?'

'Have you?'

'Maybe not.'

'There's no 'maybe' about it, Danny. This is a rough business. Are you in, or are you out?'

'In, for sure. But, good God, Irene, how can either of us handle all this?'

'Either of us? What about your father?'

'What about him?' Danny asked, angrily.

'We could use him better,' she replied. 'Just think it through. You're too busy visiting sites. This business is going to need a lot more controlling, and we can't afford to have you out travelling the country when we've got to be dealing with our customers. Not to mention the bank, especially when we get the Ormskirk contract.'

'When?'

'Up to you, Danny.'

'But if I don't visit the sites, who will? You're not suggesting…?'

'Exactly,' she answered. 'Your father. It's what he'll be best at. After all, he's taught all our gangers, except Steele. They look up to him. That's what you said. Whatever about the ganger meetings, we need reliable figures week by week, and someone to look over the sites and spot problems before they arise.'

'But what of mother? How will we take care of her, with father out travelling?'

'Get her working. There's plenty of cotton mills in Stockport.'

'Like hell. She doesn't stand a chance, and you know it. The mills are laying off people at a desperate rate. There's thousands of mill-hands out of work in Stockport alone. Thousands. And there's more lay-offs coming. The big mills are on the edge of bankruptcy.'

Irene arched her fingers, thinking.

'Fine,' she said at length. 'We won't put her out working.'

'Then what...?'

'What you said already. Get a nurse to look after her.'

'The maid will be fine. She can keep an eye on her.'

'Maybe she can for a while. But one way or the other, we get your father out on the road. That's where we need him.'

It was decided that Murtybeg would accompany his father on his first round of inspections. One morning, they left early.

Murty was astounded as the train crossed Edgeley Viaduct. Far below, he could see the black greasy waters of the Mersey.

Murtybeg could see the look of amazement in his father's eyes.

'Quite something, isn't it?'

'It's strange,' his father replied. 'Every day I've seen it, but it's not until you're going over it you see just how high it is.'

'You've been over it before. Remember when you first came.'

'I never noticed it then. Maybe I'd other things on my mind.'

They changed trains in Manchester.

They came to the end of the line where the construction began, and began to walk. At McManus' site, everything was straightforward, since Murty had already seen the site with Danny. They met with McManus, checked through wages paid and required, timber on site and various other items on a list which had been prepared by Irene.

'And many more men on site, I see,' Murtybeg commented.

'We could use more still, if we could get them,' McManus replied. 'Isn't it strange though, us needing so many men, with sites closing all around us?'

'I know,' Murty said. 'It's Danny's opinion that the faster we finish, the less likely we are to be suspended.'

'Aye, there's logic in that,' McManus said.

That afternoon, they travelled on to Kearney's site. They saw a line of mud huts alongside the edge of the construction site. Murtybeg could smell the raw sewage, running out the front of the shacks, and forming a stinking rivulet, which looped between the huts, running down towards a distant canal.

'What the...?' Murty exclaimed.

'The Irish Camp, they call it,' Murtybeg replied.

'They live in those? Mud cabins! Just like in Mayo.'

'Sure it's the same all over. And not just the Irish neither.'

Murty walked over towards the huts. Murtybeg grabbed his arm.

'No, father.'

'But we're supposed to be checking the sites.'

'Not these. There's fever here.'

'But...'

'Come on, let's see if we can find Tim.'

They spotted Kearney. Murty shouted at him. He came over.

'Master!'

'You don't need to be calling me that. But tell me, I hadn't known about this camp here.'

'Not our concern,' Kearney said.

'What do you mean? Aren't these our fellows working here?'

'They might be, but the huts are for their families, and the women and children sure as hell don't work here. And I wouldn't go near them.'

'Murtybeg says there's fever.'

'Most certainly.'

'Wouldn't it spread to the men on the Works?'

'We do all we can to stop that,' Kearney replied. 'Any fellow who shows the slightest sign of fever, we send him back to his hut. The last thing we want is to have it spread through all the workers.'

'So what if he dies at home?'

'It's like I said. Not our concern.'

Murtybeg and Murty copied down Kearney's figures, and then travelled on towards Lavan's site. Here they could smell the huts, well before they saw them. It was only as they came closer that they saw the encampment, just below the top of the embankment. The railway construction was continuing just above.

Lavan spotted them.

'Master!' he exclaimed. 'I wasn't expecting you today.'

'Nor was I expecting to be here myself,' Murty said. 'It's just that Danny is too busy now. He's got a big business to run, as you can understand. He wants to have a better understanding of the books, week by week.'

Lavan reached into his jacket, and pulled out a wad of papers.

'Everything's here,' he said.

Murtybeg looked at him in surprise.'

'You must be the only one who does that.'

'I have to. I wouldn't remember it all otherwise.'

He waved them across to a water barrel, and spread the papers on the lid.

'Now, what do you want to know?'

For a half hour, they went through the figures.

'I can see I taught you well,' Murty said with satisfaction.

'I wouldn't be here otherwise,' Lavan said. 'Danny expects us to know our sums.'

At that moment, the rough door of one of the huts was flung open, just below them.

'Oh God, not again,' Lavan exclaimed.

A priest came out, followed by four men carrying a rough-made bier, a ragged body laid on top. Then the keening began, as two women followed the bier down the embankment, one grasping the hands of two children, the second carrying an infant on her hip.

Murty strode across. Murtybeg followed his father, but Lavan did not. The funeral went between the lower huts and continued to the bottom of the embankment, where a rough grave had been dug.

The bier was laid alongside the grave. Murty and Murtybeg knelt with the rest as the priest began the funeral service.

At the end, he sprinkled the holy water over the corpse.

'Earth to earth, ashes to ashes, dust to dust.'

The corpse was taken from the bier. Carefully the woman stripped the clothes from the body, and it was laid in the grave, naked for all to see. Now they could both see the ravages of fever, and could smell the gangrene.

At the end, the family clambered back up to their hut. The work on the railway went on, with no break. No one else seemed to have noticed the little funeral, though Murty was sure they were all well aware of it.

The priest began to shovel clay onto the body. Murtybeg grasped the shovel from the priest.

'Here, Father, I'll finish it.'

Murty stood with the priest.

'A hard way to die, Father.'

'It is,' the priest replied. 'Hard for the dead, and harder for the ones left living. Though that won't last long. There's fever in that hut. There's another girl in there, she'll be dead soon. And God knows who else she'll infect before she does.'

Murty shuddered.

'You're Irish, Father?'

'Of course,' the priest replied. 'Letterfrack. Near Clifden, out the far end of Connemara. '

'You've seen worse than this, I'd guess.'

'You might say that. Connemara was bad enough, though I've been out of it this long time. I remember 1840 all too well. It's worse now, from all I hear.'

'A lot worse,' Murty replied. 'The West is in a desperate way.'

'God help them all.'

Murty gestured at the rough grave.

'How do you put up with it, Father?'

'I don't know. I just get on with it. It's a desperate hazard, I know. The fever might get me in the end. But death comes to us all, so why worry.'

Murtybeg finished the filling. He handed the priest the shovel.

'Is it like this all over?' Murty asked.

'All along the railway lines,' the priest answered. 'The English camps aren't so bad, and do you know why not? Because they keep the Irish out. They're scared of fever, they reckon the Irish carry it. And I think they're right. But if you consider this is bad, I'll tell you where it's worst. Have you ever heard of Little Ireland?'

'Up in Ancoats?' Murty asked.

Murtybeg was becoming restless. He wanted to end this conversation, but could not over-rule his own father.

'Yes, Ancoats,' the priest replied. 'They're evicting men and women to make way for the railway. They've mud cabins there. *Sceilps* alongside them, if you could call them that. Worse than the huts, they are. As bad as Connemara ever was in the hungry years. All run by this Ryan fellow. Daniel Ryan. Same as here.'

Murtybeg pulled again at his father's elbow. 'Come on, father, time to go.'

Again, Murty waved him away.

'Yes, I know Daniel Ryan,' he said.

'You know him?'

'I'm his father. And may God forgive me for that.'

Next day, Murty and Murtybeg travelled down to the Brassey site. Roughneen was in his office. For some time, they went through figures. When they were finished they walked out.

'Where are the huts?' Murty asked.

'Just over here.'

Murty stood back in astonishment. 'Good God, these are better than I expected.'

'I'd hope so.'

'I'll tell you this, Johnny, I haven't seen anything like these before. All the other sites, they're hardly better than *sceilps*. But by God, these are solid. Well-built too.'

'I don't know about the other sites,' Roughneen said, 'but you've got to remember one thing, Murty. This is a Brassey site. We'd enough *sceilps* here when we were starting, and damned lucky we didn't have an inspection that saw them. But now we're ready for anything.'

Murtybeg went to examine a shack more closely. 'Solid timber, I see. No shit out the front neither.'

'Oh no,' Roughneen replied. 'We had to buy in pipes for that. Dug trenches too. All runs down to a soak-away pit at the end of the field. It's like I say, Murty, we've got to keep Brassey happy.'

Murty took out his pipe, and tamped down the tobacco. 'There's just one thing I don't understand,' he said. 'The shacks are better than the other sites. But the wages…'

'Like you just saw. A shilling a day. A shilling and tuppence for some of them.'

'Not much, is it?'

'We feed them too…'

'Offal. Doesn't cost much to feed them kidneys and livers.'

'True.'

'So what does Brassey think of that?' Murty asked.

'I don't think he wants to know. The food and wages are no concern of his.'

Murty lit his pipe.

'But you fellows. You've worked with Brassey. What was he paying you?'

'Four shillings a day, sometimes five shillings. But that's a different matter. You've got to understand that Brassey has two different ways of working. Before we came working for Danny, we'd been working with Farrelly, before he went to America. The same gang that Luke and Danny worked with, in years gone by. But we were running a butty gang, working for ourselves, and contracting direct to the agents of the big railway contractors – Brassey, Mackenzie and the rest of them. Surprising, isn't it, a gang of twelve or fifteen Mayo fellows working direct with the big contractors. We always elected our own gangers, Farrelly in the past, Tim Kearney until he came over to work with Danny, Joe Gilligan now, I believe. Healthy fellows we were, no question of hunger or fever. Farrelly, or whoever, he'd quote per cubic yard to be removed. It's great working that way. We could work as hard as we liked, and we'd be earning the best wages on the railways. And that's where you come in.'

'Me?'

'Yes, Murty, all the fellows on the butty gangs, you taught us, we'd never have book learning without you. There were no government schools in Mayo when we were being educated. If it wasn't for you, we'd be working as low Irish navvies, just like this lot.'

'I can see that,' Murty said. 'They've not much strength, that's for sure.'

'It's not only a matter of strength, it's everything else they're missing. These are landless men, and you know yourself what that means.'

304

'I do,' Murty said. 'Sure I've seen it all around back in Mayo.'

'I'm sure you have. I know for a certainty your brother Michael had a fellow on his land, growing a patch of potatoes every year, and paying in labour. Isn't that so?'

'He had. I'm not sure that he still has. It was a woman, anyhow. Her man was well past working, so she worked Michael's land for him instead. She went to the Workhouse long ago.'

'And how much was she paid?' Roughneen asked.

'Paid! Nothing. Sure she was glad enough to have her potato patch to live on and feed herself and her man.'

'Some class of slaves then?'

'I wouldn't have said that.'

'Let me ask you this, so. Your school. How many children would you say were from landless families?'

'None I'd say,' Murty said. 'They wouldn't be able to pay a penny for the schooling.'

'And that's the point, isn't it. They come over here, and they've no book learning at all. Can't add or subtract, read or write, they can't even speak English. There's no way any of those fellows could form a butty gang and work direct with Brassey's agents, or the like. Danny knows that, and he knows it well.'

'So why do the big railway contractors put up with Danny when they could be working with proper gangs?'

'That's not fair, father,' Murtybeg interrupted.

'Maybe not,' Murty said, 'but the question stands.'

'It's just what's been happening over the past two or three years,' Roughneen replied. 'We've had this Railway Mania and a massive need for navvies. None of the contractors could get enough of them. At the same time, we've famine in Ireland, and hundreds of thousands of Irish navvies pouring into England, looking for work. The big contractors, they knew they had to use them, but they couldn't do it direct. You don't think Tom Brassey speaks Irish, do you?'

'Of course not.'

'And it's not just that. There's the fear of fever. Riots too. No, the contractors know they can't get these fellows direct, so what do they do? They find Irish labour contractors, that's what.'

'Like Danny?'

'Just like Danny. To be a labour contractor, you might need to be able to play one side against the other. You have to be able to speak Irish, and deal with the Irish navvies. On the other side, you'll speak English and have proper book learning, so you can negotiate with the big contractors. They know the wages we're paying, but they don't want to pretend they know. They want to keep the Irish navvy at arm's length, that's what.'

'So, if the money was so good over around Leeds, why did you leave?'

'One simple answer, Murty. Money. Danny's paying his gangers six shillings a day. We can't get that anywhere else.'

'Is it worth it?'

'By God, it is. Don't forget, all of us are sending money back to Mayo. And it's not just our own families. You know how it works in Mayo. My mother, for example, she's helping to feed our other kin around. There's never enough money, and we have to earn it where we can.'

'So how do you find working for Danny? It must be damned rough, directing starving men, working them at starvation wages.'

'I just don't think about it. Do you, Murteen?'

'Never,' Murtybeg replied. 'We're giving work, aren't we?'

Murty shook his head in despair.

'I don't know about ye, I never stop thinking about it. And it's worse for me. Danny is my son. And I'll tell you this, I don't like his way of working. That woman of his, too, she's just as bad. And it's not that I blame you for what you're doing, Johnny, but I'm seeing it all the time.'

'Yes,' Roughneen said. 'I can understand that. But what else could you do?'

'I don't know. I was thinking of doing some sort of clerking around, but there's nothing going. What do you think?'

Murtybeg looked at his father in astonishment.

'You were thinking what?'

'You heard, Murteen. But it's Johnny's opinion would interest me.'

Roughneen looked from father to son.

'In confidence?'

'Of course,' Murty said. Murtybeg only nodded.

'Fair enough so,' Roughneen said. 'Why don't you go over to Yorkshire? Leeds, Bradford, Halifax, wherever. Work with Joe and the lads?'

Murty's eyes opened.

'Are you mad? I'd never be able for that kind of work.'

'I don't know about that,' Roughneen said. 'You're an able enough man...'

'At my age!'

'And you mightn't have to work as much as you think, neither. I know one thing, the fellows are trying to grow the gang, maybe twenty in all. And they'll easy get that. There's enough lads around Kilduff would work with them.'

'Landless men? They'll get plenty of them.'

'No way. They'll have no rednecks in the gang. The only ones they're interested in are the fellows with book learning. All your pupils, Murty. But they've a problem if they have twenty working.'

'What's that?' Murty asked.

'Too much paperwork,' Roughneen replied. 'They're all young lads, strong and able. They want to be out with a pick and shovel, earning high wages. They need a fellow like you to do the paperwork. All the bidding, paying out the wages, and sending the money back to Mayo. There's a lot more work than you think, and from what I know of the lads, they don't want to be doing that class of work. Look, Murty, why don't you write to Joe Gilligan. Better still, go over and see him.'

Murtybeg was stunned. He looked from Roughneen to Murty.

'I don't know, father. I don't...'

'*Arra*, what,' Murty said, before Murtybeg could continue. 'So what now, Johnny?'

'Hold on,' Roughneen said. 'He went inside the hut, and rummaged through some papers.

'You'll need Joe's address. I'll write it out for you.'

He handed the address to Murty.

'Now, go on. Drop him a line and see what he says.'

'I don't know. I'll think about it.'

They left Roughneen.

'Will you do it, father?'

'What?'

'Leave us?'

'That all depends,' Murty replied. 'It depends on whether there's other work to do. It's your mother I have to consider first. But I'll tell you this, Murteen, we were talking about how much your mother has changed. I'm thinking, it's you who has changed the more.'

Murtybeg stopped.

'You might be right,' he replied. 'In fact, you are right. Perhaps I don't see things the same way as you do any more.'

'That's only natural between father and son.'

'True, but when you've been out of Ireland as long as I have, you'll see things in a different manner. All I see around us are workless navvies, and even if they are working, it's for very little. Danny doesn't want to be like that, and I sure as hell don't. I don't know about yourself, father, but your opinions may change in time. Or...or...'

'Or maybe I'm too old to change?' Murty said. 'Isn't that what you're thinking?'

'Maybe, or maybe not. There's many ways of looking at life. You have yours, I have mine. But one way or another, I'm not leaving Danny. Edwardes & Ryan is the future, I know that.'

'Well, be that as it may, it's your opinion. But there's one other thing I'm asking of you.'

'What's that?'

'Secrecy. Not a word of this gets out to Danny. And I'm not just asking you, I'm ordering you, as your father.'

'Fair enough,' Murtybeg replied. 'I won't breathe of it to a sinner. But what about Roughneen?'

'He's an honourable man. He'll keep his mouth shut. But it's not just his silence I'm worried about. It's your loyalty. Do you see yourself as a loyal son, or is Danny more important to you?'

'Now that's an unfair question, father. You know my first loyalty would be to you and mother. Always.'

'And what of your other loyalties? Is it money that's most important? Or your own conscience?'

'Damn it, it's not that simple.'

'Oh, but it is.'

That evening, Murty and Murtybeg met with Danny and Irene.

'I've just come back from Roughneen's site,' Murty said.

'Well, what did you think?' Danny asked.

'Better lodgings, that's for sure. Better than the other sites.'

'That's because it's a Brassey site.'

'I know.'

Irene was checking through the figures.

'They're using a lot of timber.'

'I know that too,' Murty said. 'It's needed for the shacks.'

'Shacks?'

'Shacks for the workers. We can't have mud cabins on a Brassey site.'

'But our profit margin is down.'

'Not much we can do about that.'

'Oh, but we can. We can charge the men.'

'Charge…'

'Penny halfpenny a night for a bunk. A farthing for sleeping on the floor. It's the going rate with all the contractors.'

Danny cut across them.

'We'll see. One way or another, we have to complete the North Staffordshire for Brassey. All the railways are watching us on this one. And so are Brassey's inspectors.'

Chapter 24

Morning Post, London, March 1848:
Riots in the North. Manchester, Friday afternoon. The energetic conduct of the police during the whole of yesterday, has wonderfully cooled the ardour of the disorderly crowds who still make New Cross their headquarters. The last deliberate and organised act of violence yesterday was the turning out of the hands at a mill in Blackfriars Street. The police force from the Town Hall were upon them in an instant, and took most energetic measures to clear the street. The miscreants here, as elsewhere, were mostly youths. A great many of them got a severe drubbing, which compelled the whole band to rush through the bridge into Salford, where they dispersed through its narrow streets in knots of two and three. Towards five o'clock they mustered courage to return to New Cross by way of Market Street, at which time, and for a few hours after, several hundreds of the police were drawn out in single or double file.

One morning, Murtybeg was woken up by his father.

'Come on, Murteen. We've got a site visit.'

'I didn't think we were planning one today.'

'We are now. We're going to Ancoats.'

'Danny never said anything about Ancoats.'

'Never mind Danny.'

They walked rapidly to Stockport Station, where Murtybeg purchased two third class tickets.

They arrived at Oxford Road, and stood at the edge of the Works. The stink of the place hit them at once. Pigs were snorting at sewage in the drain in the centre of one of the roads. They could see a number of houses had already been reduced to rubble. Navvies were lifting broken bricks into wheelbarrows and wheeling them in the direction of the rails that had already been laid. More navvies were shovelling the rubble onto wagons. Even from here, they could hear the Mayo voices, as the work went on.

A group of people were sitting and standing twenty yards from the

Works. They too had the accents of County Mayo.

A well-dressed man came over to them.

'Who the hell are you?'

Murtybeg stiffened with anger. He had hoped to come anonymously, but now decided to abandon all caution.

'Who am I? Murtybeg Ryan is my name. And if you don't know who I am, you damned well should. Now who are you?'

'Ryan!'

'Daniel Ryan's brother. And this man here is our father. Now I asked you...'

'Steele is the name,' the man answered. 'Samuel Steele. I'm the ganger on site.'

'Yes, I've heard about you,' Murtybeg said. 'Now, if you don't mind, we've been looking around.'

'I'll show you.'

'If you wish,' Murty said. 'We'll need to see your figures first.'

'My figures?'

'Wages, costs for timber, horses, food...'

'Fine, so. I'll show them to you after.'

For some time they followed Steele around the site, taking in everything with a mixture of interest and horror. Murty noticed that one of the doors on the surviving houses was barricaded. Steele saw where he was looking.

'I wouldn't worry,' he said. 'That won't take long. The police will have that cleared soon enough.'

They went back into a small house that Steele had cleared for his own office, and for some time they went through figures and timing.

They heard the tramp of men outside.

'Time for an eviction, gentlemen,' Steele said. 'Do you want to stay?'

'We might as well,' Murtybeg said, feeling he should at least witness what was being done here. They followed Steele outside.

More police had arrived, accompanied by six armed soldiers. The police started to take down the barricade, as the soldiers stood guard. People rushed out from the other houses, but a fusillade, shot in the air, stopped them. The soldiers reloaded, and pointed directly at the crowd. There was complete silence. The police entered the house, and then the screaming started. They watched as women and children were dragged out. One man tried to resist, but he was flattened by a blow from a tall, heavy constable.

'There's few enough would stand up to a man like him,' Murty said.

'Aye, not many would be able for it.'

The eviction went on, until no one was left in the house.

'They'll lodge in that again,' Murtybeg said.

'Not if we demolish it fast enough. And that's where the problem arises.

If we do it brick by brick, the workers would be attacked.'

'So what do you do?' Murty asked.

'Blast it.'

'Blast it!'

'A few ounces of blasting powder. That's all.'

A gang of workers smashed small holes beside each of the four corners, enough to take out one brick. Blasting powder was tamped into the holes, and fuses attached. At a shout from Steele, each of the four fuses were lit simultaneously. The evicted family and the other inhabitants ran. There were four explosions over a few seconds, and the building collapsed.

'Doesn't take much powder for a job like that,' Murtybeg said.

'Nothing like what we're used to on other parts of the railways,' Steele said. 'If we used anything like that, it would break half the windows in Manchester.'

Already the inhabitants were making their way back to the shattered house and their scattered possessions. Through all this time, Murty noticed that most of the navvies worked on, without comment.

At length, they left the site and walked to the Cat & Cage bar nearby. Murtybeg felt deeply depressed. He ordered two beers, and two pork pies.

'I never thought I'd see anything like this outside of Ireland,' Murty said. 'Evictions too. I've seen enough in County Mayo, but to see them here in Manchester, in the industrial heart of the Empire! It's unbelievable. What do you think, Murteen? What do you really think?'

Murtybeg sipped at his beer.

'It's like you said, father. From County Mayo to the slums of Manchester. They don't stand a chance. It's what Roughneen told you. They're all landless men. They don't have any land, rented or otherwise. They're nothing but the starving of Mayo. Why? Just think – what do they have in Mayo? Nothing. No land of their own. So they rent a tiny patch to grow a crop of potatoes for themselves, and pay their rent in labour. Do you know, some of these people have never seen money before they came here?'

'How did they get here so?' Murty asked.

'Any little bit of money that's earned here might be sent back to Mayo to bring out brothers or sisters. Walking across Ireland, then the cattle boat to Liverpool. They can't speak English, so it's hard to get work. No book learning neither. And if you think this place is bad, they might look at it in a different way. They have brick houses here, at least when they're not being evicted. What did they have at home? Nothing but mud cabins. Whole mud villages all across the mountainsides. And while you might think it grim to see the pigs in the street here, it's better than having no pigs at all. Isn't it?'

'You might have the right of it,' Murty said. 'But still, men and women from Mayo being evicted, while Mayo navvies just carry on working on the railway, pretending not to see anything.'

'It's their own families they're thinking of. They need the money – here and back home. They have their eyes tight closed against anything else.'

'So why not use English navvies? They'd have no problems with watching the Irish being evicted.'

'Two reasons. You'd have to offer them three times the wages. Even then, they're terrified of fever. And I'll tell you this, father, these people have fever.'

For an hour, they sat talking of Manchester and Mayo. Then they shared a third class carriage back to Stockport Station.

'What will you do now, father?' Murtybeg asked, as they walked back to the house.

'I'll write to Joe Gilligan. I'll do it tonight. And not a word to anyone.'

Next day, Murty brought up the subject of Little Ireland.

'We went across to see the Ancoats site,' he told Danny.

Danny looked at him, startled. 'I never asked you to do that.'

'You asked me to visit your sites. You never said anything about not visiting any of them.'

'So what's your problem?'

'The fever, Danny. Evictions too. It's worse than Mayo, and it's our contract.'

'None of it has anything to do with us. The railway is going through, so the houses have to be demolished. And if you want to call that evictions, that's up to you.'

'And who's doing the demolishing?'

'It's part of the contract. If we don't do it, someone else will. What would you want us to do, stand back and wait 'till the houses are demolished, knowing well that they're only being demolished for us to put a railway through? And that's the reason I never asked you to visit Little Ireland. I knew it would only upset you.'

'So why do you use Steele? A ganger who doesn't come to any of our meetings. Why is that?'

'It's easier that way. That's why.'

When Gilligan's reply arrived, Murty discussed it with Murtybeg.

'Gilligan's answered me, and asked to meet.'

'Where?'

'Over on the Leeds & Thirsk. He's sent directions.'

'Will you go?'

'I have to, Murteen, but I doubt I'd be able to find my way on my own, so I want you to come with me.'

'Me?'

'Remember what we said about loyalty?'

Murtybeg knew he was trapped.

'But what will Danny say? He'll know we're gone. We'll have to stay a night away at least.'

'I doubt Danny will care much.'

Murty was right. He simply said that he was interested in meeting his old pupils in Yorkshire, and Danny accepted this. He also accepted that Murtybeg would have to travel with him, since Murty was not yet used to travel on English railways.

On the following Sunday, they took the first train from Stockport into Manchester Piccadilly station, and made their way to Victoria station, the terminus of the Lancashire & Yorkshire Railway. Then they took the train across the Pennines, past Bradford to Leeds.

Watching the mountain scenery, Murtybeg felt more torn than ever. Yes, his first loyalty was to his parents, but he could not face the life of a navvy, even as part of the Gilligan gang. Danny gave him an opportunity of living a life far removed from all of that. And even further removed from County Mayo.

When they reached Leeds, they left the station, walking through Swinegate, the Calls, and past the lower end of Kirkgate.

Murty held his nose against the stink of raw sewage.

'Good God! Is this the mighty Leeds we hear all about? Woollen capital of England?'

'You get used to it,' Murtybeg answered.

'I'm sure you do. Danny's huts would get you well used to all sorts of things.'

Following Gilligan's instructions, they left Leeds behind, and walked another hour until they found the lodging house.

The men were still at their mid-day meal. Jim Doyle looked up in surprise.

'The Master!'

Gilligan swung around in surprise.

'By God, you made it.'

'Did you think I wouldn't?' Murty asked.

'And who's this?'

'This is my other son. Murtybeg.'

'Danny's brother? I remember you now.'

Murtybeg found the next ten minutes bewildering, as Murty shook hands with one man after another, sometimes hugging them tightly. Then one question after another about relatives and friends in Mayo. This was a little more difficult, in that Murty knew that some were dead, but it seemed in these cases, the men already knew.

Then Gilligan raised his hands.

'Enough of this. What kind of men are we? They've travelled across the mountains to see us, and we haven't even offered them food.'

Within minutes, they were cutting into pork chops, with fried eggs and potatoes alongside.

'Ye eat well here,' Murtybeg said.

'Sure why wouldn't we?' Ed Higgins said. 'Good lodgings, I'll say that.'

'Better than you'd see elsewhere,' Doyle said. 'Wait 'till you see how the Irish have to live in Kirkgate.'

'I know,' Murtybeg said. 'We came across the side of it, and that was close enough.'

'Enough of that,' Gilligan said abruptly. 'I'd never have believed we'd see the Master over this side of the sea.'

'And so you shouldn't,' Murty said, 'except the Government is bringing in new schools back in Mayo. They want their own teachers, no time for an old fellow like me.'

The landlady brought out another bowl of potatoes. Murtybeg was surprised, but took two more, leaving the rest for the others.

'So, you're working with Danny, the pair of ye?' Doyle asked.

'We are,' Murty replied. 'And I'll tell you this, I must have sinned grievously to be working for my own son.'

'The other lads don't seem to mind. Jamesy, Johnny, Tim. All making good money, I hear.'

'Yes,' Murty said, 'and in the worst way possible. Taking advantage of penniless men at a shilling a day. Danny pays his gangers a lot more than that, as well ye know. And I can't complain about what he's paying me. Still, Danny's way of working is a terrible one, and I don't want any truck with it no more.'

'I can well understand that,' Gilligan said. 'And I've no doubt about one thing, you'd be far better off over here. Not the same as Danny is paying his gangers, that's for sure, but we'd not be abusing Irish navvies the same way he does. Not that I've much time for them myself.'

'No?'

'They deserve all they get from Danny and the rest of the contractors. You've seen Kirkgate, have you? Go over to Bradford and see Broomfields. It's worse, and full of Mayo men too. Not like us though. Rednecks. The lowest of the low, that's what they are.'

'I'm surprised you'd think that,' Murty said.

'It's not surprising at all. The navvies hate the butty gangs, and we hate them. There's no love lost either way. They reckon all we're doing is spreading piecework, like was done on the Famine Roads in Mayo. But I'll tell you this, there's nothing wrong with a man being on piecework, so long as the man is willing to work.'

'And if they're not?' Murty asked.

'Well, what do you think?' Higgins asked. 'You've seen them on Danny's gangs.'

'That's different,' Murty said. 'They're starving.'

'Yes, and fever-ridden too,' Doyle answered. 'And working for a shilling a day. And you know what that does to us? Here we are, working for four shillings a day. The contractors keep asking us why we can't stop working as a butty gang, and work for a shilling a day instead. They know damned well what kind of work they'd get from us for that kind of wage though. Still, it's hard competing with fellows who've been used to working for nothing at all back in County Mayo. Slavery, I'd call it.'

Gilligan stood.

'Enough of that. It's not them fellows we should be thinking of. The Master is here, and we need a man like him. Ye all know that.'

'I'm not sure I'd be so good at hard labour myself,' Murty said.

'*Arra*, it won't be difficult,' Gilligan said. 'You're a strong enough man.'

'I wouldn't be up to the likes of you young fellows, though.'

'Sure you'll do some. And anyhow, it isn't that we're talking about, is it? It's all this paper that's drowning us. We need a man like you for that. Then the rest of us can do the hard work, and get more hardworking fellows on the gang from Kilduff, Carrigard and around. And to hell with those fellows from West Mayo.'

'And what of this fellow here?' Higgins interrupted. 'Murtybeg, he'll work with us too?'

'I wish he would,' Murty replied, 'but he's got a mind of his own.'

Murtybeg looked up at them all. 'It's kind of ye to offer it,' he said, 'but I'm working with Danny now, part of the business. I'll take my chances with him for now.'

'Fair enough,' Doyle answered, 'but if you change your mind, let us know. We've a powerful need for strong fellows on the gang here.'

'Yes,' Higgins said, 'and we want only the best. Kilduff and around. The men we know.'

Over the next few hours, Murty and Murtybeg visited the site with Gilligan.

'It's mainly the Lancashire Yorkshire and the Manchester Leeds lines we're working on,' Gilligan told them. 'The main lines have both been completed, but it's all the branches off them now that we're building, linking up with the smaller towns and tying one railway with another. There's plenty of work for years to come around Bradford and Leeds.'

They returned to the lodging house for a good dinner of steak and potatoes. Gilligan proposed terms of employment to Murty, and this was voted on over the table, with all in favour.

They spent that night in a spare room at the lodging house. They rose before dawn, and Gilligan walked them back to Leeds station, carefully avoiding Kirkgate.

At the station, they shook hands.

'We'll all be looking forward to having you as one of the gang,' Gilligan said to Murty.

'I'll need time, Joe. It's not that I'm undecided, but I've got Aileen to think of. Danny too. Give it a week.'

They shook hands with Gilligan, and returned to Stockport.

Other matters arose, when Winrow requested Danny's presence for an urgent meeting.

When he arrived at the bank, he was ushered into a large office, where Winrow introduced him to two bank directors. Danny began to lay out his cash position on the various sites, but Winrow waved it aside impatiently.

'We can discuss those some other time. In the meantime, we'd like to discuss another contract with you.'

'Which one?' Danny asked, though he was beginning to suspect he already knew.

'The Ormskirk Cutting on the East Lancashire line. You had already done costings on it?'

'I had. Preliminary only. You did request though that we not proceed on it.'

'Yes,' Winrow replied. 'At the time, we thought the Brassey contract was a large one for you, and any more would stretch Edwardes & Ryan beyond what might be acceptable in terms of risk. But from what you say, the Brassey contract is going well, as well as your other contracts.'

'That's true,' Danny said, wondering how Winrow could have known that, since he had not even looked through the accounts Danny had brought with him. 'I'd be delighted to go ahead with it, if you wish to lend on it.'

'So what was your borrowing requirement for it?'

'Three thousand pounds. That of course would be on a rolling basis, to be run down to nil at the end of the contract.'

He was beginning to suspect that Roscoe had been correct about Baxendales. Were they bankrupt?

Winrow was speaking again.

'Perhaps if I could ask you to submit detailed costings for this contract, on the basis that we are inclined to go ahead with the loan.'

'I'd be delighted, of course,' Danny said. 'I had understood though that the Ormskirk contract had already been awarded to another company.'

'Rumours only,' Winrow said, impatiently. 'The question is, do you wish to bid for this contract? If so, the bank will most likely support you.'

Yes, Danny thought. Baxendales are gone.

When he left the bank, he walked towards Manchester Piccadilly Station.

The city was in turmoil.

First, he saw debris all over the road. Then he came on a crowd of hundreds of young men, yelling at the police, and hurling bricks and stones.

The police were preparing for a baton charge. Danny ran out of the way, and stood back into a crowded doorway, where others sheltered from the batons and bricks.

The police charged, but they were driven back under a shower of bricks, followed by a mob wielding sticks and metal bars. Danny realised he was now trapped.

There was a woman beside him, carrying a baby.

'What's happening?' Danny asked.

'There's fighting all over the city. They've been attacking the mills. Kelly & Gilmours. Kennedys over in Ancoats Street. Clark's too. They've been stoning the courts all day. Tried to burn the Workhouse...'

Police reinforcements had arrived. Danny watched as they charged again, batons slashing wildly. This time the mob broke, screaming as they ran.

'They're rough, the police,' Danny said.

'Nothing like Peterloo,' the woman said. 'The dragoons used sabres then. We wouldn't run before wooden sticks at Peterloo.'

'Peterloo? But when...?'

'Thirty years ago.'

'Before my time, I'm afraid.'

'I was only six myself. But even a child remembers the sight of blood.'

Danny was startled.

'I've heard of Peterloo,' he said, 'but never spoken to anyone who was there.'

'You never had much interest in it neither, I'd warrant.'

'Perhaps you're right,' he said.

'Well, let me tell you, the times were just like this. Thousands out of work and starving, right across Manchester. Then the political fellows came to talk to us. A peaceful meeting. The powers-that-be could have left it at that. They could have let us all finish with it, and go to our homes. But no, they wouldn't have that. They had to send in the dragoons with their sabres. The Manchester & Salford Yeomanry, no less. Brave men they were, cutting down innocent men and women.'

The Manchester & Salford, Danny was thinking. He tried to imagine Winrow as a dragoon, but the idea was too ridiculous.

There was a hail of stones, from a different direction now. Some hit the people in the doorway. Instinctively, Danny pulled the woman and child down, and sheltered them behind his coat. After a minute, he looked out. The mob were retreating before another police charge.

'You're safe now,' he said.

She stood up. 'And I must thank you for that,' she said, 'but I'm wondering what your accent is? I think it's part Irish.'

'It is,' Danny said. 'I was born here, though.' He was lying, but there was no need to upset this woman.

'Of an Irish mother and father, I'd say.'

'You're right,' he said.

'Well I won't blame you so. This whole mob, it's the Irish they're rioting against. There's thousands of English men and women out of work in the mills and on the railways. And do you know why? It's because the Irish come in and work for nothing at all. It's not that I'd blame them either, it's the mill owners and the railway contractors, getting in starving Irish people to steal our jobs. They're the guilty ones, the ones who bring hunger and rioting to Manchester.'

The mob was more distant now.

'I think it's safe to go,' Danny said.

They stepped out of the shelter of the doorway.

'I must thank you, Sir,' she said. 'You protected me and the baby, when we needed it. Irish or not, you are a gentleman.'

Then she left.

Danny made his way to Piccadilly Station and home to Stockport.

The family were at dinner when he returned.

'You've heard about the riots?' Murtybeg asked.

'Heard about them? I was right in the middle of one of them.'

'A big mob, was it?'

'Hundreds, but the police were well able to deal with them.'

An excited conversation began around the dinner table, as everyone exchanged rumours and opinions about the riots, but Danny was only half listening. In his mind, he could still see the woman and baby, and what, to him, was a picture of innocence and helplessness.

But he was a railway contractor, and there were things that could never be.

After dinner, he discussed the Winrow meeting with Irene.

She did not seem surprised.

'Didn't I tell you we'd be offered the Ormskirk contract again?'

'You did,' he answered. 'What else could they do when Baxendales went bankrupt?'

'But no one else knows that. What did the bank say about them?'

'Nothing. Baxendales was never mentioned, neither by them nor by me. They offered me the loan for Ormskirk, but wouldn't discuss the original contractor.'

'That's good,' she said. 'Now, from here on, we can be sure that Ormskirk is ours. It's exactly like Nick Roscoe said. Mackenzie is under desperate pressure to complete it. Now, with Baxendales gone, he'll be months behind, and we're the ones who can do it fastest. They know that, and so do the Manchester & Salford. And if there were to be any further delay, Mackenzie will sue.'

'Starting with Baxendales, no doubt.'

'Yes,' she said, 'but they're bankrupt, and it's doubtful they'll pay out more than a shilling in the pound. So there's only one other company they can sue for this delay. Which is...'

'The Manchester & Salford Bank.'

'Exactly. They're in trouble, Winrow is in trouble, and we're the only ones who can pull the fat out of the fire for them.'

Danny was still concerned about the general prospects for Edwardes & Ryan. He found it hard to accept Irene's logic on the business. They were caught between enormous opportunity and enormous risk. Yes, many of the railways were pushing for rapid completion on contracts so as to open long sections of rail to traffic. Equally though, there were suspensions on the railways all around them.

There was great opportunity too in driving down prices of supplies. Danny wondered though how long this could continue, and what might happen if suppliers went bankrupt. Cash on delivery meant there was no financial risk to Edwardes & Ryan, but if a supplier stopped trading, could he be replaced in time?

And the banks? The Manchester & Salford was desperately important to them now. Yes, they had to lend to Edwardes & Ryan because of the consequences to the bank if they did not. But what would happen if the bank itself went bankrupt? The Royal Bank of Liverpool had been thought to be indestructible. Was the Manchester & Salford solid? Would any other banks lend to an unknown employer of Irish labour?

But were they unknown? Working for Brassey – that had startled many of the other labour contractors. It was desperately important to finish his contract on time and on budget. Now Irene reckoned they had wider opportunities. The Ormskirk Cutting meant working with Mackenzie too. That put Edwardes & Ryan at the top table. High level contracts, low wages, low supply prices. The future was open, but it was terribly risky.

*

319

The next week was a busy one for him. He travelled to Ormskirk to get more detailed information on the site. Afterwards, he hand-delivered detailed costings to the bank. Next day, the letter confirming the loan was hand-delivered to his office.

On an impulse, he decided to travel to Mackenzie's Manchester office, and was not surprised when he was invited in at once. What did surprise him was that the East Lancashire line was being built jointly by Mackenzie and Brassey. The office manager was well aware of Danny's work for Brassey on the North Staffordshire.

They spent an hour going through the contract. Then Danny was asked to bid. He decided to add two hundred pounds to what he and Irene had already agreed. His bid was accepted at once, and a contract was drawn up and signed.

He returned to Stockport.

'That's splendid,' Irene exclaimed. 'More profitable than ever. And now we're working with the two top contractors in England. The future is open.'

And it only got better.

One day, Danny received a letter from Roy Anderson, requesting a meeting. They met in the Midland Hotel in Manchester.

'I've another contract for you, Danny,' Anderson said. 'And it's urgent. You've heard about Baxendales?'

'I've heard rumours,' Danny answered.

'Seems the rumours are true. Baxendales are bankrupt, which creates a hell of a problem for the railway and the bank. They've a site out by one of yours.'

'I know, Jamesy McManus is running it for me. You might know that we've had problems there. Rioting between our fellows and Baxendales.'

'Well, you won't have problems there anymore. Can you take over the Baxendales site? Perhaps we could do it together, splitting profits half and half.'

'Of course.'

That afternoon, Danny travelled out to see McManus. The two men stood together, watching the navvies streaming out of the Baxendales site.

'No point in going in there 'till they're gone,' McManus said. 'They'd only kill us.'

It was late in the afternoon before the site was totally empty. Danny spent the last hours before sunset, measuring out the site with McManus, estimating the remaining cubic yards to be excavated until he felt he had a good understanding of it.

That evening, over dinner, Irene was elated.

'Our first competitor gone,' she said. 'Didn't I tell you we could pick up bankrupt contracts?'

'You did,' he said. 'It's just like on the Ormskirk. Now Roy needs us. Otherwise the Railway has a logjam on the line. We've done the costings already, we know what's involved. And we're just beside them, it's only an extension to our site.'

The next morning, he and Irene went through the figures. When they were happy, Danny met with Anderson again, and after they added an amount for Andersons, and two fair copies had been made out by the clerk, they sent a copy to the railway contractor's office. A week later, Anderson wrote to Danny, saying their bid had been accepted.

'Nothing can stop us now,' Irene said.

'It's like I told you before,' Danny said. 'We make one hell of a team, the pair of us.'

'And isn't it time we made it more lasting. We'll have to set a date for a wedding and tell everyone.'

'You're right,' he said. 'Let's go for July, so. That should be good timing.'

'Why July?'

'We'll have finished the Brassey contract by then.'

A few days later, Danny was startled to be told that Inspector Crawford was looking for him.

'Show him into the living room,' he said, irritably.

He and Irene descended the stairs. 'What in hell does he want this time?' Danny asked.

'Whatever it is, I doubt it's going to be good.'

Crawford was standing as they entered. Danny waved him to an armchair, and they all sat. Danny smiled. 'Well, Inspector, I hope it's good news you're bringing this time.'

'The worst,' Crawford replied. 'I've just had news in from one of your sites. Your ganger – Mr. McManus – has been killed.'

'Jamesy,' Danny gasped. 'Killed!'

'Shot in the back with a shotgun. Died in minutes. Another murder case, I'm afraid. The second on your site.'

Danny could hardly speak with the shock of it.

'But...why?' he asked. 'Why...?'

Irene spoke for him.

'You must understand, this is terrible news for us, Inspector. Mr. McManus had been a close friend, and we had not been expecting this. Have you been able to make an arrest?'

'I'm afraid by the time I got to the site, there was no sign of the killer.

He would hardly wait around, would he?'

'But surely you have some idea of the motive?' she asked.

'We can't be certain,' he answered, 'but there is one very obvious possibility. He was killed in revenge for Eckersley's murder.'

'Does that mean that the killer thought Mr. McManus was behind Eckersley's murder?' she asked.

'Not necessarily,' the Inspector replied. 'But he was the nearest and most senior victim, though, as you might know yourself, there was more to Mr. McManus than meets the eye. We've been watching him for a long time.'

Danny was more alarmed than ever.

'But why?' he asked.

'He was a known member of the Molly Maguire gang.'

'But...the Molly Maguires? They're all back in Ireland.'

'Most are,' Crawford responded. 'All up the north west. Including Mayo, where Mr. McManus was from. You too, I believe.'

'What? You're not suggesting...'

He realised at once that was the wrong thing to say.

'Not necessarily, Mr. Ryan, though I can say at this stage the enquiry is open. It's quite possible – likely even – that Mr. McManus killed Mr. Eckersley, or at least ordered it. But even if he did, the question is, who ordered him? We know the Molly Maguire gang are well established in Liverpool. They're in the process of establishing themselves in Manchester too. Clearly we can no longer question Mr. McManus, but what we really want to know is this. Who was his chief? Bodymaster, as they call it. Yes, Mr. Ryan, there is one mastermind controlling the gang in Manchester. We do not yet know who he is, though we have our suspicions. And we will get him, have no doubt about that.'

The maid showed the Inspector out. Danny was stunned. He could not say that he knew who the Manchester bodymaster was. To do so, could incriminate him, and imply he himself might have been behind the Eckersley murder. Worse still, the Molly Maguire gang had ways of dealing with informers, and Danny knew that he would spend the rest of his life on the run if he informed on Sheridan. Or die if they caught him.

After some moments of silence, Irene spoke. 'Calm down, Danny.'

'I am calm,' Danny said, without conviction.

'You're white in the face. Crawford saw that.'

'Well, I was shocked, wasn't I? Hearing Jamesy was dead, that was shock enough. You reckon it goes further, do you?'

'I think so,' she said. 'He certainly suspects you. What he suspects you of, is not clear, and perhaps even he doesn't know yet. One way or another, we've got to be very careful. Crawford is no fool.'

Danny was more than alarmed. He was becoming terrified. He had started a chain of events which had ended in two murders. He convinced himself that it was not something that he could ever have foreseen. He had asked Sheridan to remove Eckersley, not to kill him. All he had wanted was to eliminate the shebeens on his sites and stop the gang riots. His objective was quite right, even Crawford would have agreed with that. But Eckersley had died, and, while he had not wanted that, it had happened. He had always prided himself on being tough on his workers, but in spite of his toughness, he felt a certain guilt about Eckersley's death. Now Jamesy was dead too. An old friend for many years, and no matter which way he looked at it, he himself was guilty of his death.

He could only hope that this was the end of the chain. Or would it turn into an endless series of tit-for-tat killings?

Murtybeg too was shocked by McManus' murder, but he said nothing to Danny. There were other matters on his mind, less shocking, but more immediate.

He had been disturbed by Murty's discussion with Roughneen, and even more so by the meeting with Joe Gilligan and the gang in Yorkshire. He had never expected the way they had scorned other Irish navvies and the Irish of the slums. In some ways, he could see the logic of it, in that men on good wages were afraid to be undercut by those who were used to working for nothing at all in County Mayo. 'Slaves', as Doyle had put it. Roughneen too.

What disturbed him more was that it was something he had never considered when he was in Mayo. Landless men and their families had been all around him there, but he had had little interest in them. Those in school were the ones who could afford to pay, not the children of rednecks.

The families who paid might have paid very little, and a few even paid in kind – potatoes and cabbages in season, sometimes labour – but even these were families who valued the benefits of education. But what of the rest? The people in mud cabins? Roughneen had been right. Michael had had a landless couple living in a mud cabin in Carrigard. *Sorcha* was the woman's name, but he had forgotten the name of her husband. She had been a hard worker. But what had happened to them? He had some recollection of them being sent to Knockanure Workhouse, but that was all.

Did he care? It no longer mattered whether he did or not. He had a straight choice – work with Danny, or work with the gang in Yorkshire. But which was the lesser evil?

One evening, he stood on the path outside the house. It was a clear, starry night, and bitterly cold. Murty came out.

'There you are, Murteen. I thought we'd lost you.'

Murtybeg laughed. 'You'd be hard put to lose a fellow like me.'

'What's up with you, standing out in the cold like this?'

'Just thinking.'

'About McManus?'

'That, and other matters.'

'Jamesy's murder was a terrible thing.'

'It was,' Murtybeg replied. 'It shocked us all.'

'There's only one thing I'm wondering, Murteen. Why was he killed?'

'Damned if I know,' Murtybeg replied.

For some time, Murty said nothing, then he spoke again.

'Remember what we said about loyalty, Murteen. I'll ask it another way. Who murdered him?'

Murtybeg knew he was caught.

'I'd be telling the truth if I said I don't know, but I've got my strong suspicions. It was someone from the English gang that were working next to Jamesy's site. As yet, I doubt if anyone knows the exact man.'

'And why would any of those fellows want to kill Jamesy?'

'In revenge for Eckersley's murder.'

'The shebeen fellow?'

'Yes,' Murtybeg replied. 'The shebeen fellow.'

There was silence again, as Murty knocked his pipe on the heel of his shoe and watched the still-glowing ashes on the ground. Then he tamped more tobacco into the pipe, and slowly lit it.

'Yes,' he said, 'that fellow got one hell of a beating. Died afterwards. Just the same as happened to Jimmy Corrigan, after you and Danny beat the hell out of him.'

Murtybeg was angry now. 'Well I can tell you one thing for sure, father. It wasn't me nor Danny beat Eckersley.'

'Fine,' Murty said. 'I believe you on that point. But the question is, who did beat him, and under whose orders?'

'Not mine anyhow,' Murtybeg said, knowing well that that left only one alternative, and Murty was shrewd enough to work that out for himself.

'Well, enough of that for now,' Murty said. 'What did you think of our visit to Gilligan and the rest of them?'

'It went well,' Murtybeg replied. 'You've sure got a job there, if you want it.'

'Yes,' Murty said. 'And that's the question, isn't it?'

'But why wouldn't you?'

'Quite a few reasons, Murteen. One is the question of your mother, and how she would take it, moving from site to site.'

'They mightn't move as much as you think,' Murtybeg said. 'After all, they've been on the Leeds & Thirsk for a year or two. Good lodgings too, as we both saw.'

'Maybe you've the right of it,' Murty answered. 'But there's other questions too. Did you hear what they were saying about the other Irish navvies? They hold them in utter scorn.'

'Yes,' Murtybeg answered. 'I noticed that fast enough. I've been thinking about it ever since.'

'It's not much different to what you fellows think over here, is it. Though mind you, at least the Gilligan lot aren't exploiting them, though their hatred is bad enough.'

'It is.' Murtybeg took out his own pipe, tamped it and lit it. 'So have ye decided?'

'I have,' Murty said. 'Have you?'

'Damned if I know what I want,' Murtybeg said.

That night, Murtybeg lay back in his bed, staring into the darkness. He felt more conflicted than ever. He had told his father that he held his first loyalty, but still his actions showed a closer loyalty to Danny. If he was loyal to his father and mother, he could leave Danny and work in the Gilligan gang. They were still looking for strong fellows from Kilduff, and Murtybeg was sure he could work with them, and stay with Murty and Aileen. He knew Aileen would be delighted if he did, and this would help her out of her misery. But then what? Whatever Gilligan said about it, he would be working as a navvy, even as a highly paid one. How long could that last? Twenty years until he could do it no longer? Perhaps more, but even so, it would come to an end. He had better chances with Danny, and could become a wealthy man, and retire when he liked. Which was the better?

Next evening, Murty was alone with Danny, as the maid was clearing up the dishes after dinner, and the rest had gone to bed.

'I'm leaving here,' he said.

Danny looked up in surprise. 'Leaving?'

'Leaving,' Murty repeated. 'There's nothing to keep me here. I've had enough.'

Danny put down his pen. He could see from his father's face that this was deadly serious.

'But surely…you're making good money, more than you'd ever make in Mayo.'

'True,' Murty said, 'but then I see where it's all coming from. This is an evil place, Danny, and you've made it so. The way you treat your men, the way you pay them, the condition of the navvy huts, the evictions, what could be worse? All these years I've been a teacher…'

'Yes,' said Danny angrily, 'but that's over. Isn't that why you're here?'

'It is, right enough,' Murty answered, 'but it doesn't mean I have to stay.'

Danny stood, and walked over to the fire.

'But where would ye go? Times are hard now, you know that. The Stock Market…'

'I know,' Murty said, 'I read the papers too, you know.'

'Well, then?'

'I'll be working with Joe Gilligan and the rest of the lads…'

'You'll what' Danny exclaimed. 'You'd work on the rails, would you? And you're the one saying you're a teacher.'

'Yes,' Murty said, 'I'd work on the rails. They need someone for all the paperwork, and God knows I'm well able for that.'

'But…in Leeds. Sure that's miles away. The other side of the Pennines.'

'So it is,' Murty said, 'but what of that? We can start over again, this time with a respectable job. Yes, it's less money – just over half what I'm getting here. But who knows, Aileen might get a job in the mills too and make up for it.'

'There's no work for mill-hands.'

'Not now, there's not. But there will be again. Give it time.'

'And…where would you stay?'

'Their lodgings are fine. A good house, good landlady, good food. What more could a man want?'

Danny had a sudden thought. Why was he arguing? If Aileen went, it would solve any problems between her and Irene.

As indeed it did.

'Thank God for that,' Irene said to him afterwards. 'Now we'll be able to live the way we want, without having to look back over our shoulders every hour.'

But Danny did not look at it that way. His family was close to him. Nessa's death had hit him very hard, and he and Murtybeg had beaten a man for it, a man who died soon afterwards. Danny saw no conflict in this. His duty was to protect his family, and if others must suffer for it, so be it. One way to protect the family was to make enough money to ensure they had enough to eat. He knew the Hell that County Mayo had now become. He had taken his parents out of that, given them food and lodgings and good pay. The fact he was exploiting helpless men to achieve this was not a problem to his mind. Yes, he had had differences with Murty, and even Murtybeg in the past, but he had never seen these as serious opposition.

But now, Murty was leaving. He saw this as a betrayal of everything he valued. That it was done by his own father was even worse. He knew now he was alone, or almost so. Irene would stay, but was that only for his money?

Murtybeg might stay too, but was he tough enough for this business?

And all this, coming on top of Crawford's visits. Perhaps he was reading too much into Crawford's questions, but the more he thought about it, the more convinced he was of it. Crawford suspected him of Eckersley's murder. He also suspected him of being the bodymaster for the Molly Maguire gang in Manchester. The only way to prove otherwise, was to inform on Sheridan.

Either way, he could die for it.

No time was wasted, as Murty and Aileen left a few days later. All their possessions were packed in trunks and loaded onto a hansom cab, which Murtybeg had been instructed to order.

'It's not too high a cost for getting what you want,' Danny said to Irene.

'I suppose you're right,' Irene said. 'Not that I like paying it.'

Danny and Murtybeg kissed Aileen, and stood by the door as the cab left. Irene was already back working on accounts.

A few minutes later, she came across to his desk.

'Have you seen this?'

She handed him a letter from Birkenhead. Brassey's head office.

'What does it say?'

'They want completion by the end of May.'

'The end of May? Are they mad?'

'They might be. But one way or another, we have to do it.'

Danny shook his head. 'My God, that's impossible.'

'We're going to have to make it possible,' she said. 'So first, we'll have to get an awful lot more navvies.'

'Yes, I know, there's thousands around, but we won't be able to pay them the wages we're paying the west Mayo fellows. Even if they're desperate, it'll be at least two shillings a day, maybe half a crown.'

'I wouldn't worry too much about that,' she said. 'Sure, it'll cost us, but we've got the margins built in.'

'Ah yes,' Danny responded, 'your contingencies.'

'Exactly,' she said. 'Though less than before, now. Aren't you pleased they were there though?'

'Indeed. But there's another problem now. Even if we take on new navvies, it'll have to be four or five hundred.'

'There's plenty of jobless men around here. We won't need any direct from Ireland. They're all over here already.'

'True. But then – at the end of May – we'll have to fire the lot of them again. Seven hundred men, or more. And how the devil can we do that? There's nowhere else they can go for work, that's for certain. And the Parish won't take them.'

'Send them back to Ireland,' she said 'It's the only way.'

'But think of the cost. And anyway why send them all the way to Ireland?'

'You're right. So just put them on wagons back to Liverpool. Let the Workhouse take them. They can do what they like – send them back to Ireland or feed them, or just let them beg.'

'We'd have to get someone to go with them though.'

'How about Murtybeg? He was good enough at getting them over from Liverpool. And he knows the Workhouse staff.'

'Yes,' he said, 'we could do that. But first they'd have to be fired.'

'Get the gangers to fire them.'

'They've too much to be thinking about already.'

'Let's use your own family again, so. You keep going on about how educated they are.'

'Who so?'

'Your cousin…'

'Luke. He's gone to America.'

'I know. He's not your only cousin. Is he?'

'There's Pat.'

'Pat, so. Why would he want to stay in Mayo?'

'I understand he's got a position in the Poor Law Union.'

She snorted. 'And how long is that going to last? From all we hear, half the Irish Unions are bankrupt already. What we should do is write to him, offer him good pay. It'll be better than Union rates anyhow, and he'll be over here in a flash. We don't have to tell him what his duties will be, he can work that out when he gets here.'

'Maybe,' Danny said. 'That might work. Let me think about it.'

'Don't think too long.'

'Don't worry. Our next problem though is Jamesy's site. We've no ganger there. There's a few foremen, but I doubt they're much good.'

'So what do we do?'

'We'll just have to split it between Murtybeg and myself for a while.'

Danny's next shock came when he received a letter from Roy Anderson. In it, Anderson explained that the crash on the railways was now causing severe problems. There was an on-going threat of suspensions on their sites. The only exception was the Little Ireland site in Ancoats, which was going well.

On the other three, Anderson wrote, the only way to avoid suspensions was to cut the price. He suggested a reduction of twenty percent.

Chapter 25

Montreal Transcript, January 1848:
From Grosse Île, the great charnel house of victimised humanity, up to Port Sarnia – along the borders of our magnificent river, upon the shores of Lakes Ontario and Erie, and wherever the tide of immigration has extended, are to be found the resting places of the sons and daughters of Erin – one unbroken chain of graves where repose fathers and mothers, sisters and brothers in one comingled heap, without a tear bedewing the soil or a stone to mark the spot.

One morning in February, one of the Quebecer overseers came up to Luke. Wordlessly, he handed him a letter.

Luke looked at it in astonishment. He saw the Castlebar postmark.

'Where did this come from?'

'*Pour vous? Oui?*'

'Yes, yes, for me. But where...?'

'Quebec.'

Luke stared at it, still unable to comprehend it. The address on the front was very short. It read –

'Luke Ryan, Gilmours, Quebec, Canada.'

There were scribbles on the front in English and French:

– Unknown. Try the shipyard.

– *Pas ici.*

– Not here either. Try Wolfe's Cove.

– *Irlandais?*

– McGowan might know.

He turned it over. There was another note on the back of the envelope –

'You were fortunate this landed on my desk after all this time. Hope it reaches you now. Mary says to send our best wishes to you and the lads. Write us when you get to New York. Larry.'

McGowan, he thought. He knew where I was. Damned lucky, that. He opened it.

Luke Ryan   Carrigard
Gilmours   Kilduff
Quebec   County Mayo
Canada   Ireland

11 December 1847

My Dearest Luke,

I am sending this letter in the hope that it will reach you. Perhaps it will, who knows. We well received your first letter, and were more happy to have it than I can tell. We had heard such terrible stories about the Quebec ships. Your mother says the Good Lord was looking over you. Your second letter was welcome too, we had not expected another so soon. Your father directs me to say the price of corn is high, and we have much need of money for the rent too. I am happy to say that all here are well. The fever around is less than it was, and thank God for that. Pat is well, and Sarah has visited us twice since you left. Neither of them will say anything, but I'm sure she's not coming over just to visit your mother and myself, and like I told your mother before, there is too much making eyes between them. I think you may now think her your sister-in-law. Your father still works the farm and quarry. Your mother says he is doing too much, and Pat helps whenever he can. Your father says that we have enough potatoes for our own needs. There has been no rot this year past, but we have had to bring them all in to the house, for they would all have been stolen by now if we had not. There were far too few potatoes planted around Kilduff, and whatever there were would be gone before it even got out of the ridge, except it was guarded at night. But now we are in a good way, though I fear the hunger goes on around us, and it will do for some time yet. I pray the next harvest will be a good one, for everyone's sakes.

I note that you say that I must wait until you have a fixed address before I leave, but how long will that be my love? My plan would have been to leave in April, a month after our son is to be born, but this will no longer be possible. (Your mother has just asked how I know it is to be a son. I just know, and there's an end to it). But if I do not leave by August the season for crossing may be over and so we may not meet until 1849. So please give me a fixed address as soon as you can.

If your friend *Conaire* is still with you, you may tell him that we sent a letter to his family after your first letter but have had no answer yet, and are sending another letter tonight.

Your mother and father join me in sending all our love.

Your loving wife,

Winifred

He looked at the date. Two months past. There was nothing surprising in that. Five weeks at least on the Atlantic. A week overland from Halifax, because the St. Lawrence was frozen. A week or two going in circles around Gilmours in Quebec, and more time to make it out to the Gatineau.

And all alive, too. Potatoes enough – for the family at least. And Winnie coming out in the summer. That would be best. What a risk she would be taking though, with a young baby. Would they meet in New York, or miss one another? Would he get there in time? How long was he himself going to stay in New York if she had not arrived? Could he get work in New York? Would it not be better to go straight to Harrisburg, and meet with Farrelly and the gang?

One way or another, Winnie could not leave until he had a fixed address. But when would that be?

He put it in his pocket, and returned to work. He hefted a sack of flour up to Jack.

'Well, who was it?' Jack asked.

'My wife. Writing from Mayo. It's a miracle I got it at all. She just sent it to Gilmours, and Larry saw it. At least he knew where I was. No one else would have.'

'So what's she got to say? How's Mayo?'

'Better and worse. The fever is less than before. There was no blight in the last harvest, but it seems there was very little planted, so the hunger goes on.'

He leaned against the side of the horse. He was thinking about Winnie, and the whole family. Could the farm survive? There was little he could do about that, but it was crucial to get Winnie out to America as soon as he could.

He lifted another sack of flour.

'There's one thing that still worries me though. We won't have a fixed address until June at the earliest. That's assuming we make New York, get work and have somewhere settled to stay. What do I do then? Buy the ticket for her, and send it over? Or just send her the money?'

'Best send the money,' Jack said. 'Then she can make her own choices.'

'That's true. But if she doesn't move fast enough, it'll be a winter crossing.'

'I don't know that it has to be,' Jack said, 'and even if it is, we'd be talking about New York, not Quebec. Direct from Westport too, on a proper passenger ship. No, I wouldn't worry about a winter crossing. All she'd have to do is get to New York, money in her pocket, and all will be fine.'

He found his way to the office shanty and agreed a price of two cents for a sheet of paper, and the loan of a pen and ink. He sat at a desk and started to write.

Ryan Family   Gatineau Forests
Carrigard   Canada
Kilduff
County Mayo
Ireland   10 February

My Dearest Winnie, Dear Mother and Father,
I have just received your letter, and was most surprised that it arrived. A friend
in the Gilmour offices in Quebec saw the address, and sent it on to me here in
the forest. By rights it should never have arrived, but I was mighty glad to see it.

I was happy to hear that all are well, in our family at least. The stories we
hear here of famine and fever in Ireland are terrible though, and I pray to the
Lord it will ease soon. Perhaps the early harvest will be a good one.

As for you travelling, Winnie, I am not so certain when this will be
possible. Like I said it would be better to wait until I have at least a fixed
address, and at present I do not know when I will arrive in New York, nor
indeed whether I will have an address I may call my own for a good time after.
I do not know what the chances of work in New York are, nor when I will
travel to Harrisburg or wherever Farrelly and the boys are, so I may be only
a few days in New York. I would ask you for patience therefore, and wait until
I can give you more certain information. I have heard of many families who
have been separated in this way, and are forced to advertise in the newspapers
for their husbands or wives.

I hope too that I will be able to send you more money, when I am paid
and can buy a bank draft. I still work with *Conaire*, who is now learning
English, and I am sure he will speak it better by the time he arrives in New
York. I also work with a man of the name of Jack Kilgallon who comes from
Turlough, beside Castlebar.
I have nothing more to say, but remain your loving husband and son,
Luke Ryan

He went to post the letter. It was more expensive than it had been in Quebec.
'Twenty per cent for commission,' the clerk explained to him.

Luke cursed. He had not enough money. 'You can sign for it,' the clerk said.

Luke signed for the amount to be deducted from his wages.

Afterwards Luke shook hands with *Conaire*, though the other Mayo
men stayed away. He thought it better not to mention Winnie's letter to
Conaire, since she had no news of his family in Erris.

Then he scrambled up the sleigh, sitting on top of a pork barrel, and
whisked the reins. Breslin went ahead of him, leading the horse. They were
only half way up when it began to snow. They went on through it. This time,

they had no one following them to offload and reload the sacks when they came to the steep part.

They pulled the sleighs in to the side and unhitched the horses, tying them to the side of the sleighs.

'There's no shelter,' Luke said.

'Just shelter as best you can.'

Luke sat down in front of the barrels and pulled his coat up around his cheeks and neck. It was bitterly cold, and through the night he kept rubbing his face to keep the blood moving. But his feet were numb.

'You fellows awake?' Jack whispered.

'Never more so,' Luke responded.

'Now you know what cold is,' Jack said. 'I'll wager it was never as cold as this in Mayo last year.'

'Not as cold. More snow though. And we'd houses and cabins to live in. Turf to burn too.'

Breslin had woken.

'But when you were coming across from Quebec, was it as cold then?' he asked.

'Not so cold,' Jack answered. 'There was almost a warm spell.'

'I remember,' Breslin said. 'It was strange, that. Ye were lucky to come over at that time. It got a lot colder for us fellows who came later.'

'I can believe that,' Luke said.

'Yes, we had to walk the whole way, the ships were frozen hard. But even before we left Quebec, you could see the bodies frozen in the snow.'

'Bodies?'

'Men, women and children. Irish, I'd say. All the way along the road to Montreal. If the fever didn't get them, the cold did. You were lucky you didn't have to see the likes of that.'

Luke rubbed his legs. He had heard of frostbite. He didn't know if rubbing would help, but there was no way he was going to take off his boots.

'I won't say we saw bodies on the way across. We saw enough men, women and children who wouldn't have long to live. I know the smell of fever. People who are weak like that, they don't fight it off.'

'Nor would they be invited into anyone else's house,' Breslin said. 'All along, they're terrified of fever. Why would any man save another life, only to risk his own family?'

'They wouldn't, is the answer,' Jack said. 'There's those who would though. The Grey Nuns, that's who. Luke will tell you all about those.'

'Will I?'

'Well, you know more about them than any of us.'

'What's he on about?' Breslin asked.

Luke shook his head.

'He's on about the Emigrant Hospital in Montreal. A place you wouldn't want to go.'

'I would not,' Breslin said.

'Well, I had to,' Luke said. 'One night, when we were lodging close to it, without even knowing it, two nuns came over to us, looking for someone Irish, able to write. The other fellows here weren't too eager to say they could write, so I had to go with them to the hospital. A terrible place it was too. They gave me a pen and paper, and I had to go around the beds, writing out letters as best I could, and taking down the addresses in Irish, but I'd have to put the addresses in English also for the envelopes. I did as many as I could, excepting those that were past talking.'

'And where were these fellows from?'

'The West. All the way from West Cork to Donegal.'

'And what kind of things were you writing?'

'Only to tell their families that they were alive and well. None of them wanted to tell the truth. And sure why would they? It'd only upset people.'

By morning, the blizzard had cleared. They went on, and reached the shanties as the sun was high.

Three times more, Luke brought timber down to the river dock, and provisions back. Then he was sent back to the higher trails, hauling the longer logs from the edge of the forest down to the first assembly station.

Late one afternoon he was skidding a sixteen foot log as dusk came on. Without warning, one of the horses stumbled and fell. The log kept moving. Panicked, the horse tried to get up again but the log had already caught one of his legs. Luke heard the sharp crack as the cannon bone snapped. The log came to a stop, as the horse whinnied wildly.

Luke saw the next gang hauling a log behind him. He ran back up

'I've a horse down. Stop, stop.'

With difficulty, the next teamster brought the log to a halt. Within minutes, the trail was stationary, six teams of horses behind.

Jack arrived from one of the teams.

'We have to shift the log,' he said. 'There's no other way. It's too much to go forward, we'll have to drag it back.'

They unhitched two horses behind, and attached chains to the back of the log. Then they were driven back. Slowly the log moved, as the horse whinnied. Almost like a human sound, Luke thought.

'I'll go for the gun,' one of the other men said. They waited, watching as the horse tried to stand, but each time it collapsed again. Time dragged.

At last the man arrived back with a shotgun, and leading another horse. They placed the gun to the horse's forehead, and shot it. It whinnied, and rolled over kicking. A second shot silenced it. Six men dragged the horse's carcass well in off the trail.

'Do we bury it,' Luke asked.

'Not a chance of that,' Jack said. 'It'll be frozen hard in a day. When spring comes, the foxes will see to it.'

Foxes! He thought of Lisnadee. Croghancoe. No, that's all in the past. Forget that.

He hitched up the fresh horse and started driving the log down to the shanties.

Roarty was waiting. 'So who's responsible for this little mess?'

'It slipped on the snow,' Luke said. 'I couldn't stop the log.'

'And where do you think we get fresh horses up here?

Luke said nothing.

'Right,' Roarty said. 'What's done is done. Two weeks wages deducted.'

'Two weeks…?'

'Yes. And more if you go on about it.'

'Rough on you,' said Jack, that night.

'Two weeks,' Luke said. 'As if they didn't need all that back home?'

'I know,' said one of the other men. 'They're right hoors, the lot of them.'

'Only because the Gilmours drive them to it.'

'I don't think they need to be driven,' Jack said. 'That's the class of man they take on for this kind of job.'

'I know,' said Luke. 'The Wrights, Gilmour, Egan, the whole damned lot of them. Never giving a thought for the men under them, though they pretend they do.'

'Roarty and his breed too,' the other man said. 'And none of the gangers have to pretend anything.'

Luke did not go down to the river again. He and Jack stayed working as teamsters in the forests, skidding the loads down from the forest edge to the first assembly station at the shanties. Often in the morning, they carried meals for the axe-men working in the bush, and sometimes carried the axe-men too. Luke was surprised to note that the weather had become colder, even as it went into January, though by February the extreme cold was lessening.

Often in the evenings, he would take out Winnie's letter and read it, again and again.

'You'll have it worn out,' Jack said.

'*Arra*, what.'

'Sure you know every word that's in it now. You could say it back to me backwards without looking at it at all.'

'Maybe you're right,' Luke said, 'but it's the only news I have from home.'

Yes, the only news. The only hope of meeting Winnie again. And a new child too by then. He wondered how he would find that, holding a son or a daughter. His own and Winnie's.

Still, not all of the news was good. The family would not starve, he knew that, but the talk of local starvation was disturbing. How many people he knew around Carrigard and Kilduff would be dead by now. Was the fever worse? Winnie had not said anything about that. Was it still going on? Who knew? And Winnie had not said anything about Brockagh either. He thought of Winnie's family and wondered.

It seemed that the winter dragged on forever. He was getting hardened to the conditions though. He felt he was stronger than he had ever been working on farms and quarries in Mayo, but there it hadn't been as cold. Or had it? He remembered the desperate winter in the mountains of Mayo last year. The worst in memory, everyone had said. Was the Gatineau worse? Maybe, maybe not. One way or another, he was used to freezing cold by now.

After that, he had no more accidents, though there were a few frightening moments from time to time. Yes, Roarty was tough as a ganger, but even this no longer bothered Luke.

In April, the thaw began. Fewer logs were being taken down from the forest, and Luke was not surprised when he was asked to take a twenty foot log down to the Gatineau. This time, Jack came with him.

When they arrived at the dock Luke unhitched the horses as Jack went to one of the shanties. Luke asked a group of men for *Conaire*. No one answered. Still bitter, he thought. They still remember Lisnadee. Who can blame them for their bitterness?

Finally, Jack joined him. 'He's gone.'

'Gone where?'

'No-one knows. All they'll say is he's gone.'

'Damned bastards.'

They walked to the end of one of the piers. All along the Gatineau, the ice was breaking, pools of melt water on top of the floes, the black water of the river showing through in parts.

'Won't be long now,' Jack said.

'Aye,' Luke said, 'and time to leave this damned place.'

'I wonder how much better New York might be.'

'Isn't it bound to be better? All the stories back in Mayo – they tell us great things about New York. And it sure as hell can't be as hard as this.'

They slept in one of the lower shanties that night, but the other Mayo men did not talk to them. Early the following morning, Luke and Jack left before the other men were awake, and led the horses back to the higher shanties.

They did not stay long.

Luke had been wondering when they would have the chance of travelling to New York, but the decision was abruptly made for them. Roarty came into the shanty one evening.

'Some of you lads were talking of going to New York?'

'What about it?' asked one of the other men.

'The Gilmours and Egan are talking of sending a cargo of lumber down from Bytown. They're looking for men to float rafts down towards Montreal and over the Champlain to the Hudson.'

No one said anything.

'Of course' said Roarty, 'once the news gets out, everyone on the Gatineau will want to be on it. You'll have to move fast. Now who wants to sign?'

Luke and Jack joined the lengthening queue at the table by the camboose. Luke was disturbed to see that many of the men were being refused.

When they got to the top, Roarty asked them if they could read and write.

'We can,' Luke said. 'Both of us.'

'Well sign your names here.'

Luke signed.

'What about our wages?'

'You'll get them down at the dock.'

Jack signed.

'You've a good hand,' Roarty said to Luke, 'but this fellow would need to work on his writing though.'

'I'm sure it's good enough,' Luke said.

'Fine,' Roarty said, 'get moving. There's more waiting.'

They walked back and sat on Luke's bunk.

'Hard to believe, isn't it. We might even get to New York,' said Jack.

'You're right,' Luke said. 'There were times I was starting to wonder if we'd get there at all.'

'*Arra,* it's too gloomy you are, always thinking the worst. We'll get there now, that's for sure and certain.'

Next morning, they took their packs over their backs and walked the trail down to the river. It was muddy as the snow melted.

'We were lucky,' Luke said.

'Indeed. I wonder what the other fellows will do.'

'Go back to Gilmours at Quebec? Who knows?'

'I was just thinking about *Conaire*,' Jack said. 'He can't read nor write.'

'No, not a chance. It's a miracle he can speak the little English he can.'

'I wonder if he'll get to New York.'

'We'll see. One way or the other, we've got his brother's address, and that's something to go on.'

They walked on.

'God Almighty, would you look at that,' Luke said.

They looked down at a park full of sleighs along one side. Directly back from the pier, there were lines of logs – short logs, long logs and a few very long.

'They'll be for masts, those big fellows,' Jack said.

'I'm sure you're right,' Luke said. 'Forty foot if they're an inch.'

On the river itself, rafts of timber were being assembled. Further out, rafts were floating down the river, five or ten men on each.

'Seems that's the way to New York,' Jack said.

'Looks good to me,' Luke answered.

They went to the office. Both were paid, signing their names again.

'Ye can both write, can ye?' the clerk asked.

'Sure enough. That's the reason we got on the rafts, or so I understand.'

'Could be you're right,' the clerk said. 'They're always short of men to keep an eye on all the cribs and rafts, and make out what's in them.'

'And what about our letters?' Luke asked. 'Would ye be able to forward them on to us?'

'Doubt it, but we can try.'

'Fine so,' Luke said. He wrote down Farrelly's address in Harrisburg. 'This is where I'm headed. If any turn up, just send them on.'

'What of New York?' Jack asked.

'I doubt I'll be there for long enough.'

They walked out.

'Money at last,' Jack said.

'Aye, and more than I was expecting.'

'What? Why's that?'

'They never took off the two weeks that I was supposed to pay for the horse.'

Jack looked at him in surprise.

'But if they didn't take it…Will they take it from some other poor fellow?'

'*Arra*, no. Unless they get Roarty for it, for being so damned careless.'

Jack checked his own pay.

'He was smart enough to take the three days for the riot, though.'

'Aye. I saw that right enough.'

They slept in the shanty with the Mayo men that night.

'Still no sign of *Conaire*,' Jack said.

'I don't think we're going to see him now. We're going to have to wait 'till New York.'

'We don't have his brother's address in New York.'

'Damn it, you're right,' Luke said.

'Can you remember it?'

'I can remember his name was Costello, since that's *Conaire*'s name. The only other thing I remember is about Five Points. That's the part of New York the bar was in. Who knows, maybe we'll find it there. Can't be too many bars with the name of Costello.'

Chapter 26

The Times, London, April 1848:
They represent, they carry with them, misery and degradation, a visionary temperament and a factious religion, a deep sense of injury and a burning hatred of the British name. Centuries will not efface from their vindictive memories and their inventive imaginations the dark circumstances of their banishment, their landing, their dispersion over the inhospitable wild. Let anyone read the extracts from Canadian journals in our columns last Friday, and find a parallel, if he can, in any annals. Is it possible that it should ever be forgotten? These hundred thousand, after the loss of thousands by disease on the passage, and as many more in hospital sheds, are forwarded up the river to Toronto, and thence to the Upper Provinces, still perishing, still scattering disease wherever they go, and entirely dependent for support on the piety and alms of the benevolent. The clergy, the medical men, and other charitable persons who have tendered to their wants, have fallen by wholesale, martyrs to that service.

They were put to work, assembling a crib. Twenty pieces of squared timber were locked between two larger logs. Oarlocks were fitted. Planks were fitted on top, and the crib was ready.

Then they were pushing off into the Gatineau River. As they did so, Luke noticed a small cross nailed onto one of the uprights on the pier.

'What's that,' he asked an older man.

'Oh, that? That's for O'Shea. Killed there five years ago.'

'Killed?'

'Caught between a log and the pier.'

'Poor fellow.'

'And not the only one either. A hundred men get killed on the river drives in Ontario every year. You should know that.'

'I do now,' Luke said.

When they reached the Outaouais River, the crib was floated across to Bytown, and tied up.

Luke and Jack met a group of three other men on the quays, who had rowed in from another raft. Luke knew they were Irish from their accents, but certainly not Mayo.

Bytown was a rough looking place, but no one seemed to mind.

'There's a place I know down here,' one of the men said, leading them into a side alley. He pushed at a door. Luke entered, Jack following.

It was a bar. Luke was surprised, since there was no name over the door, but guessed at once it might have been more of a rough shebeen than a bar. He wondered what the citizens of Bytown used instead of *poitín*. The other man put a sixpence on the counter.

'We'll have whiskey for all my friends here,' he said. Jack winked at Luke, but within a minute they were sipping at whiskey.

There were two old men in the bar. They both finished their drinks and left.

'Don't seem to like us shanty fellows,' Jack said.

'No way do they like us,' one of the other Irishmen said. 'Frightened would be more the word. Especially when we finish work.'

'Finished work, are ye?' Luke asked.

'Dead right, we are,' one of the other men said. 'Had enough with sawing for one season. And what about yourselves?'

'We're going with the rafts,' Luke said.

'To Quebec?'

'Not a chance,' Jack said. 'New York is where we're heading for.'

'New York? What's bringing you there?'

'More money,' Luke answered.

'Have they fever there?'

'Damned if I know,' Luke said. 'I haven't heard about it, if there is.'

'Couldn't be any worse than what we had here last year. God knows how many died in Bytown. Toronto and Kingston too. Thousands of them were buried in mass graves.'

'I can guess what it was like,' Luke said. 'We've come through Quebec and Montreal. I saw what happened there.'

'Ye don't have fever, do you?'

'Not now, we don't,' Jack answered. 'If we had it last year, we'd either be well mended or dead.'

Luke and Jack paid for a round of drinks. A while later, they left.

'That's lightened our pockets a bit,' Luke said.

'*Arra*, not much. I'm sure we'll earn plenty in New York.'

'I suppose you're right,' Luke said. 'And now for a bank.'

'Just what I was thinking,' Jack replied. 'It's dangerous, walking around with this money in our pockets.'

'It is. Though if we weren't jumped back there, I think our prospects are better now.'

They searched for some time, without success.

'Let's ask someone,' Jack said.

'They'd only jump us if they know we need a bank.'

'Good point. Let's ask a woman so. She wouldn't jump you, even if you asked her.'

'Good idea,' Luke said.

He saw an elderly woman across the road, and walked over to her. She looked apprehensive at his approach. At that moment, it struck Luke that his appearance, after all those months in the forests, might be a little off-putting.

'Not meaning to alarm you, ma'am,' he said. 'I'm just looking for a bank.'

'Which bank would that be?'

'The Bank of British North America.'

'You're outside it.'

Luke looked up.

'By God, so we are. Thanking you, ma'am.'

They entered. Luke took out his savings book from Quebec. He passed across his money, and asked for a banker's draft for most of it, keeping a few dollars for himself.

They found a post office, and Luke borrowed a pen and ink.

Carrigard	Bytown
Kilduff	Ontario
County Mayo	
Ireland	28 April 1848

My Dear Winnie, Dear Father & Mother,

I hope ye are all well. The bank draft I am now sending you should help, though it might be best to hold most of it for the boat ticket for America.

We are now finished with working in the forests, and heading to New York. We heard that the Gilmours were intent on sending a cargo of lumber from Bytown to New York. The cargo was to be assembled on the river, and when word came out that men were needed to travel with it, there was a race to be on it, but we were preferred to many others because we could read and write and add. We did not see *Conaire* again though, and I doubt we ever will.

I will travel to New York with Jack Kilgallon, where I intend to write to Farrelly, and will travel out to Harrisburg after I hear back from him.

Should you have sent any letters to me at the Gatineau camp, I have already asked that they be forwarded to me in Harrisburg, but I do not know if they will be sent, nor whether the gang will still be in Harrisburg. I can only pray.

I hope I will have a fixed address for you to write, and so Winnie can come to America. It will be two or three months' time though, so please stay until you hear from me again.

I remain, your loving husband and son,

Luke Ryan

When they returned to the docks, Luke saw their crib was assembled together with other cribs.

'We make a real raft now,' an older man said.

'Some raft!' Jack said. 'I thought there were enough logs in a crib but how many cribs are here?'

'I've not counted them,' the other man said. 'Fifty, sixty, something like that.'

'Where are they all coming from? Luke asked.

'Where have you come from?'

'Down the Gatineau.'

'Well, half of these are down the Rideau – the Wrights' concessions. Most of the rest comes down from the Bonnechere – John Egan's lot. Lost a lot in the Falls too. And there's talk they're opening up the Petawawa all the way back to Lake Nipissing, but I don't know if there's any of them here yet.'

'You know a lot about it,' Jack said.

'Sure why wouldn't I? I've been here long enough. Now can any of you fellows read and write?'

'Both of us,' Jack said, surprised.

'Add and subtract?'

'Of course,' Luke said.

'Ye've been drinking.'

'Not much,' Luke said.

'Not much, says he. You sure?'

'Sure, I'm sure. We're not into that class of thing. Are we Jack?'

'Not much,' Jack said, copying Luke.

'Right, I want you two working with me.'

'You? Who're you then?' Jack asked.

'Mick Conlon. Your ganger since you ask.'

'Our ganger!' Luke exclaimed.

'Yes. Do ye have a problem with that?'

'Well...no.'

'Good. Now listen. We're trying to work out how much timber is in this beast. We've got to divide it down too between the Gilmours, the Wrights and Egan. Them lads won't be too happy if we start making mistakes.'

He gave them both pencils and notebooks, and Luke and Jack followed him. Luke was intrigued by the process. Each crib had been marked with the name of the owners. Their task was to work out the amount of timber in each crib, as well as the quality of it, the length of the logs and the type of pine – white or red. All the logs had already been planed square.

Luke noticed that Conlon knew the lengths of the logs without even measuring them.

'It's easy enough,' Conlon told him. 'They're standard lengths. It's the diameters that are important, but even that, you get used to.'

'I'm sure we will,' Luke said, 'though a square diameter isn't something I'd come across before.'

'*Arra* what, enough of your guff. Just write down what I tell you.'

'Fine so,' Luke said, as he wrote down the figures Conlon called out.

The raft had begun to move.

That evening, Luke and Jack sat inside one of the shanties that had been erected on the raft.

'Our office,' Conlon explained. 'You sober now?'

'Never better,' Luke said.

'We're going to be doing a lot of arithmetic so you might as well understand this. Simple enough. For square logs you're given the figures in feet – breadth by depth by length gives you the volume.'

'Fair enough,' said Jack.

'Now sometimes breadth and depth will be given in inches, so once again, multiply out and divide by one hundred and forty four. Think you can do that?'

Jack looked hesitant.

'Well, I can anyhow,' Luke said.

'A smart fellow so,' Conlon said. 'Where did you learn that class of thing?'

'My uncle used to run a kind of a school back in County Mayo. He'd be giving us problems like that all the time. Expected us to be sharp, right enough.'

'Fine,' Conlon said, 'now, do you know how to measure a round log? See if you're smart enough for this?'

'Damned if I know,' Luke said, 'but try me.'

'Right. You take the girth at both ends.'

'Girth?'

'Circumference,' Conlon explained.

'Ah yes,' Luke said.

'You take the girth at both ends, add them, and divide by two which gives you the average girth. You then multiply the length in feet by the square of a quarter of the average girth.'

'I'd better write this down,' Luke said.

Conlon repeated it. 'Just remember it.'

'So, that's it,' Luke said.

'Yes. That gives you four fifths of the cubic volume.'

'Only four fifths?'

'That's to allow for waste in sawing. Can't be charging our customers for waste, can we?'

They spent the next hour going through figures, multiplying figures and adding columns so as to work out the number of cubic feet of each type of log to be allocated to each of the lumber companies.

'Quite some business this,' Jack said, that night.

'That's for sure,' Luke said.

He was thinking of other times, multiplying figures and adding columns on Famine Relief Works. Starving people, frozen people. Men, women and children with fever. The dying and the dead.

And the man from Lisnadee who had recognised him back at the Gatineau dock in the winter. To hell with that. I'll not meet him again. Nor any of the other Mayo fellows there. And thank God for that.

How could it have come to this? County Mayo, his own county, his own home. Yet he had had to leave it because so many hated him. And even here, even in the forests of Canada, the hate still followed him.

And what of *Conaire*? Anything could have happened to him. He might still be alive, but Luke was beginning to doubt it. He thought again of Conaire's hard opinions about his own people. He had not started that way, Luke was sure of it. Was it all just the bluster of a man who was frightened, trying to put on a front of uncaring coldness? That kind of attitude could get a man a knife between the ribs.

Conlon entered. 'Come on you fellows, time to get moving.'

Then they were outside, casting off the ropes, as the more experienced men began to pole the raft towards the centre of the river.

They left Bytown, moving down the Outaouais River to the St. Lawrence, through the Lachine Canal and past Montreal to Sorel.

They came to the mouth of the Richelieu River.

'Seems like we're changing here,' Conlon said. 'This lot is going up to Quebec, and you fellows are trying to get to New York. Right?'

'Right,' said Luke.

'There's another raft behind us.'

Two men rowed out to the raft. Luke and Jack followed Conlon onto it, and they arrived at the village of *Sorel*.

Another office. A clerk went through Conlon's figures.

'All correct, no doubt?'

'As near as I can get it.'

'Sign here so.'

Conlon signed, leaving a space for Luke's signature as witness.

They were taken out to another smaller raft of cribs. A steamboat was being attached to the front.

They travelled the *Richelieu* River, through the Chambly Canal, back to the *Richelieu*, to *St. Jean-sur-Richelieu*, and then up to Lake Champlain.

The raft was far too wide for the canals, and had to be broken up into the smaller cribs again, and each poled separately through the canals.

'Hard work,' Jack said.

'I'm sure we'll get used to it.'

'Still – all these canals. Can you picture the work it took to dig them out?'

'Sure wasn't that what I was doing on the railways?' Luke answered. 'Hard work right enough, digging it all out, shovelling it up into the wagons, I'm well used to it. And so will you be, if you want to work the railways.'

'Ye're lucky, ye're coming this way,' Conlon said one morning.

'What else would we do?' Luke asked.

'Well, ye might have been thinking of going down to Quebec. God knows, enough of the lads did, to their eternal sorrow. Or if I might put it this way, by the time they get to Quebec, there'd be no work for any of them. The good times are over, and they don't even know that. They say there's twenty or thirty million feet of logs piled up in the docks in Quebec, with no market. There'll be damned little sawing done in Quebec this summer, I can tell you. And even less logging up the Gatineau, or anywhere else for that matter.'

Jack looked up from the figures he had been adding.

'But why would that be? Weren't they just crying out for shanty men in '46? They couldn't even get enough of us.'

'Ah yes, but that was then. Now the Quebec trade has collapsed. The most of it was going over to England, and from all I hear, there's no market for it in England anymore. They were buying millions of cubic feet of it for railroads, ships, building and all, but there's little of that being done now. Especially railways.'

'You mean...?' Luke gasped.

'Just that. It's in all the Quebec papers. The English markets are failing, the banks won't lend any more, England nor here. So none of the lumber you're seeing on the St. Lawrence is going to Quebec. The most of it is following us down to New York.'

Luke watched the sun rising above the forest-lined shore. He was thinking of the days he had worked on the railways himself. Working as a navvy on the rail gangs. Hard work, but well paid. But then Danny had gone off contracting on his own, and invited Luke to join him. But Luke knew Danny's methods. So what of Danny now? If the railway companies were collapsing, how much work would Danny's business have today? And what of his workers? Danny was far too tough and ruthless, but for the Mayo men who were working for him, it was better to be worked hard by Danny than starve in Mayo. He wondered what would happen to them.

And what about Harrisburg if railway companies were collapsing?

When they entered the United States, he was not even aware of the fact. They both staggered out of the shanty one morning. Conlon was outside, leaning against the side of the wall.

'That's Rouse's Point over there,' he said. 'We're in the United States.'

'United States!' Luke exclaimed.

'None other. State of Vermont to your left. New York on the right.'

'But…the border…' Jack asked.

'We passed through it a while back.'

'But I thought we had to get off and slip around the border?'

'That was last year. From all I hear, appears they've ended it now. At least for anyone coming down from the Canadas. And it's the same with the lumber. Used to be that they had a tariff on Canadian lumber going into the United States, but they've given that up, and that's why we're heading south to New York. Some years back, it would never have been possible. Back then, the *Richelieu* and Champlain timber went straight to Quebec. Quebec only.'

'You seem to know a lot,' Luke commented.

'Only what I hear from the fellows on the ship, and the towns along the shore. I've been on this journey many times before.'

'So have I,' Jack commented, 'but only the once. Still, I'd never picked up so many facts.'

'That's it,' Conlon said. 'You have to keep your ears open, you know.'

Luke reckoned Conlon was the best ganger they had ever worked under, in Quebec or the Gatineau. Apart from Farrelly, he was also the only ganger Luke had any liking for. He was tough and hardworking, and expected the same from all the other men, but often, he would join them, sometimes playing cards, more often just chatting.

'Did you have a hard crossing?' he asked Luke one night.

'Damned hard,' Luke said. 'I was on the Centaurus.'

'I've heard of that one. Most everyone has.'

'Yes,' Luke said. 'Many died on the crossing. Well over a hundred.'

'Were you travelling long?'

'Long enough.'

'Was there anyone travelled with you.'

'Not from home. But I met a fellow on the boat – *Conaire* he was – from the far end of Mayo. He lived, and came with us to the Gatineau.'

'Where is he now?'

'I don't know any more,' Luke replied. 'Jack and myself were put working on horses, and *Conaire* was sent loading and unloading supplies at the dock. We never found him when we got down again. God knows where he's got himself to. I don't think we've a chance of finding him in this land.'

'Not an earthly,' Conlon said, 'The United States of America – it's one hell of a big country.'

As they passed through the lake, Luke stood at the edge of the raft, watching the shore. There were forests on the hills, stretching almost endlessly along the edge of the lake, and high into the mountains behind. Late at night, there were purple sunsets, as the sun touched the hills and mountains, its reflection shimmering across to the raft.

'Some country, this,' Jack said.

'It is,' Luke said. 'Just like on the St. Lawrence, the Outaouais and the Gatineau. Seems to go on for ever.'

From time to time they passed farms, interspersed by small villages.

'Maybe we should take up farming?' Jack said.

'Not enough money in it.'

'There might be a lot more than in County Mayo. I'd say the farms over here are more than a few acres.'

'A hell of a lot more. Still, I didn't come to this country to farm.'

At Plattsburgh a canoe came towards the rafts. There were two men in it.

One scrambled onto the raft. He came to Luke and Jack.

'Are you fellows in charge?' he asked, in a clear Irish accent.

'No, he is,' Jack said, pointing to Conlon.

'I'm looking to cross the river. Burlington, if ye're going that way.'

'We are,' Conlon said.

The stranger introduced himself as Tom Lynagh, from Sligo.

'Are you over long?' Conlon asked.

'Since last year only. I travelled with my wife. We were aiming to find my brother, who lives in Burlington. We arrived in this country in early August.'

'A month before I arrived,' Luke commented. 'How was your crossing?'

'In a word – dreadful. We travelled on the Larch, and a more accursed ship you never saw. Four hundred...five hundred people, God only knows how many, left Sligo on that hell-ship. Only the half of them ever got to

Quebec. And you know what the strange thing was? It was a fast crossing – four weeks, I'm told, though truth to tell, I never kept track of it.'

'All I know is that by the time Ben Bulben had disappeared behind us, the dying had already started. The fever ran riot through the ship. Every day, men, women and children, thrown to the sea. When it first started, they were wrapped up in canvasses – old sails cut apart, but they ran out soon enough. After that, they were just thrown overboard, naked. Their families would auction their clothes before they were thrown over – if there was any family left. Otherwise, everyone just fought over their clothes. At first it was only one or two bodies a day – by mid-Atlantic it was running at five or six. Every day. Can you imagine it? They say a quarter died on the voyage, though I'm inclined to think it was more.'

'Then we arrived at Grosse Île. They took one look at the ship and quarantined it at once. The bad cases, they were left on board to die. The rest of us were taken off by boat and rowed to the fever sheds on that hellhole of an island. And you know the one strange thing about that island – it was the most beautiful place any man could want. The smell of the pines, the lapping of the water, not that you got much of either of those when you were inside the sheds. It was still warm, it was only early August, but the inside of the sheds was like a furnace.'

'I thought at first we were fine, I thought we were only being held for a quarantine period to see if we had fever. And then, God damn it to hell, I got it. I'll never forget it. The savage pain, the nightmares. But lucky for me, I had had it as a child, and I was tough enough for it then, and thank God it toughened me up to have it a second time. Margaret nursed me all through it. So I lived. But when I came back to myself, the nightmare just went on. The stink of those sheds, it was something terrible. I saw men, women and children around me, raving some of them. Just lying in their beds, dead included, until someone noticed, and had the time to take them out. I don't know how many of the ones left in the ship survived, but I know many more died in the sheds. Margaret was lucky then, she never got the fever. But at last, they took me out, and put me in another shed for getting better. So I was alive, and thankful. Then the ones of us who still lived, we were put back on the Larch and told to clear off the corpses. When we were finished that job, they started moving again and brought us to the docks at Quebec.'

Luke threw a piece of bark into the water and watched it float into the distance.

'A hard story. Not so different to my own. I was on the Centaurus, out of Liverpool. It was just the same. There's no point in repeating it, you've put it so well. The ocean voyage. Grosse Île too, the lot. Then we worked in the forests for the winter.'

'Tough work, I'd wager,' Lynagh said.

'It was,' Luke said. 'Kept us warm though. What about yourself? How did you get down to the United States from Quebec? Rough travel, was it?'

'Rough enough, I'd say, though at least we didn't freeze. Margaret and myself, we stayed a few weeks in Quebec with a fellow we'd known back in Ireland. Then we went up to Montreal in a steamboat, and stayed there a few weeks. I was lucky enough to get a few weeks work on the Lachine Lock.'

'Yes,' Jack said. 'We know that one. We came by way of the Lachine.'

'Ye'd know it, so. But after that, we got as far as Bytown, but then Margaret was sick with the fever. We found lodgings with a kind Irish family, and I was able to take care of her with the help of the woman of the house. Then a terrible thing happened. Margaret mended, but the woman of the house died, after Margaret infecting her. I dug a grave, and we buried her. Then we left the family and travelled further up the St. Lawrence, where I got some work on a building site. But then I caught the fever again, so we had to stay a few weeks? After that, we crossed the St. Lawrence, into the United States.'

'When was that?' Luke asked.

'Oh, a few months back. Early February I'd say.'

'A lot of ice then?'

'Not so much. We hired a skiff to go across, but the ice was very thin. Wherever it stopped us, we just rocked the boat from side to side to break the ice, while the boatman paddled us across. From there we travelled, hitching lifts on wagons, being shaken to pieces on the corduroy roads. We'd stop off at farmhouses, when we'd enough of being shaken. I'd stay a week or two in each, working for board and lodging for the two of us, feeding the hogs and the like, while Margaret worked for the woman of the house.'

'You were working without pay?'

'I was,' Lynagh replied. 'Margaret too. But it was no great harm. There wasn't a huge amount of work in the winter. At least we had food inside of ourselves, and that was a lot better than back home. But Margaret got fever again, and died. I buried her in a field, and I left her there. I've been working this past two weeks with a farmer just outside of Plattsburgh.'

At Burlington, they stopped for supplies and went ashore. Lynagh left them there.

'A rough story, he had,' Jack commented.

'Rough indeed,' Luke commented. '*Conaire* would have silenced him soon enough.'

'If *Conaire* were here.'

There were many men in the street outside a building site.

'All looking for work,' one told them. 'They're cutting back on the railroad building here.'

'I didn't know they were building railroads around here,' Luke said.

'There's two big ones building up country – the Central Vermont and the Vermont & Canada. You'll soon be able to travel the whole way from Montreal to New York by train. But with all these cutbacks, it might be a while.'

Luke was more concerned than ever. If railroad building was cutting back in Vermont, what of Pennsylvania? What of Harrisburg?

They left Lake Champlain, entering the Champlain Canal at Whitehall, poling the cribs down to Fort Edward. Then at last – the Hudson River.

Forty miles downstream, Conlon pointed out the entrance to the Erie Canal.

'Clinton's Ditch, they call it. Runs all the way from the Hudson to Lake Erie. Many Irish worked on that back in the 1820s and 1830s. Scotch Irish. They died in their hundreds of swamp fever.'

Through Albany to Poughkeepsie. Then on to West Point, Tarrytown and Yonkers.

From time to time, there was hard labour, as cribs were floated off from the main raft, and Luke and Jack had to help the other men in disentangling the cribs, or rowing them to shore.

Once the quantities of timber had been checked at each landing, even the clerical work was very limited.

'They're only small towns,' Conlon told them. 'We're keeping the most of the lumber for New York.'

Chapter 27

Telegraph & Connaught Ranger, March 1848:
Our brave military are brought low indeed when they are
about being encamped in our mud wall cabins to fight the
fleas for the filthy blankets which cover the fever patients in
these wretched hovels.

Eleanor took out Danny's five pound note and pinned it to the inside of her shift.

'*At least no one will see it,*' she told Winnie, '*though if word got out I was carrying this amount of money, I'd never get near Knockanure.*'

It had been suggested that Michael might accompany her, but Eleanor had thought he would be needed for guarding the growing crops, so she went on her own.

When she arrived at the Workhouse, Pat looked up in surprise.

'Mother! What the devil...?'

'I'm going to the Hibernian Bank, and I was hoping you might help me.'

'Help you with what?'

'I'm trying to set up an account.'

'For yourself?'

'No, for Brigid.'

'For Brigid!' he exclaimed. 'Are you mad?'

'Yes,' she answered, 'and so are all the rest of us in Carrigard.'

'But...But how did you get here?'

'Walking. How else?'

'Were you alright?'

'Not so bad? I met dragoons, marching the other way. They all started whistling me. Their officer tried to stop them, but they wouldn't have it.'

'A bad lot, them fellows.'

'Oh, I don't know. At least they thought I was worth whistling, and isn't that something? Helps you forget all the other things you see on the road. And I can tell you, I was glad enough to see them too when I got here too. I wouldn't have got in the gate with that crowd there.'

She unfastened the note, and took it out.

'Five pounds!' Pat exclaimed. 'Where the devil did you get that?'

'From Danny.'

'Danny!'

'Maybe he's mad too. What do you think?'

Pat shook his head in bewilderment. 'Fine so,' he said. 'I'll go with you. They know me well there. The only way I can see of opening an account for a baby though, is to not mention her age. They're hardly going to ask for her baptism papers, are they?'

'Just what I was thinking,' Eleanor said.

'We'll say she's a minor. All that means is she's under twenty one.'

'Which she surely is.'

Eleanor followed Pat to the front gate, where he requested two dragoons to accompany them for security. When they reached the Hibernian, Eleanor placed the five pound note on the counter.

'We want to set up an account,' she said.

The clerk looked at Pat. 'Mr. Ryan. You know this lady?'

'She's my mother.'

The clerk turned back to Eleanor.

'So it will be in your name, will it?' he asked.

'No, it will be in the name of Brigid Ryan.'

'A minor, not yet of age,' Pat added.

The beneficiary was given as Brigid Ryan of Carrigard, with Patrick Ryan and Eleanor Ryan, as authorised signatories. Then Eleanor was given the savings book for Brigid.

Luke's letter from the Gatineau Dock arrived in Carrigard. Michael slit it open and glanced through it.

'Come on,' Eleanor said, 'what does it say?'

'He wishes us well...Hopes conditions around may get better...Says you should not go to America...says...'

But Winnie had already pulled the letter from him.

'Let me see.' She read rapidly through the letter. She looked to Eleanor. 'He says he might have no fixed address in New York, and to wait until he tells us he is settled...'

'Yes,' Eleanor said abruptly, 'it would be many months yet.'

'And even more for the letter to cross the ocean and then...then it'll be too late in the year.'

She sank her head into her hands. 'Oh Lord, how long? How much longer must we wait?'

'And no money, this time,' Michael said. 'We'll still have to depend on Pat.'

'Did he get your letter?' Eleanor asked Winnie.

'Yes.'

'We should be thankful for that,' she said. 'To be honest with you, I never thought it would get through, and you sending it to Quebec, when he would have been up the forests.'

'I knew it would arrive,' Winnie said. 'Sure he's working with Gilmours, isn't he? They're in Quebec, and they own the forests too. I knew they'd get the letter to him.'

'You've more of a belief in human nature than I'd have,' Eleanor said. 'I still think that letter was a lucky one. It had the Good Lord looking after it.'

There were tears in Winnie's eyes.

'Whatever about the letter, it's bad news it brought back from Luke. I've still to wait, and that's the beginning and end of it.'

Eleanor sat down beside Winnie, putting her arm around her shoulder. '*Whisht, alanna, the time will come. It will, it will.*'

The two women were alone with Brigid when Winnie's waters broke. Eleanor was taken by surprise, and from the condition of Winnie, she knew there was little time.

Desperate, she brought Winnie to the bed in the back room. Through the window, she noticed a young lad walking. She went to the door and called him inside.

'*Mícheál isn't it?*'

The lad nodded, a look of puzzlement on his face. She poured a cup of buttermilk.

'*Here, get this inside yourself.*' She put a farthing alongside.

'*I want you to run up to Kilduff for me. You know Sabina Ryan?*'

He nodded again.

'*You're to talk to her direct, no one else. Tell her Winnie has a baby coming. Tell her she's to come right away, and bring the midwife with her.*'

The rest of the buttermilk was gulped down, and he was gone.

Sabina arrived, accompanied by the midwife.

'*That was sharp of you,*' Sabina said, '*telling me not to come down without Siobhán here. Did you think I'd not have sense to work that one out for myself?*'

'*Who knows?*' Eleanor said. '*I thought you were wet-nursing*' she said to the midwife.

'*So I am, but midwifing too since my husband died.*'

'*Died?*'

'*Fever. Not that the rest of us are much better with the hunger.*'

There was a scream from the back room. The midwife went in.

Eleanor filled a small pot with water and swung it out over the fire, waiting impatiently until it boiled. She brought it inside with a towel. She sat down, holding Winnie's hand.

'*Push, Winnie. Push.*'

Another scream.

Brigid was crying in the kitchen. '*Don't worry,*' Sabina said, '*I'll look after her.*'

For an hour, the struggle went on. Eleanor stayed, mopping Winnie's brow with cold water. She was thinking now of Nessa's death. All this time she had thought it ridiculous. She had thought Winnie was too strong. Now she no longer knew.

Then it was over. Deftly *Siobhan* cut the umbilical cord, slapped the baby's bottom, and there was a wailing sound. She placed the baby in Winnie's arms. A son. Winnie tried to smile, but could not. But Eleanor knew the worst was over and that Winnie would live, and Luke had a son.

For some time, Winnie continued very weak. For the first day, Eleanor fed her with buttermilk, sometimes with broken brown bread mixed through. Sometimes she gave her mashed potatoes. Over the days though, Winnie started to eat more solid food.

At first *Siobhan* had come around once a day to feed the baby, but as Winnie's strength increased, she took over. Eleanor was relieved. Yes, Winnie would live, and she would recover her strength.

During this time, Kitty came to Carrigard every few days. The first day she went to the back room to see Winnie.

'*I know, I've heard all about it. You're to get better now, do you hear me?*'

Winnie nodded weakly.

Kitty took the baby from the cot. '*What are you calling him?*'

'*We don't know yet. Liam we were thinking of.*'

'*And a nice name it is too.*'

The baby had begun to cry, but Kitty rocked him, singing softly. Winnie recognised the tune at once.

'*Mná na hÉireann,*' she exclaimed. Women of Ireland.

'*Yes,*' said Kitty, '*and we might as well get the little mite used to women and to music. We'll have him singing before he can talk. Now you'll want to sleep.*'

Winnie flopped back into the pillows.

Kitty took the baby out to the kitchen, still singing. Eleanor was playing with Brigid on the bed in the outshot. Brigid spotted Kitty.

'Kitty,' she cried.

She saw the baby, and started to cry.

'*I think someone here is very jealous,*' Eleanor said. '*Aren't you Brigid?*'

She tickled Brigid's toes.

Kitty's reaction to Winnie's baby was more nuanced. Winnie was her friend, and Luke's wife, but Kitty had been Luke's lover. Now Winnie had his baby.

She herself only had Fergus, and no wish to have any of his babies. But still, they all had Brigid, and their ambitions for her future.

And Winnie would have her own ambitions for Liam, though that would be in another country.

'*I'm hoping they have good schools in America,*' Eleanor said.

'*They'll need to,*' Winnie responded, '*or else I'll want to know why not. I wonder are they bringing in government schools in America.*'

'*Maybe they are,*' Kitty answered, '*but will you have to pay for them? That's the question, isn't it?*'

Eleanor waited some days. When she was sure of Winnie's recovery, she asked Michael to write a note to Winnie's family. In it, he simply stated that Winnie had a son called Liam, and that she and the rest of the family were well.

He wrote another letter to Sarah in Westport. At first he had been uncertain whether he should do this, but Eleanor convinced him that if Sarah was not part of the family yet, she soon would be.

The next time Pat arrived, Winnie was fully recovered. Though it was late at night, she had been feeding the baby, and he was still awake. She stood as Pat entered.

'Your first nephew, Pat.'

Pat observed the crinkled face.

'And he looks a Ryan too,' Eleanor said. 'Look at that nose – you take your nose after your Uncle Pat, *alanna*, do you know that?'

Winnie handed the baby to Pat, who drew back in astonishment, but finally took him.

He sat beside the table, holding the baby on his lap.

'I must tell Sarah about this little fellow.'

'No need,' Winnie said, 'your father has already written to her.'

'He has? And he never wrote to me.'

'Sure what need was there,' Michael said. 'We knew you'd be through soon enough.

Eleanor placed buttermilk and brown bread beside Pat. He handed the baby back to Winnie and started to eat.

When he was finished, Michael tapped him on the shoulder. 'I want a word with you.'

Both men stepped outside. It was a starlit night, the stars over the Mountain showing through the bare branches of the ash trees, quivering slightly in a gentle breeze.

356

'What's this I hear about the Union working on road contracts?' Michael asked.

'I don't know,' said Pat. 'It wouldn't be my office anyhow.'

'They're undercutting us,' Michael said angrily. 'How do you think the County fellows are going to react to that? I'll tell you what they'll do. They'll take our contracts away, that's what they'll do. They can't afford to spend anything now, why would they go on paying us for stone and labour when they can get the stone from the Workhouse with no charge for labour at all.'

'I thought you had a contract, father.'

'We do. A three year contract. Runs from April of 1845.'

'But won't they renew?'

'The devil they will. They wrote me, said they were bankrupt, couldn't afford our charges and asked us to revise them. The old ones that we had, and the ones that Bensons had before they emigrated, and that's where the second problem is. Bensons never had a written contract. We thought they had. So they can drop both contracts. And that's what they'll do.'

Pat was staring at the Mountain, remembering nights when he could see lights right across it. Weak enough perhaps, but on dark nights they could be seen. How many houses were there then? How many were there now? The lights around *Gort-na-Móna* – they had all disappeared.

'I'll tell you what, father, I'll talk to Voisey. He'll know about roads contracts.'

'Will you do that so? Because one way or another, we need the cash. Sure, you bring enough and Luke sends it too, but damn it, Pat, a man must have some pride, some way of earning his own keep. And God knows your work in the Union is well paid, but how long will that last?'

Pat returned to Knockanure Workhouse. As he walked to the Administration block, he saw two lines of young girls coming out of the Industrial School. They were unnaturally quiet. A young woman was watching them as they walked back towards the dormitories. When they had entered, the woman came back towards the School. She nodded as she passed by Pat.

'Excuse me,' Pat said quickly.

She turned around. 'Yes?'

'I thought all the teaching stopped a year or two back.'

'You're right,' she said. 'But this is a special group. They're all orphans.'

'Orphans!' Pat exclaimed.

'Most of them. Or just abandoned. Either their parents are dead, or disappeared, or just don't want to know, who knows. So they're sending them to the colonies.'

'The colonies?'

'Port Phillip Bay. Somewhere in Australia. Colony of New South Wales, I believe.'

'A convict colony so?'

'Who knows? Some Lordship in England thought it all up. There's too many men in the colonies, and too many girls in Irish Workhouses. Stands to reason, doesn't it?'

'I don't know,' Pat said. 'Shipping them off to marry convicts…'

'They're not all convicts, you know,' she said. 'That's what they're telling me anyhow.'

'Ticket-of-leave men so?'

'Perhaps.'

They walked on towards the school.

'So what's this all got to do with schooling?' Pat asked.

'Seems the settlers want the girls to be trained. Some very basic arithmetic and reading before they go. Two to twelve times tables maybe, though I'm not sure how much we'll manage. They want them to have domestic training too. Domestic servants. Biddys, if you like. No point in sending them to other side of the world if they can't get work.'

'That's a hard life for anyone,' Pat said.

'Better than starving here in County Mayo, isn't it?'

'Perhaps.'

'Anyhow, you're very curious. What business is it of yours?'

'I work in accounts. They expect me to watch costs.'

'I wouldn't worry,' she said. 'My wages won't bankrupt the Union.'

'I don't know,' Pat said. 'Money is tight enough as it is.'

'Well, once we get these girls away, it will help your accounts, no end. There's not many will return, that's for certain.'

The next day, Pat was called to the Guardians Meeting. For some time, he went through the accounts. As he spoke, the tension in the room increased. When he had finished, they questioned him on the figures.

At last, Clanowen brought up the subject of the Port Phillip Scheme.

'That will be all,' Voisey whispered to Pat.

Pat returned to his office.

An hour later, Voisey entered.

'You did well there, Pat.'

'Thanks, Mr. Voisey.' He decided to press further. 'I just wanted to ask you about this Port Phillip scheme. I met a young lady this morning. She said she was teaching here. I guess her salary will be additional now?'

'Indeed it will,' Voisey said. 'We'll be employing her for six months to give the girls basic literacy. Five shillings a week, she's earning, with food and lodging. But in the long run, the Port Phillip scheme will save us a vast amount of money.'

'I'd hope so,' Pat said.

'Yes, it's something that's been on my mind, ever since you first pointed out to me how close we were to the edge. Every time you go through the accounts with the Guardians, it alarms them.'

'But this Port Phillip…?'

'Ah yes,' Voisey said. 'That's all to do with Earl Grey. He wrote to all the Irish Workhouses a few weeks back, and proposed we should select girls for the scheme. We're intending on sending fifty girls out. They'll be sailing before Christmas, God willing. They'll work there as domestic servants.'

'And save a lot of money here.'

'Yes,' Voisey said. 'At least it will reduce the food and fuel bill, though I'm sure we'll have enough new inmates to keep the pressure up.' He glanced at the letters that Pat had been writing. 'Keep some of the damned merchants happy too'

Pat was surprised. Voisey never used bad language. 'And what about the boys?' he asked.

'They're not part of the scheme,' Voisey replied. 'But we'll be fostering out some of the younger ones around the county. It's not so easy, though. There's few enough families with the means to foster children. Some of them expect payment. They also have a strong liking for the very young – infants and the like, so it doesn't reduce cost very much. But for the girls, the idea of sending them to the colonies seems to be a better solution for them.'

He leaned over to see what Pat was working on.

'Still on accounts? He asked.

'That, and correspondence. It's the accounts that worry me.'

'Yes, I know. We've been thinking a lot about your reports. The Guardians are most concerned. We decided to start bidding on road contracts around the county.'

'I know. I'd heard of that?'

'You had?'

'Yes, my father told me about it. You're bidding contracts around Carrigard. Father says it's impossible to bid against you.'

Voisey looked at him in dismay.

'I hadn't known your father was working on road contracts, now that the Relief Schemes are finished.'

'We always worked on road repair,' Pat said. 'We've a quarry on our land.'

'I'm very sorry, but you can realise the position we're in. The Workhouse is desperate for money. All your reports say so. There's little I can do about it.'

'I know,' Pat said. 'You're doing what has to be done. I don't blame you for it.'

Pat went to visit Sarah again, travelling first to Carrigard.

It was dark when he left the Workhouse, and raining heavily. There were still people huddled outside the Workhouse wall, hunkering down under rough shelters or carts.

He pulled the collar of his greatcoat up and pulled his hat down, but the rain dripped down on his nose, and within a mile, his trousers were soaked through.

When he reached Carrigard, his mother wrapped him in a blanket by the fire, and hung up his clothes to dry.

Next morning he left early for Westport.

It was still raining as he left, but before he reached Castlebar the sun was out, and by the time he reached the town, his greatcoat was dry. He walked down the Green, watching the soldiers march and counter-march. Then past the Workhouse, with the usual crowd outside it.

It had begun to rain.

At Ballymacrath he saw the first body of the day. It was just visible up a side boreen, two feet sticking out of the drain, but no boots. He knew from the condition of the feet and ankles that the dogs had already been there. He walked on.

At Islandeady he came to the remains of an eviction. He saw the ruins of many houses on the side of the road and further back. He could see men, women and children trying to pull timber out of the houses. In the open field were two timber shacks made from the ruins of rafters that had already been half burnt. Inside, he could see children lying on the ground. The timber was not enough to keep the rain out.

There was a family sitting beside one of the ruined houses, on the roadside.

'*What happened?*' Pat asked.

'Sir Roger Palmer,' the woman answered listlessly. '*He's trying to prove he's as good an* Exterminator *as* Lord Lucan.'

Pat shook his head in despair, and left the ruins behind him.

At Westport Workhouse, he was recognised. The gate was opened by one inmate while two other inmates with sticks drove back any of the crowd who tried to follow him.

As he entered the office, he saw the Clerk at his desk. Sarah was on a high seat, sitting at a high sloping desk against the wall behind the door.

'See who's here, Sarah?' the Clerk said.

Sarah looked around. She jumped, and stumbled off the stool. Quickly Pat caught her. She recovered and threw her arms around him. 'Pat! Oh God...'

'Sure you knew I was coming, didn't you?'

'But sneaking in on me like that!'

'How else could I sneak in?'

They both sat at the Clerk's desk as he went to the corridor, and called for tea. He came back in.

'Well, what news have ye?' Sarah asked.

'Ye heard about Winnie's baby.'

'I did,' Sarah said. 'Didn't your father write to me?'

'Indeed. Well that's the news and...Oh, father's mad at me.'

'But why?'

'The Union at Knockanure. They're bidding contracts on the roads around Carrigard...'

'But how can they do that?' the Clerk asked. 'Aren't the Relief Works over?'

'Maybe so, but they're calling them road repairs now. They're paying for yearly maintenance. And they're paying the inmates almost nothing. So anything father can bid, he can be undercut.'

'That's terrible,' Sarah said.

'I wouldn't worry too much,' the Clerk said, 'they'll cut back on that soon enough.'

'Why's that?' Pat asked.

'No new contracts. The county and the baronies are as near bankrupt as the Unions.'

'But you're still breaking stones.'

'And why not. We might have call for them, whenever they start building and repairing roads again. Anyhow, it gives them something to do, doesn't it? It is a Workhouse, you know.'

An inmate came in with cups of tea on a tray, carefully placing them on the Clerk's desk. He went out without a word.

'We've news for you too,' Sarah said.

She passed a page over to Pat.

'Danny!' he exclaimed. 'Now what the devil does he want?'

'We'd written to him,' the Clerk explained. 'Asked if he'd like to take more men for the railways.'

Pat read through the letter. 'Seems a certain 'no'.'

He looked up at the Clerk. 'I wonder why this should be.'

'Haven't you heard?' the Clerk replied. 'There's a desperate collapse in the markets in England. The railway companies are in a terrible state. Some of them are even bankrupt. One way or another, they're stopping contracts all over the country.'

Pat read further. 'And he might let men go?'

'I know,' the Clerk said, 'and that worries me. Last year in Liverpool the Workhouses were sending men back to Mayo.

'I know,' Pat said.

'I don't know what Stockport and Manchester are like, but by God, I wouldn't like to have more men back here. We couldn't let them in anyhow. And one way or another, what's going to happen to their families now, in England or Mayo?'

Pat slept in Westport Workhouse that night, slumped over a desk in the Clerk of Union's office. The Clerk had offered him a bed in one of the dormitories, but Pat was still too much afraid of fever to want to take it.

Next morning, Sarah accompanied him across the breakers yard to the gate. 'Now you take care of yourself,' she said to Pat. She kissed him on the lips.

'You too,' Pat said, as he and the horse were led out of the gate.

He held his nose against the smell of Westport's streets. There were the usual crowds of people waiting for admission to the Workhouse. As he got further from the Workhouse, the crowds lessened but there was still the smell of shit mixed in with mud. He saw a woman at the side of the street, lying on straw. She was clearly far advanced in fever. Shortly after, a man's corpse.

All along the road to Castlebar, were the signs of famine, but he no longer noticed them now. Beggars everywhere, and the silence of the roads between. He wondered about it, as he passed quiet mud cabins. People starving, or in fever inside? Who knew? Who cared?

At Castlebar Workhouse there were now thousands of people outside. He could see children screaming in the crush of the crowd, women shrieking as they tried to protect them. Approaching the Workhouse from the streets around were dozen of donkeys, side panniers holding one, two or three children. Some donkeys carried only animal bones, the remains of donkeys or cattle that had been eaten, Pat guessed. Bones to be crushed for animal meal? Or bones for glue?

He travelled the direct route back to Knockanure, but avoiding Kilduff and Carrigard. More families staggering towards Castlebar, more donkeys.

There was one thing that cheered him. There were men working the potato fields. The spring planting was going ahead. He wondered how much it would be, and whether the people had saved enough seed potatoes from 1847. If they had, there was cause for hope, and three years of famine and fever would come to an end in 1848.

Yes, he thought. If there's enough planted, and the blight doesn't return, then it'll be over. Then we'll have a future.

Chapter 28

Dublin Weekly Register, May 1848:
Famine in the West. We copy the following extract from a letter from Newport, Mayo, received this morning: 'The distress in this part of the country is awful. Deaths by starvation are of daily occurrence. Here is a terrible instance: An entire family consisting of five souls died here of starvation ten days ago, and it was only on Friday the priest could procure a cart, and had the bodies carried to the graveyard, where they were all deposited in the one grave without coffins. Death by famine and un-coffined burials take place here every day. Fever, too, is awfully prevalent through the district. Notwithstanding, the people are making a good sowing here.'

As it turned out, that future was to be very different for Pat.

One morning Voisey entered the office. He threw a sheaf of papers on Pat's desk.

'I've been looking through these figures of yours, Pat. They're terrible. They mean only one thing. We're bankrupt.'

'I know,' Pat said.

'What's worse is the merchants know it. They're refusing credit. Stanton & Hyland are refusing to supply us. Dillon's too. We'll just have to cut back. Otherwise they're all out in the rain.'

'But what can we do, Mr. Voisey,' Pat asked.

Voisey picked up the sheaf of papers again, riffled through them, and took one out.

'We could cut back on what we're feeding them. Not that I want to, but I have to.'

Pat was stunned. What were they feeding them already? One meal a day, and little enough in that. Most of the inmates were very thin, especially the children.

'But what about the roadworks?' he asked. 'Aren't they bringing in money?'

'Very little, I'm afraid, Pat. There's little work being done – the men are too weak. We might have to stop the roadworks, I don't know. The question is – what else can we do to bring down our expenditure?'

'We could stop taking in any more people.'

'We've already done that,' Voisey said.

'So what now?'

'We're cutting back on staff.'

'Teachers…?'

'We can't. The Port Phillip scheme must go ahead. You know that.'

'Orderlies? Kitchen staff?'

'They're all inmates this long time, working for nothing. Mrs. Trinder is working for no salary. Mr. Trinder is on half salary. And so am I. So that leaves you.'

'Half salary?'

'At the very most.'

Late that afternoon, Pat walked back to Carrigard. Once he saw a pig sniffing at a corpse, but he no longer cared.

They sat around the table that evening, talking quietly. Michael had come back in from the fields. Winnie was feeding the baby, saying nothing.

'So what now?' Michael asked. 'The quarry's gone with Knockanure underbidding us, and now this. Half salary. They cut you back already. It's hardly worth it what you're earning now.'

'You're right,' Pat said. 'Still, it's getting harder for Knockanure to bid against us now. They're cutting back on feeding the inmates. I doubt the most of them would be able to work on roads anymore. And even if they do, they'll be too slow for the contract.'

'We had starving people working on roads through the winter.'

'Yes, but that wasn't for the purpose of profit. No – from all I hear I reckon it'll be impossible for the Union to keep this up.'

Pat wrote a letter to Danny.

Eleanor watched as he folded it, and inserted into the envelope. She saw Danny's name. 'Does your father know about this?'

'Not yet, and let's keep it that way until we have a reply. There's little chance of work in England now, but I must try. Any work with Danny will be better paid than Knockanure. Have we stamps left?'

She walked to the dresser and pulled a drawer open. 'Three.'

Carefully, she took the scissors and cut one off. Pat stuck it on the envelope – one black portrait of Queen Victoria.

He walked up to Kilduff with the letter, accompanying Winnie.

'At least we have Luke's money,' she said.

'Yes, but where will he go next? When will he have settled work?'

'I don't know,' Winnie said. There were tears in her eyes.

'Oh, I'm sorry,' Pat said, 'I didn't mean upsetting you.'

Winnie joined the corn line. Pat posted the letter, and then returned to the line. Winnie was at the top, and soon they were inside.

'Tuppence ha'penny a pound!' Winnie exclaimed. 'That's robbery.'

'Take it or leave it.'

They walked back. Inside the well, there were only three women talking.

'Hold on here,' Pat said. He ran to the house, left the corn in to Eleanor, and grabbed four pails. He returned to the well, and he and Winnie filled the pails with clear spring water. None of the women said anything. They walked back up the track from the well. Winnie pointed across the road. Two men had just come out of a cottage, bearing a child's corpse on a roughly-made stretcher consisting only of a few branches roped together.

'Johnny Tolan,' Pat said. 'Éamonn too.'

The men were followed by one woman, two children alongside her. She was holding their hands as they walked along. Pat nodded at them but no one seemed to see him.

'They used to be great friends of ours,' Pat said. 'Playing cards every week. Now no one talks to anyone. Especially us.'

A few days later, Danny's reply arrived. Michael opened it, even though it was addressed to Pat.

'You hadn't told me you were writing,' he said to Pat on the Saturday. 'Now Danny's asking you to England.'

'I didn't want saying anything until I had his answer,' Pat answered. 'I'd thought he wouldn't be taking anyone. I only wrote on the off-chance.'

'Six shillings a day. It's better than Knockanure.'

Pat took the letter.

'Six shillings. By God, I wasn't expecting that.'

'Well, that's what he says,' Michael said.

'It is,' Pat said. 'Between this, and whatever Luke can send back, ye shouldn't be too bad.'

'Where will he have you working though?' Eleanor asked. 'Out shovelling in the rain?'

'No,' Pat replied. 'Some kind of clerical work I'd think.'

'It won't be too hard on you so,' Eleanor said. 'But you won't be returning weekends to work the farm.'

'We've not so much call for him now,' Michael said. 'There's not much need for extra labour when the quarry's not working. And any which way you look at it, we've no choice.'

'We've not,' Pat said.

'There's more news yet, though,' Michael said.

'What's that?' Pat asked.

'It seems Murty and Aileen have left them. Murty's gone to work with the gang over in Yorkshire.'

Pat read down further down the letter.

'What! The old gang? Joe Gilligan and the lads?'

'Seems so. Ed Higgins and Jim Doyle, they're there with the gang too.'

'And Murty's working with them! But sure that's impossible. He wouldn't be able to swing a pick at his age. And the life of a teacher, that'd never toughen a man up for anything like that.'

'I don't know how much he'll be working on the railways though. Seems to be mainly there as some class of a clerk.'

Pat felt torn. He knew now he had no choice, but still it meant he was leaving Mayo, and leaving Sarah. But he reasoned that he would be back soon. There was a good potato harvest coming, he was sure of it. Yes, when that happened, he would come home for Sarah. Marry perhaps? Why not? What would she think of the life of a Mayo farmer's wife, though? Strangely, he felt confident of that. Yes, she would wait for him. The main thing was to get back to Mayo as soon as possible.

There was only one disturbing aspect. He knew from Sarah and the Clerk in Westport that Danny was not taking on new workers, and was even reducing what he had. Why would Danny offer him a job so? Because he himself had asked for it? Perhaps. Still, Danny had replied at once.

He wrote a letter back to Danny, indicating his acceptance of his offer. Within days he had another letter from Danny confirming it all.

On the Monday, he gave in notice to the Poor Law Union, and left Knockanure for Carrigard.

A few days later, he went to Westport once more. Eleanor gave him a small package of brown bread and cold cooked potatoes. It was early, and Kilduff was silent. The sun was well up by the time he had walked to Castlebar. The town was even filthier than he remembered. He saw the usual crowds outside the Workhouse and a detail of soldiers, but fewer this time, probably ten or twelve, he reckoned. He went out the Westport road.

As he walked, he saw again that many potato fields had been planted, and in more the planting was still going ahead. He wondered where the seed potatoes had come from, but one way or another, it gave some hope for the future. Certainly, more was being planted than in 1847.

Yes, 1848 would be a good year, no doubt about it.

At Westport Workhouse he was admitted with little difficulty. When he reached the Clerk of Union's office, he was surprised to be told that Sarah was not there, but was spending the morning working with her mother in the fever sheds. Concerned, Pat left the Union building, crossing the stone-breaking yard to the fever sheds. At the third shed, he found Mrs. Cronin with Sarah. Mrs. Cronin was directing three inmates as they cleared the straw and faeces from the floor, and carried sheets to baskets for the laundry.

Sarah was standing beside her mother, a notebook in one hand and a pen in the other. An inkwell stood on the window-sill. She looked up as Pat came in.

'Pat! What are you doing here?'

'And what are you doing here?' Pat replied.

Mrs. Cronin nodded at him briefly before turning back to her task.

'I'm still working on accounts,' Sarah said.

'Here?' Pat exclaimed

'We still have to keep the figures. Numbers in fever, numbers dead. The Union wants the reports.'

She opened the door and stepped outside.

'You said you weren't working in the sheds, Sarah.'

'And what of it? There's work to be done.'

'You'll get fever.'

'Maybe I will. And maybe mother will too. It's what we have to do, isn't it?'

They walked down between two of the sheds, out of sight of the stone yard and the Union building.

'I've other news for you,' Pat said. 'That's why I'm over. I'm finished with Knockanure.'

'What!'

'They're bankrupt. Can't afford me anymore. Not at any real wage, anyhow.'

'Oh God, Pat, what now? When?'

'A few days back.'

'Why didn't you tell me?'

'That's why I'm here.' He had never expected to see her quite as shocked.

'But what will you do?' she asked. 'Work with your father?'

'I would, if I could. But the quarry's stopped for now. And while there's money coming from Luke, we can't rely on it. And anyway, once Winnie and the baby go to America, he won't be able to afford much to be sending back to Ireland. No, I've no choice in the matter. I'm going to England.'

'England!'

'Working with Danny. He's offering me six shillings a day. I couldn't possibly refuse.'

'But what will we do, and you in England?'

'Don't worry, I'll be back.'

'But when?'

'Sometime. I have to come back. Someone's going to have to run the farm when father isn't able for it anymore.'

'But...'

'Or otherwise you could join me in England.'

She shook her head. 'I couldn't do that. Not as long as mother is here.'

Yes, Pat thought, as long as Mrs. Cronin lives. That's it, isn't it? But working in the fever sheds like that. How long will she live? More important, how long will Sarah live, if she doesn't keep out of them?

Pat grasped her by the arm.

'For God's sake, Sarah, we're young yet.'

'Even so.'

He opened the Workhouse door. They went to the gate, and were let out.

They walked down towards the docks, talking quietly.

There was a small shed, with one door open. Pat could see a heap of sacks inside. There was no-one there. He grasped her arm again.

'Come, Sarah,' he said. 'It's time.'

'In this cold!'

'It's not cold. And anyhow, we'll warm ourselves soon enough.'

'Fine so,' she said, and followed him inside.

He stayed in the Union building that night. Dinner with the Workhouse and Union staff was very quiet. Neither the Clerk nor Mrs. Cronin asked him of what he had seen around the county, nor did Pat wish to say much about it. It was clear they knew enough already.

Sarah roused him before dawn. She brought him to the kitchen and buttered a slice of bread for him. For some time, they spoke of Westport, of Carrigard and of England but there was no certainty of the future. The only thing they knew was that Pat would have to leave Mayo within a few days.

At the door of the Union, they kissed. Sarah hugged him closely.

'God bless you, Pat, and always remember me.'

'I'll write, I promise.'

He walked to the gate. A soldier let him out. He slipped through, stepping over sleeping forms outside the gate, and walked out the Castlebar road.

He wondered if he would ever see Sarah again.

When he arrived back at Carrigard, his father handed him a letter. He glanced through it.

'The Contract!'

'Yes,' Michael said. 'It's ours again. Ours and Benson's old one.'

'But – how?'

'God only knows,' Michael said. 'Perhaps it was something you said.'

'Damned if I know,' Pat said.

'Or maybe it was that Voisey wanted to keep you in Mayo,' Eleanor said.

'So what should we do?' Pat asked. 'Should I not go to England after all? There'll be plenty of work in the quarry.'

There was a silence.

'I think you should still go,' Michael said. 'I know your mother's worried about all the work with two quarries, but the spring planting is done, and there's little enough work on the farm 'till the main harvest. No, I think the best thing is to go over for a few months anyhow, see what the lie of the land is, and we'll see how things turn out back here. I reckon by August you'll be home.'

Through all the horror, the women still met. Now there were two babies, and the women's ambitions increased.

'*We mustn't let Brigid think we'll want any the less for her,*' Kitty said one day.

'*I don't think there's any fear of that,*' Sabina replied. '*And anyhow, it's Winnie who'll have to worry about Liam once the pair of them are settled in America.*'

'*True for you,*' Winnie said, '*but the poor fellow will only have one mother, and he'll be used to four.*'

'*Sure he'll have Luke as well,*' Eleanor said. '*A man with his schooling, he won't let ye down. And he'll be proud of his son, you wait and see. No, there'll be no problem with little Liam's schooling, nor your hopes for him.*'

'*Nor Brigid's schooling, neither,*' Kitty said.

Eleanor put more turf on the fire.

'*So what about ye?*' she said to Kitty.

Kitty sank her head. Eleanor saw she was crying. She put a hand on her shoulder,

'*I'm sorry, alanna. I didn't mean upsetting you.*'

'*I know you didn't,*' Kitty said, still sobbing. '*It's only how everything's against us. If it wasn't the hunger, it was the cold and the fever. Now the hunger is back again. Half the villages are gone. They tell their stories walking down off the Mountain and past our house. Gort-na-Móna, there's still families living in the wreckage after the eviction. Or at least there were. The half of them are probably dead now. Baile-a-Cnoic was wiped out by the fever. Sliabh Meán too. Even today, and I coming over to you, I saw them tumbling a cabin. I could see from the smell of it there were people inside, or at least what was left of them. Only the dogs are living, and you know well why that is. I met Tiernán O'Ceallaigh too coming down from* the Mountain, leading a donkey, his wife and daughter slung over the back of it. Dead. Where he was bringing them to, I just don't know, it surely wasn't to a grave in Kilduff. A hole in the bog somewhere…'

She was crying again.

'Hush there, alanna,' Eleanor said. She had flinched at the O'Ceallaigh name, though no one had noticed. O'Ceallaigh was her maiden name, and she too was from the Mountain. But she knew no Tiernán. Perhaps a distant cousin, she thought. Who knows? We never will now.

Sabina poured a small amount of poitín and handed it to Kitty. Kitty pushed it away.

'And the way we're living, it isn't living at all. Fergus is drinking more, God only knows where he gets it from, and not a penny to his name. I've heard he does be distilling it himself further up the Mountain, but I find that hard to believe. He's not eating enough, all he's doing is drinking, and he gets thinner every day. But still he lives on. I wish he'd die.'

'You mustn't say things like that,' Sabina said. 'Bad and all as he might be, we shouldn't wish him dead.'

'Yes,' said Kitty, 'you have the right of it. And it's not Fergus we should be thinking of, it's these. Our little ones here. They're our future, our only future.'

After Sabina and Kitty had left, Eleanor and Winnie were surprised to see the door open. Without asking, Fergus entered.

'Where is she?'

'If it's your wife you're seeking, she left some time back.'

She saw Fergus was already drunk.

'I told her never to come here again,' he said.

'And why wouldn't she? 'Tis only the baby she wants to see.'

'Sending her to America, are ye?'

Both Eleanor and Winnie were surprised at the question.

'Sure why would we do that?' Winnie asked, 'I never heard Kitty had that intention.'

He had spotted the cup of poitín on the table. Quickly, he reached for it and swallowed it.

'You could have asked,' Eleanor said.

For a moment, Winnie thought he was about to strike Eleanor.

'Well, I don't want her coming here again,' he said.

'Is it so we can't see the beatings you're giving her?' Eleanor asked.

Once again Fergus went as if to strike her.

'I wouldn't do that if I were you,' Eleanor said. 'Bad enough attacking two women when there's no men here, but Michael and Pat will hear of it, and they'll have the beating of you.'

'I beat Luke when he was seeing my wife.'

'So you did,' Eleanor replied, 'but that was before you started beating Kitty. A powerless woman, that'd the only kind you can fight now, is it?'

For a moment, Fergus glared at the two women. Then he made for the door, and went.

They sat by the fire. *'He was angry enough,'* Winnie said.

'He was,' Eleanor said. *'He'll never forget Luke and the business with Kitty. But that was before Luke knew you.'*

'I know,' Winnie said, *'and there's many thought I should hate Kitty for it. But how could I do that, seeing the kind of woman she is, and the dreams she has for little Brigid too? And living with a brute like that. No, Kitty has paid the price, and she'll go on paying it for many years yet.'*

That afternoon, there was a knock on the door and Eleanor went to answer it. An old woman stood outside.

'The hunger is on me.'

Eleanor poured a cup of water and brought it to the woman who drank it quickly. When she was finished, Eleanor took the cup back and closed the door.

'It was food she was looking for,' Winnie said.

'I know,' Eleanor said, *'but if we gave her food, we'd have a hundred back in the morning. And one way or the other, we'll be needing it ourselves. We can't be giving it away.'*

'But...'

'There's no buts about it. I gave her water, and God knows on a dry day like this she needed it. At least we gave her one blessing.'

'Yes,' Winnie said, *'I suppose you're right. Still, with all the hunger around us, I almost feel bad about eating the little we have. What will the neighbours think when this is all over? They'll be looking at us, saying we could eat when so many died.'*

'I know. But it's little enough food we have, and little enough money to be buying food. And any money we have, we must save for the ticket for yourself and Liam.'

It was late May when Luke's letter arrived from Bytown.

'So what does he have to say?' Eleanor asked.

'He's left the forests. Gone to somewhere called Bytown.'

'I've never heard of it,' Eleanor said.

'No, me neither. But wherever he is, or whatever he's doing, he's still sending us money. He says too he's hoping to have some kind of fixed

address whenever he manages to get to meet up with Farrelly and the lads, but he says that may be three months. And you know what that means.'

'I know, alanna,' Eleanor said. 'It'll be too late in the season. There's no chance of a winter crossing, even when we do get a lasting address from him, in Pennsylvania or anywhere.'

'I've heard there are winter crossings to America.'

'There might be, but what of the storms? And it's not just yourself, it's little Liam too. No, you'll just have to be patient.'

'But for how long?' Winnie asked. 'Next year? A sailing in March or April? It'll be May of next year before I get to America. That's still a full year away.'

Chapter 29

Staffordshire Advertiser, April 1848:
The line from Stoke to Norton Bridge forms part of the contract of Messrs. Brassey & Co., and has been completed in a style that fully sustains the reputation of that celebrated firm. The government inspector, who passed over the line last week, said it was one of the best he had ever travelled upon.

Raining again. The Edgeley Viaduct was nearly invisible in the grey. Danny stood by the coal fire, watching the barely visible outline of a train pulling out of Stockport Station in the direction of Manchester.

'Can't you sit down?' Irene said.

'Not while I'm thinking,' Danny replied.

'So what do we do now? You tell me.'

'Damned if I know,' Danny said. 'You were the one who said we should keep our prices high.'

'I did,' she said, 'and we have a contract with Andersons to that effect. How could I have known he'd drop the rates like this? He's in breach of contract.'

Danny turned, gazing into the glowing centre of the fire. He could hear the distant hooting of another train on the viaduct.

'And what of contingencies? Didn't we build in a contingency?'

'We did,' she said. 'But a twenty per cent reduction, we'd have needed a very big contingency to allow for that.'

'We could, of course, take Roy to court.'

'And what good would that do? It'll cost a fortune, and one way or another, Anderson can outspend us on lawyers.'

'So what then, Irene? What can we do?'

'Reduce the wages.'

'Have sense, would you. They're at the lowest they can be. We can't reduce them anymore.'

'But we're losing money now on every cubic yard,' she said.

'I know.'

'So we'll just have to start firing men on all the Anderson sites.'

'But that'll slow them down.'

'Not if we increase the hours by a quarter.'

'A quarter!' Danny exclaimed.

'Why not? Less men, more hours, same rate of work.'

'By God, Irene, you are one tough lady.'

'Any objection?'

'No.'

'So that's agreed then. We start firing men on these three sites, and that's just a slow build-up to what we'll be doing when the Brassey site finishes.'

The rain was clearing. Another train was crossing the viaduct, this time in the direction of Stockport Station. A local, he wondered, or a long distance? Stopping or express? Heading south. London or Birmingham?

Pat left for England.

As he walked across Connaught he saw all the evidence of a country shattered by famine. East Mayo, Roscommon, East Galway – nothing but starving people on the roads, hundreds of them outside the Workhouses. Twice he saw dead bodies by the side of the road.

The Workhouses in Leinster did not seem as crowded as those in Connaught. When he arrived in Dublin, he walked to Kingsbridge Station, reckoning from the front of it that it was very new, and very costly too. He hailed a hansom cab, which brought him to the Dublin Docks. He bought a ticket for the upper deck on a cattle boat. Then he fought his way through the milling crowd, and carried his bag aloft. During the crossing, he stayed at the rail above the cattle hold, which was crowded with cattle and humanity.

He watched the people, and thought of the time he had spent working on the harvest in Castle Bromwich. That was two years back, just as the hunger was starting. Even then, the cattle boats had been rough for those who had to travel with the animals. Was it worse now? Or was it just that he was more accepting when he was younger? The hold was far more crowded with people, and less cattle maybe? But the people were the real difference. He reckoned their clothes were more ragged than he remembered, their bodies thinner, their faces more etched with the signs of hunger. When he had first travelled, he went with harvesters to work on the corn and potato harvests in England. They were strong young men then, nothing like this pitiful crowd of men, women and children. He knew few of them would earn much on the harvest, let alone the railways.

In Liverpool he tried to avoid the worst, but it was impossible. He had to force his way through more crowds of Irish emigrants. He walked to Buckleys' in Scotland Road. Shocked at the conditions of the surrounding tenements and of Buckleys' itself, he walked towards Lime Street Station.

He could not understand what had happened to Buckleys'. There was a time he would have been happy to stay there, but within one or two years it had become run down in a way he could never have expected.

He stayed that night in Brown's Temperance Hotel, close to the station. He woke late, and ate a cold, greasy breakfast, still glum from what he had seen of Liverpool. It was not until he was aboard the train to Manchester that he felt he could relax.

At Manchester he changed to the Manchester & Birmingham travelling south across Edgeley Viaduct to Stockport.

That evening, Pat met Danny for the first time since Danny had left for England. His first surprise was the quality of the lodgings, though he had heard that Danny was building a private house. As he soon found out though, even these were not just lodgings. Danny and Irene were renting the entire house.

Danny met him at the steps.

'You're most welcome,' he said to Pat, extending a hand. 'Did you have a good journey?'

'Good enough,' Pat said. 'I'm getting used to it.'

Danny ushered him into the hall.

'How did you come?'

'Walking across, from Mayo to Dublin. Cattle boat to Liverpool, but I stayed on the upper deck, then train to Manchester and Stockport.'

Danny's appearance surprised him. Yes, he was certainly taller – far taller – than he had been when he had left Mayo. He was dressed in a well-cut suit, a white shirt with a winged collar and cravat. What struck Pat most was Danny's face, most of all his hard, gleaming eyes. No tears here. This was no heartbroken *spailpín* leaving Carrigard for the unknown.

'What's Mayo like?' Danny asked.

'Terrible. It's getting better though. There'll be a great potato crop this year, and I reckon the hunger will be over soon.'

'Well, I'm delighted to hear that,' said Danny. 'Now, come on in and meet everyone.'

Pat followed him into the living room. Murtybeg was there, a glass in his hand. He jumped up.

'Pat. At last.'

'Murteen.'

'It's lucky you're meeting me too. I'm only back here on Sundays now. Come on now, a drop of whiskey surely.'

He poured a glass.

'Best Irish too,' Danny said. 'It's one thing we stayed true to.'

'I'm sure,' Pat said. He felt the deep cut crystal glass, and held it up to the light. 'Irish glass too?

'Of course,' Danny said, 'Waterford, what else.'

They sat on easy chairs. Pat sipped at the whiskey.

'It's good,' he said. There was no sign of Murty or Aileen though.

'Murty and Aileen aren't coming across, are they?' he asked.

'We didn't know when you were coming,' Danny said. 'If we did, we'd have had them over.'

'They're a fair distance, are they?' Pat asked.

'Far enough,' Murtybeg said, avoiding his gaze.

'And Irene?'

'Still working, I think,' Danny said. 'She'll be along shortly.'

Over dinner they spoke of many things. The maid served them oxtail soup, followed by steak and vegetables on china plates, all on a linen tablecloth. A six stemmed candelabra in the centre of the table lit the room.

Murtybeg thought that Danny would talk business, as he always seemed to do these days. He was surprised when he opened up with the subject of Nessa. So too was Pat.

'You can have little idea how that shocked me,' he said.

'Yes,' Pat said, 'it was a horrible shock for us all. We hadn't expected it.'

'It was,' Danny said. 'And it was only when I heard the news that I realised how many good times we had together then. Of course, we were all young when I left. I often wondered what kind of young woman she had become since I left. Now I'll never find out.'

'We heard you sought your revenge,' Pat said.

'Of course we did, Murtybeg and me. We couldn't let Corrigan away with that. He was the father, and what good was he for her when she needed him. Cut and ran, he did. We had to do something.'

'I'd have preferred you hadn't,' Pat said abruptly.

Murtybeg looked up in surprise. 'But we had to, Pat...'

'No ye didn't. That was not called for.'

'But Corrigan was the fellow who killed her,' Danny said.

'Killed her!' Pat exclaimed.

'Killed her,' Danny repeated. 'If she was never with child, she'd be alive today. Wouldn't she?'

They were half way through the main course when Irene entered the room.

A tall woman, Pat saw, nearly as tall as Danny. Thin too, but not from hunger. She wore a purple dress, tucked closely under her breasts. This was a woman who knew how to impress and excite.

'I'd like you to meet Irene,' Danny said. 'You've heard of her, I'm sure.'

Pat stood as Irene held out her hand.

'Of course.'

He took her hand and stepped back, looking into her eyes. Hard eyes. A tough woman. But what else had he expected of Danny's woman?

'So this is Pat?' she said, icily. 'I'm delighted to meet you.'

'And I'm delighted to meet you,' Pat said. 'Murtybeg has told us much about you.'

She did not smile. They sat down to dinner again, as Irene was served soup.

'How are your mother and father getting on?' Pat asked.

'Not so bad,' Danny answered. 'Over with the gang in Leeds, like I wrote you. They seem to be well enough.'

Pat noticed the frown on Irene's face, and he wondered what the story there was. Best not to ask yet.

'Nice lodgings you have here,' he said.

'Not too bad,' Irene said, sharply. 'It'll be better when we have our own.'

'Yes,' Pat said, 'I'd heard about that too. Still, if it'll be better than this, ye must be doing well on the railways.'

'Well enough,' Danny said. He was about to go further when Irene interrupted him.

'There's excellent opportunities on the railways,' she said, 'and Edwardes & Ryan are the best. Our competitors, they can't keep up with us. We'll drive them all out soon enough.'

Pat could see the fear now in Danny's eyes. He wondered about that. Did he not agree with Irene? Or was he afraid of her? Danny? Afraid?

'Keep the prices up so?' he said.

'Yes,' Irene said, emphatically. 'Once we get rid of all the muck-shifters, we'll have the prices as high as we like. It'll be hard work, but that's where you're going to help us. Keeping costs down, that's where you come in.'

'What costs?'

'Never mind,' Danny said. 'We'll explain it all later.'

That night Pat shared a bedroom with Murtybeg, using a small camp bed in the corner.

'How's your father?' Pat asked.

'Why do you ask?'

'Why did they leave?'

'I don't think either of them are very happy to be in England at all. You know mother, you know how she is.'

Pat folded his shirt, and left it neatly on a small chest-of-drawers beside his bed.

'And your father?'

'It's just like I told Luke it was going to be, before he left for America.

Father is trapped. With his school gone, it seemed his only future was working with Danny. Once he saw how cruel Danny was though, and the way he was treating his workers, he couldn't stay.'

'So what happened?'

'He reckoned that the fellows in Yorkshire might need someone to do their clerical work for them. Roughneen's idea, it was. Quite right he was too. So the two of us went across to Leeds, met up with Gilligan and the other fellows, and they agreed to take him on, not so much as the ganger, as a paid clerk. It might involve some other labour too, but I don't think they'd ask much of him.'

'Sounds like he did right.'

'Oh, I don't know,' Murtybeg said. 'There's one other thing he's playing down, I think. Mother is in a bad way, though I don't have to tell you that. The question in my mind is – how long will the lads stay on any single site? They might have a good lodging house now, but what happens when they have to move on?'

'It'll be hard on them, one way or another. I'm not sure your mother would be up to all that moving about.'

'That's what I'm thinking.'

'So where are they right now?'

'The gang are still working on the Leeds & Thirsk.'

'They've been there a while so. Wasn't that where they were going when Luke came home?'

'That's right. It's coming to an end soon though. September or so, that's what they're saying.'

'Do you have an address?'

'They're lodging at Barretts, three or four miles out of Leeds on the railway. If you're writing, just address it to him at care of Joe Gilligan at Barrett's Boarding-house, care of the Leeds & Thirsk.'

Murtybeg licked his fingers and quickly doused the candlewick.

Pat stared into the darkness, finding it all difficult to understand.

'What makes you think I'll be able to work for Danny?' he asked.

'I think you're better able to keep control of yourself,' Murtybeg said, 'and anyway you don't have to deal direct with the workers. Roughneen, Lavan and Kearney – they come into head office to make their reports, settle up all their accounts and take their orders. They're the fellows who'll have it hardest, not you.'

Next morning, Danny took Pat out to see one of the sites. Murtybeg had already left.

'We're going out to see Bernie Lavan,' Danny explained. Fifty thousand cubic yards to be removed for the railway.

'Fifty thousand cubic yards?'

'Yes, it's a good contract. We've a hundred and twenty men working on it at the moment.'

Yes, he thought, and less later. But now was not the time to tell Pat about the sackings, and his own future role in them.

They walked out along the newly laid rails. Half an hour later they were passing a group of mud huts. Pat could see they were all roughly built, for the most part using rough cuts and discards of timber for the roof, with sods on top. Behind the huts a group of women were washing clothes in the stream. Even from twenty yards, there was a marked smell of cabbage and sewage intermingled. Pat stopped.

'Come on, Pat,' Danny said.

'What's this?' Pat asked.

'Workers lodgings.'

'But they're hardly better than *sceilps* back home. Have they been evicted or what?'

'Evicted is right. That or the hunger forcing them out. They're from out west Mayo – Erris, Achill, Partry, down around Killary – all those parts.'

'Yes. I'd heard that. But are these your workers then? The fellows we sent across. Surely not?'

'Some are,' Danny replied, 'though some of those lads are working on other contracts.'

He saw the shock in Pat's eyes.

'Are you paying them at all?' Pat asked. 'How much are you paying?'

'Plenty enough,' Danny replied. 'Ten pence, eleven pence, a shilling a day.'

'But that's hardly more than what they'd be getting on Famine Relief.'

'Don't forget two things though,' Danny replied. 'First, we have to feed them, and by God, they need it when they arrive here. We have to strengthen them up. And the other thing is there's damned little Relief out in west Mayo. Even during the worst of it, there was none. And I'll tell you another thing, if we weren't employing them here, most of them would be dead, their families too. Just think about it, Pat. The men came over here, they arrived at Liverpool, and what happened? They tried to get into the Workhouses in Liverpool, but most of them wouldn't be let in. And for the rest of them, either they emigrated to the Canadas, or the Workhouses in Liverpool sent them back. Some of them weren't even being sent back to their own parts, just dumped in Kerry or Clare or anywhere that the ship's captain decided. And for the ones going to Quebec or Montreal, you've heard of the ships there. Hell holes is all they are. We're always hearing stories of the lumber traders going back to Quebec with their cargoes of the starving.'

They walked on.

'You know that Luke was going to Quebec?' Pat asked.

'Yes, father told me. Johnny Roughneen told me too. He had a letter from home. But I'll tell you this, Luke was a fool to go, and it wasn't just because of the condition of the ships. He had other chances.'

'Other chances?'

'Yes. I offered him a position, but he wouldn't take it. Damned fool, he was. If he had taken it, he and the wife could be here now, living in comfort.'

Pat stopped to observe the rock-cutting.

'It's deep,' he commented. 'I wonder what father would think of this if he saw it.'

'Yes,' Danny replied. 'It makes the quarry look small. But your father never had a hundred men working it.'

'Not usually,' Pat replied, 'though he had many enough when they were running the Relief Works. They were building the new road out from the quarry towards Knockanure, and there was a heavy call for rock on that.'

'So I'd heard.'

Pat shook his head.

'But tell me this. What were you saying about Johnny Roughneen? I thought he'd been with Martin Farrelly.'

'He was,' Danny replied, 'but the time Farrelly went to the United States, I saw a good chance for getting men who were able to be gangers. Lavan and Kearney, like I said, they're here too. You'll meet them. Good men they are too. And if Luke had had sense, I'd have him working as a ganger. He'd be well able for it. I even offered him a share of profits, but do you think he'd take it? No way.'

'Do you have many Kilduff men around here so?' Pat asked.

'Only the top fellows. The ones I know. The ones I can trust. And they're the only Kilduff men working here. The rest are west Mayo, like I told you. Those fellows, they're able for nothing else.'

They had arrived at the new cutting. Pat saw dozens of gaunt men swinging picks at loose shale. Further on, more men were shovelling broken rock onto a rail wagon. The larger rocks were being carried across in wheelbarrows, and lifted into the wagons.

'I'm surprised that men like that can work at all,' Pat said.

'Oh, they can work fine,' said Danny. 'Like I say, we feed them well, and that strengthens them. You'll see the fellows loading the wagons are strong enough.'

There was a man by the wagons, shouting orders at the working men. Danny waved to him and he ran over.

'You know who this is, Bernie,'

Lavan stared at Pat, slowly realising. 'By God, Pat Ryan!' he exclaimed.

'I'd heard you were coming, but I didn't believe it.'

'Well, you may believe it now,' Pat replied. 'But to hell with that. Tell me how you're doing yourself?'

Lavan looked at Danny with a smile. 'Well enough. Six shillings a day. It's good money.'

'It is,' Pat replied.

'Exciting too. We're just preparing a blast. Would you like to see it?'

He followed Lavan over to the side of the cutting.

'They're just getting the blasting powder into place.'

There was a screech from a siren. Work stopped, and all the men walked back behind the safety of the wagons.

'Come on,' Lavan said. 'Let's get back a bit.'

They walked back to Danny, and scrambled up the cutting on the other side. Lavan raised his arm. The man with the gunpowder lit the paper quill, and ran back. Half a minute later there was a violent explosion, and a thousand tons of rock shattered and collapsed.

They walked back along the line to Stockport.

'Irene's a hard worker,' Pat commented.

'She's all of that,' Danny replied. 'Keeps the office well in control, she does. No slacking when she's around, I can tell you.'

Yes, thought Pat. And I wonder who else she might keep in control.

'Ye're to marry, so?'

'We are,' Danny replied.

'I'd understood that was to be some time ago.'

'So it was. But with all the new contracts we got, we didn't have a chance. It's brutal work this, you have no idea. And you can't turn down breaks that might never come again. So we decided it would be wiser to put it back for a while.'

'To when?'

'July, we're intending.'

They arrived at Stockport. Roughneen was there, poring over the accounts book with Irene. Two police constables were sitting in the corner.

Danny noticed Pat's surprise. 'It's normal,' he said. 'Johnny will be taking the wages back out the line to the men, it'd be far too dangerous to let him out on his own with all that money.'

'But all they're carrying is night-sticks. Would that be enough?'

'What do you mean?'

'Back home we'd have more than constables if cash was being moved around. Especially the amount you might be taking out.'

'What then?'

'Militia at least. Well-armed too, I can tell you.'

'Militia,' Irene exclaimed. 'Now there's an idea.'

'It's an idea right enough,' a constable said. 'I rather doubt the army would like it though, and anyhow we've had little trouble yet. Nothing we couldn't handle.'

Irene unlocked the safe. Roughneen took sacks of coins out, and started to count them out. Farthings, halfpennies, pennies, sixpences and shillings. No half crowns, as Pat noticed, and sure as hell, no sovereigns.

Danny led Pat across the office to a high desk. Carefully he cleared some wage sheets to the side.

'I was going to show you these, but a better idea perhaps might be to see what Johnny here is doing.'

He called Roughneen across.

'Now, Pat, your main duties in this instance would be to check the wage sheets, calculate them, and make sure they are correct. I know I can depend on you for that.'

Pat rapidly checked Roughneen's wage sheets, and found no errors of consequence.

After Roughneen left with the constables, Pat spent the rest of the day under Irene's instruction, going through requisitions. Most concerned implements, explosives, heavy boots, working clothes and provisions. Then he came across an invoice from the butcher.

'Twenty sheep heads caught his eye. He made no comment but read through the rest of the list – sheep and cow livers, kidneys, crubeens, and many other items. He checked for steak, bacon or lamb, but there was none.

That evening in their bedroom, Danny and Irene spoke quietly.

'I don't like this,' he said. 'I think he's curious about mother and father.'

'Well, let him be curious,' Irene said, 'what harm does that do?'

'I don't know,' Danny said, 'but he seemed disappointed when he heard they weren't here to meet him.'

'How could they have met him? We didn't know when he was coming, did we?'

Danny lay back, thinking. Yes, Irene was certainly the woman to have as a partner in this business. Ruthless? Most certainly. Cruel? Perhaps. She certainly didn't care about his family, and even treated Murtybeg with some contempt. And what about the workers? She knew how to handle men, how to push the gangers to get the most out of them at the least cost. He could protest, of course, but with the present state of business there was no other way. The railways had to be built, cuttings dug, and the most work forced out of every man. Yes, and push the costs down too, just as Irene wanted.

So what about marriage? He knew he needed her. But what kind of need was it? Desire, perhaps?

And for the business? A need stronger than desire.

Pat quickly settled down to the work required of him. Still, the wages and the cheap food unsettled him. The visit to Lavan's site unsettled him too. He had to find out more.

On a Saturday afternoon, as he left the office, he told Irene that he was going out to find a beer. She did not question him.

A few hundred yards away he found a bar. He entered, ordered a whiskey straight, and sat at a table in the corner on his own, still thinking.

After half an hour he stood up, and left the bar, circled around away from their lodgings and scrambled up an embankment to the railway line. For two hours, he walked out along it until he came to the Irish huts. There was an open drain running down between them. The stink was overwhelming. A small group of women stood by the drain, smoking clay pipes. He could see the look of alarm on their faces as he approached.

'*Do ye have Irish?*' he asked. '*Can ye speak it?*'

A tall woman stood forward. '*What if we do?*'

Pat caught the accent clearly. Mayo? Could be Galway, but unlikely. No, Mayo for sure.

'*Nothing at all,*' he replied. '*I was just trying to be friendly.*'

'*Friendly, is it?*' she said, irony in her voice.

'*Friendly, yes. And why shouldn't I be? I'd heard there were people from Mayo out this way. I'm Mayo myself, so I thought I'd drop out and see ye.*'

'*Is it a whore you're seeking?*'

'*It is not.*'

Three men approached from behind a hut. Two carried sticks.

'*He says he's from Mayo,*' the woman said.

'*He is for sure,*' said one of the men. '*Ryan's cousin, that's who he is.*'

Some of the women backed away. Pat decided to appeal to their sympathy.

'*Yes, it's true,*' he said. '*Daniel Ryan is my cousin. I'm over here working with him, the same as ye.*'

'*But with better lodgings,*' the man said.

'*Perhaps,*' Pat said, '*but the reason is the same. I've no work back in Mayo now, nor any way to make a living or to eat. Isn't that why ye're here too?*'

'*So state your business.*' Pat was surprised by the question. What was his business?

'*So as to see how you're living.*'

'*And report back, is it?*'

'Perhaps I should,' Pat said. '*What do ye think?*'

'*Yes, perhaps you should so. Let* Mr. Daniel *know the way we're living here.*'

'As if he doesn't already,' the woman said angrily. She grasped Pat by the hand. '*Come on so,*' she said, '*Come on, and I'll show you.*'

Pat shook his hand free, but he followed her.

She led across to one of the huts, and flung the door open. Pat stepped inside. At first he could see nothing. It was dark, and smoke stung his eyes.

Mingled with the smoke was the smell of cabbage. Turnips too. He was surprised that he could distinguish them all so clearly. There was also the strong smell of shit. Trying to trace it, he saw a rough box built into the back of the hut. He could see daylight through it. He drew back.

'*Is that what you wanted to see? Is it?*'

'Yes it is,' Pat replied. '*Everything. I want to understand it all.*'

He noticed the fire had been built up on some rough blocks, more of them behind to keep it away from the timber. A rough shelf had been built alongside. There were two pots on top, a sheep's head between them.

On the other side of the hut there was a bed. It was only then that he heard a moan coming from under a blanket.

'Fever,' the woman said. '*She's only eight years old. What chance does she have?*'

'*I'm sorry,*' Pat said.

'*It's for this we left Torán.*'

'Left...?'

'*Evicted, more like. Evicted at Christmas.*'

'That's terrible,' said Pat. '*And it's no better for ye here, is it?*'

'*Oh yes, it's better,*' she said. '*Much better. Here we eat. There we didn't.*'

There was a shout from the door.

'*Are you alright there, Síle? Is he attacking you?*'

'He is not,' the woman replied. '*Now ye may go away and leave us in peace.*'

She pulled out a wooden box and put it by a rough cut table made from a single crate. She placed a gin bottle on the table, alongside two chipped cups.

'*Here, sit yourself down. What else do you want to know?*'

She poured out the clear spirit, offering one to Pat.

'*Look,*' he said, '*I'm only just come over myself. Like you, only because I had to. I'd starve in Mayo. But I'm trying to understand – just what is happening here?*'

He sipped at the spirit. *Poitín!* What else would be kept in a gin bottle? It was raw, but the rawness had quality.

'I'll tell you about Edwardes & Ryan so,' she said. 'It's a grand business – for the owners. Very able they are too, Mr. Daniel, Miss Irene and Mr. Daniel's brother. The way they work it is this. First Mr. Daniel sends his brother up to Liverpool. You've seen Liverpool, I'm sure. When he gets there, he works out which ships have come in from Mayo – Westport, Killala, wherever. That's his favourite stalking ground. Finding men who are desperate and starving. He offers them wages which seem high to them, and brings them back here. He has a preference for married men, travelling without their families, though there's many families on this site. Mr. Daniel knows how desperate they are, especially with family back in Mayo. If he can't get enough men at the docks, he goes to the Workhouse. He has good contacts there, young Murteen has. He finds out soon enough which of the married men are to be sent back to Ireland. He does the same trick with them, offering them ten pence a day. He knows they have no choice. If they're sent back, they'll die. And they can't speak English either, so they're trapped. He promises food,' she pointed at the sheep's head, 'but as you can see, it's only the cheap cuts we ever get. But I'll say one thing, there's always plenty of it. He wants to build up his workers, Mr. Daniel does. He can work them harder that way.'

'And what about you and the other women?' Pat asked. 'How did ye get here?'

'No thanks to Mr. Daniel, that's for sure. Whatever our husbands sent back was never enough for more than food, though some of us starved to get the money to leave. Some of us were cleared by the landlords who paid the money to go, though that was rare enough – the half of them are bankrupt. Some got money from other relatives working in England, though few of them would stay working with Mr. Daniel. And some were evicted, and we were in Liverpool in the Workhouse already.'

'Why wouldn't they all leave Edwardes & Ryan?' Pat asked. 'Surely, when they've their strength, they can get better wages on other cuttings.'

'Yes,' she said, 'you'd think so. But you must remember two things. First, none of the men speak anything but Irish. Mr. Daniel makes sure there are no English speakers in the gangs. But also, he helps the men with sending money back to their families in Mayo. He gives them cash advances for that, then he holds back their wages. Then they are really trapped. They moment they leave Edwardes & Ryan, their families are cut off from any cash.

When Pat left the hut, there was still a group of men and women outside. Shouting erupted.

'Well, what did she tell you?'

'Did she bed you?

'Did she feed you well?'

'I'd lay a bet that you never ate any of that at Mr. Daniel's *dinner table?'*

Pat pushed his way through, without saying a word. He scrambled up the embankment. A number of the men followed him onto the track, but he ignored them and kept walking. A stone flew past his head, close enough for him to hear it. He stopped, and turned back to face them. The men stopped too. For a few moments there was a stand-off, then Pat turned again and walked towards Stockport, no one following him now.

It was getting dark. As he passed the office, he noticed a single candle burning. Curious, he entered. Murtybeg was there on his own, writing in a ledger. He looked up.

'Not had your dinner?'

'I thought I'd have a look around first,' Pat said. 'See the cut of the place.'

'Stockport?'

'No. I took a walk out along the track.'

'What did you do that for?'

'To have a look at the *tigíns* they live in and have a chat with them while I was at it.'

Murtybeg slammed his pen on his desk.

'Damn it, you shouldn't have done that. Surely you know better.'

'Sure how would a poor *amadán* from Mayo know any better?' Pat said. 'But yes, I've stayed in those kind of huts myself. Working the harvest – shacks, booleys, whatever. But I'll tell you this, Murteen, they're nothing like these. These are disgusting. The slop Danny calls food, and the stink of shit everywhere.'

'The food is grand,' Murtybeg replied. 'The meat's more than they ever had out Erris. It might not be steak, but it's wholesome food, and it builds them up. Far better than starving in Mayo, I'll tell you that.'

'And what about the wages?' Pat asked.

'It's a free world. They can leave whenever they like.'

'And your own father and mother left ye? Isn't that it? Went away, rather than work with their own sons.'

'I can't deny it,' Murtybeg said. 'But I don't know why you're so surprised, Pat. I told you about father already. Why do you think he wouldn't work with Danny?'

The following morning was Sunday. Pat was awake early. He got up.

'What the…' Murtybeg said.

'I'm going to Mass.'

He left the house quietly, and walked along the tracks into Stockport Station. When he reached the station, he took the train into Manchester. He was just in time for the Leeds train, having to run hard to catch it.

'That was a dangerous thing to do,' the conductor told him.

'I'm sorry,' Pat said. He bought a ticket to Leeds.

When he arrived at Leeds station, he asked direction for the Leeds & Thirsk Railway, and walked through Kirkgate, then along the tracks until he came to the Works. A number of times he asked for directions to Gilligan's gang, and after some time he found them. Doyle spotted him first.

'Pat! Pat Ryan.'

Gilligan strode over.

'Well, by God, we don't see a Ryan for ages, and now we get flocks of them.'

'So maybe you should count yourself lucky.'

'Are you coming to join us?' Doyle asked.

'I'm afraid not. I'm working for Danny.'

'Danny,' Ed Higgins exclaimed. 'You'd have your work cut out for you, working for him. And he'll need you too, now the Master has left.'

For a few minutes, Pat stayed with them, chatting about the gang. Then Gilligan stood.

'Time to go back to work, I'm afraid,' he said.

'Work on a Sunday?'

'Why not. But I suppose you're looking for your uncle?'

'I am.'

'He's back at the lodging house, working I think.'

Pat followed Gilligan's instructions and soon found the house. The landlady admitted him.

'Last door on the left,' she said.

Pat knocked. Murty opened the door to him, and gaped at Pat for a moment.

'Pat!' he said at length. 'What the devil…'

'Just dropping by to see you,' Pat answered.

'Are you looking for work, is it?'

'I'm with Danny.'

'But…oh, to hell with it, come in, come in.'

Pat ducked to enter. Murty took his coat, hung it, and ushered him into the room. It had whitewashed walls, mullioned windows and a rough dresser on one wall. On the lower shelf, there were glasses, clay pipes on a small wooden rack, and tins of tobacco.

For the furniture, three stools, a low table in front.

'Sit down, sit down,' Murty said to him. 'You'll have a drink.'

'I will,' Pat said.

A spirit was poured, and placed in front of Pat. He sipped at it.

'*Poitín*! Where the hell do you get this?'

'Oh, there's a lad from West Cork, works near us. Gets it from his father, I believe. You have to be able to trust your source, you know. Turn you blind otherwise.'

'Indeed it would,' Pat said, 'but not this stuff you say.'

He sipped again at the rough spirit. Even for double-distilled *poitín*, it was rough enough.

'We only take it out for special visitors.'

'Of course,' Pat said.

All this time, he had been expecting Aileen to enter, but now he realised she was not in.

'Where's Aileen?' he asked.

'At Mass.'

'At Mass?'

'Indeed. Gone all religious. First Mass on a Sunday, and God knows how many more. Then all sorts of devotions or whatnot for the rest of the day. Reckons the Sabbath must be kept holy. I think it's the fright of all that's happened. Seeing the way Danny is, and then the shock of leaving him again. Still, religion seems to calm her, and who am I to say there's anything wrong with that?' He raised his glass. 'She'd kill me if she saw us drinking this of a Sunday.'

Pat sniffed at it. 'I never thought I'd be drinking this in England either. But the strange thing is, this is the second time I've had it since yesterday.'

'Don't tell me Danny has been leading you astray with *poitín*.'

'Oh, it wasn't Danny. I went visiting his huts though. Got a sip of *poitín* there.'

'Not from Cork. I'd guess.'

'No,' Pat said, 'more like Mayo, I'd say.'

Murty stood up and took two clay pipes, handing one to Pat. He opened a tobacco tin. Pat pinched at it, taking a quantity and pushing it into the bowl of his pipe.

'So you've seen Danny's huts?'

'I have. Mostly mud cabins.'

Murty lit a match, holding it across to Pat. Pat drew at it, tamping it down and drawing it again until the tobacco glowed red.

'So what did you think?'

'Pretty rough conditions, I'd say,' Pat replied. 'Danny sure as hell has no great *grá* for his workers, nor for their families, however many of them manage to make their way over.'

'Have you seen what he feeds them?'

'I have. Dreadful slop.'

'It is.'

'But that's not the worst. They've fever in the huts. Only a little, as far as

I can see, but by Christ, if it spreads, what happens then?'

'That's the question, isn't it?'

There was a rattle at the front door and a squeak of hinges. The door opened.

'Aileen!' Pat exclaimed. He stood, went over to her and hugged her.

'It's great to see you,' he said.

'Pat...' she said, faintly.

Pat recalled the times before Murty and Aileen had left Mayo. In recent years, she had been held to be 'weak in the mind', a remarkable fact given that she was Eleanor's sister. He wondered how they could be so different. Perhaps it was what she had seen on the Mountain in her childhood. She had had fever as a child, but so had Eleanor. She had suffered hunger in the 1820s famine, but so too had Eleanor.

When she had married, she might even have had an easier life than Eleanor, not the tough life of a farmer's wife. But she never had Eleanor's strength.

'Pat...' she repeated. Murty came across and took her by the arm. He sat her down. Pat noticed the two glasses of *poitín* had disappeared.

'A cup of tea for everyone,' Murty said.

Pat expected Aileen would get it, but Murty went out to the kitchen. He thought of following him, but felt that would be hurtful to Aileen, so he sat down beside her.

''Tis well you're looking,' he said.

'Yes,' she said, 'the Good Lord helps.'

'You were at Mass, I hear.'

'Indeed. And it's a cause of great heartache to me that my own husband will not do it.'

'Why is that?'

'There's few enough of the fellows in the gang go to church. Murty did back in Mayo, but now he doesn't have the courage to stand up for his own beliefs.'

Pat wondered what Murty's beliefs were. He doubted if Murty ever had any deep religious conviction.

Murty re-entered, carrying a tray with tea, milk and sugar. He placed a cup in front of Pat, and lit his pipe again.

'So what about Carrigard?' he asked. 'How's everything there?'

'As well as might be expected,' Pat said. 'Father had lost the contract on the quarry for a few months, but he's got it back again. There's starvation around, no doubt about that, but we're doing well enough.'

'It's a curse, this damned famine. No end to it.'

'I don't know,' Pat said. 'There might be less need to worry about it soon. There's any amount of potatoes planted, and the blight has gone. Come the early harvest, and things will be easier. By August it should be all over.'

Murty tamped down his tobacco. 'I hope to God you're right,' he said, 'because, by Christ, there's enough hungry Irish over here, that's for certain.'

'Yes,' Pat said, 'I'd noticed. Liverpool is in a terrible state.'

'I know,' Murty said. 'We've only seen it the once, but God, it was awful then.'

'Sugar, Pat?' Aileen asked quietly.

'Just the one,' Pat replied.

She spooned it into his cup and stirred it for him.

'What are you doing here in England?' she asked.

'Working.'

'Was it Danny tempted you?'

'It was,' Pat said, surprised she had not considered he might work on the Leeds & Thirsk. Had she realised that he had come to replace Murty?

'Didn't you have work in Mayo?'

'I did, but that was a while back, and now the Workhouse is bankrupt. They're letting people go, staff and inmates, both. I was earning very little. So you needn't think it was Danny tempting me. I wrote to him, asked what was possible, and it was only after that he offered me a position.'

'Out of the goodness of his heart, no doubt,' Murty said.

It was very late when Pat returned to Stockport. Danny and Irene were sitting in the living room with Murtybeg, a candelabra sparkling in the corner.

'That was a long Mass,' Danny said.

'Who said anything about Mass?'

'Murteen here was getting worried about you.'

'*Arra* what,' Pat said, 'it isn't worrying about me you should be. Don't you know I'm well able to take care of myself? It's just how I got this idea I might go over and see my uncle and aunt...'

Danny jumped up.

'Damn it, Pat, you should have told us you were going to do that.'

'Sure what's the harm,' Pat said, feigning innocence. 'They're family after all.'

Danny sat again.

'They're my parents first, and I'd still have preferred if you'd told me. One of us might have gone with you.'

'I didn't think you'd want to,' Pat said. 'After all, you haven't been across since they left.'

'That's none of your business,' Irene said sharply. 'How we conduct our lives over here is our affair. You're only over because you couldn't live in Mayo.'

Pat said nothing for a while. 'Maybe you're right, Irene,' he said at length. 'Maybe you're right.'

A few days later, Pat went out to discuss the wages with Kearney, and collect the wage sheets.

As he walked along the rails, he saw a Works locomotive at the end of the line, three wagons behind it, being filled with spoil. Further on, dozens of men were digging into the side of the cutting with picks, while others shovelled away the spoil. Already along the cutting side, there was a long concave space as the pick men dug into it. Above, more men were driving metal stakes into the ground above, hammering them deeply so as to start to separate the shale and rock.

Pat had seen this type of working before, though his father would never allow it in their own quarry in Carrigard. He knew the real trick was to let the pick men dig in as far as was safe, before the men on top brought down the 'lift'.

He saw Kearney, and both went into the office. For some time, they went through the figures. There were no errors. Kearney too, had been educated by Murty.

There was a roar from outside as the lift collapsed.

'Good work,' Kearney said. 'They were fast getting that lot down.'

There was a scream.

For one terrible moment, Pat and Kearney stared at each other. Then they rushed to the door.

Already, men were hacking at the edge of the collapse. Without waiting, Pat grabbed a shovel and went to join them.

He saw a rough pair of boots sticking out. The man was not deeply buried. Within seconds they had him out, and he started to breathe convulsively. There were deep gashes on his head though, and he was still unconscious.

'*Is this Mícheál O'Brogáin?*' Kearney asked.

'*It is,*' a man answered.

Already Kearney was taking a rough roll-call, using the wage sheets he and Pat had been checking only minutes before.

'*Aedán Ó'Cadhain,*' he shouted.

'*Anseo.*' Here.

'*Ciarán MacCoinín.*'

'*Anseo.*'

'*Seán Ó'hUigín.*'

'*Anseo.*'

'*Diarmuid Ó'Céirín.*'

There was no answer.

'*Diarmuid Ó'Céirín,*' Kearney shouted again, but the men were already back at the collapse, shovelling faster than before.

Pat walked along the entire line.

'*Diarmuid Ó'Céirín,*' he called, again and again.

Still no response. At length, another man came to him.

'*He was over here. Just here.*'

'*God protect him,*' Pat said.

Kearney continued through the list, one by one. Before he had finished, there were already two corpses lying where they had been dragged out.

'And we reckon there's three more as well as them,' Kearney said. 'If they haven't had their necks broken, they'll be well suffocated by this time.'

He left the wage sheet back into the office, then he and Pat joined the workers, shovelling hard.

After all the bodies had been dug out, they walked back the tracks together. Kearney was clearly upset.

'Don't say it to anyone,' he said, 'but I blame myself for this. This way of working, it's terrible dangerous. We should just be digging it straight, not trying to bring hundreds of tons down at once. Those men digging in under, they never had a chance.'

'So why do you do it then?' Pat asked.

Kearney stopped. 'What kind of *amadán* are you to ask me a question like that. You know well why it's done this way. Your cousin insists on it – may God damn him. It's faster, gets the job done quicker, and all for less wages. But you're right, you know. I should stand up to him...'

'What good would that do?' Pat asked. 'He'd only fire you, wouldn't he?'

'I'd guess you're right,' Kearney said.

They walked on.

'So what about the dead fellows?' Pat asked. 'Are they bringing them back to Stockport tonight?'

'Not a chance of that, I'm afraid,' Kearney said. 'They'll take them out to the far end of the cutting, that's what they'll do, bury them deep under the embankment. It's much easier, no questions asked that way. And yes, before you ask it, that's the way Danny wants it.'

'You're a tough fellow, Tim,' Pat said.

'Not tough enough,' Kearney answered, 'and I'll tell you this, Pat, any ganger has to be tough in this business. It's not as easy as back in Mayo. If we weren't tough, the railways would never get built.'

A few days later, Inspector Crawford visited.

'I understand you had a number of deaths on one of your sites, Mr. Ryan,' he said.

'It was an accident,' Danny replied. 'You know that.'

'Perhaps. You seem most anxious to convince me it was an accident though. Did you think I'd have thought otherwise?'

Danny felt himself tensing.

'Damn it, what else could it be?' he said. 'You don't think it was deliberate? Do you?'

'No,' Crawford replied. 'Though with the conditions those men work under, it was to be expected.'

'Expected?'

'At the very least, it shows a great lack of respect for human life.'

Irene interrupted.

'Is this the only reason you have come here, Inspector?' she asked. 'Criticising us for accidents?'

'No, no,' Crawford responded. 'In fact, it wasn't the reason at all. I just wanted to let you know that Mr. Brady has been arrested.'

Danny was quick on this one.

'Mr. Brady? Who is Mr. Brady?'

'Oh, I forgot' Crawford responded. 'You wouldn't know him, would you?'

'It's a common enough name in the west of Ireland,' Danny responded. 'I can't say I know any over here, but it's possible I've played with some as children.'

'I see,' Crawford said. 'Well, just in case you might know any over here, I'm referring to Gene Brady, a resident of Vauxhall in Liverpool.'

'Can't say I know him,' Danny said.

'In that case, it'd be of no interest to you to know that we have arrested him. He's definitely the leader of the Molly Maguire gang in Liverpool. We're questioning him. Inspector Lloyd is very good at that. And I can assure you, Mr. Ryan, we will trace the leader of the Molly Maguire gang in Manchester.'

He stood, and made to the door.

'But I forgot. None of that is of any interest to you. Is it?'

Chapter 30

Hereford Journal, May 1848:
State of Greater Manchester. Everything commercial and manufacturing is literally at a standstill here. Nothing is doing on 'Change, and great numbers of the mills and workshops are either wholly closed or working only for a short time. About ten thousand operatives are at present working short time, and nearly the same number are wholly out of employment. The operative population are not the principal sufferers; the shopkeepers and tradesmen generally are deeply distressed, and hundreds know not how to turn for relief.

If Danny had been concerned about Crawford's previous visits, he was now very badly shaken. Even Irene's attempts to calm him had little effect. Crawford would certainly not stop until he had his man. The only minor comfort was that Danny was not the key man he was seeking. That was Sheridan – he was the bodymaster in Manchester. Danny could only pray that Crawford would find him, and be happy to terminate the investigation at that.

But then another thought struck him. Even if Crawford got Sheridan first, he would question him intensely too. He would want to know more about the murders of both Eckersley and McManus. If Sheridan was facing the rope, he might try to make some sort of settlement with the police, to tell them all they wanted to know, in return for a commutation from a death sentence to life imprisonment.

Then what? Could Sheridan lead them to Danny?

He was becoming suspicious of everything. One day, he noticed a man across the road, watching his window. He pointed him out to Irene.

'Don't be silly, Danny, he's only waiting for the coach.'

As indeed he was.

But the following day, when Danny went into Manchester, he felt sure he was being followed. He could not say why he felt this, but could not shake off the sensation.

As he returned that evening, he saw a man standing outside his door.

It was a face he had not seen before. As he made to enter his door, the man stopped him.

'A message from Mr. Sheridan,' he whispered. 'Just keep your damned mouth shut. We all know the fate of informers.'

Danny said nothing, and the man left. He entered, but found he was sweating heavily. Again he thought – what if Crawford gets Sheridan? He had no doubt that the Molly Maguires had been watching the Ryan house for long enough to know that Crawford had visited him on a number of occasions. They could well assume that Danny was collaborating with Crawford on his investigations. Yes, if Sheridan was arrested, it would be a race between the Molly Maguire gang and the police to see who got him first.

He was more frightened than ever.

As the financial markets continued to collapse, the cash supply in both the banks and the large contractors tightened. Then the Newcastle Bank collapsed. Irene pointed out that the Royal Bank of Liverpool had re-opened its doors in December, but Danny knew this was only with government support. He found it impossible to convince himself that the Newcastle Bank would re-open, or that more banks would not collapse.

Also, he had not been able to hold pricing on the Anderson contracts, as Irene had been so confident of doing. What of his other contracts now?

At first he had hoped sackings would not be necessary. Further discussions with the Manchester & Salford Bank had convinced him they would. The banks would not lend further. As Winrow had explained to him, there were two problems. The first was that at present contract prices, it was impossible for Edwardes & Ryan to make a profit with so many men. The second was even simpler – the bank had no money.

The third, which Winrow did not know, was that Edwardes & Ryan was finishing the Brassey contract in May. Danny had agreed staged payments to the bank, month by month, until September, when the contract had originally been projected to finish. But the massive increase in labour that the early finish of the contract had forced upon him, meant that the loan had all been taken up, and there would be no means of repaying the rest of the loan after May. At least not from the Brassey contract, whatever about other contracts. But the Anderson contracts would barely be profitable, even after firing so many men.

Irene and Danny had requested Pat to come to Stockport in order to assist in sacking men, though they had not informed him of this.

Over dinner one evening, they discussed it with both Pat and Murtybeg.

'It can't have come as a surprise to you fellows,' Danny said. 'You've seen the figures yourself. Anyone with a bit of sense can see that the figures can't add up, especially since we're in danger of losing the Anderson contracts.'

'I didn't know that,' Murtybeg said.

'Not all of them,' he said. He handed Anderson's letter over to Murtybeg.

'All except Ancoats. We just got this a few weeks ago. Times are changing, Murteen. At Andersons' new rates, we're losing money on all of the other three contracts. It can't go on like this.'

'But…But if we don't finish them out, that means they can't complete the line.'

Irene snatched the letter angrily. 'Maybe they can't complete the line. Or maybe they can get someone cheaper to do it for them.'

'Who in God's name could be cheaper?' Pat asked.

'Anyone who employs less men,' Danny said. 'That's who.'

There was silence around the room, then Murtybeg started to drum his fingers on the table.

'So, we're over-manned, that's it. But by how many?'

'Maybe Pat could answer that,' Irene said.

Pat looked up in surprise. 'I could?'

'It's very simple,' Irene said, 'you know how much we're taking in per week on these contracts. You know how much is going out, and you certainly know the difference.'

Pat nodded, feeling rather gloomy. He took out a pencil and scribbled figures in a notebook. No-one spoke.

'The difference,' Pat said at length. 'Twenty pounds. At least. Could be twenty five.'

'And the wages?'

'Varies.'

'You can give us an average?'

'A shilling a day. Six shillings a week,' he said. 'Average.'

'So now, since you know the wages we pay, divide one into the other and what do we get?'

Pat thought for a few seconds.

'Hard to be exact. Eighty perhaps. Seventy five to eighty certainly.'

'So there's your answer,' Irene said. 'We have to sack eighty men. Now.'

'But we'd still be losing money.'

'Not if we increase the hours they're working.'

Pat cut into his beef. He dipped it in the gravy and started to eat.

'So what next?' he asked, speaking and eating at the same time.

'We've got to tell them,' Danny said.

'And who will do that?'

Danny put down his knife and fork. 'Look at it this way, Pat. We've all got hard jobs to do. I have to keep negotiating with the banks, I can't stop that. Murtybeg has taken over from McManus…'

'And the gangers?'

'They've work to do too. There still has to be someone for the calculations and accounts out there. You know that as well as I do.'

'So that leaves you, Irene,' Pat said.

'Yes, Pat, very funny you are too. You know what a rough lot they are. How many women have been abused out there already?'

Pat had not heard of any women being abused, but he did not say so.

'So ye've obviously been doing all the thinking,' he said. 'Ye know all the answers. Ye know what comes next.'

'Well, there's one simple answer,' Danny said. 'Just stop paying them. They'd leave soon enough. But Irene has convinced me that that's not the best way to do things. And in any case, we should have proper legal dismissals.'

Pat was observing the candle light refracting through the crystal chandeliers. He brought himself back to what Danny was saying.

'And how would you do that?'

'Give each of them a legal document – a few lines on a page would be enough. We can get some of the young clerks to assist you on that. All you've got to do is to decide the eighty names.'

'But how would I know?'

'Go out and ask the gangers to decide.'

'And after that? Sack them? What do they do then? Where would they go?'

'That's not really our problem,' Irene said, 'but if you want us to be generous, we could organise wagons back to Liverpool for them. Most of them came from the Workhouse, and they can take them back. And if they don't like it, they can send them back to Dublin. Or Mayo.'

No one mentioned the Brassey site. That was still running flat out. The sackings there were some weeks away yet.

Early next morning, Pat walked out to the cuttings. As he went through the streets of the town towards the line, it was raining. He pulled his hat down on his head, but the rain still dripped down along his nose.

He scrambled up onto the railway line, and started walking out along it. The rails glistened in the rain. The sleepers, which were all neatly cut and impregnated with creosote, glistened too, since no train had ever been over them except the work wagons. The crushed grey rock dripped.

He walked and walked. At last, he saw the lines of men working, picks rising and then shovelling the spoil away to the waiting wagons. They were all saturated. 'No money if you stop for rain', as Danny used to say, though Luke too told him the same whenever he spoke about his years on the railways.

Kearney looked up from where he had been measuring out the distance from the track to the rise in the side of the cutting. He glanced up.

'Pat?'

'Indeed.'

'What brings you out these parts this time of the week?'

'Danny thought I should have a word with you. A little bit of planning.'

'Is there something wrong?'

'I think so, Tim.'

Kearney ushered Pat into the tent. Rapidly, Pat explained the situation. He did not wish to give away too much about the overall financial situation of Edwardes & Ryan.

'So there's sackings,' Kearney said, twisting his fingers around a pencil. 'Isn't that it, Pat?'

'That's it,' Pat said. 'But not necessarily everyone.'

'How many are you looking for?'

'Twenty five off this site.'

'Twenty five!'

'That's the number. Can we do it? Or sorry, to put it another way, we have to do it.'

Kearney had been looking into space, counting on his fingers. 'Well, we've about a hundred and twenty men here. If you take twenty five out, we'll still have ninety five left. What do you propose to do with them?'

'We'd have to work them twelve hours a day,' Pat said. 'That way, we might be able to finish faster, and get paid the sooner. I wish we could do that with all of them, but we can't.

'Well, I'll say this,' Kearney said. 'It's not your fault, you don't control the banks. Nor the railway companies for that matter.'

'I'm not too sure I'd wish to either,' Pat said.

'But one way or another, it's pretty savage. But we have to do it, don't we?'

'That's it,' Pat said.

'I'm just thinking though,' Kearney said. 'Perhaps we'd be able to get rid of the weaker ones, and the trouble-makers. Then we keep only the men we want to keep.'

'Which ones though?' Pat asked.

'I thought you were going to ask me that,' Kearney said. 'And you know the answer as well as I do. The Madden huts, both of them. That'd do to start.'

He looked around at Pat, who was a little puzzled.

'They're the real trouble-makers,' Kearney said. 'And their women? They're even worse.'

'Worse?' Pat asked.

'Well, you should know. You've met them.'

'Have I?'

'Yes, Pat, you have. I might even say you're a trouble-maker yourself, but you're too good a friend to say that to.'

'Me? A trouble-maker?'

'That time you visited their huts, and talked to the Madden woman. *Síle* Madden. It was all over the site on the Monday. We'd real problems getting them back to work after that. Once you start showing concern, they're out of control. There's only one way to keep these bastards working. Be tough. Never let up.'

Pat stayed on with Kearney, going through pages of names and wage rates. The two Madden families together came to eleven, including four working men. More were selected by Kearney as either trouble-makers, or too weak to work.

It was already dark. It was agreed that Kearney would meet Pat back at Head Office the following morning, where he and Pat could discuss their plans with Danny. Then the foremen from the other sites would have to be called in.

For three days, the planning continued. One by one, the gangers came in, and discussed who was to be released. All of this was conducted in the greatest secrecy.

On the Saturday morning, Pat walked back out to Kearney's site. After another discussion, they started walking along the line of workers, distributing the notices of sacking. At first, there was little reaction. As Kearney had already pointed out, none of them could read, and certainly not in English. At last, he snatched one of the pages from one of the men and read it out in English. A few of the men understood.

Within seconds Kearney and Pat were surrounded by angry men, jostling them. Then Kearney jumped up onto a barrel, shouting.

'*And there's fifty more where these came from,*' he said. '*And if you want them all to be given out here, this is the way to do it. So I'm warning all the rest of ye, get back to work.*'

A voice came from the back of the crowd.

'*And what are we supposed to do now?*'

'*For those of ye leaving, get your things together,*' Kearney said. '*We have places booked from* Stockport *to Liverpool.*'

'*Why* Liverpool?'

'*The* Stockport *Workhouse won't take ye.*'

'*The* Liverpool *Workhouse won't take us either.*'

'*Well, they'll know what to do with ye,*' Kearney said.

Yes, Pat thought, send you all back to County Mayo. And God help you there.

The next day, he returned to the site, accompanied by the constables. The men were paid off for the week, including those who had been sacked.

One of them held his wages out for all to see. '*Nine shillings. Not much to bring back to Mayo.*'

'*If ye spent the rest, it's not our concern,*' Kearney said.

On the Monday, Pat accompanied Murtybeg, Lavan and Kearney to Stockport Station.

As they walked through the streets, Pat noticed women begging.

'*Tá an ocras orainn,*' one woman said to him. The hunger is on us.

Pat gave her a farthing. She said nothing.

Before they reached the station, they had passed many such women.

'Why are there so many women?' Pat asked.

'Because their men are abandoning them, that's why,' Murtybeg said.

When they got to the station, they walked across to the freight yards. There was a crowd of hundreds of men, women and children, most carrying packs or other possessions. The rain had eased, and as the day started to warm, steam was rising from the crowd.

At last the wagons were shunted in, and the men began to board, taking their packs and children from their wives and then pulling the women up last of all.

'At least the rain is cleared,' Pat said.

'Indeed,' Murtybeg said, 'and they might even be dry by the time they get to Lime Street Station.'

Before the end of the loading, a woman broke away from the crowd and ran across to the two men. She spat in Pat's face.

'*And that's for you, you bastard. You were the one was going to talk to your damned cousin and do great things for us.*'

She screamed again, as Murtybeg and Lavan pulled her away.

'*You're no better than the rest of them, you filthy son-of-a-bitch.*'

Pat felt he was being ground to dust. The sackings had taken a toll on him. He was sickened by Danny's methods, but now he was on Danny's side, whether he liked it or not. His own work meant that people were being sent back to Ireland – County Mayo. If they got that far.

But Danny too was under stress.

The financial markets dropped further. Pat would not have noticed it, but Murtybeg mentioned it to him. That night, Danny said nothing over dinner.

It had been a warm day. Afterwards, Pat and Murtybeg stood together outside the house, smoking their pipes.

'He's taking it badly, I'd say,' Murtybeg said.

'And how,' Pat responded.

'God knows, the sackings were bad enough, but Danny was hoping things could only get better from here. And now this. The banks, the railways, they're all dropping. Things are going to get an awful lot worse, Pat, before they get better. And I'm not sure that Edwardes & Ryan can take it.'

The sun was setting in the North West. Pat could hear the screech of a train whistle from the tracks.

'I'm not sure Danny can either,' he said. 'But it surely can't be that bad.'

'Oh, I don't know,' Murtybeg said, 'I'm not a money man, I don't understand all these things. But from what I read in the Guardian, they're saying it's the worst crash ever.'

'I didn't know you read the Guardian.'

'I wouldn't, but Danny has it in every day. The Times too. First thing in the morning, last thing at night, he sees how the markets are, what the banks are doing, how the railway shares are. I think he's obsessed. And I'll tell you something else, Pat, that woman of his gives him damned little support. Danny's an ambitious man, I don't need to tell you that, but between the banks, the markets and Irene, he's being torn asunder.'

The sackings eased the pressure on Edwardes & Ryan, but only for a few weeks. More railway contracts were being suspended all around them, and those that remained tightened in price. As time passed, Danny became more desperate.

He thought of Irene's assumption that the increasing pressure would bankrupt their competitors first. In certain ways she had been right, Baxendales had proved that, but it was not enough. He had been able to convince himself that Irene was right at first, but as the squeeze went on, he found himself less and less able to do so.

He thought of her utter callousness. Surely there were other ways out. He would have liked to discuss it further with her, but by now he no longer wanted to know whether she had any answers, nor what those answers might be.

There was also the question of their forthcoming wedding, even if it was still a long way off. Now the date had been agreed. Yes, the business needed her, but did he? He could walk away from it all, just tell her it was over. Or tell her to leave. That would result in one hell of a row. And what then?

She would leave the business, that's what, and take it all with her. Even without taking the papers, Irene, he was certain, had it all in her head. She knew the contractors, she knew the competitors, the rates charged and all the details about the contracts still running. What was worse, she might take his top men too. And what could she do with them? Roughneen, Kearney and Lavan, the best in the business. Steele too. Yes, Irene could set up as a competitor, and bankrupt Edwardes & Ryan all on her own.

What then? It was not as if he was any less tough than he had been in 1846. It was only that Irene was tougher, and he was going to marry her?

A few days later he received a letter from the Manchester & Salford Bank. In it, Winrow explained that it had come to their notice that the Edwardes & Ryan contract on the North Staffordshire Railway was nearly finished. Danny wondered how he could have known that, but then remembered being told that the bank was acting for the North Staffordshire on a share issue. But one way or another, Winrow was aware of the contract finishing, and pointed out that, as per agreement, the full loan had to be repaid within two weeks. He requested confirmation that this would be done.

Just as he was considering the implications of this, the maid knocked on his door.

'A Mr. Crawford to see you,' she said.

Danny looked at her in horror.

'Show him in,' he said at last.

Crawford shook his hand.

'You seem in a bad way, Mr. Ryan,' he said. 'Perhaps I should come back at a more appropriate time?'

'That's fine, Inspector,' Danny said. 'I've just had a rather bad shock. Nothing to do with you.'

'A personal bereavement?'

'Something like that.' He waved Crawford to a chair. 'I don't suppose you're going to bring me good news, are you?'

Crawford shook his head. 'I'm afraid not, Mr. Ryan. There's been another murder.'

'Another!'

'A Mr. Worsley. He was a ganger with Baxendales on the site beside yours, where Mr. McManus was killed.'

'Oh God...'

'We've only just started the investigation, Mr. Ryan. We can only conclude that it was done in revenge for Mr. McManus' death. We think it must have been a professional killing. He was shot at close range by a shotgun, fair tore him asunder. Not only that, whoever it was had taken trouble to trace him, since, as you know, Baxendales are no longer working on the site beside yours.'

'Where was he so?'

'He was working on the Manchester South Junction Railway, just beside your site in Ancoats. Little Ireland, as we say. It seems Mr. Worsley was being watched for some time.'

'This is unbelievable,' Danny said.

'Only too believable, I would say, Mr. Ryan. We know Mr. McManus was a member of the Molly Maguire gang. We know too, that they always exact their revenge. The question, once again, is – who is the bodymaster in the Manchester area?'

'You had been questioning someone on that,' Danny said, careful not to mention Brady's name.

'We have indeed, Mr. Ryan. We've been making excellent progress too. Inspector Lloyd in Liverpool has passed information to our Manchester branch. We hope to make an arrest soon, and hang the bastard.'

For many days Danny turned it over in his head.

Could he buy off Crawford by means of fingering Sheridan? No. That was far too dangerous. The threat from the Molly Maguire gang had terrified him.

But what if the police arrested Sheridan anyhow? How could he prove he was not involved? Would they suspect him, and kill him anyhow? Would Sheridan talk? Would Brady? Would Crawford arrest him on a hanging charge?

Could Irene save him? Did he want that? To admit that she was, after all, the strongest.

He was surprised to find that he was becoming more fretful about firing Irish navvies. For the first time ever, he felt he himself was vulnerable. He was facing death, as so many in West Mayo were facing it. Would he be forgotten, like so many thousands of them were? Or just reviled?

When would Winrow realise that Edwardes & Ryan had finished the Brassey contract? Did they have enough cash to repay the loans? Day after day, he went through accounts, until the figures swam in his eyes.

Then he would start thinking again. His thoughts were going around and around, faster and faster.

Anderson. Brassey. Winrow. Would they bankrupt him?

His father and mother. Did they despise him now?

The threat from the Molly Maguire gang. The threat of a trial on a hanging offence.

Brady. Sheridan. Crawford. Who would get him first?

One evening, he left the house. He went by back streets around the south of Stockport, and strode away from the town until he came to railway tracks. He walked along between the tracks, still heading south.

It was the Manchester & Birmingham line. This stretch was said to be one of the longest straights in England, and when the train's headlight appeared it was still miles distant, running along the straight at full steam with nothing to slow it.

He stood to the side, watching the distant light, transfixed by it. For three minutes, he waited, until the train was only seconds away. Then he stood out between the rails.

He heard the high pitched screech of steel on steel, then all was black.

Chapter 31

Brooklyn Eagle, New York, June 1848:
If our Irish fellow citizens were to be controlled by priests, and obey conduct dictated from the pulpit, the naturalisation law would be changed in a year, and no man would ever cast a vote who was not born in this country. We have seen murder preached by a minister of God in Ireland within a year, not in such bold terms, but in equivalent language. We have seen humane men shot in open day for some slight supposed wrong, and a neighbourhood leagued to protect the offender. Such things cannot be and will not be unavenged.

Luke was intrigued by New York's shipping. He knew London was larger, and Liverpool much larger, but the activity inside New York's harbour fascinated him. Manhattan, surrounded by the shorelines of New Jersey, Staten Island and Brooklyn created a harbour far vaster than the Pool of London, and comparable even to the anchorages on the Mersey Estuary. These New York place names were familiar to him from stories in emigrant's letters, through all the extended family of the Ryans' and the many people they knew around Carrigard, Kilduff and the Mountain. Even in Knockanure Workhouse, people knew of Staten and Brooklyn.

When they arrived at the Box Street Lumber Terminal in Brooklyn, there was another day of rough work sorting out the logs, and Conlon still expected Luke and Jack to help out with measurements and calculations when called upon.

Next day, they went to the pier, and walked to the end to the pay office.

'United States dollars,' Jack said, as he came out, waving a roll of notes.

'Yes,' said Luke, 'I thought the day would never come.'

They slept on one of the rafts that night. They rose early next day, shook hands with Conlon, left the lumber terminal, and asked their way along the pier until they found a ferry to Manhattan.

They disembarked, and asked directions to Five Points. Luke noticed that the man they asked had looked strangely at them, but he thought no more of it. They followed the directions, then asked again, and again.

It was still early. Sometimes they saw men walking towards the terminal.

Further on they saw single women or groups of women, dressed in black, some with white pinafores, walking towards the city.

'It's a long way,' Luke said.

'And I hope we get there soon,' Jack said. 'These packs are getting mighty heavy.'

Luke was uneasy.

'This territory is getting mighty rough,' he said. 'Better watch your pack, or it won't be its weight you'll be worrying about.'

'*Arra*, don't worry. Two strong lads like ourselves would scare the devil out of any of them.'

'Watch your pockets too, that's all I'm saying.'

There were fewer working men or women now. Those they met wore ragged clothes, and some were very thin. A group of lousy children played at a street corner, but their play was sluggish and limp.

There was garbage everywhere, and the stink of shit. Four dogs were scavenging a heap of rubbish and waste food, growling at each other. They heard the squealing of pigs.

'A lot of four legged bacon in there, I'd say,' Jack said.

'Two legged too, I'd say.'

On a street corner, two girls eyed them.

'They don't seem to have too much to do,' Luke said.

One of them lifted her skirt above her knees.

'I'm sure they would if we asked them,' Jack said. 'I wonder how much they charge.'

'Not much from the look of them. And with lice like that, it's I who'd need the paying.'

They passed an alleyway, hardly wide enough to take a man walking. At the end, there was more squealing of pigs.

'I wonder how they get them fellows out.' Jack asked.

'A hell of a lot of pushing, that's what I'd say,' Luke said.

They passed a bar. Four men stood outside. Luke asked directions, but there was no answer.

'Damned Irish,' one snarled. 'Over to steal our jobs.'

A big man, Luke reckoned, well built at the shoulders too. He thought of the fight in Quebec. No point in trying that again. They were outnumbered twice over.

He pretended not to have heard and walked on.

They reached Five Points.

'I can see why it's called Five Points,' Jack said. 'The question is – which point do we take?'

'Hold on a moment,' Luke said. 'Do you see the name of that street?'

'Orange Street. What of it?'

'I'm just doing a bit of hard remembering now,' Luke said. 'What was the name of the street that *Conaire* said to me, the time we were still on the ocean?'

'How would I know? Orange Street, you're going to say.'

'Come on,' Luke said, picking up his pack. 'Can't be far now.'

He was more anxious now. Whatever he had expected of Five Points, it was not this. All he could see around him were derelict tenements. This was not what America was supposed to be. Once again, he recognised Irish voices, though that was not surprising. Still, the poverty was extreme. It brought to mind the Irish tenements of Liverpool along Scotland Road. Could it be that bad?

Could it be worse?

There was one difference though. Black people. He had never seen so many before. Yes, he had seen them in Liverpool. But that was normal in Liverpool, once a major centre of the slave trade. But New York?

Jack had been asking directions for Costello's bar. Luke followed, saying nothing. At length, they stood outside Costello's.

'Doesn't look great, does it?' Jack said.

'I wouldn't be fooled by that,' Luke said. 'I'll wager it's a damned good business for the Costellos, and we know *Conaire*, don't we? Come on, let's go in.'

They walked into a thick haze of tobacco. The bar was crowded, and Luke noticed the Irish voices at once. Also, all the faces were white, and, unlike the street outside, there were no exceptions. Jack sat at a table with their packs while Luke went to the bar. He ordered two beers. When they were delivered and paid for, he asked for John Costello.

'Who's asking,' the barman asked.

'Luke Ryan's the name. Mr. Costello wouldn't know me yet. I'm a good friend of his brother *Conaire* though.'

The barman looked at him in surprise.

'Hold on a moment,' he said. Luke returned to the table.

A man came, and sat with them. He was well-built, with grey, wiry hair. His clothes were spattered, trousers held up with a broad well-worn belt.

'So which of you knows *Conaire*?'

'We both do,' Luke said.

'So you know *Torán*?'

'Well, no...' Luke said. 'I met him on the Atlantic back in July, coming over to Quebec.'

He was beginning to feel something was amiss. One thing was certain, *Conaire* had not arrived in New York before them.

'Quebec,' the man exclaimed. 'So he's left Mayo.'

'That's right,' said Luke. 'The same ship that I travelled on. Left Liverpool back in July.'

'Before the evictions?'

'What evictions?' Luke asked. The man groaned.

'I can see this is going to take time,' he said. He signalled to the barman who nodded. 'But first, let's sort ourselves out. I'm John Costello...'

'Luke Ryan,' Luke said, 'and this is Jack Kilgallon.'

'Both from Mayo then?' Costello asked.

'Of course. I'm Kilduff myself, over the east side. Jack is from Turlough, just beside Castlebar.'

The barman had arrived with another beer. Costello grasped it.

'*Sláinte mhaith*. To your very best health. And may ye do well in America.'

They clinked glasses. Costello took a long draught, and wiped his lips.

'Right,' he said, 'let's start again. You left Mayo in July.'

'He did,' Jack said pointing to Luke. 'I'd been over in Quebec from long before.'

'Let me give you the story so,' Luke said. 'I met *Conaire* on the ship. We were about half way across when we met. He told me he was trying to find his brother who ran a bar in New York. As it happened, I was planning to link up with friends I have working on the railways out at Pennsylvania. I had thought of going to Pennsylvania by New York, so we thought we'd go together.'

'There's just one thing I don't understand though,' Costello said. 'Why did I never hear of any of this?'

'Had they not written to you?' Luke said.

'Now, what do you think,' Costello answered. 'Do you think anyone in *Torán* could write? Still, you'd have thought he'd get someone else to write for him.'

'I think he was intending on that after he got to Canada, perhaps after we left the forests. But then we lost him.'

'Lost him?'

'We were working in the forests, up the Gatineau from Montreal. They separated us – *Conaire* was put working loading and unloading on the river dock, but Jack and I were sent up to the forest as teamsters.'

'Teamsters?'

'Yes,' Luke said, 'driving teams of horses, pulling the logs out of the forest. One time we had to go down to the dock, and met up with *Conaire*, but when we went down the last time as we were leaving, he wasn't there.'

'Where had he gone?'

'God only knows,' Luke said. 'We asked around but no one knew a thing.'

'So when did ye leave the forests?'

'In April.'

Costello ordered three more beers.

'There's little chance we'll see him so,' he said. 'If he isn't here, and we've no letter, he's dead.'

'Perhaps,' Luke said. 'But when I wrote home first, *Conaire* couldn't pay his own postage, so I asked my people to send a note to a Mr. *Tomás Ó Coisteala* in *Torán*, through the Parish Priest in Belmullet, to say that he was alive and well.'

'When was that?' Costello asked.

'When we were yet in Quebec. He may have intended that your family would write direct to you when they heard of it.'

'Sure how could they do that when they couldn't write, and they wouldn't have the money for a stamp anyhow. Or maybe they were just evicted first, and the letter from your people never arrived.'

'I don't know,' Luke said. 'But I never heard of him having any letter sent direct to you, though I know he had your address – he showed it to me once. I reckon he would have asked me to write the letter for him, if there was to be a letter. But then we lost track of him, so there was nothing sent that I ever heard of. Letter or no letter though, he was intending to come to New York, I know that for certain.'

'Well, he's not here, and we don't know where he is. Do we?'

'We don't,' Luke said, 'but one thing I would like to know – what's this you say about evictions.'

'You haven't heard then?' Costello said. 'The Walshe Evictions, just before Christmas. Cleared the lot out, including all my family and friends, the bastard. Pretty well all dead now, from what I can gather. Two lads turned up here with my sister to tell us the story. She was the only one left. They'd lived in Ballina Workhouse for the rest of the winter. They saw it all. They saw what they did to the people, and the way they let them freeze and die on the sand. Pure murder it was, my own family too. I'll never forgive it.'

'And why should you?' Jack said. 'It's a bad story, and we hear them often enough.'

'Well, enough of that,' Costello said. 'It wasn't to hear stories like that that you came here.'

'No,' Jack said. 'We came here in the hopes of finding *Conaire*, or at least hearing he was coming. But now we know he isn't here.'

'So what will ye do now?' Costello asked.

'Find work...' Luke answered.

'Not in this hell hole, you won't,' Costello said. 'Or should I say, ye'll find work right enough, but it'll pay little, and the rookeries ye'll live in would make sure life's not worth living. Not that ye'd last long anyhow. There's fever enough to kill any man, the longer he stays.'

Jack started to pick up his pack. 'Well, we'll just be moving so.'

'Hold a while, why don't ye? Ye can settle down here for a few days 'till you find work elsewhere. We'll fit ye in some way.'

'But, how much...?' Luke started to say.

'Look, if ye're friends of *Conaire*, I'd like to hear more about him. Ye can share a room for a day or two, and work the bar at nights if ye want. That way, we'll all be happy.'

'Fair enough,' Jack said.

That evening, they both slept in an upstairs store-room above Costello's bar. The beds were squeezed tightly, with bunks running four high on one wall. Under the bunks of the beds, there were chamber pots, some empty, some full.

Three children sat on one bunk, their mother alongside them. She was very thin.

An old man lay on one lower bunk, breathing harshly. Luke walked past, sniffing close. Above the stink of human sweat and shit, it was difficult to pick anything up. He leant closer to him.

'Checking for fever, are you?' Jack said.

'You're quick,' Luke said. 'He's fine though. Old age only, that's all that's wrong with him.'

'There mightn't be fever here right now,' Jack said, 'but I reckon if we hang around long enough, there will be. It's like Costello says, we might not live long if we stay.'

The next morning, Luke requested a pen and ink from Costello, and wrote to Farrelly in Harrisburg, requesting information on the railway building there. He gave the address at Costello's in Orange Street.

He explained his plans to Costello, and it was agreed that they might stay in the room until a reply had been received. They decided to find work.

'And where better than the lumber terminal,' Jack said.

Before they went, Luke borrowed a needle and thread from Costello, and stitched his trouser pocket with his dollars inside. Jack looked on in surprise. Then he did the same.

They left the bar.

More dogs and more pigs. And always the fetid smell of garbage, shit and piss. It was already warm.

Many of the hovels they passed were mere wooden structures built up against the walls of the squalid tenements. On street corners they saw beggars, mostly young girls, some as young as five, Luke reckoned, though even this was hard to determine given their stunted growth.

He noticed too that the prostitutes did not stand on the same corners as the beggars. He found now that he could identify prostitutes from the other women, though he could not work out why this would be so since there was little difference in their appearance.

At last they left Five Points and the squalid tenements around it.

'And thank God for that,' Jack said. 'All we've got to do now is find the ferry.'

They walked, trying to follow the route they had come by.

At last they found the piers. Luke saw a post office, and sent the letter to Farrelly.

They went to one ferry, but it was larger than the one they had taken the previous day. Jack went over to ask a sailor, and came back.

'He doesn't know about any lumber terminals.'

Nor did anyone else. They walked along until they saw another ferry.

'That looks a little more like it,' Jack said.

It was three cents for the crossing. They came to the terminal, but it seemed too quiet. Men were working, but less than the previous day.

A line of men stretched back from the gate. Jack went to the end while Luke stayed at the wharf, watching.

Jack came back. 'They're saying there's no new rafts in, only the one they're unloading there, and they don't know when another is coming.'

'So why are they waiting?'

'They're hoping one'll be along shortly. When there is, the gangers come out and chose who they want to work. One way or another, we're too late for today – they started lining up hours ago.'

They returned to the ferry.

'Well, that didn't take long,' Luke said, 'and if they're only choosing men by the day, how do we get to be chosen? Why would they take us above any others?'

They returned to the bar.

'Ye're back early,' Costello said.

'We tried the lumber terminals,' Jack said. 'Thought we could get work there easy enough. No chance.'

'Don't worry. Ye'll have work soon enough. '

They worked that evening in the bar, sometimes serving customers, but more often washing up. The bar intrigued Luke. As the evening wore on it became more and more crowded.

Sometimes they worked alongside Costello's sister, Catherine. Luke was still curious about the *Torán* evictions, but he felt it was not the time to ask. Catherine certainly knew all about it, but why distress her asking about things she would prefer to forget. Losing *Conaire* was bad enough.

*

They were still concerned about carrying cash. They spoke to Costello about it.

'Ye'll need a bank,' he told them. 'Many of them don't deal with the Irish, but I reckon ye look respectable enough. It'd be best to talk to the Irish Emigrants Society first, they'll give you the best advice on the matter. There's some talk of them setting up a bank for the Irish, but I don't know that they've done it.'

They followed Costello's instruction to Chambers Street, less than half a mile from Costello's bar. There was a line of men and women inside the door, many poorly dressed. They waited in line for an hour, at last being directed to a man at a table.

'You're busy enough today,' Luke commented.

'We certainly are. There's many looking for lodgings, and those that have found them have been shocked at the conditions of them, and are trying to find somewhere else. Happens all the time. And then there are the ones that have been robbed, lost everything. Sometimes we give them a few cents to help them on their way. I'd say from the look of ye though, ye'd not be having that kind of problem.'

'We might be close enough to it,' Jack said. 'We're carrying our wages, don't want to lose them. We're looking for a bank. Heard you might have one.'

'Not yet,' the man replied. 'We're close enough to setting one up. Are you thinking of sending money home, is that it?'

'That, and having somewhere to keep our money that would be safe.'

The man took out a scrap of paper.

'This is where you'll go so,' he said. 'The Chemical Bank is where we send everyone.'

'A strange name,' Luke commented.

'It is, isn't it? They're reliable though, they won't run off with your money.'

He scribbled the address and gave it to Jack.

'It's on Broadway, near Ann Street. Not far to walk.'

They left.

'Might as well do it at once, so.' Luke said.

They found the Chemical Bank, where Luke explained what they needed.

'Are you looking for a draft for Ireland?' a clerk asked them.

'Not yet,' Luke answered. 'We're only looking for a secure place for our money for now.'

Within a few minutes, the business was done.

That evening, Luke was serving behind the bar with Catherine.

'Have you been here long?' he asked.

'Three months near enough,' she said.

'Direct from Ireland then?'

'Indeed. An early crossing.'

'A bad crossing, was it?' Luke asked.

'The crossing wasn't so bad' she answered. 'The food wasn't the kind you'd want to eat, but there was food, and that was more than we had in *Torán*.'

He flinched. *Torán*! Better not press her on that.

He waited, as she served beer. When she returned, she grasped his hand. *'You've heard of Torán then?'* she asked, speaking in Irish.

'Yes,' Luke said, *'didn't Conaire tell me enough of it, and I crossing the ocean with him.'*

'Yes,' she said, *'but he never knew what happened after.'*

'I know,' Luke replied. *'John told me of that.'* He decided this time to press on. *'But only the fact of it happening, none of what really happened.'*

She said nothing.

'It's all right' he said. *'There's no need to talk.'*

'But there is,' she said. *'If I don't tell you, who will I tell? And if I don't tell anyone, the world will forget it. Yes, it was a bitter time. Christmas-time too. We all thought Mr. Walshe – a Catholic – would never evict us. What fools we were to even think it. They came with their soldiers and guns and their crowbar brigade, and destroyed every cabin in Torán. Mullach Rua and Clochán too. All the animals were taken for rent. Then they just went off and left us there. Some of the people tried to scramble back under what was left of the cabins, but it was desperate cold and they died. Others dug into the sand dunes along the Mullet and the Great Ocean, they thought it was warmer, God help them. And I – to my eternal shame – I left Torán. I walked to Belmullet and found the hotel there where they were throwing out scraps for the starving. From there I walked to Ballina, fifty miles, every single mile of it. Why they let me into the Workhouse, I'll never know, but they did. But I knew I had a brother in America. I'd repeated the name so many times over in my sleep, how could I forget it? By February, I knew there was no hope in Torán, that there would be no people alive. So what was there left but to go to America? So I walked to Killala, found an early ship, but I had no money, so I found a sailor and became a ship's wife, and...'*

'Oh, God...'

'Think nothing of it,' she said. *'It was the price I had to pay to leave Ireland. And in the end I found John, didn't I? Not like most, who lost their families in the wide open spaces of America.'*

They were down early for breakfast.

'Letter for you, Luke.'

He saw the postmark. 'My God, that was quick.' He slit the envelope and sat at a bar table.

Mr. Luke Ryan   Harrisburg, 5 June
Costello's Bar   Orange St.
                                                         Five Points
                                                  City of New York

Dear Luke,

We received your letter, and it was well you wrote to us, since matters here
have changed greatly since I last wrote to you.

I must tell you that rail building is finishing in this place. It appears from
what we hear that there has been a crash in the money markets, and this has
carried through to the rail companies, who have little money to spend on
further rail building. Your letter therefore arrived only just in time, since we
will be leaving this site in one week.

We are now going to a township called Lackan, which is in Pennsylvania,
convenient to Wilkes Barre and Scranton. I understand they supply the
anthracite market in New York from there. We will therefore travel to Lackan
to work in the mines. We hope to be working as contract miners, the same as
we worked on the railways in England and God knows, we made good money
there. Mikey Jordan, Matt McGlinn and some other Kilduff men will travel
with me. It might seem strange to you to have railroad workers going to work
in mines, but from what I understand, much of the work will be shovelling
anthracite onto wagons, and we're all well used to shovelling.

My suggestion therefore to you would be to join us in Lackan. Should
you wish to remain in New York though, you will find work difficult to get at
this time. You might find a job at the anthracite terminals either in New Jersey
or New York. I know the Morris Canal has an anthracite terminal at Jersey
City. Many other men we have met have worked there, though I understand
the wages are low. In this way though, you may well be able to save enough
to travel to Lackan, where we should be well settled by then. I hope this is not
all disappointing for you, but perhaps my idea will help.

From your good friend,

Martin Farrelly

P.S. I will write the moment we arrive in Lackan.

Luke was concerned by the reference to Matt McGlinn. They had been old
friends in Carrigard, and worked together along the railways in England,
but when McGlinn had come to him, looking to work on the Famine Relief
Roads, Luke had not been allowed to select him. He remembered the despair
in McGlinn's eyes that day. Would they be able to work together? The famine
still followed him.

He showed the letter to Costello.

'It might not be too bad an idea either, working the anthracite docks,'

Costello said. 'They'll certainly pay more than I'm able to pay you, though they won't give you board and lodging.'

Yes, Luke thought, but it will get us out of Five Points.

'So what's he saying in the letter?' Jack asked.

'They're going working in the mines. They'll be contract miners there.'

'What does that mean?' Jack asked.

'It means they work for themselves as a gang. Same as we did in England. Contract by the ton, not just being paid by the day.'

'Sounds like piecework. Like the Relief Works in Mayo?'

'*Arra*, no,' Luke said. 'That was a different business. From what Martin says, this is better. If you're strong you'll have no difficulty with that. It's like on the railways. A good gang can earn far more than anyone else. We were damned near the best paid on the English railways then, working hard for long hours, I'll tell you, but no complaints from us. And from all I see here, it's the same in the mines.'

'I hope you're right,' Jack said. 'It's piecework all the same. A brutal way of using fellows to get the greatest number of tons for the least amount of dollars. That's all it is. You'll see.'

'We'll both see.'

'Who said I was coming?'

'You're not?'

'And have the mining bosses abuse me like that? No way.'

'Well, I'm going,' Luke said.

'So when will you leave?'

'I'll have to wait 'till I hear from Lackan first. After that, it'll be as soon as Winnie arrives.'

Chapter 32

Dublin Evening Post, June 1848:
New York besieged. Since Saturday morning, the lower part
of the city – say from the Battery, through West Washington
and Greenwich Streets, up as far as Washington Market –
has been kept in constant motion. Steamboats, lighters,
periaugers, scows, clamboats and nondescript water-witches
of every sort, have arrived almost hourly from quarantine,
loaded with almost entire villages of men, women, and
children, some of the larger steamers having emigrants
packed in every part like bales of cotton on a Mississippi
cotton-boat.

Next day, New York was hot and humid. Luke and Jack walked over to
Cortland Street and found a coal terminal.

'Christ, I've never seen so much coal in my life,' Jack said. 'There's any
amount of shovelling here!'

'And any amount of men to shovel it too. Must be a hundred here
waiting?'

'And none of them looks as if they've eaten for a long time.'

As they watched, the gate was opened, and the men lined back against
an outside wall. Luke and Jack tried to join it but were quickly elbowed to
the far end.

'Damned bastards,' one man shouted at them. 'Think you can come here
and take our jobs. It's scum like you who are stealing the food from our
mouths.'

Neither Luke nor Jack responded. They had noticed the Irish accent
though. Was this what Irish men thought of their own?

One man came out of the terminal, accompanied by two men with
sticks. He walked the line, pointing at each man required. They never got as
far as the end of the line.

Luke felt sickened. Now he had been through a selection, he knew what it
felt like. At least he could understand McGlinn better, when they finally met.

'What now?'

'Now we find the terminal on the Jersey side,' Luke said.

Soon they were standing in an empty anthracite lighter, crossing the Hudson River. They found the anthracite terminal. There was no line of men waiting for selection. They were sent to the ganger and asked for work. Luke was rather surprised when they were both given shovels, and told to get on with it.

They joined a group of men and started shovelling. After a while, Jack stopped, wiping his brow.

'This is hard work,' he gasped. 'I thought we knew what work was up the Gatineau. I don't know how long my arms will take this.'

'*Arra*, pay it no mind,' Luke said. 'You'll strengthen up quick enough. I'm well used to this kind of work, shovelling rock and dirt on the railways. There's a trick in it, you know. Your muscles will tell you how, and once you understand what they're telling you, there won't be much pain.'

As they discovered, the anthracite terminal was a mixed kind of place. All kinds of immigrants were there, many hardly able to speak English. Luke heard many 'Dutch' speaking Germans. Other immigrants too from all over Europe – Scottish, Swedish, Danish, French, Russian and Hungarian.

But the Irish outnumbered all the rest by far.

Half way through the morning, they stopped for a break. Hot tea and bread. Luke realised three men across from him were speaking in Irish. He listened closely. West of Ireland definitely. He walked over.

'*Are ye long working here?*' he asked.

'*Long enough,*' one of the men replied. '*A year if it's a day.*'

'*Where are ye from then?*'

'*Tourmakeady and around.*'

'*Down by the Partry Mountains.*'

'*That's it, right enough.*'

'*Are things so bad there?*' Luke asked.

'*Worse than bad. The fever was murdering us last year. We were lucky enough to get out of Ballybanane. Sure there'll be none of it left if it goes on like that. That's where my father and mother live, four children too when I left. No word from them since, only silence. The same with Bornahowna, that's where Éamonn and Seán are from. Silence there too. Not a word. Three families. Flanagans, Derrigs, and Shaughnessys. What's left of any of them? No one knows.*'

'*Can they write?*'

'*Write? Not a chance. They get the priest to do the writing, when he's passing through.*'

Back shovelling coal. Luke was working beside one of the Tourmakeady men.

'One thing I don't understand is how easy it was to get working here.'

'Did you think you wouldn't?'

'We tried the other side. There were dozens of men ahead of us, and the gangers were only selecting some. They never got down as far as us.'

The man stopped shovelling for a moment, and leaned on his shovel.

'Well there's two reasons for that. First of all, they're all from Five Points, and they're all far too lazy to come over this side.'

'They weren't as lazy as that.' Luke said. 'Standing outside in the cold that early was hardly easy.'

'Sure, but what kind of condition were they in? And there's another reason too. We're paid damned little here.'

'I never even asked...'

'Maybe you should have.'

'Like – how much?'

'Fifty cents a day, if you're lucky.'

Lines of barges along the piers had to be worked. Sometimes they shovelled the anthracite out directly to the lighters, sometimes they filled carts and wagons, and sometimes they filled sacks and heaved them onto the wagons.

Some barges came with anthracite in large chunks, and the coal heavers had to break them with sledgehammers before shovelling them further. Young boys worked the smashed anthracite, searching for 'slate' – rock mixed in with the anthracite that could explode with heat.

It was no different to Mayo, Luke reflected. Breaking rock and shovelling it, whether in their own quarry or on the Famine Relief Works in the mountains. Children working too. That was no different either, but, while their blackened grimy faces looked ghastly, at least there was none of the hair growing along their cheeks to show the later stages of starvation.

Their foreman was American. His only concern was to get them to work faster.

'Another hard man,' Luke said.

'They're the same all over,' Jack said.

'What's that ye're saying?' one of the other men asked.

'Just talking about the foreman, that's all,' Luke replied.

'Arra, they're nothing as bad as the fellows on the Relief Works back home. They were the Devil in Hell, every single one of them. Drive you to hard work, and you starving.'

'I know what you mean,' Luke said. Best not talk about that.

Ten hours was the usual working day. Even Luke found his muscles were aching at the end.

'So how does this compare to the railways?' Jack asked him one day.

'Tougher, I'd say. On the cuttings, you'd get a chance of a break from the shovelling. Like using the pick in under the front of the lift of rock, but I preferred the shovelling anyhow.'

That night, they returned to Costellos.

They rode on an anthracite lighter back to the New York side. It was full, and they sat on the anthracite, looking back over the harbour as the sun set over New Jersey.

When they returned, Catherine looked at them in disgust.

'Ye're looking as black as coal, the pair of ye.'

'Sure it is coal,' Jack said.

'Enough of that guff out of you. Get down to the courtyard and clean yourselves up.'

They stripped off their shirts, and washed at the hand pump in the courtyard. Then they carefully returned to their room and changed their trousers.

'Time for a drink,' Jack said.

They sat with Costello, as Catherine served the beer.

'Ye got work, did you?' Costello asked.

'We did. Not that it pays a lot, but it'll do for now. And at least we'll be settled, so we can stay around New York for a while. It might be better than going to Lackan straight away.'

'It might,' Costello said. 'You're still thinking of bringing out your wife?'

'Of course.'

'You can use this address so,' he said, 'and if you're not here, we'll know where you are, and be able to send her on to you.'

After a few days working and travelling back at nights, one of the Tourmakeady men suggested they should stay on the New Jersey side of the Hudson.

'Not a bad idea either,' Jack commented to Luke.

After work that evening, they accompanied the three others to a lodging house on Steuben Street. It was a square-built building, just across from a shipyard.

'And if ye don't like shovelling anthracite, ye might try building ships instead,' one of the others said. 'Whenever they start building them again, of course.'

They entered the house and met the landlady, a Mrs. Gleeson. A rate was quickly agreed. It was cheap, but at their wages they could afford no more, and Luke reckoned Mrs. Gleeson knew that. They followed her up to the

419

bedroom. There were six bunk beds around the walls.

'You can have these two,' she told Luke and Jack.

'I'll take the top one so,' Jack said rapidly.

'And there's one other thing,' Mrs. Gleeson said. 'I expect my lodgers to be clean. Very clean.'

She brought them back down the corridor to a small room in the end. Inside was a large copper tub, three pails of water beside it. The floor was covered with damp coal dust.

'Now you can wash each other here,' she said, 'and make sure you're scrubbed clean before dinner.'

'We best have a clean suit of clothes so,' Jack said, half joking.

'Ye can come down naked, as far as I'm concerned, but you don't come down in filthy clothes.'

She left them.

'I'd hoped she was joking about the naked bit,' Jack said.

'I think so,' Luke replied. 'But still, staying here might be better to where we are. I never wanted Winnie to see Five Points.'

'I'm not sure that this'd be much better for any lady,' Jack said. 'Coal dust and naked men, eh?'

'We'll see.'

That night they travelled back to Five Points and explained their plans to Costello.

'Yes,' he said, 'it would make sense too. But ye'll come back and visit now and again.'

'Sure why not,' Luke said.

He had decided now that Farrelly's suggestions were for the best. He could stay waiting in Jersey City and New York until Winnie arrived with the baby. He had a fixed address at last, two if he included Costellos. Now too, he knew there was no problem travelling in winter. The ships came straight from Mayo to New York, all year round. With his own money, he would be able to ensure that she would travel on a passenger ship. No coffin ships for his wife and child. Yes, one way or another, it would be best to have her come to New York and meet her in New York or Jersey City. That would be far better than waiting 'till he moved to Lackan, and have her take a train to the mines in Lackan on her own.

Early on the Monday morning, he got a bank draft from the Chemical Bank.

Then he returned to Jersey City. That evening, he bought a pen, ink and paper, and returned to the lodging house. He washed, went down to the dining room, and wrote.

Carrigard   Gleeson's Boarding House
Kilduff   Steuben Street
Co. Mayo   Jersey City
Ireland   New Jersey
                                                             United States
                                                             7 June 1848

My Dearest Winnie, Dear Mother and Father,

At last, I have some good news for ye. You will notice the address above, and
this will be my fixed address until at least Winnie and the baby come out to
join me in America. It is only just across the river from New York. A second
address worth noting is that of Mr. John Costello, who owns Costellos Bar in
Orange Street in the city of New York. If there is any problem, he will always
know where I am.

I enclose a bank draft, which should cover more than the price of a ticket
to New York. It may help you through the present hard time too. I would send
more, but the work we are doing is not well paid.

There is no problem with winter crossings to New York, because the
rivers here do not freeze like in Quebec. So Winnie may leave at whatever
time she pleases, but should take a good passenger ship, direct to New York,
and from Mayo if possible. At any cost, avoid the lumber ships, where the
passenger quarters are worse.

Now for other news. We have had a good journey from Bytown, with
little to do except for some labouring work when we had to break up the
lumber rafts, and by God, that was hard. We also did a little clerking for
the ganger. For the rest of the time, we were able to watch the country we
were passing through. There are now many farms along the rivers following
the line of the logging in Canada, and along the rivers in the United States too,
and many Irish farmers have settled the land, I hear.

At Lake Champlain, we passed through the border of the United States,
but it seems that things are easier now than they were in 1847, and they no
longer stop Irish people from entering. We then followed the Champlain Canal
down to the Hudson River, which runs straight down to New York. When we
got to America, there was some work breaking up the timber, and floating it to
towns on the river bank, and the same when we reached New York.

Jack and I are now working on the anthracite terminals in this town,
shifting anthracite to carry across to New York City. It is hard work too.

I have to tell you that Martin Farrelly has gone from Harrisburg, since
the rail building has stopped in that town. He is moving to a place called
Lackan in Pennsylvania, and Mikey Jordan and Matt McGlinn are going
with him. They will work in the anthracite mines there, making up their own
gang. Ye may tell their people if they have not already heard.

It is my intention, Winnie, that as soon as you join me in New York, we might afterward travel to Lackan so that I may work with old friends who I have known so long in County Mayo and the English railways.

Please God I will write again before the end of the summer and send more to ye, and by that time, Winnie may already be with me here in America.

I have no more to say, but remain your loving husband and son,

Luke Ryan

When he had finished writing, one of the Tourmakeady men approached him.

'*You can write?*'

'*I can.*'

'*Would you write a letter for us?*'

'*For all of ye?*'

'*Why not? There might be one of us with family still living.*'

Luke took a separate page, and wrote out the address –

Ballybanane, Tourmakeady, Partry, County Mayo, Ireland.

He then went on in the Irish language, writing separate letters on the same page for the three families, first horizontal, and then vertical. He wrote on both sides, and when there was no more room he wrote again across the back.

When he was finished, he wrote an extra note on his own letter.

I would also ask ye, as a favour, to send the enclosed letter down to Tourmakeady. The fellows I have written it for, are working with me here in Jersey City. They would consider it a great kindness if you could do this for them.

A cheaper way,' Luke explained. *It'll only cost a penny for the postage from one part of Mayo to another, rather than us having to send two letters from here.*'

One of the men insisted on giving Luke two cents to pay the cost.

Every week, they visited Costello's at Five Points. Partly this was to catch up with any news Costello might have, partly to find out what had happened to *Conaire*.

'I doubt we'll see him now?' Costello said one day. 'He's lost in getting to New York. Though I reckon it's worse than that. The forests are deadly dangerous, aren't they? He might have met with an accident.'

Luke remembered the axe-man who had been killed in the forest, and the Quebecer who had died in the fight, as well as the many he had heard of being killed on the river drives.

'Yes,' he said, 'that's likely enough.'

'In fact, he could even have got this far,' Costello said. 'For a fellow like him, not knowing New York, he could have got knifed for his pack. This place has the highest murder rate in America.'

'I'd believe it,' Luke said.

'And it shows you the dangers of travelling this country. Once you're on the road, no one on earth can find you.'

'But he knew you were in Five Points, I tell you,' Luke said.

'Maybe he did. But that doesn't mean he'd be able to get here on his own.'

'He could have gotten someone to write.'

'Or maybe he didn't want to.'

'But why? Why would he not want to?'

'Any number of whys. Someone might have told him about Five Points, and scared him off. Or he might be making money in a way he wouldn't want known. Or maybe he's living with a woman he doesn't want us to meet.'

'Or he might be dead,' Jack said.

'Yes,' Costello said, 'he might be dead.'

Dead, Luke thought. Killed by a falling tree? Crushed by logs on some river drive? Frozen on some Canadian trail? Killed by fever? Axed in a fight? Knifed on a street in Five Points?

There were many ways to die.

Chapter 33

Telegraph & Connaught Ranger, June 1848:

State of Erris. There are some very miserable places in Ireland just now, but not one that can bear a comparison with Erris for poverty and neglect. And yet they are talking of building a Workhouse there. We wonder how such an establishment would be supported; certainly not by the occupiers of land, for they have not as much property as would enable them to supply themselves with the commonest necessaries of life. It is a wretched district, sunk in the lowest depths of misery, and unless some active and immediate steps be taken to bring about a wholesome change in its condition, its inhabitants will, ere long, be swept from the face of the earth.

Kitty came on mid-summer's day. She grasped Brigid and hugged her close.

'*There now, little Brigid, you're not to be jealous of your little brother now, do you hear me?*'

'*If you keep on spoiling her like this, it's Liam who'll be the jealous one,*' Eleanor said.

'*Arra, not at all,*' Kitty replied. '*Sure at Liam's age he wouldn't even know what jealousy is.*'

She reached into the pocket in her skirt and pulled out a potato.

'*Isn't this a grand size, for the early crop?*'

'*Where did you get this?*' Eleanor asked.

'*In our own potato garden,*' Kitty replied. '*It might be early, but by God, it's a good size already.*'

Winnie took the potato and washed it. She brought it back to the table and sliced right through it. The flesh was firm and white.

'*Not the slightest sign of blight,*' she said, '*that's for certain.*'

'*I know,*' Kitty said. '*And it's like this all over. The blight is gone, well and truly gone. By the time we get through to the main crop, the hunger will be gone with it.*'

And so it went on. It was still too early for the main potato crop to be dug, but even so, hungry people dug out the still growing potatoes to allay the hunger. Others dug up one plant from time to time, if only to wonder at the quality of the potatoes and the size of them.

Then Luke's letter arrived.

Winnie took it from the postman, and ran inside. Eleanor took a knife and slit it open. The letter and bank draft fell on the table.

Winnie started reading the letter.

'Well, he's given us a fixed address...so we can write to him. We can write straight away. And he says...he says I can sail to New York at any time.'

'Through the winter season...'

'He says there's no ice. There's nothing about storms, but he says I may cross as soon as I like.'

Eleanor took the bank draft and went out to the fields.

'Michael, Michael...'

When they returned to the house, Liam was crying. Winnie was sitting at the table, trying to console him while still reading the letter.

Brigid was pulling at her skirts.

'*Shush, shush there,*' Eleanor said to Liam. 'What more does he have to say, in the name of God?'

'He's working at shovelling anthracite.'

'Shovelling what?'

'Anthracite.'

'What's anthracite?'

'He doesn't say,' Winnie said, 'but whatever it is, they're shovelling it. And he'll stay around New York until I get there with Liam. It'll be a while yet, but at least there's a chance of it now.'

'But what else...?' asked Michael.

'I'm getting there,' Winnie said, 'there's more news yet. Martin Farrelly has left Harrisburg. Mikey Jordan and Matt McGlinn too. They've gone to some other place in Pennsylvania, Lackan it's called. Seems there's better chances there, as the railways are coming to an end all over. They're all going to be miners.'

'Miners!' Michael exclaimed.

'Yes,' said Winnie. 'Luke's intending we should join them as soon as I arrive in New York. They'd be better paid, I'm guessing.'

That afternoon, Winnie went down to Kilduff for corn. An hour later, she arrived back. She handed the corn to Eleanor.

'*I saw a notice stuck to a wall across the street from Dillon's,*' she said.

'*What was that?*' Eleanor asked.

'*It was telling of a ship leaving Westport for* Philadelphia, *by way of* New York.'

'But...when?'

'*Leaving on the twenty first of July to arrive in New York sometime late August. Long before any winter season.*'

Less than a week away, Eleanor thought.

They discussed it in Carrigard that night.

'It would be a great chance for you, surely,' Eleanor said. Not that she really felt it. She would be sad to see Winnie go.

'It is, mother.'

'I wonder what late August means,' Michael said. 'Could be the twentieth or the thirtieth. And how could they know anyhow?'

'Well, there's only one way to find out,' Winnie said, 'I'll have to go over to the passage brokers in Castlebar.'

'You will not,' Eleanor said. 'You've little Liam to be minding. You'll stay here, we'll go across for you.'

Early the following morning, Eleanor and Michael travelled to Castlebar in the horse & cart. Luke's bank order was tightly wrapped inside Eleanor's bodice.

Michael took a whip for the horse, together with a short whip and two sticks for protection. He drove the horse down towards Kilduff, passing men on the road, but no one spoke to them. There were three women outside Dillon's, far less than the longer line of some months earlier. Less money, Eleanor reflected, but some at least should have had remittances. Perhaps they were too late for many.

Out the Castlebar road they twice met carts coming towards them, dead bodies piled inside. Eleanor gagged at the smell from one of them.

'There'll be no coffins for those,' Michael said.

When they arrived in Castlebar, they asked their way to the passage broker's office.

'Are there no later crossings to New York?' Michael asked the clerk.

'Not until mid-October out of Westport, that's for certain,' the broker answered. 'This is the only one.'

'And what time for the crossing?' Michael asked.

'Four weeks. Certainly less than five. The ship is well able to travel the Atlantic, no matter what the weather.'

'The price is high,' Michael said.

'What do you expect? There isn't steerage, like on other ships. This isn't the Ashburton.'

'What of fever?' Eleanor asked.

'In a ship like this? The slightest sign of it, they'd quarantine them at once. This is a passenger ship, not one of those wrecks out of Cork or Liverpool.'

'Fine so,' Michael said, 'we'll come back in a while.'

Eleanor and Michael discussed it. Then they found the Castlebar branch of the Hibernian Bank, and cashed the full amount of the bank draft. Then back to the passage broker, where Michael walked to the desk and put most of the money on the counter.

'One for New York.'

It was late when they arrived back in Carrigard.

'Well?' Winnie asked as they walked in.

Eleanor placed the ticket on the counter.

'*The thing is done,*' she said.

Winnie picked up Liam who was still awake. '*We're going to America,*' she said, '*and you're going to meet your daddy.*'

Eleanor hugged both of them. Tears were rolling down her cheeks, though whether from joy for Winnie, or her own unhappiness at the loss of her, she could not tell.

Next day, Winnie sat down to write a letter to Luke. Eleanor sat alongside her, Brigid on her lap. Young Liam was asleep in the bedroom.

Mr. Luke Ryan	Carrigard
Gleeson's Boarding House	Kilduff
Steuben Street	County Mayo
Jersey City	Ireland
New Jersey	
United States of America	16 July 1848

My Dearest Luke,

I hardly need to tell you that we were delighted to receive your letter and the money with it. So now at last I have enough for myself and Liam to travel to New York. I must therefore tell you of our present plans.

I intend on leaving from Westport within six days on a ship called the Vega. They expect it to arrive in New York, perhaps towards the end of August. So the moment I arrive in New York, I will make my way either to Costellos, or direct to your address in Jersey City, and we will then be united again, my love.

But first, some happier news. You now have a son called Liam. He was born in March and he is getting on well. I had always said it was to be a son, even though your mother said I could not know that. She says he has your face, and that is no bad thing.

Your mother and father join me in sending our love and best wishes to you.

And so, until we meet again, I remain your loving wife,

Winifred Ryan

'You know,' Eleanor said, 'with your letter and the ship being so close together, you might even be in New York before he knows you're coming.'

Winnie went to Kilduff and posted the letter.

Early next morning, Michael went out to dig potatoes. There was a low mist lying above the crop, a sort of miasma, with a sweet fragrance. He could feel the tremor in his body as he saw it.

Anxiously, he dug into the potato ridge, carefully easing the potatoes out. Then he picked one potato, held his hand against a clear blue sky, and squeezed hard. The potato disintegrated, a grey slimy mess seeping out between his fingers and running down his forearm. He flung it on the ground, picked up a second and did the same. Then a third.

He moved around the field, but everywhere he dug, the result was the same. He thought back over the past week. In Kilduff he had heard reports of an excellent potato crop, bigger potatoes than in previous years. All seemed to be in excellent condition, no mention of blight then. At that time he had decided to leave the potatoes in the ground to get a little more growth before digging them. But now it was over.

He felt a cold fear like he had never felt in his life before. Even 1846 – that had been terrible, but this was worse. The crop in 1847 had been a good one, and all had thought the failure was over. But now? What future for Mayo? What future for any of them?

He picked up some potatoes, and carried them home in one hand, his spade over his shoulder. He left the spade in the cowshed and went to the house. Eleanor was making brown bread. He placed the potatoes on the table. She saw the look on his face.

'No, Michael,' she gasped. 'Not that.'

She took a knife and cut one of the potatoes cleanly in half. It was grey all the way through.

'All gone,' he said. 'Not a single one left.'

Winnie came out from the back room, where she had been feeding the baby.

'What's wrong?' she asked.

She saw the rotten potatoes.

'Oh, Mother of God...'

Michael picked one, and squeezed 'till the slime oozed out.

Winnie staggered back, stunned by the shock of it.

'Sweet Jesus, no.'

Glossary of Words and Expressions

Acushla: Darling.

A ghrá: My love.

Alanna: Dear child. My love. From *A leanbh* (child).

Amadán: Fool.

Arra: Implies 'No' or 'don't be silly'. From *Aire* (care).

Biddy. Short for Brigid, but also used as a slang word for a maid.

Boreen: A narrow road or track.

Bytown: Original name of Ottawa before Federation.

Camboose: Either living quarters for lumbermen, or the open fire inside it.

Clochán: A tiny settlement of primitive houses.

Crubeens: Boiled pig trotters. From the Irish *Crúibín*.

Eejit: Idiot. From the English word.

Gossoon: Boy. From the Irish *Garsún*, and originally, Old French.

Grá: Love.

Hoor: Irish slang, mostly for a crafty fellow who is not to be trusted. Not related to 'whore'.

Lumper: A large potato.

Molly Maguires: A nineteenth century Irish terrorist group.

Musha: Indeed. Probably from the Irish word *Muise*. Mainly used by older women.

Outshot: A bed built into the inside of a wall, often in the kitchen.

Piseóg: Superstitious story.

Poitín: An illicit spirit distilled from potatoes. Moonshine.

Rath: The remains of an ancient fort or settlement. There are about 30,000 in Ireland.

Sceilp: A primitive lean-to shelter made of branches and sods.

Shebeen: A small or unlicensed bar or pub. From *Síbín*.

Sleán: A special spade for digging turf.

Spailpín: A seasonal or migrant harvest worker.

Sláinte mhaith: Good Health, as in a drinking toast.

Ticket-of-leave men: Ex-convicts, released on condition of good behaviour.

Tigín: A tiny house.

Townland: A rural sub-division of land.

Trawneen: Something or someone of little value. From Tráithnín, a blade of grass.

Turf: In Ireland, peat dug from a peat bog for burning as fuel.

Union: Organisation running the Poor Law. Also a word for Workhouse. Not related to Trade Unions.

Whisht: Hush. Silence. Be quiet. From Middle English.

If you enjoyed *The Exile Breed* don't miss
The Killing Snows and *Cold is the Dawn*

CPSIA information can be obtained
at www.ICGtesting.com
Printed in the USA
BVHW071141220520
580032BV00001B/28

9 781781 324523